TRANSPLANTED MAN

wm WILLIAM MORROW   *An Imprint of* HarperCollins*Publishers*

SANJAY NIGAM

TRANSPLANTED MAN

HarperCollins books may be purchased for educational, business, or sales promotional use. For information please write: Special Markets Department, HarperCollins Publishers Inc., 10 East 53rd Street, New York, NY 10022.

FIRST EDITION

Printed on acid-free paper

Library of Congress Cataloging-in-Publication Data
Nigam, Sanjay.
Transplanted man / Sanjay Nigam.—1st ed.
p. cm.
ISBN 0-688-16819-1
1. East Indian Americans—Fiction.   2. Transplantation of organs, tissues, etc.—Patients—Fiction.   3. New York (N.Y.)—Fiction.   4. Physicians—Fiction.   5. Hospitals—Fiction.
I. Title.

PR9499.3.N48 T73 2002
813'.54—dc21   2001051394

02   03   04   05   06   SPS/RRD   10   9   8   7   6   5   4   3   2   1

· For my PARENTS and π^3 ·

. . . not till we have lost the world,
do we begin to find ourselves . . .

• HENRY DAVID THOREAU, *Walden* •
•

CONTENTS

1

DAYS AND NIGHTS

2

STATES OF AWARENESS

3

HIGHS AND LOWS

4

COMPLICATIONS

5

SLINGS AND ARROWS

6

RESOLUTIONS

7

HERE, THERE—ELSEWHERE

DAYS AND NIGHTS

1

Stuck

MORNING RUSH HOUR.

Dr. Sunit "Sonny" Seth stood in the crowded, rattling car, his hand gripping the cool steel support rod. As he stared out the window at the blurry subway walls, he half-closed his eyes and fell into a light trance. His mind drifted, no longer aware of the mingling of human and subway smells, the flickering lights, the bold rhythm of the train racing over the tracks.

When the train slowed down for its next stop, the spell broke. Sonny's whole body felt stiff, sluggish. The percolator in his apartment had gone on strike, so he hadn't had his usual three cups of coffee before leaving for work. But caffeine deprivation wasn't the only reason he felt tired. He hadn't gotten much rest last night. Around 2:00 A.M. he'd gone sleepwalking through the neighborhood.

Again.

Sonny had no reason to suspect this as a cause of his fatigue. Since he lived alone, he wasn't aware of his nocturnal behavior—even though he was able, in his sleep, to put on his shoes, leave his apartment, avoid being hit by taxis as he crossed neighborhood streets, and safely return home. In some respects, his sleepwalking was like a deeper version of the trance he'd just been in.

The train stopped. Sonny stepped aside to make room for exiting passengers. For the first time he glimpsed a man standing a foot or so from the open doors. Stone-faced, whole body rigid, the man looked like a statue wrapped in a thin layer of flesh. Some psychiatric disorder, guessed Sonny. But before he could develop a clearer sense of what was wrong with the man, the car filled, blocking his view.

The train gathered speed. Vibrations from the steel support rod traveled into Sonny's wrist, his arm, his shoulder. His mind returned to coffee. On days like today, when he'd be on call at the hospital all night, he would finish six or seven cups before lunchtime.

Sonny liked being on call. For those twenty-four hours he was in his element. He thrived on the here and now of the hospital, a battlefront with all the intensity of a real war—though no visible enemy. But his tour of duty would be over in less than a year. He didn't often think about what to do next, though, oddly enough, he was considering reenlistment: another residency. His colleagues shook their heads in disbelief. Was he crazy? Who'd want to fight the war all over again? But Sonny understood exactly where the battle lines were in this war.

Beyond hospital walls was a different matter.

• •

At the next stop more than a dozen people got off, and only two got on. Now Sonny had an unobstructed view of the motionless man. Although the man's skin was pinkish white and Sonny's was deep brown, both men were about five eleven and lithe, with black, uncombed hair hanging over their ears. Both men's eyes, mildly bloodshot, were dark, and their lips had even curled into a similar, somewhat puzzled, expression. In the minute and a half since Sonny had first noticed him, the man had moved no more than a foot. Yet the movement had direction. In his own hypokinetic way, this man was going somewhere.

By the time the train slowed for its next stop, the hypokinetic man had inched all the way to the doors, which now parted before him. The tip of his right shoe managed to creep out. Suddenly the doors closed, clamping his foot. The safety mechanism responded, and the doors rebounded. Then they closed again and, after slamming the man's foot, squeaked open once more. Instead of withdrawing his foot, the man pushed it forward—ever so slightly. The doors shut, bashed his foot, then reopened.

The man and the train were stuck. The doors kept opening and closing, causing a sickening thud every time they hit the hypokinetic man's foot. But the man didn't utter a sound or change his expression.

Over the loudspeaker the conductor repeated, "Please stand clear of the closing doors." He sounded more agitated with each repetition. When the hypokinetic man still hadn't moved, the conductor bellowed, "Make up your mind and get on or off!"

The other passengers appeared hypokinetic, too. Not one rose to help. Perhaps suffering from urban neurasthenia, not to mention legitimate fears of bombs and semiautomatic rifles, they watched the rhythmic pounding of the strange man's foot with guarded concern. Resigned to showing up late for work, they stopped checking their wristwatches.

Sonny wanted to help. But he worried that if he gently pushed the hypokinetic man onto the decaying subway platform, the man, stiff as he was, might trip and break his neck. Or, because he was so thin, his leg might slip into the larger-than-usual gap between the car and platform. Sonny could almost visualize the man's severed limb lying in a pool of blood. Maybe he should just lift the poor guy onto the platform. How heavy could he be?

While Sonny debated, the doors kept smashing the hapless foot. The hypokinetic man still wasn't moving—or, rather, he was moving extremely slowly. And the conductor was now yelling, "You're holding up the train!"

Sonny had finally decided to carry the hypokinetic man to safety. But just as he stepped forward, the hypokinetic man managed, somehow, to stagger onto the platform.

The doors closed.

"Amen!" shouted the conductor. The train started to move.

While the train sped over the tracks, Sonny chided himself for not coming to the aid of the hypokinetic man more swiftly. Could the man understand the anxieties of his fellow passengers, their inaction? *His* inaction? After all, the hypokinetic man simply needed a little help. A nudge.

The train began to slow. His stop: Esmoor Street. Sonny stepped onto the platform and fused with the crowd climbing out of the subway station.

Sunlight.

At the street corner was a roadside vendor, and Sonny stopped for a cup of coffee. He drank slowly, savoring the steaming concoction. After draining the last drop, he tossed the paper cup into a garbage can and made his way down Esmoor Street. In a couple of hours Hindi film songs would be blaring from stores with names like Raju's Paan Shop, Desi Dosa Palace, and Aap Ka Dukaan, as old Lata and Kishore melodies competed with the latest disco-bhangra rhythms. Menus in restaurant windows advertised tandoori chicken, alu chaat, uttapams, and kulfis—and every restaurant claimed to offer the best lunch special in town. With last night's trash stuffed in bins up and down the street, that Indian bazaar smell of spices and fried sweets, mixed with more disagreeable odors, was present as well. On humid days like this, when the air soaked up every odor, that smell became overwhelming—as if compensating for something that was amiss. Perhaps all that was needed was the sight of an autorikshaw belching black exhaust to dispel the sense of incongruity between place and smell. Whatever the reason, the smell wasn't quite the same as the original, and it brought to mind all the other things that were different.

In this tiny enclave, known to taxi drivers as Little India, Sonny's destination was the tallest building: a fifty-five-year-old hospital. And last night it had admitted one of the most unusual patients in the history of medicine.

• •

THE CHAOTIC MAIN LOBBY that Sonny entered resembled a bus terminal. Uniformed security guards interrogated suspected vagrants. A newsboy who'd made acceptable financial arrangements with the security guards hollered the latest headlines of metropolitan and Indian American newspapers: "Six Arrested in Drug-Prostitution Ring" . . . "More Tension on Indo-Pak Border" . . . "INS Changes Rules Again."

Custodians mopped up spilled coffee and tea. The old linoleum floors, originally off-white, had turned light bronze. The ambulatory entrance to the emergency room was through the main lobby, and the darker color of the floor along the way was due not only to petrified layers of dirt, hot drinks, and colas but also to blood, vomit, and other human secretions. Yet the color had character.

Patients, relatives, and friends encroached upon the circular information desk. "Excuse me!" they kept saying to the volunteer, a man of Indian origin who had immigrated from Malaysia, one of a corps of octogenarians who staffed the information desk. People asked for the locations of rooms, specialty clinics, this or that doctor's office, the Sleep Studies Lab, the X-ray department, the dialysis unit, the outpatient pharmacy, where to get change for parking meters. To almost every question, the old man smiled benevolently and gave the same reply: "Down the corridor, turn right at the end."

No one had ever done a survey to find out how many who went down the corridor and turned right arrived at their intended destinations—or how many, frustrated and late for their appointments, came back to the information desk, only to be told once again, "Down the corridor, turn right at the end."

The issue was not trivial. Although the hospital had once been among the finest in the city, its reputation was on the decline. Flowers were frequently delivered to the wrong patient, and last year the wrong person (a visitor who didn't speak English) ended up on the operating table. The hospital had such serious image and financial woes that the CEO had recently told the governing board that if they didn't control the damage they'd go bankrupt. The board, mostly businessmen who knew a great deal about circumventing import-export regulations but little about running hospitals, debated passionately. Treating the patient as a consumer, they adopted the strategy of luxury goods manufacturers: Packaging was everything. The consensus was that improving the look of the place might do wonders. But the planned renovations required the kind of money the hospital couldn't spare. So the refurbishing project kept getting postponed.

Nevertheless, as hospitals go, it was still a good one. The senior doctors, foreign medical graduates, had been doubly trained—first in India, where they learned how to heal by touching people, and again in the States, where they became proficient at treating based on computer printouts. The expert medical staff made the hospital's residency training program highly regarded—one reason Sonny had chosen to come here. And the hospital's reputation back in India remained untarnished; it was still a frequent choice of Indian luminaries who sought medical treatment abroad. Within the city, however, it had become known as a hospital for foreigners.

• •

SONNY JOINED THE STREAM of people in the corridor. He passed a poster that read, CHEWING BETEL NUTS IS HAZARDOUS TO YOUR HEALTH, then went by a door marked PLACES OF WORSHIP. The door opened into a hallway, which bifurcated twice and led to rooms dedicated to four different faiths. If God was anywhere, staff agnostics argued, it was somewhere in that branching structure.

Unlike others, who turned right at the end of the corridor, Sonny turned left—the direction of the staff locker room. As he rounded the corner he was forced to leap out of the way of a racing stretcher. The stretcher's rash driver was Manny, a young Trinidadian orderly whose life's ambition was to become a playback singer in Hindi films.

"Watch where you're going, you mad doctor!" yelled Manny.

Before Sonny could reply, Manny turned to the nervous woman on the stretcher. "Relax, ma'am. We won't let this doc operate on you."

Sonny patted the woman's shoulder in a doctorly way. "I'm not a surgeon."

"Thank heaven for that!" said Manny.

Sonny's eyes flashed in anger.

Manny offered a placating smile. "Looks like you left your laughter in bed this morning."

"I brought my venom instead," muttered Sonny.

Manny turned to the woman in the stretcher. "We'd better move on. This snake has big fangs. Besides, we can't keep the operating room waiting, can we? If you're late, they might grab someone in the hall and do your operation on her. Do you know they really did that once?"

At last in the staff locker room, Sonny dialed 2-24-10 on a red combination lock and jiggled the latch. When the locker door opened, his nostrils detected a pungent odor; he couldn't tell where it was coming from. He pulled out his white doctor's coat, noticed a smudge, and reminded himself to exchange the coat at the hospital laundry later in the day. At the beginning of his residency, he found that if he kept his doctor's coat buttoned, few noticed that he didn't wear a tie and came to work in jeans and running shoes. After buttoning up he made sure his stethoscope, penlight, and reflex hammer were in the appropriate coat pockets. Then he reset his pager. It emitted a series of high-pitched beeps.

As he was about to close the locker, he realized that he didn't have a pen. So he dug through the mess at the bottom in search of a working ballpoint. Two slips of paper turned up with phone numbers of women he'd considered dating in recent months. One he crumpled and tossed into the garbage. The other he placed in his wallet; he hadn't had much of a love life lately, and the once-discarded number seemed worth saving. Continuing to rummage through the locker, he found the source of the smell: a bag of decaying samosas that he'd bought at Tiger Raj's restaurant but forgotten to take home. Now the rank bag suffered the fate of the rejected phone number. Still searching for a pen, he came across an overdue phone bill and a pamphlet published by Americans Against Columbus Day. The last thing he found was a blue ballpoint.

Sonny went to the wall phone and dialed the page operator. Pinned to the bulletin board in front of him was a calendar put out by New Dariba Jewelers, "experts at blending Eastern and Western traditions into the finest ornaments in the world." Nine rings later an operator came on the line. Sonny asked her to page Dr. Bhandari, who'd been on call last night. Bhandari would update him on how his patients had fared overnight and inform him of new admissions.

While he waited for Bhandari to answer the page, Sonny poured a cup of coffee. The coffee in the staff locker room was widely regarded as the worst on the planet, to be consumed only when absolutely necessary. Now was such a time. With a monstrous grimace he swallowed the stale brew in a series of quick gulps. Then he refilled his cup.

The phone rang. "How'd it go last night?" asked Sonny.

"Busy," replied Bhandari. "Eight admissions. One patient was really complicated. Normally he would have gone to Mirza, and next in the rotation would have been Venkataraman, but the word from higher up is that *you* are supposed to be his doctor."

"That's odd. Who's the patient?"

"A big-shot politician from India."

"And who's the higher-up? I can't think of a single higher-up who likes me."

"They don't have to like you. It's a tough case, an important patient, and they don't want someone to make a mess of it."

"So what's the case?"

"First, listen to this," said Bhandari, snickering. "Last night, I covered the ER for an hour, and in came this guy and his wife. The guy had taken a bite out of his wife's rear!"

"He bit her *there?*"

"Believe me, it was hard to keep a straight face while I sewed up the wife's buttock with her husband looking on."

Sonny knit his brow. "Are you sure that was a good idea? When bite wounds get infected—"

"Yeah, yeah, I know. But the wound looked clean, and the husband insisted that it be sewn up. Poor guy, he was *so* upset. He held his wife's bloodstained nightie like it was evidence in a murder case. Embarrassed mainly, I guess. They seemed proper professional types—engineers, I think, both of them."

"How'd it happen?"

"Neither would say. They must have been having pretty weird sex."

"Sounds a bit fishy. . . . Sleep any?"

"Not a wink. Get here earlier next time, will you?"

"Sorry—I had a strange experience on the subway. This hypokinetic guy . . . Actually, he was probably catatonic, but how does one know for sure? Anyway, he got stuck between the doors. The doors kept smashing his foot— I can still hear those awful thuds! I really wanted to help. Instead, I just watched. No different from the rest. I mean, I was about to help, but by then he'd managed to get out on his own."

"I've seen that guy on the subway, too—white, dark hair, thin, about your height? The man I'm thinking of is as hypokinetic as they get."

"That's him! You can't get any slower without reversing time."

"If it's the same guy," said Bhandari, "he's been like that for a while."

"Oddly enough, I had the feeling he was trying to go somewhere."

"Could be. A shrink friend of mine thinks it's important for homeless schizophrenics to choose a neighborhood, a street corner. A home. Anchors them while their minds are all over the place."

"I wonder what goes on in the head of a guy like that."

"You sound bothered."

Sonny sighed. "We handle weird stuff all the time in the ER, but it's different out there. On the street, we're like everyone else. It's hard to know what to—"

Bhandari's pager beeped. "I'd better answer this right away," he said. "Whenever I see this number flash on my pager, my sphincters loosen."

"Why?"

"It's my wife. She thinks I screw around when I'm on call."

"Do you?"

"No. But the more she accuses, the more I think about it. Home has become hell."

"Just give me a quick rundown of last night's cases."

"All routine, except for your special patient. A cantankerous guy, but he has reason to be. He's damn sick. Right now, his main problem is failing kidneys. Get this: They call him the Transplanted Man."

• •

THE TRANSPLANTED MAN was known not only as a medical curiosity but as one of India's most powerful, popular and, some said, wiliest politicians. His political success was in no small way related to his many successful organ transplants. His body now harbored seven organs—a heart, a pancreas, a liver, two lungs, and a pair of corneas—that had once belonged to different people. Blood from Ladakh to Kanya Kumari, from Goa to Kolkata, had been transfused into his anemic vessels. Not only did the Transplanted Man freely admit to his disease—something that might have turned into a political liability—but he campaigned on it.

The strategy was brilliant. He made his condition, along with his political agenda, sound spectral—pluralistic. What might have easily turned into an absurdity had become a symbol of mosaicism that resonated throughout the land. No other politician could so credibly claim to represent everyone.

He liked his nickname. The Transplanted Man: It sounded heroic, like that of a comic-book superhero, Batman or Superman. Better yet, a Hindi film hero. He especially relished that thought, the lust for film stardom being another affliction the Transplanted Man had battled. Over the past few decades he had watched film star after film star turn politician—and unseat veteran politicians. It should go both ways, he thought. Where was the politician who'd made it big in Bollywood?

But the hormonal decline that accompanies aging tempered that dream. The reality of disease chewed up what was left. Years of illness had not only drained his life, they had ravaged his once not so bad looks. As much as his well-guarded bungalow in New Delhi, the intensive care unit—with all its beeping machines and blinking lights—had become his home. He had suffered horribly: the relentless decline of his organs, one transplant after another, each followed by agonizing bouts of rejection. A veritable swamp of pathogenic bugs had been cultured from his blood and other body fluids. Disease had incited his heart to pump every which way, engaging in perverse frenzies of electrical activity that stumped renowned cardiologists. Countless tubes and wires had coursed through his veins, arteries, and orifices; at times the paraphernalia seemed to become part of him. Half the organs in his body had been pierced by biopsy needles. Rivers of tears had flowed from his eyes—not only because of his light-sensitive corneas but out of sheer misery.

Each triumphant return from near-death, often with yet another organ stitched into his viscera, brought national attention to the once local politician who had, until then, done more for his own good than for that of the landless farmers who'd elected him. Somehow the cravings of both public and press for high drama relentlessly fed each other: Soon he was heralded as a great man. "Superleader Survives Again," proclaimed one magazine when it featured the Transplanted Man's face on its cover. "The Phantom Returns," shouted another. "Let us hope he imparts his own resilience to the nation," wrote the editor of a respected national daily.

The myth grew. A once obscure politician from a largely agrarian district in central India (who, years ago, had nearly lost his state assembly seat over corruption charges) had managed to build a national following. People began to say he was the last of the great leaders, the only one left who could mobilize a fractious nation and chart its future. In the last election the Transplanted Man had won his parliamentary seat almost without campaigning. But there were no majorities in Parliament. As a result of the usual postelection machinations and deceptions, the Transplanted Man's party became the power broker of a six-party coalition. Of course, it was taken for granted that the Transplanted Man would occupy a key cabinet post. But the Transplanted

Man didn't think the new government would survive long and at first declined any portfolio, including Home and External Affairs. However, at his party's urging, he reluctantly accepted the less visible post of Health. Opposition leaders joked that his only real qualification for the job was that he happened to be the sickest member of Parliament.

Despite his prior lackluster record, he proved an able minister. "For many," reported a highly regarded foreign weekly, "the performance of the Indian Minister of Health and Family Welfare has been a pleasant surprise." Even the Transplanted Man was surprised. Perhaps, he reflected, all his suffering had given him insight into the maladies of the country. He did not know how a mother felt after losing her month-old baby in a diarrheal epidemic that might have been averted simply by boiling drinking water, but for the first time in his thirty-some years in politics, he woke up at night wondering how that mother felt. And now that he wielded power—in a coalition too confused to worry what his ministry was up to—the Transplanted Man wanted to do something for that baby, that mother. Something important that would put a stop to such unnecessary misery. The subtle wisdom of his own pain hadn't been lost upon him. A man of mediocrity had transformed into a man of noble ideals, and the hour of his greatness was approaching.

But he was dying. This time he feared it would really happen.

• •

THIN BLADES OF LIGHT escaped the drawn blinds, crossed the room, and bisected the face of a man snoring in bed. Sonny quietly watched medication drip out of inverted vials, then course down the plastic tubing into his new patient's veins. Asleep, with puffy eyelids and a deeply creased face, the Transplanted Man looked older than the sixty-four years recorded in his hospital chart. He had a full head of thick gray hair, untidy, sticking up in spots. His chin was unevenly covered with white stubble, though an occasional blackish hair peppered the lawn. Even in the wrinkled, blue-striped hospital gown that diminished most patients, the Transplanted Man seemed important in an indefinable way.

Sonny cleared his throat. The Transplanted Man opened his eyes, blinking a couple of times.

"I'm Dr. Seth. I'll be one of your physicians while you're here."

The Transplanted Man suppressed a yawn. "You sound like you expect me to leave soon. In what form do you think I will be reborn?"

"That's not what I meant," said Sonny, smiling.

"You didn't answer my question."

"I don't know the answer to that question."

"A doctor of the body but not the soul?"

"You might say that."

The Transplanted Man appeared to be mulling over something. "You're a resident, aren't you?"

That question automatically put Sonny on the defensive. He was ready to reply that resident doctors *ran* this hospital—supervised, of course, by senior physicians—and if His Highness, great man from the Mother Country, didn't like that, he could go elsewhere. But all Sonny said was "Yes."

"How old are you?"

Another question Sonny didn't like. Still, he supposed patients had the right to know their doctor's age—to the extent it bore on clinical expertise, which was highly debatable. "Twenty-nine," he finally said.

The Transplanted Man seemed to become lost in thought for a moment. "My son would have been twenty-nine this year."

Sonny waited for more, but the Transplanted Man shut his eyes and muttered inaudibly. When his eyes opened again, they were watery. He remained quiet for a while, then said, "So tell me, young Dr. Seth, are you Indian or American?"

Sonny wondered why this very ill patient was asking his new doctor personal questions that, in another tone, might be viewed as antagonistic. But he felt sorry for the Transplanted Man—especially for whatever had happened to his son.

"Well, Doctor?"

"It isn't that simple," said Sonny, allowing irritation to creep into his voice.

"I can see my scalpel cuts the doctor too deep, too soon. Excuse my invasion into your life. I am a politician, but I am neither polite nor politic. One would get nowhere in my line otherwise. Now tell me, is there anything else?"

"*Everything.* I need to know about your medical history."

"I spent hours last night recounting it to Dr. Bhandari and the medical student. Both still felt compelled to examine my prostate gland! The medical student was very rough."

"I'll leave your prostate gland alone."

All at once the Transplanted Man appeared drained. "I've told a hundred doctors the same story. Look for yourself. Am I any better for it?"

"I only want to——"

"You want to encapsulate my life into a page of notes, correct? A history, you call it. I am not a fool. I know the workings of hospitals. A specialist will further reduce that history—my life, mind you—to a few sentences. And then a surgeon will shrink it into one line—just before slicing me open. Am I right?"

Sonny gave no reply.

"Have you any idea how many volumes of my medical records there are?"

"Twenty-four, I'm told."

"*Twenty-five.* And you are beginning the twenty-sixth. A volume for each letter in the English alphabet. An encyclopedia! Someone should make an index. Then I won't have to go over the whole thing every time I'm in the hospital. It *hurts* to remember. An old man should be allowed to forget the past—to imagine the future. May I suggest that you ask someone to create an index to my records? Perhaps that medical student with the thick fingers." The Transplanted Man paused for a moment. "Oh, what's the use? I'm sure some physician has already condensed the entire encyclopedia into a single sentence. True?"

"I wouldn't know."

"You wouldn't tell me if you knew!" The Transplanted Man was breathing rapidly. "An outrage! Everything is condensed these days: milk, dictionaries, life. A man's life is many stories. I am aging fast, but few stories in my life are over yet. And you propose to distill everything into a few sentences!"

"Your medical history, that's all."

"As if my spleen does not say anything of who I am!"

"By that logic, your heart, actually another man's, should say a great deal about you."

The Transplanted Man coughed twice. "It does, don't you see? Maybe the creature I have become is more than one heart can bear. Maybe my own heart was too good for the man God placed it in. Now I have another heart, a heart torn from the chest of a man I do not know, a heart that has come to the same conclusion as my own heart, which long ago decomposed in a garbage bin. This new heart is also trying to escape from my body. Witness the episodes of rejection. It's all in my medical history."

"Yes, about the history——"

The Transplanted Man coughed again—violently. A tear crept down his left cheek. "I have nothing to add to the doctors' summaries that arrived with me. Read them."

These last words were almost gasps.

"I'll make it quick," said Sonny. "How long have you been short of breath?"

"Three days."

"Are you nauseated?"

"A bit."

"Itching?"

"Worse than a street dog."

"Chest pain?"

"On my left side when I take a deep breath."

Sonny stepped back and observed the Transplanted Man's labored breathing. Sickness did not diminish the dignity of each breath. Finally Sonny said, "Sit up and let me examine you. Then I'll leave you alone."

With difficulty, the Transplanted Man sat on the side of the bed. Sonny placed his stethoscope on the patient's chest. He immediately detected a sound made by the inflamed membrane surrounding the Transplanted Man's heart as it scraped against the pumping ventricle, accompanied by crackles in the fluid-filled lungs. In the background he heard the Transplanted Man's gurgling stomach. It sounded awful, like a group of amateur musicians struggling to play together.

"Someone must have told you already that your kidneys have failed," said Sonny. "I hope it's only temporary. In the meantime, to remove excess fluid and cleanse waste products from your blood, you're going to need dialysis. Do you know what that is?"

The Transplanted Man nodded. He had become passive, a sick child with the face of an old man.

"You can rest now. I'll be back after I discuss your case with the doctor who handles dialysis arrangements."

Sonny placed his hand on the Transplanted Man's shoulder for a moment, then left the room. As he passed an open door in the corridor, he detected a spicy scent. That usually meant someone was getting better. The hospital offered both American and Indian fare, the latter prepared on a spiciness scale from one to ten. Although sick patients generally couldn't tolerate anything spicy, they found spiceless Indian food inedible, too. So they often switched to American diets for the first time in their lives.

At the doctors' station Sonny spent half an hour leafing through the last five volumes of the Transplanted Man's medical records. Too much to make sense of in the time he had; he'd have to return later to study each volume. He

ɔ the phone and called the dialysis unit to find out if there was an
ɩn the schedule.

ɩave a dialysis machine available later this morning," said the nurse,
"but Dr. Rajchand must approve it."

"I'll be working with Dr. Rajchand on this case," replied Sonny, miffed by
the nurse's tone. "As a matter of fact, I'm meeting him for staff rounds in a
few minutes. So count on doing the dialysis."

After he hung up Sonny added his own words to the newest volume of the
Transplanted Man's medical records:

> This is a 64-year-old Indian male suffering from a highly unusual syndrome
> (that has so far defied a clear diagnosis), who has undergone cardiac, hepatic,
> pancreatic, lung, and corneal transplantations for complications due to his
> disease, and now presents with progressive renal dysfunction, most likely
> caused by nephrotoxic drugs, along with signs of pulmonary edema and
> pericarditis, and requires urgent dialysis.

Sonny quickly read over his note and signed it. As he started to walk away,
his conscience pricked him. Exactly as the Transplanted Man had predicted—
accused—he had reduced the man to a single sentence. He sat down again,
opened the chart, reconsidered the long sentence. First he crossed out two
conjunctions, then added a couple of pronouns and periods. One sentence
became three.

· ·

SONNY ARRIVED TWELVE MINUTES late for staff rounds with Dr. Rajchand.
Since the early days of his residency, he'd been feuding with Rajchand, an
Oxbridge-educated kidney specialist who cultivated a Renaissance-man
image. Sonny had little tolerance for the older doctor's haughty ways; their
mutual dislike was widely known. Through either rotten luck or the mischievous designs of someone involved in scheduling, the two had been forced to
endure each other yet again this month. Luckily, only a week remained.

The thick-fingered medical student who'd been on call with Bhandari last
night was about to discuss the Transplanted Man's case. "This is a sixty-four-
year-old Indian man with multiple organ transplants," began the student.
"His social history is remarkable for the fact that he is a major political
figure—"

"And we are to deny his presence here if asked by anyone not on the hospital staff," said Dr. Rajchand. "A security issue."

The student nodded solemnly.

"Continue."

"The exact nature of his disease remains a mystery. He has suffered damage to many organs and undergone numerous transplants. His medical history is a nightmare of rejection and infection, complicated by . . ."

The medical student went on to describe the circumstances surrounding each transplant. Dr. Rajchand periodically interrupted to quiz the student or digress upon some topic. After twenty minutes they still hadn't begun to discuss the Transplanted Man's current problems.

More impatient than usual, Sonny said, "Can we stop for a moment? We need to make a decision *now*. His condition is worsening. He's shot his beans."

Furrows suddenly developed on Dr. Rajchand's forehead. "Beans! How dare you! Would you malign the heart or the brain? The kidney is like the brain, except it doesn't think. Nevertheless, our director of research, Dr. Ranjan, has informed me that the brain and kidney express similar genes. Perhaps your own cranial vault contains such an organ, Dr. Seth. By that I mean you may have three kidneys but no brain: That would explain a great deal, wouldn't it? There is hope for you, though. The kidney can almost think. It probably *could*—under appropriate stimulation. The fact that the kidney has been subjugated to the seemingly menial task of making urine, while moronic poets have elevated the heart, a sorry excuse for a pump, to a powerful metaphor, has given the kidney an undeservedly poor image. Hearts and brains—that's all the world cares about! God had the choice of endowing the kidney or the brain with the power of thought and chose the brain. Who am I to criticize this choice? But it saddens me. The kidney is full of wonders! Consider the glomerulus. What a beautiful structure, more beautiful than a sunflower! It filters nearly two hundred liters of plasma every day through its delicately fenestrated capillaries. Then there are the tubules, a million of them finely compressed together, as though fashioned by an emperor's goldsmith. Have you seen Fabergé's eggs, the very best of them? Imagine Fabergé stricken by an obsessive mania, creating thousands upon thousands of convoluted tubes, thin, intricate structures, tightly packed, all dedicated to the supreme function of acid-base and electrolyte balance—so the lungs can breathe, so the heart can beat, so the brain can think! That marvelous organ is the kidney. And we are blessed with two. Possibly three in your case, Dr. Seth."

Sonny cursed under his breath.

Dr. Rajchand may not have heard Sonny, but apparently he had absorbed the gist. An acerbic smile crept across his face as he turned to the medical student. "Now, what is the cause of this man's kidney failure?"

"Maybe an immune complex lesion from a tropical disease," said the medical student. "Malaria, perhaps."

"You're searching for unicorns among mules," said Dr. Rajchand. "How about a simpler explanation?"

"I only suggested it because he's from the Third World."

"Yes, yes, I know! Where do you think I'm from? And where, Mr. Asian American, do you think your parents came from? Even Dr. Seth can lay claim to Third World origins, though perhaps the Third World will not claim him. Definitely not from this world, though."

The medical student's face turned red. Sonny scowled.

"In case you don't know," Dr. Rajchand went on, "diseases in the so-called Third World are not limited to parasitic infestations. People get diabetes and high blood pressure there, too."

"Come to think of it," said the student, "he has had terrible hypertension for years."

"That's only part of it," said Dr. Rajchand. "Even more significant is the treatment he has undergone. Some of the drugs he has received are very toxic to the kidney. We're all aware of the mechanism by which immunosuppressant drugs damage the kidney, aren't we?"

The medical student nodded vigorously, a sign that he had no idea.

"Another possibility," continued Dr. Rajchand, "is kidney failure due to his underlying disease—whatever it is." Dr. Rajchand turned to Sonny. "His current cardiac dysfunction is due to an episode of rejection, I imagine?"

"Probably," replied Sonny. "It's a heart of a different flavor. It'd be great to save his heart—just to prove peaceful coexistence isn't psychologically impossible."

"Inappropriate comments, Dr. Seth! Not the first time, either."

Sonny was fed up, too. For a moment he teetered between engagement and restraint. It was hard to put over two years of antipathy behind him. "What I just said is as germane to the case as anything discussed so far."

But Dr. Rajchand was not to be further engaged. He addressed the medical student. "So you see, we don't have to invoke mysterious tropical ailments. In all likelihood, the treatment did this to him."

"His blood potassium is sky-high," said Sonny. "And he's fluid-over-loaded. I heard a pericardial rub, and he's nauseated, itching—overtly uremic."

"Let's talk about the uremic syndrome."

"Let's not!" said Sonny. "This guy needs dialysis. Right now! He's suffering unnecessarily. There's a dialysis machine available this morning—I checked. If we don't stop bullshitting this second, I'm going to wheel him over to the dialysis unit, stick a catheter in him, and do the dialysis myself."

"Enough!" said Dr. Rajchand, without looking at Sonny. "Send him to the dialysis unit in half an hour. Rounds are over."

• •

ALL AFTERNOON SONNY was on duty in the emergency room and, one way or another, involved in the care of thirty-three patients, almost twice the usual number. He desperately needed another cup of coffee, for he'd soon take over as senior medical resident on call, ultimately responsible for all the internal medicine patients in the hospital until tomorrow morning. He was about to go upstairs to survey the wards when an ER nurse handed him one last chart.

The nurse smiled apologetically. "It isn't a *real* emergency. But if you don't see her now, she'll end up waiting another hour for the next shift to get settled."

Sonny snatched the chart and called out the patient's name. A small, thin man shot up from a chair in the waiting area.

"There must be a mistake," said Sonny. "The chart says the patient is female."

"That is correct, Doctor," stammered the man. "My wife is over there." He pointed to a woman in a black blouse and denim skirt who was leaning awkwardly against the wall.

Sonny turned to her. "Please follow me."

The patient and her husband followed him into an examining room. Sonny read the comments scribbled on the chart by the triage nurse: "Infected laceration. Patient won't say where."

"Please seat yourself on the examining table," Sonny told the woman.

"I prefer standing, if you don't mind."

"The chart says you have an infected cut. May I see it?"

Her face reddened. "The cut is in an odd place, Doctor."

"Where?"

"It's a trifle embarrassing," said the husband.

Sonny smiled politely at the husband and once more turned to the woman. "If you want me to help you, I must see it."

Again it was the husband who answered. "Can't you just prescribe something?"

"I'm sorry, no."

"Oh."

"Let's start with something else," said Sonny. "Why don't you tell me what happened? How did you cut yourself?"

The woman just looked at her husband, who answered, "That's embarrassing, too."

Sonny gave the man a long stare. "I'm not a mind reader—"

"I bit her!" shouted the husband. "Go ahead, Sonali, show it to him! Let's get this over with and go home. Hopefully it won't take as long as last night. I could have punched that smirking Dr. Bhandari!"

Only then did Sonny realize that this was the case Bhandari had told him about. He did his best to look serious as the woman lifted her skirt and leaned over the examining table. The husband watched intently while Sonny inspected the sutured laceration on her ample left buttock. When Sonny poked the inflamed wound with his gloved fingertip, the woman squealed. A drop of pus oozed out.

"It's infected, all right," said Sonny. "You need a full course of antibiotics."

"You'll write a prescription?" asked the husband.

"I'm afraid it won't be so simple. It's unusual to see a wound infection develop so rapidly. The stitches will have to be taken out. Bacteria love to cling to those stitches. When human bites get infected like this, we admit the patient to the hospital for antibiotics infused directly into the bloodstream. You see, the bacteria from the teeth can cause gangrene."

"Gangrene?" said the woman.

"The skin tissue could die and, well—"

"Fall off?" said the husband.

"Oh, no!" gasped the woman.

"I really doubt that will happen," said Sonny. "But in this kind of situation, it's always best to—"

"Can't we first *try* pills?" said the husband.

"You can try anything you want, but I wouldn't advise it."

"Nishad, he said my . . . could fall off!"

"I didn't quite say that—"

"We'll take the pills."

"But, Nishad!"

"Sonali," the husband warned in a stern voice, "it will be okay."

"I want to stay in the hospital, Nishad. Enough has happened down there already."

The husband's lips rearranged into a profound pout. He glared at his wife, then marched out of the examining room, slamming the door.

Sonny considered giving the couple some time to discuss the matter in private, but he was worried the husband would prevail. "Would you like me to talk to your husband?" he said. "Maybe I can explain more clearly why you need to be here."

"Don't worry, Doctor. He'll be all right. I'm sorry you got caught in the middle. This business has been very difficult for him. He has no recollection of what happened."

"What exactly did he do?"

"I don't know, either. I was asleep until he bit me."

• •

AROUND 2:00 A.M., Sonny stepped into an on-call room on the eighth floor. Except for a toasted sesame seed bagel, he'd eaten nothing all day. Now exhaustion overwhelmed his hunger. His back ached; the spasm ran into his neck and shoulders. He placed his pager on the side table next to the phone, fell into bed, and sandwiched his head between two thin pillows. But his back was too stiff for the soft, lumpy bed. He turned from side to side, couldn't get comfortable. So he tossed the pillows onto the floor and lay down on the dusty tiles. The cool floor soothed his back. Sleep came in minutes.

His pager shrieked.

He opened his eyes in the dark and groaned. His body felt glued to the floor. On his knees at last, he groped for his pager. He pressed a button and squinted at the phone number on the illuminated display. Even before he comprehended the number, the pager shrieked again. That usually meant something bad. Now the number registered: the ER. He dialed the emergency room. Busy. His pager went off once more. Same number. He dialed the ER again, a different extension. Busy, too. He quickly slipped on his shoes and darted from the room. Since the elevators couldn't be trusted in emergencies, he took the stairs. Still groggy, he stumbled the first few steps but descended the rest of the seven flights in half a minute.

The ER smelled of stool, vomit, mentholated disinfectant, ammonia and, because there was nowhere set aside for the staff to eat, food. Sonny squeezed through a crowd of doctors, nurses, and technicians. Everyone was saying something, however unimportant. All spoke English, but with different accents—American, Indian, Caribbean, British, East African, reflecting whatever routes they or their ancestors had traveled between the Indian subcontinent and this corner of New York City. Usually Sonny found the variety interesting, but right now he thought even Babel couldn't have sounded this bad.

Lying on a stretcher at the center of the crowd was a stocky man in his forties. He'd been stripped except for his socks—a dark blue sock on the left foot and a gray one on the right. Wires ran from rubber suction cups stuck on his arms and legs to a cardiac monitor. A plastic endotracheal tube protruded from his mouth. A blue oxygen bag was being squeezed by a respiratory technician, while the intern, a tiny woman named Kapoor, performed chest compressions. Meanwhile, Moorty, the night resident in the ER, stared at the fluorescent tracing on the cardiac monitor.

"Another amp of epi!" yelled Moorty in a thick New Jersey accent. He glanced away from the cardiac monitor and spotted Sonny. "Where the hell have you been?"

"What's the story?"

"This guy came in with no pulse. We've been resuscitating for five and a half minutes, but nothing—nothing at all. His family is out there. One of the kids can't be older than six. This man seems awful young for a heart attack."

"That's what we get for coming here," interjected an older nurse from Guyana. "We leave our own land, work hard in someone else's, and die young."

People rolled their eyes.

Kapoor was starting to tire from all the chest compressions. Moorty ordered another intern to relieve her.

"The man is actually forty-seven," said Kapoor, still huffing. "This happened in a hotel room with his mistress. She rode with him in the ambulance. She said he developed chest pain in the middle of his orgasm."

The cardiac monitor screen still showed a flat line.

"What have you given him so far?" asked Sonny.

"Name it," replied Moorty. "Bicarb, glucose, epi, calcium chloride, atropine, liters of saline—"

"How soon did the paramedics get to him?"

"They said he was conscious in the ambulance. He arrested en route. The paramedics started resuscitating right away. His brain may still be okay."

"He needs a pacemaker," said Sonny.

Moorty nodded his agreement. "I paged the cardiologist on call. He's twenty minutes from the hospital."

"If this guy isn't dead already," said Sonny, "he can't have more than a couple of minutes left. Someone get me a pacemaker kit. And prep his groin."

"Have you ever done this before?" asked Moorty.

"No."

"Shit," said Kapoor.

"Are you sure you don't want to wait for the cardiologist?" asked the head nurse.

"Do you see any point in pacing a dead man?"

"The policy—"

"Listen, I'm the senior doctor here. If you can find someone to overrule me, fine. Otherwise get the damn pacemaker! Now!"

The head nurse went to get the pacemaker kit. Another nurse scrubbed the man's groin area with an iodine solution.

Now gloved and gowned, Sonny made a tiny incision. Deep purple blood trickled down the side of the man's thigh. Sonny dabbed the blood with cotton gauze, then picked up a thick-needled syringe and aimed for the femoral vein. Blood filled the syringe. He held his gloved palm open and gazed at the nurse.

"Guide wire."

He inserted the guide wire into the pierced vein, then slid the plastic catheter over it. He tried to imagine it snaking up the tree of blood vessels on its way to the man's heart. Twisting the catheter according to his mind's-eye, he navigated branches of the venous tree. Satisfied the catheter was in place, he threaded the pacemaker wire through the tube until he thought it had lodged in the heart muscle.

"Let's give it a try."

All eyes focused on the screen of the cardiac monitor. The pacemaker created regular spikes, but it didn't induce any electrical activity in the man's heart.

"Damn, it isn't capturing," said Kapoor.

Sonny stared up at the bright ceiling light, then closed his eyes. It hadn't worked. What now? All of a sudden his whole body felt heavy, aches growing by the second as if toward a final, infinite ache. He opened his eyes. Blind for a moment, he eventually saw the man lying before him, nearly dead.

Maybe he was dead.

"Turn it off," said Sonny. "I'll try again."

He shut his eyes, once more attempting to visualize the anatomy of the blood vessels in the man's chest. He saw nothing. He opened his eyes, tried to feel the resistance of the vessels as he jiggled the wire. It slid a bit, then stopped.

"Turn it back on."

The monitor screen still showed no response.

"Maybe we should quit," said Moorty.

Sonny glanced at other faces in the room. Like Moorty, they had given up this man for dead.

Sonny continued to play with the pacemaker wire. Suddenly his fingers sensed something: a faint shudder . . . *A plea?*

"Let's end this," said Moorty.

The intern stopped the chest compressions.

"No!" shouted Sonny. "Keep going! I feel something!"

"*Feel* something?" said Moorty. "What the hell are you talking about?"

"Keep going, I said!"

The intern started the chest compressions again, though not energetically.

"Do it like you want to save a life!" yelled Sonny.

The intern pushed harder, faster.

A few seconds later Sonny stepped back. "Turn it on again—last time." He closed his eyes, listened to the reaction.

A collective sigh passed through the room as a new pattern of spikes appeared on the monitor screen.

"Quick!" said Moorty. "Someone listen for a heartbeat."

Kapoor placed her stethoscope on the man's chest. "Eighty beats a minute, regular."

A pleasant chill passed through Sonny's body. He studied the monitor screen for two full minutes—160 beautifully paced spikes—while Moorty took over again.

Sonny went out to the doctors' station, plopped on a chair, rubbed his eyes. It seemed like he hadn't breathed so deeply in months.

"Where's the patient they called me about?" barked someone.

Sonny looked up. It was the cardiologist, Mitra.

"I just put a pacemaker in him."

"*You what?*"

"Paced him."

"That's what I'm here for!"

"He went flat line more than half an hour ago. What are the chances he would have survived without a pacemaker?"

"Zero."

"So?"

Mitra stomped off to the resuscitation room. A minute later he came out.

"That guy's incredibly lucky," said Mitra. "And you are, too. I can afford to be frank at three A.M., so a word to the wise. A hospital is like the army. There are standard procedures, majors and captains to make sure things are done a certain way, generals to watch over the majors and captains. I've heard that you're damn good, but you're just a foot soldier. It won't matter how good you are if you piss off the wrong people."

"I'm already on the wrong side of all your generals, majors, and whatnots. They won't need this excuse to go after me."

Mitra shook his head disbelievingly and went back into the resuscitation room. All Sonny could think of was returning to sleep on the cool, dusty tile floor of the on-call room.

A nurse came up to him. "The patient's wife is waiting to speak with a doctor."

"Let Moorty take care of it. It's his case."

"Dr. Moorty will be tied up for another hour."

"Then ask the intern, Kapoor."

"This isn't for an intern," said the nurse. "It's very tense in there. The woman the patient was with—his mistress—is in the room, too."

"Hell."

"I've never seen such icy looks."

Sonny tried to make his body rise, failed. He put all his energy into it, grunted, and finally stood up. He took a moment to steady himself, then trudged over to the family waiting room.

• •

THE CUBICLE RESERVED for discussing serious matters with families had a couch on either side. A woman occupied each. The woman to Sonny's left looked fortyish. Three children sat with her, the youngest, a little boy, in her lap. Across the room was a woman who could easily have passed for the other woman's sister. The two had similar figures, complexions, hairstyles.

"Mr. . . ," began Sonny, suddenly realizing he didn't know the patient's name. "He arrived in the ER with no heartbeat . . ."

Slowly, in a clinical monotone, he began to recount what had happened, doing his best not to focus on one woman more than the other. But he tended to look people in the eye, and soon he was favoring the wife. This angered the mistress. And when he made the mistake of referring to the man as "your husband," the mistress rose and yelled, "He may have been her husband, but he loved *me!*"

Now the wife stood up and shouted, "How could he love filth like you?"

The mistress smiled. "Ask him."

Both women now turned to Sonny for news of the man's condition. As Sonny stared back at them, he began to wonder if he'd done the poor man a favor. If the man ultimately survived—and the chances were minimal—it might be only the beginning of his suffering.

· ·

SONNY LEFT THE HOSPITAL just before 6:00 P.M., having gone thirty-five hours without sleep. He lived outside Little India. On warm evenings he often walked the eighteen blocks home. But today he was too tired and took the subway.

As soon as he entered his apartment, he checked the answering machine. No messages—as usual. He emptied his pockets onto a small dresser, then undressed, tossing his clothes on the floor. In his underwear he went to the kitchen and returned with a glass, a corkscrew, and a bottle of Bordeaux. He placed everything on the coffee table, then sat in an easy chair. He had a large collection of original jazz recordings and was particularly fond of Charlie Parker's improvisations. He reached for the remote and pressed some buttons. The stereo began to play "Embraceable You." He uncorked the bottle, let it air for a minute—he was too tired to wait any longer—and poured. Thick rivulets streamed down the sides of the glass as the deep red liquid settled. His nostrils took in the aroma. At last he sipped. He held the liquid in his mouth for a long time, sensing the flavor as it crept along his gums, up to the roof of his palate. He didn't like the wine: too acidic, the tannins too strong, too rough a finish—a nineteen-dollar bottle no better than a four-buck special.

His neck was locked in spasm. He rubbed it and swiveled his hips in the chair until he felt comfortable. Deciding to make the best of the inferior wine, he put his feet up on the coffee table and drank in the dark. His thoughts drifted back to Arizona, where he'd grown up. On warm, clear nights he used to lie on the ground and watch stars dance across the sky. Back then he could recognize every constellation. Here in the city he missed the solitude of the Arizona desert. Still, when he was there he'd been drawn to New York City, just as now, sitting here, he felt the pull of Arizona. Would it always be that way?

Sonny's thoughts were interrupted when his left foot knocked over the wine bottle. A ruby puddle ballooned on the floor. He was too exhausted to clean up the mess and fell asleep in his chair.

· ·

A FEW HOURS LATER Sonny stood up, smacking his lips. All he had on was his boxers. He slipped into his shoes. In less than a minute he was out the door.

Sleepwalking.

It was a warm night, nobody on the streets. Homeless dogs followed Sonny as he headed in the direction of Little India. The restaurants had been closed for hours, the scents of tandoori-grilled meat and fried sweets no longer saturating the air. Without those powerful smells—or the Hindi film music booming from stores, the newly arrived brothers-in-law of appliance merchants yelling "Sale! Sale!" the out-of-towners rushing from shop to shop—the neighborhood had a mysterious stillness. Neither American nor Indian, it seemed like an original settlement, an outpost in the New World set up for a specific purpose—even if that purpose was unknown to its settlers.

Departing Little India, Sonny sleepwalked through Little Korea and Little Vietnam. Along the way he passed the hypokinetic man, stalled on the opposite side of the street. In one of the working-class white neighborhoods wedged within the growing Little Asia, a drunken man sitting on a doorstep shouted, "Where're you going in your underwear, nigger?" The man heaved his empty beer bottle at Sonny. It shattered on the pavement. Dogs barked, and one mutt with burgundy fur broke from the pack and took a mean nip at the man's right hand.

Sonny wasn't conscious of the drunken man, the broken bottle, or the dog, but his mind was far from blank. Into his dream strode a man with silvery hair. He and the man were somewhere in the desert, surrounded by saguaro cacti. The man had dark brown skin, deeply furrowed by the sun. His eyes gleamed, almost aflame, as if the light that bleached the desert came from those eyes, not the sun. The man was saying something. Sonny couldn't make out the words. But he was sure his whole life depended upon those words. Could the man speak louder, more distinctly? The cracked lips curved into a warm, fatherly smile. Then the man rested one hand on Sonny's shoulder and, with his other, pointed at a patch of sky just above a ridge of beige hills. Sonny stared at that patch of spotless blue for a long time, but to him it looked no different from any other part of the sky.

"What is it?" asked Sonny, still gazing into the distance.

All he heard was the silence of the desert.

Eventually he realized that the warm hand was no longer resting on his shoulder. He turned his head.

The man was gone.

• •

WHEN SONNY'S ALARM went off four hours later, he had no recollection of his sleepwalk. He did, however, remember his dream in great detail. Lying in bed, he stared at the ceiling. This was the fourth or fifth night in a week that he'd dreamed about the old man in the desert telling him to go somewhere. But where?

2

Visiting Hours

PATIENTS AND VISITORS SURROUNDED THE INFORMATION DESK IN THE hospital lobby. Nishad squeezed through the crowd. "Where can I buy flowers?" he asked the aged volunteer.

"Go down the corridor, turn right."

When Nishad arrived at Sonali's private room, a dozen roses in hand, she was still asleep. Not wanting to disturb her, he stood outside. Every time nurses walked by, though, he noticed their smirks. Occasionally they whispered or giggled. He was sure they were talking about him. After fifteen minutes he couldn't endure the humiliation. He went inside.

Sonali was lying on her right side. Her eyelids fluttered, then opened. "Hello, Nishad."

She turned on the reading light as Nishad approached the bed. "Roses! Nishad, you shouldn't have!"

While Sonali sniffed the roses, Nishad watched a solution of antibiotics drip down the clear plastic intravenous line feeding into a vein in her wrist.

"What I shouldn't have done was *that*," he said, pointing to her left buttock.

"I'm sure it was beyond your control. Have you been able to recall anything at all?"

"Uh . . . no . . . How does it feel?"

"Quite raw, still. When Dr. Seth last examined me, he said it was very inflamed."

Nishad didn't care much for Sonali's young doctor. "Does he know what he's doing? He doesn't look like a *normal* doctor."

"He seems quite competent. Fortunately, he has gentle hands."

Doctor or not, Nishad didn't like the idea of a good-looking man touching his wife's rear with gentle hands. "So what does he say?"

"Dr. Seth is worried about a collection of pus. He hopes these antibiotics will kill the bacteria. If not, a surgeon may have to drain the wound. They'll make a cut in my bum and—"

"Oh no! . . . Sonali, I'm so, so sorry! I . . . I . . ." He began to sniffle.

"Don't cry, Nishad. Come to me, my cute little man."

While Nishad knelt on the floor embracing Sonali, his guilt became unbearable. He was on the verge of confessing when, clumsy with emotion, he managed to yank the intravenous line from her left wrist. Blood trickled down her hand and soaked into the bedsheet; the bottle of antibiotics emptied through the swinging intravenous line onto the floor.

Color drained from Nishad's face at the sight of Sonali's blood.

"It will be all right," said Sonali, as she pressed the nurse's call button. "A little blood, that's all."

Sonali got out of bed and went to the bathroom, where she pressed a tissue against her still-oozing wrist. After the bleeding stopped, she removed a gold bangle and washed away the drops of blood that had clotted on it. She took a moment to brush her teeth. Then she combed her long, wavy hair and fixed it into a bun. Looking into the mirror, she thought she appeared too healthy to be in a hospital—except, possibly, the maternity ward.

When Sonali emerged from the bathroom, she was horrified to find Nishad lying flat on the floor, his face ashen. Two nurses hovered over him. Red rose petals were scattered everywhere.

"Nishad!"

"Don't worry," said one of the nurses. "I caught him just as he was passing out."

"Are you sure he's okay?"

"Only a fainting spell," said the nurse. He and the other nurse lifted Nishad, who weighed a mere 134 pounds, onto the bed. "There! Strange that he did this. The sight of a few drops of blood, I guess."

Sonali sighed in exasperation as she gazed at her husband, who was now regaining consciousness. She, too, was beginning to wonder why Nishad did strange things.

· ·

AT THE OTHER END of the hall, the Transplanted Man slept peacefully. When at last he opened his eyes, his dream lingered: It was a scene from a film he'd seen over three decades ago, except that he, not Dev Anand, was the hero—singing *"Gatha Rahey Mera Dil"* to the actress Waheeda Rehman while she glanced coyly at him between flourishes of her filmi dance.

It was love.

A trace of a smile remained on the Transplanted Man's face as he returned to the present. After several sessions connected to a dialysis machine, his blood had been cleansed of waste products—at least temporarily—and he felt better. But his heart suddenly sank when one of the most recognizable voices in all India boomed his name. For a second the Transplanted Man thought he might be still dreaming: a nightmare now. Then the door squeaked open, and light from the corridor invaded the room.

"*Arre bhaiyya*, are you awake or no?"

The words pierced so cruelly they had to be real.

"Ronny?"

The intruder switched on the light. When the Transplanted Man's eyes had adjusted, he saw a small man, who was a hero to millions, standing before him.

"Who else?" said Ronny Chanchal, grinning.

That legendary grin had made mush of women's hearts in India and beyond. And while Ronny Chanchal could no longer claim to be number one, among the older generation of film heroes, he alone had withstood the onslaughts of youth. He still refused to play any role other than the young hero.

But the Transplanted Man knew the other side of the man standing before him. And now he was a member of Parliament. Owing to preelection deal making, the Transplanted Man had, despite serious reservations, agreed to support his candidacy. But a few months ago Ronny Chanchal's party had withdrawn from the ruling coalition, leaving the already shaky partnership with a very slim majority. In the meantime Ronny Chanchal had quietly managed to unite the Opposition. Everything seemed to be going his way . . .

"You look quite well, *bhaiyya*."

"And you lie better than ever. Politics suits you, Ronny."

Ronny Chanchal smiled. "It is all due to you."

"One makes mistakes."

Ronny Chanchal slapped the Transplanted Man's shoulder—not very gently. "Always a joker!"

The Transplanted Man rubbed his shoulder. "How did you find me? No one is supposed to know I'm here."

"Not many know—yet. They will, of course. You are, after all, the head of a ministry. Suddenly the prime minister has to answer questions about the absent Health minister."

"There are no secrets about my condition, and I've left dedicated civil service officers in charge. The only secret has to do with my specific whereabouts."

"As if anything in our business can remain a secret! But why?"

"Threats. The CID thinks I ought to take them seriously. They started after the last elections—when there was speculation about me as a potential PM."

"Frankly, *bhaiyya*, I never understood why you opted for the Health portfolio when you could have taken Home or External Affairs."

"Look at me! A Home or External Affairs minister can't be incapacitated. Besides, in a weak government more can be accomplished in a ministry like Health than a more prominent one—where you and your new allies are not constantly trying to subvert every move."

Ronny Chanchal could not suppress a smile. "But from a purely political standpoint—"

"From a political standpoint, the timing wasn't right."

Ronny Chanchal raised his eyebrows. "Oh?"

The Transplanted Man kept quiet.

"New Delhi is full of rumors about you," said Ronny Chanchal. "And now that you mention the threats, I remember hearing speculation that you might have been kidnapped. Someone even suggested that it could be in the government's interest to cover it up, since your ministry's new look is making everyone else appear bad these days."

The Transplanted Man rolled his eyes. "As it is, the government can't manage its cover-ups."

Ronny Chanchal sat down in the chair beside the bed. "There is even talk of a foreign mistress."

"How outrageous! Were it only possible for me to—"

"Others say that, if it really is the illness, then why must the minister go abroad for treatment? Doesn't he have faith in the capability of the health care system of which he is in charge?"

"The reason we've always given is that it's such a rare disease."

Ronny Chanchal nodded. "*Yeh phir bhi kaha gaya tha.* But then people ask, If it is so rare, how can anyone outside India have much experience treating the disease?"

"They have a point."

"Some say you finance your medical treatment abroad by accepting money from foreign companies."

The Transplanted Man winced. He'd once been guilty of corruption, but he was clean now—had been for years. Because he was a minister, the government would pay a large chunk of his expenses, but if his illness dragged on, his own pockets would eventually dry up. True, some of that money had been ill-gotten—in an ultimate sense, long ago. It was hard to give up the money when you needed it so badly. He was uninsurable, and not only had his illness feasted on his body but it had digested his savings and inheritance. If this particular flare-up lasted, he might be forced to obtain personal loans from wealthy well-wishers. Of course, no one just handed out money without expecting a favor or two . . .

"Then there's the rumor—"

"Please, Ronny!"

"All right. I'll spare you. How long will you be here?"

"This time I'm afraid it will be long."

"Are they taking good care of you?"

"I have a good doctor. Young, but good."

"Is there anything I can do? *Anything.* Just tell me."

"Get me a part in a film with Shahina."

"Such a joker!" Ronny Chanchal squeezed the Transplanted Man's hand. "You must be tired. I'll come back later."

The Transplanted Man almost told Ronny Chanchal not to bother.

As the actor-politician rose to leave, a nurse entered. She was young, pretty, with a sandy brown complexion and black hair down to her hips. Ronny Chanchal lingered.

"Sorry to interrupt," the nurse said to the Transplanted Man. "It's time to check your vital signs. Won't take more than a couple of minutes."

"My friend was just leaving."

But Ronny Chanchal just stood there and watched while the nurse bent over to check the Transplanted Man's blood pressure. She kept glancing back at his lascivious gaze. Finally she faced him, folded her arms, and glowered. Without a word Ronny Chanchal backed out the door.

"I hope you aren't a lecherous old prick, too," she told the Transplanted Man.

"No," he replied. "Just old."

· ·

Ronny Chanchal traipsed down the hospital corridor, past reeking rooms that emitted groans of pain accented by anger over the unfairness of life. He didn't notice. Having evaluated the Transplanted Man's condition, he was optimistic about the future. His future. Even though it was still a bit early for lunch, he felt like treating himself to a fine meal with expensive wine.

Outside the hospital, he hailed a taxi. "Take me to the best restaurant in Manhattan," he told the driver.

"I ain't no goddamn tour guide," replied the man.

Miffed, Ronny Chanchal muttered the location of a posh Midtown Indian restaurant. But as the cab sped down the street, Ronny Chanchal realized he didn't feel like Indian cuisine. He wasn't sure what he wanted anymore; this rude driver had spoiled his mood as well as his appetite.

"Please drop me off at the next intersection," he said after the taxi had gone several blocks.

"What the—?"

"Just drop me off *here.*"

"Pay me full fare—eighteen bucks."

"The meter says three fifty."

"Keep your dough, asshole! And go back to where you came from! Damn Indians have got their hands into everything in this town. Newsstands, gas stations, cabs—everything!"

As soon as Ronny Chanchal shut the taxi's door, the driver floored the gas pedal. Startled, Ronny Chanchal tripped and fell into a gutter. Fortunately, the gutter was dry. But the hero was red in the face. He got up as fast as a fifty-two-year-old man could, glancing around anxiously. A couple of people had seen what happened, but luckily he was outside the Indian neighborhood, so he went unrecognized.

Across the street was a coffee shop. He went in and sat at the counter.

"Your order?" asked the waitress.

"Coffee. The blackest."

"There are lots of shades of brown, but black and white come in only one."

Ronny Chanchal was in no mood to debate this sassy waitress. He kept quiet.

Soon the waitress returned with the coffee. The hot brew was unexpectedly delicious, soothing. Still a bit ruffled, Ronny Chanchal asked for refills. After his third cup he began to feel better. He sighed aloud.

His original intent in coming to America had been to lead a song-and-dance extravaganza with performances scheduled on both coasts and major cities in between. Never married and without children, he had no family responsibilities and had been looking forward to his month abroad. But things had changed since he signed the contracts a year and a half ago. Politics. Now he was a member of Lok Sabha, and with so many performances so far from home, he was vulnerable to the charge of neglecting his legislative duties in New Delhi. He had tried to get out of his American tour altogether, but the sponsors had threatened to sue for millions. Fortunately, the contracts allowed for rescheduling, so the tour, originally planned to last four weeks, was adjusted to accommodate his political career: a schedule requiring frequent travel between India and America. Here in New York his performance next month had nearly sold out. Huge posters depicting Ronny Chanchal's face had been plastered all over Esmoor Street for months.

Lately, though, Ronny Chanchal's mind had been on matters other than the show. Since learning of the Transplanted Man's desperate plight, he'd been preoccupied with something greater. Monumental. It was only a matter of time before the flimsy coalition currently governing India fell, and years of mass adulation had convinced Ronny Chanchal that he was the man to take charge of the country amid its present sickness. Besides, so many film stars had found their way into Parliament—and Ronny Chanchal was never satisfied being one among many. Of course, there were other aspirants for the biggest prize. In order to position himself he needed the blessing of the only man who could sway virtually every bloc of voters in the country.

Ronny Chanchal believed that blessing could be negotiated. It would, however, require tact and time. During the many trips he'd be making to America, he would find time between shows for the Transplanted Man. In India scores clamored for the *neta's* attention. Here he had the Transplanted Man's ear to himself. He knew that the Transplanted Man saw through him— and further complicating their relationship was the fact that he had recently joined the Opposition. Even so, Ronny Chanchal was confident that he and the Transplanted Man would eventually come to an arrangement. For Ronny Chanchal was privy to information about the Transplanted Man's past sins— fiscal, carnal, other. Though the sins had occurred long ago, they were still valuable bargaining chips, especially with the Transplanted Man now presenting himself as a model leader. If Ronny Chanchal had to cash in those chips, he wouldn't hesitate. Somehow he had to create the impression back in India that he was the Transplanted Man's heir apparent. When the Transplanted Man retired due to illness or died, Ronny Chanchal figured he was unstoppable.

3

Unhealed Wounds

RUMORS WERE CIRCULATING, AND THE PRESS HAD BEEN CALLING THE hospital. Administrators denied that the Transplanted Man had been admitted and even started a counterrumor that the illustrious patient was in a Boston clinic. At the same time the Indian government maintained that he was somewhere in Europe. Soon dozens of other rumors were floating around, eventually putting a stop to inquiries at the hospital.

In the meantime the Transplanted Man was improving. His much-tortured body, skeptical of doctors, had also learned to recognize the authentic healing hand. Something in Sonny's touch seemed to penetrate his diseased tissues, assuage his aching bones. The Transplanted Man was convinced that Sonny possessed a gift. His body told him so.

He knew next to nothing of Sonny's background but had nonetheless surmised a great deal. His uncle had been a professional physiognomist, and the Transplanted Man always paid attention to facial details. The slight asymmetries in Sonny's features suggested a breach birth, lending support to the Transplanted Man's conjecture that Sonny's compass was deviated. But it was Sonny's eyes that he found most striking. Deep within those eyes lurked a wild longing, evident even while Sonny was absorbed in the day-to-day details of doctoring. It was the look of a young man searching for something beyond what the rest of the world was satisfied with, yet at the same time unsure what that was. Grateful for Sonny's attentive care, the Transplanted Man wanted to help, if he could.

One morning the Transplanted Man preempted Sonny's routine by asking outright, "Why so troubled?"

In a testy voice Sonny replied, "I'm not."

The Transplanted Man smiled faintly. "Tell me about your family. Where does your father live?"

The question made Sonny freeze. At the same time he was struck by the Transplanted Man's talent for locating the jugular. "I don't know," he finally said.

"I'm sorry."

"Nothing to be sorry about."

"My father died when I was five," said the Transplanted Man.

"I have no memory of mine. He left soon after I was born."

"And your mother?"

"She lives in Arizona."

"Do you go back often?"

Sonny glanced away. "We don't have much contact."

"It is hard for a mother to raise children by herself," said the Transplanted Man. "Luckily my family owned property that yielded a steady income, allowing me to finish college. I was the youngest of four brothers and two sisters. And you?"

"Just me."

"Your mother didn't remarry?"

"She did, recently—for the fourth time. . . . Look, can we stick to a doctor-patient conversation?"

"You needn't be angry. Perhaps you are angry because you know it is different between you and me. You wouldn't get angry if I were simply any old man."

"You're a patient. And I have fourteen more to see in the next two hours. So would you please sit up, raise your shirt, and shut up?"

"Certainly," replied the Transplanted Man, smiling.

Sonny smiled back, then rested his hand on his patient's arm. He kept it there for a while, absorbing the Transplanted Man's warmth. Then he placed his stethoscope on the Transplanted Man's chest. In a gentle voice he said, "Take a deep breath."

The Transplanted Man inhaled.

"Your lungs sound better," said Sonny, putting away his stethoscope. "Let's try to hold this course."

As Sonny walked away he became aware of a bitter feeling growing inside him. The Transplanted Man's questions had reopened old wounds. For one, his mother. Not inviting him to her wedding was only the most recent thing he couldn't forgive. He hadn't even met Stepfather Number 3. Then again, anyone would be better than the one before that. When Sonny had visited his mother and Number 2 a couple of years ago, it had been a fiasco. He'd planned to spend the weekend, but he stormed out of the house after just three hours. Of course, he hadn't been entirely innocent in the matter. Number 2 didn't know much about the family past. It was just like his mother to gloss over it, if not misrepresent it. As always, an additional presence sat at the dinner table that night—invisible but all the more powerful for it: his real father. When Number 2 assumed a patriarchal tone and tried to defend his wife against Sonny's not-so-subtle insinuations, Sonny hurled sharp words. He was in top form that night: *Outsider* quickly escalated to *jerk*, then *sonovabitch*. The two of them almost came to blows. His mother made him leave.

• •

SONALI SAT PROPPED UP in bed, answering the questions of a very inquisitive social worker. After six days of intravenous antibiotics the wound in her left buttock was finally healing. However, two scars remained, each the shape of a crescent moon, the exact dimensions of Nishad's jaws.

Sonali had already told Ms. Evans-Puri what had happened in general terms, hoping that would satisfy the small, fidgety social worker. It didn't.

"Tell me again. How *exactly* did it happen?"

"Frankly," said Sonali, "I don't know *exactly* how it happened. I was sleeping at the time, and Nishad doesn't remember anything. The surgeon who examined me said he could have been acting out a nightmare. That may be it, you know. He flips around in bed a lot and grinds his teeth all night."

"Grinding his teeth is one thing. Grinding *your behind* is quite another."

"It wasn't as you think. Nishad has never been violent with me."

"What do you call this, then?"

Sonali shrugged. "Nishad is an honest man. I have no reason to disbelieve him."

"I can give you hundreds of reasons," said Ms. Evans-Puri, shaking her head from side to side. "Men, my dear, are sick—and this city harbors the very worst of them. A man like that should be locked up."

"Oh, my God, no!"

Ms. Evans-Puri removed her eyeglasses, leaned forward, and in a confidential-sounding voice said, "At the very least, your husband should get psychological help."

"I agree he needs to see a doctor, and I must ask Dr. Seth to recommend someone, but sleep specialists and neurologists, not psychotherapists, treat these problems—"

"You're telling me he's psychologically healthy?"

Sonali took a moment to reflect. "He may have a problem or two. Nothing serious, though."

"And I suppose they aren't related to what happened?"

Sonali was about to say no but hesitated.

Ms. Evans-Puri smiled. "Tell me about it. Don't be shy, my dear."

"Nishad has been after me to lose weight," Sonali finally admitted. "He's particularly concerned about . . . uh . . ."

"About what?"

"He wants me to look more like women in designer jeans commercials."

"Those are prepubescent *girls* the Madison Avenue people try to pass off as women! They probably don't even menstruate yet!"

"Nishad's preoccupation isn't *that* unusual," replied Sonali.

"Don't I know! We live in a culture of starvation. The tyranny of it! In the world's wealthiest country, half the population is suffering from a *man*-made famine!"

Sonali nodded solemnly. "But . . . oh, how can I say it? I think we—Indian women—have bigger . . . er, hips. I'm an engineer, not a geneticist, but I'd venture it's a hereditary thing. Our genes are simply different. It isn't right for Nishad to hold me to an American standard."

"It isn't right for *any* man to hold *any* woman to such an *unnatural* standard. And you're so beautiful!"

Sonali blushed.

"*Really!* Have you ever seen the nudes by Rubens hanging at the Met? Your figure is exactly like his depiction of Venus. If your husband doesn't see that—"

"Sometimes Nishad can be a bit silly."

Ms. Evans-Puri shook her head disbelievingly. "My dear—my poor, poor dear—don't you see? Your psychopathic husband committed a most hostile act when he took a bite out of your rear end. It was calculated. Wicked! How can this be coincidental? I'll admit that his story about a transient memory loss—his alibi—is clever. It is sad that the most misogynistic men turn out to be geniuses. Take Picasso, for instance—"

"I'm afraid you're reading too much into this."

Ms. Evans-Puri took Sonali's hand and gently patted it. "I'll bring some books for you. They will open your eyes. And your husband *must* seek help. Demand it!"

Sonali let out a sarcastic chuckle. "Indian men don't go to psycho-therapists."

Ms. Evans-Puri gave her a knowing look. "There's a psychotherapist nearby to whom I've sent several Indian patients, women as well as men. He doesn't act like a psychotherapist, more like an adviser. His name is Dr. Giri. Around here, some call him Guruji."

"Let me think about all this."

"Yes, yes," said Ms. Evans-Puri. "You must think. That's the whole point. Think, think—think! I'll be back again."

• •

Ms. Evans-Puri visited Sonali every day thereafter, sometimes twice a day, and spent many hours trying to convince her that, if she didn't want to divorce Nishad, she needed to change him. What Ms. Evans-Puri did not tell Sonali was that, unhappily married to a mule-headed Indian man, she was on a crusade to fix all others, since she was helpless with her own. The social worker's motives were no longer recognizable as vengeful; they had long ago been sublimated into conviction of a just cause. All around her she saw Indian women exploited by egotistical Indian men ("Little devils who bark like alpha males"), and she was determined to put an end to it.

Daily Ms. Evans-Puri harped on the same points—the violence of Nishad's act, its perversity, its improbability. How could Sonali be so gullible as to fall for his temporary amnesia story?

Until now Sonali had never questioned Nishad's integrity. He was, doubtless, a man with many flaws, but she had always been certain he loved her deeply, which made the flaws bearable. But in the solitude of her hospital room, the social worker's arguments began to affect Sonali's thinking. And on Saturday night, while reading *The Second Sex*, one of several books lent to her by Ms. Evans-Puri, Sonali decided to take a stand.

Nishad was more than a little obtuse about important matters; he needed to be taught a thing or two. Fine, he might be able to solve nonlinear differential equations better than many mathematics professors, but she was damn good at that herself, and what was more, she had a knack for applying the theoretical to the practical that Nishad had never quite mastered. That was what counted if you were an engineer: Who cared if you understood the physics of a suspension bridge if you couldn't design one? That was the reason she advanced quickly in her profession while Nishad always got into difficulties with his bosses.

Of course, all that was beside the point. True, what Nishad had done might be merely another symptom of a society gone berserk over fat, but why did *she* happen to be married to the one idiot who nearly turned it into a tabloid headline? And, as Ms. Evans-Puri kept pointing out, no straight-forward account could explain how Nishad had bitten her buttock *while she slept fully clothed.* Maybe nipping a *finger* during a nightmare could be explained. A buttock? And Nishad, a man of remarkable memory, "couldn't recall" the event or even the moments preceding it. Very fishy indeed!

Sonali was now sure Nishad was lying. What had really happened? Her guesses, fueled by Ms. Evans-Puri's theory about the emotional underdevelop-ment of Indian men, were getting wilder every day. One night Sonali dreamed that she and Nishad had ten sons, all of whom grew up to be buttock-biting maniacs. The memory of the dream lingered through the next morning, and Sonali briefly feared that she might be going mad. She wondered if Nishad's bite had infected her with a terrible virus that devoured the nerves—like rabies but more insidious in its effects.

When Nishad arrived later in the day to take her home, Sonali couldn't help thinking that he resembled a terrier and that his voice had a yip in it. Oh, the thoughts going through her head!

"Nishad, you must see this Dr. Giri I mentioned yesterday," she said with great urgency.

"It's not *that* kind of problem."

"But, Nishad—"

"I won't see a psychiatrist—certainly not one recommended by that annoying Dr. Seth, who looks more like a homeless person than a doctor."

"Dr. Seth is the only doctor I've ever come across who listens to what I say. Besides, the recommendation came from the social worker, not Dr. Seth. And it isn't for a psychiatrist. It's for a guru."

Nishad smiled cynically. "Since when did you, Ms. Woman of the Computer Age, start believing in gurus?"

Sonali didn't like his tone, but she kept calm. "More and more I'm begin-ning to believe that there's something to our traditional ways."

"I don't care if your guru is a saint! I'm *not* seeing him."

During the ensuing silence Sonali stared coolly into Nishad's eyes. After a while she saw that he was getting uncomfortable, so she kept staring—with greater intensity. She stared until he understood that their relationship had changed, that she was now a different woman—that he would have to reckon with a new Sonali.

Then she took it all back. "Please, Nishad," she pleaded. "See this Guruji person—just once."

"No!"

It really did sound like the bark of a rabid dog.

Sonali looked away and in a slow, deliberate voice—a voice that had the rigidity of her mother—declared, "Think hard before you say no again."

· ·

THE MAN THEY CALLED Guruji had never wanted to be anyone's guru. Shaunak Giri held a doctorate in psychology. Two doctorates, actually. Since American academia refused to take his Indian degree seriously, he was forced to obtain another Ph.D. in the same field. The title of his latest dissertation was "The Inner Lives of Non-Resident Indians: A Case Study Approach." At the conclusion of his thesis defense, one of the examining professors remarked, "I commend you for raising this nebulous area of research to a new level of sophistication."

Maybe so, but Dr. Giri suffered the fate of many gifted Ph.D.s: He couldn't find a university position. And after two doctorates he was no longer young—and he had a family to boot. In the end he decided to become a practicing psychotherapist. Why not? He was gentle and personable, with a natural talent for getting people to talk, a deep understanding of human nature. It seemed logical to practice on the very group of people he'd spent seven years studying to obtain his otherwise useless degree.

The scholar in Dr. Giri found it fascinating that so many people around here operated on the edge, yet few ever fell over. Could it be the place itself—these few blocks of New York City? Perhaps the neighborhood compensated for the neuroses of its inhabitants. Nevertheless, those neuroses couldn't be neglected.

What Dr. Giri failed to appreciate was how resistant Indians were to the *idea* of psychotherapy. Months went by, but no one came to see him.

His wife said, "Shaunak, why don't we move to some New Age mecca in the Southwest where your Indian origin might be turned into an advantage? We'll mint money! You just need to learn a little about crystals, herbs, and tarot cards."

He listened to Urmila with sadness, pondering how years of marriage and child rearing had transformed an idealistic young woman into someone who could suggest such a thing.

Of course, he said no. He liked it here. The treatment of these people was his true calling. "I know we're not rich," he told her, "but we're not starving."

"Yet," replied Urmila.

Then an odd thing happened. One afternoon, someone he ran into at the local supermarket called him Dr. Guru instead of Dr. Giri. He assumed it was a simple mispronunciation. But soon others were calling him Dr. Guru as well. A week later, just Guru. Before he knew it everybody was referring to him as Guruji. And when he walked around the neighborhood, people treated him deferentially: "Whatever you say, Guruji." "After you, Guruji." "Consider my shop yours, Guruji."

Dr. Giri was perplexed. Respect was nice for a change, but nonetheless he corrected people. "I'm nobody's guru," he insisted.

Yet the forces of gurufication acquired a life of their own. Soon his first patient showed up—to see the Guruji, not the therapist. Until then he had gone nearly half a year without seeing a single patient. So when the woman said, "Guruji, I have a problem," Dr. Giri answered—in an uncharacteristic moment of weakness—"Yes, my child?"

That night, seven months ago, he was filled with guilt. He told Urmila everything. She acted so amazed that he became suspicious it was she who was behind the confusion. But he didn't accuse her, since he knew she'd deny everything, and there was no point in fighting. He just told Urmila he was going to make it clear to everyone that he wasn't a real guru.

"Think twice," she urged. "If you don't build a practice here, we'll have to move. We have three children to raise and educate, Shaunak. We *need* the money."

He said nothing, because there was nothing to say. Urmila was right. They were nearly broke.

"Besides," she went on, "*guru* just means teacher. There are secular gurus, lots of them. What is a psychotherapist if not a teacher? As you keep pointing out, people around here need someone like you. A teacher. *A guru.* Why not oblige? If you really care about them, it shouldn't matter whether or not they acknowledge your degrees. Only what you do matters."

There was logic in her words, even if they happened to be self-serving. He definitely didn't want to move or to make a living some other way. After much soul-searching, he reconsidered. Even though he never referred to himself as a guru, he let people think what they wished. But he refused to alter the sign outside his office. It still read: SHAUNAK U. Y. GIRI, PH.D.

• •

"Guruji?" said Nishad.

"Yes, my child?"

"My wife made me see you."

"Why is that?"

Nishad sandwiched his hands between his thighs but said nothing. His eyes refused to meet Dr. Giri's. Instead he glanced around the sparsely furnished room. On one side of the window was a writing desk, on the other, a densely packed bookshelf. In the far corner stood a stereo system with a collection of compact discs and cassettes.

"I bit my wife's . . . buttock."

"Please repeat."

"What you heard is correct."

Dr. Giri felt Nishad's gaze lock onto his face. So Dr. Giri bit the inside of his lower lip—hard—barely managing to thwart an incipient smile. Tactfully rubbing his sore lip, he asked, "Do you think that's an appropriate reason for you to see me?"

Nishad squirmed in his chair. "It wasn't like it sounds."

"What happened?"

"I'm . . . not sure. I had a temporary loss of memory."

"You remember nothing?"

"Nothing."

"What is the very last thing you recall?"

Nishad kept quiet.

"Well?"

At last Nishad mumbled, "I was looking at Sonali's rear while she was sleeping."

Dr. Giri ran his hand through his hair. "Do you often look at your wife's rear while she is asleep?"

"Of course not! . . . Okay, lately I have. You see, I've been trying to get Sonali to lose weight. But after I began nagging her, she took to wearing looser clothes, which made it difficult to determine what direction her weight was going in."

"Hmm."

"The night it happened, I'd already begun to think differently. Perhaps because I'm a civil engineer, I had been focused on dimensions till then. But I hadn't *really looked* at what I was measuring. If you stand too close to a van Gogh, all you see is sloppy brushwork. Stand too far away, and it looks like a child's crayon drawing. Do you get what I mean?"

"No."

"There I was, at exactly the right distance, and completely taken by Sonali's voluptuous body, her perfect curves. So I stared, reminded of the erotic sculptures at Khajuraho. What had I been thinking all this time? I began to stroke her flesh. Gently, *ten-der-ly*. It was all the more thrilling because Sonali didn't know! I got *so* excited, and when one is in that kind of mood, all sorts of thoughts enter a man's head. . . . Being so saintly, Guruji, maybe you cannot understand this."

"Fortunately the life I lead doesn't preclude carnal pleasure. I am just an ordinary man trying to help others. Please go on."

"My mind was awhirl with lustful thoughts. Such exhilaration! Suddenly I felt I must have a taste of Sonali's perfect body. But as I was gently nibbling, I experienced an orgasm. So intense! Like none I'd enjoyed before—and like none, I fear, I'll ever experience again. It happened just like that, if you know what I mean, without any direct stimulation whatsoever. I didn't know such a thing was possible! At that moment I felt immense love for Sonali—for every ounce of flesh on her delicious body. But I lost all control during that moment. My nibble turned into a bite, and before I knew it, my jaws had tightly clenched on Sonali's exquisite left buttock, and—"

"So you remember everything!"

Nishad's gaze fell to the floor. "Yes."

"Why did you lie?"

"Now that you've heard the real story, can you blame me? The matter has become so messy!"

"This kind of thing often does."

"What should I do, Guruji?"

Dr. Giri scratched the tip of his nose to pacify an itch. "There are no right answers in my business. But the truth works surprisingly well. Explain to your wife what happened. Just what you told me—the truth. I imagine she'll be flattered."

Nishad shook his head. "It's too late for the truth, Guruji. That social worker has brainwashed my wife! Sonali thinks I tried to hurt her on purpose. Can you believe it? And she's always reading a book called *The Second Sex*. Even though I now desire Sonali exactly as she is, she won't believe a word I say. She misinterprets everything! The last conversation we had was most worrisome of all. Sonali said that there were genetic differences between people, and the shape of her body was typical of our people, which meant that the ratio of her hip circumference to her height—which she claims is what this is about—was the fittest ratio for survival in South Asia, and fitness for survival is really what beauty is, and hadn't I heard of Darwin and natural selection? She said that applying Western criteria to her body was the most demeaning form of neoimperialism, since I, an Indian man, was using an American-European standard on an Indian woman. A man like that, she said, has no self-respect. A mollusk—that's what she called me. A mollusk!"

"Hmmm."

"It's not that I don't see her point, Guruji—and perhaps *the old me* is guilty as charged—but I'm different now. Oh, how I regret it all! Of course, Sonali will never know that. Things have really gotten out of hand these past few days. Sonali used to wear skirts and pants, but now she wears only saris. She speaks to me solely in Hindi. Worst of all, she keeps talking about returning to India."

Dr. Giri took off his glasses and massaged his eyelids. "This is going to be tricky."

4

Sonny's Theories

AFTER FINISHING HIS ROUNDS ONE MORNING, SONNY SPOTTED GWEN Fielding in the corridor. Gwen was new at the hospital, nearly his own height and slim, with straight brown hair twisted into a bun. For weeks he'd been waiting for a chance to talk to her. Now she was alone, no other hospital staff in sight. But something made him hesitate. Her gaze was too intense, her lips too tight, her movements too brisk—as if she was guarding a secret. And yet that intrigued him all the more. So when Gwen went into a patient's room, Sonny leaned against the wall opposite the open door, appearing to glance over some notes. Though he could see her, he didn't think she had noticed him yet.

He'd been there less than a minute when Manny came loping down the corridor behind an empty wheelchair, humming a tune that sounded familiar, though Sonny couldn't quite place it.

"Loitering again!" said Manny. "Sometimes I think orderlies work harder than doctors. But you guys get all the glory. Has anyone ever made a movie about an orderly?"

"A man pushing an empty wheelchair would make a great movie."

"It would, Sonny! Don't you see? Imagine this for an opening scene. Under a spooky, flickering light, me and an empty wheelchair are creeping down a corridor in the bowels of the hospital. All you hear are the wheels screeching—real painfully—and my sneakers shuffling over the vomit green tiles. Then a guy does a voice-over in French, and the subtitles say, 'What is emptiness?' Of course, back home in Trinidad people would laugh, but mark my words, on the West Side they'd form lines a block long in front of the box office."

"Maybe you've got a million-dollar idea."

"I'll trade that million for one shot at singing in Hindi films."

"It might be easier to make your wheelchair movie."

Manny didn't seem to like hearing that. After a while he said, "Hey, did you know your eyes are bloodshot?"

"Slept badly—not enough caffeine yet."

"Then why don't we go down to the cafeteria?"

Before Sonny could answer, Manny noticed Gwen inside the room. "You scheming devil. Be careful, though. That new English nurse is a serious one. Standoffish, too. But they say she's first-rate."

"If she's that good," said Sonny, his eyes still fixed on Gwen, "why would she choose to work here? You and I have our own reasons, but we both know the working conditions aren't great. And most of the time she's in the ICU; no one's in greater demand than good ICU nurses. Like *that*, she could land a better job across town. She must be here for a reason, too."

"I doubt you're it."

By now Gwen had noticed Sonny's stare. She looked back at him, though not with any warmth. He wanted to smile, but his lips wouldn't obey. So he raised his eyebrows, hoping for a response. There was none. At last her attention shifted to a syringe in her hand. She held it up, apparently squinting at the small bubbles inside, waiting for them to rise so she could squirt them out. But soon Sonny realized she was gazing right through the syringe—at him.

"It's probably best to stay away," said Sonny. "She's got the look that always gets me."

"In my humble opinion," replied Manny, "the look she has is homicidal. Sonny, she wants to stab you with that needle."

"Yup, that's the look."

Both grinned.

Having injected the contents of the syringe into an intravenous line, Gwen appeared ready to leave. Sonny glanced at his wristwatch.

"I guess you want me to do something with this goddamn wheelchair," said Manny.

"*Now.*"

While Manny was making his way down the corridor, Gwen stepped out of the room.

"Hi there," said Sonny, as casually as possible, though he thought his voice sounded too urgent, too high-pitched. "I'm one of the residents."

Her eyes narrowed slightly. "Is that why the identification badge on your doctor's coat says, 'Sunit O. Seth, M.D., Medical Resident'?"

He ignored her sarcasm. "This isn't your usual floor, is it?"

"I'm scheduled for another month on the regular wards. Then I go back to the ICU."

"How long have you been at the hospital?"

"Not long."

"How do you like it so far?"

"All right."

"Nice floor tiles, don't you think?"

"They're okay."

Her clipped British accent seemed to underscore her indifference. He thought she was going to walk away, but she just stood there, as if she wanted to see him admit defeat. Her lagoon blue eyes seemed to become glazed by layers of ice.

Eventually he said, "Well, do you want to go out tonight or not?"

"No."

"Why not?"

"A dozen reasons."

"Just say you're busy, then."

She gazed right into his eyes. "I'm quite free, actually. But I don't know you—so I don't know whether I want to go out with you."

"Then go out with me and find out."

"Go out with you to find out whether I want to go out with you?"

"More or less."

"It almost makes sense."

"Risk a few minutes for a lifetime."

"That sounds like a warning about AIDS."

"No. That would be: Risk a lifetime for a few minutes."

"I suppose."

"How about this, then? You can change your mind later in the day; you don't have to show up; and if you do, you can leave whenever you want."

She appeared to be reconsidering.

"Dinner?"

"No . . . uh . . . All right."

"How about Tiger Raj's restaurant? Corner of Forty-third and—"

"I know where it is."

• •

GWEN SIGHED AS SONNY walked away. As far as she was concerned, this was *terrible* timing. Whenever she was in this state, love was hit or miss. Mostly miss. Somewhere in her brain lurked a chemical imbalance that had become the story of her life. Not a pleasant story, either. Every now and then her brain went haywire, causing fits of extreme hunger and desire. For a two- or three-day stretch, she became a slave to instinct. It was an unusual syndrome that overlapped with several diseases, making it difficult to diagnose precisely—and treat. Or so explained an eminent London neuroendocrinologist who then said, "Come sit beside me"—and easily seduced her. This chemical imbalance was the reason that, upon glancing at the naked man lying beside her the next morning, she often asked herself: Why?

And yet she would not leave the man's apartment, or banish him from her bed—for the chemical imbalance inevitably overrode her better judgment. "Why?" became "Why not?" Thus began many a "relationship"—which ended after the chemicals in her brain temporarily rebalanced and she kicked whoever she happened to be with out of her life.

To protect herself, she cultivated an aloofness at work. Unfortunately that hadn't hindered Sonny. And he'd asked her out just when her instincts were shifting into high gear! She was aware of his reputation as an extraordinary doctor, most recently validated by his resuscitation of the man who'd nearly died in the ER a week and a half ago. People were still talking about that as though Sonny were a modern-day shaman. And while she found him attractive, she wondered if he was too young for her. Rather, too green. Even more to the point, how much of her attraction was because her instincts were about to break into a stampede?

· ·

LATER THAT MORNING, Gwen went into the Transplanted Man's room. As usual, he was absorbed in a book. She'd heard that, even during his dialysis session, he spent the whole time reading. In his hands today was *Wuthering Heights.*

Gwen started to dispense pills from three vials. "You read as if books will soon be banned."

"My life back home is very busy," said the Transplanted Man. "I can't read two pages before something demands my attention. It's so frustrating that I've given up even starting a book. When I'm sick, though, I read. It reminds me of the warm, quiet summers of my youth, long before politics and disease deprived me of an uneventful life, and all I did was read, read, read. There's no pleasure quite like losing yourself in a great nineteenth-century English novel."

"No, there isn't."

"You like to read, too?"

"Every spare minute."

The Transplanted Man held up *Wuthering Heights*. "Who's your favorite Brontë?"

"Charlotte, no question. It was after reading an essay on the 'madness' of Bertha that I decided to attend grad school."

"You have a doctorate?"

"I never completed my degree."

"Why not?"

Gwen hesitated. "Let's just say it got complicated. Anyway, a degree in literary criticism is hardly a guaranteed paycheck. And for a while I forgot how to enjoy what I love most: just reading."

"Nursing is certainly different from literary criticism."

"It is," said Gwen emphatically. "When I was in grad school, I went to a seminar where two professors got into a fierce debate over whether a new term, *post-somethingism*, ought to be hyphenated. The argument went on and on—to the point of absurdity. That was when I realized how much I *needed* the opposite of all that abstraction. I wanted to use my hands, touch people, care for them. . . . I know that sounds corny."

"Not to a sick man."

Gwen smiled. "How about a few pills to make you less sick?"

The Transplanted Man shrugged as Gwen handed him a cup of water, together with two round orange tablets, three square white ones, and two red capsules.

"Do you really think these will make any difference?" asked the Transplanted Man, inspecting the seven pills in his open palm.

"I hope so."

"Which means they may not. What does, in your opinion, make the difference? It is not an idle question. I've spent a tenth of my adult life in hospitals. I would have died by now, were it not for pills, doctors, nurses, and intensive care units. But I'm never sure what *ultimately* counts."

"God only knows."

The Transplanted Man swallowed the pills with two gulps of water. "Interesting that you bring God into this."

"I didn't mean to."

"I've always searched for God in hospitals," said the Transplanted Man. "Unfortunately, most hospitals seem rather remote from the realm of spirit."

"This one is certainly no temple."

"So what makes the difference? Is it the needles that stab my skin, or the blades that slice away diseased parts of my body? Is it the cylindrical red capsules I just swallowed, or the round orange tablets? Or could it be that what really matters are those hands of yours that touch people—the sense of comfort you provide when people are most vulnerable?"

Gwen sat down on the chair beside the Transplanted Man's bed. "Lots of things make a difference. But you're right: It's hard to say exactly what. The way I see it, hospitals speed recovery by providing a setting where many things can be choreographed smoothly. No doctor, no nurse, no orderly, no technician is crucial. Everyone is backed up by someone else—like in a ballet troupe or theater company."

"No one can save the show, but anyone can ruin the performance?"

"Not quite what I meant. Another way of putting it—"

"Could it be that what you really do is extract people from the lives that made them sick, so they can read the Brontës for the first or fifth time? There's something sacred about great books. At the end of *War and Peace*, how can one not feel healed?"

"I, for one, would like to believe that. While you're here, I'd be glad to supply you with whatever book you fancy. If I don't have it at home, I'll get it for you."

The Transplanted Man's face brightened. "Do you have *Emma*? *Adam Bede*? *The Mayor of Casterbridge*? I haven't read them in many years."

"I'll bring them tomorrow."

"I should read some American books as well. Any recommendations?"

"Among writers of that century, Thoreau was always my favorite. If I'd stayed in grad school, I might have done my thesis on *Walden*."

"I was talking about fiction."

"*Walden* is as good as the best fiction. I *knew* Walden Pond years before I actually went there. But if you're set on fiction, in my opinion the great American novel is *Moby-Dick*."

"Why?"

Gwen thought for a moment. "Something about Ahab and his inability to conquer his demons."

"Tell me, who has that ability?"

"Not me."

• •

SONNY SAT DOWN AT a table in the hospital cafeteria with a twelve-ounce cup of coffee. He peeled off the cover of a small plastic container of milk and poured it into the coffee. He stirred, watching the milky patch turn into a spiral, its color darkening until the coffee was a homogeneous light brown. He took a sip, relishing the warmth, the flavor. Eventually his thoughts turned to Gwen. As attracted as he was to her, he felt uneasy about tonight's date. For one thing, she'd made no attempt to hide her ambivalence. And there was an edge in her voice, a mistrust in her eyes—a fear of some kind . . .

"Dr. Seth it is, no?"

Sonny looked up at Ronny Chanchal.

The actor-politician sat down with his tea. "I'd like your opinion about my friend's condition."

"Your friend?"

"The gentleman from India."

"That's most of the people here, one way or another."

"Surely not all are the minister of Health and Family Welfare?"

Sonny took a sip of coffee. "I'd need his permission to speak with you."

Ronny Chanchal appeared offended. "He is a dear friend, very dear, like my brother. It's so sad. There hasn't been a leader of his caliber in years. Now, with the political situation so volatile, his time to hold the reins is near. So he must recover quickly. I'm leaving for New Delhi tonight to attend to my legislative duties, but I plan to be back here soon. Hopefully he'll be well by then, Doctor."

"You act."

Ronny Chanchal grinned heroically. "Yes, I do, as a matter of fact."

"You're good."

"You've seen my films?"

"A couple."

"I take it that you like them."

"Not really."

Ronny Chanchal wrinkled his brow. "Then how can you say—?"

"I wasn't talking about the films."

Ronny Chanchal's eyes narrowed. "I see."

· ·

GWEN GOT HOME from the hospital shortly after seven. She was supposed to meet Sonny in less than an hour, and she was having second, third, fourth, and fifth thoughts. Maybe she should just page him to cancel.

Still in her work clothes, she went to the closet and tried to decide what to wear. The hospital didn't allow much latitude in nurses' uniforms; the style was a bit too cute as far as she was concerned. Outside she usually wore loose clothes, sober colors: "Standard Communist Party issue," her friends teased. Were it not for her disease, she might have considered herself lucky to be born into an age that admired long, lean figures. But for her it had led from one disaster to another. That was very much on her mind as she slipped into the grayest blouse and baggiest pants in her wardrobe. Then she stood before a mirror, evaluating herself. As far as she could tell, hers wasn't a pretty face, unless its attractiveness fell into that "unconventional" category. Yes, she could almost see that, and it made her consider dabbing on makeup, just as she'd done on previous "high-risk" occasions: to bring out the worst in her features. She even owned a pair of unbecoming nonprescription eyeglasses. But as she examined her tired face, the shadowy crescents under her eyes, she decided the makeup and glasses were unnecessary.

She went to the kitchen and opened the fridge. Whenever she got into this state, she could eat just about anything. Above all she craved chocolate. She found a quarter-pound bar and unwrapped it as she walked over to the couch. She took a huge bite and savored the sweetness as the piece dissolved in her mouth. Then she nervously munched on the rest of the smooth bar, staring at the bookshelves that filled her apartment.

All those books calmed her down.

Books had always been a source of comfort for her. As a child she used to shut herself up in her grandmother's study, which was crammed with books. She would read a few pages, sometimes understanding next to nothing, then pick up something else. She loved fingering the old covers, carefully turning the thin pages, delicate as petals of a dry flower. "There is more life in books than life itself," her grandmother used to say. After her grandmother's death, many of the books were lost. When Gwen came to America, she brought along what was left of her grandmother's library. But she was always conscious of what was missing. Apart from rent, books were Gwen's greatest expense. In virtually every part of the city there was a bookstore where she was well known. In a very deliberate way she was building her own version of her grandmother's study, trying to re-create the solitude of her youth—those years before her disease had usurped control of her life.

. .

TIGER RAJ WAS EXTREMELY proud of his gray-black mustache and argued that his exuberant facial hair was evidence of descent from intrepid warriors who'd once ruled a kingdom that defied Akbar the Great. Since the kingdom was not mentioned in history books, many doubted Tiger's account. But Tiger claimed to be the kingdom's heir apparent, despite the fact that he was born in Uganda and had never been to India. A man with a theatrical flair, he often presented his story in tragic terms: He was a king without a kingdom, a ruler deprived of subjects. On other occasions Tiger told his customers, "*This* is my kingdom," leaving them to wonder whether he was referring to his restaurant, the neighborhood, or something greater.

All the royal talk lent the modest restaurant on the corner of Esmoor and Forty-third an aura of legacy. Among locals Tiger's had become the most popular eating place in a neighborhood full of such places. Not only were Tiger's prices reasonable but people liked the idea of dining on food fit for a king—which, in fact, it was.

When Sonny and Gwen stepped into the restaurant that evening, Tiger greeted them with a big grin. "Come, come, Doctor."

Sonny flashed a puzzled glance, since Tiger usually called him by first name. Then he remembered that he hadn't been here with a woman in five months—the last time he'd been on a date. All the window tables were occupied, so Tiger guided them to a table not far from the kitchen, where the clatter of utensils could be heard. On the opposite wall hung a copy of an Ajanta cave painting of a charging elephant surrounded by lotus blossoms.

"Your waiter will be here shortly," said Tiger. "In the meantime, would you like some beer or wine? Red wine is best if you take your food spicy-spicy like the doctor does."

"Red's fine," said Gwen.

"The wine here isn't very good," Sonny said after Tiger left. "Once I brought my own bottle, but Tiger didn't like that. So I've resigned myself to great food and bad wine."

"Would you prefer bad food and great wine?"

"Absolutely," said Sonny.

"I'd take great food any day."

"It seems that we have a fundamentally different outlook on this."

Gwen half-smiled. "On most things, I suspect."

"Such as?"

"You don't like small talk."

"I'm not good at it," replied Sonny.

"Me, neither."

Their wine arrived, and they sipped without a toast.

"Next time," said Sonny, "I'm bringing my own wine whether Tiger likes it or not."

"Awful, isn't it?"

Both laughed. His eyes focused on her sternocleidomastoid muscle, which jutted out when she laughed. He wondered how that edge of muscle would feel between his lips, how the skin over it would taste as he nibbled from the top of her neck, just under the jaw, all the way down to her collarbone, how her collarbone would feel inside his mouth, as he slid sideways until he got to the ball of her shoulder . . .

"You seem preoccupied."

"Usual flesh and bones stuff," he replied. "Hard to get your mind off the hospital, isn't it?"

"Speaking of the hospital, how do you think the Transplanted Man will do? Will his kidneys recover?"

"Too early to say. The problem's that it isn't just his kidneys. His heart and liver transplants are on the verge of rejection, and his intrinsic disease— whatever it turns out to be—is smoldering, too. With some patients, you get the feeling that, no matter how well they look, they could go sour any time."

As they drank more the wine began to taste better. They talked about the hospital, recent movies, the upcoming election, how unusually warm it had been, the city itself.

"So how did you end up here?" asked Sonny. "Here, as opposed to another part of town."

"I'm not Indian, if that's what you mean."

"That wasn't what I meant."

"What *did* you mean?"

"Okay, that's what I meant, more or less."

"You're wondering if I'm a standard Indophile, or if there's something more."

"I guess."

"How much does it matter?"

"When put that way, it matters a lot."

Gwen swirled the wine in her glass. "Both of my grandfathers were in the empire-building racket. So both of my parents, believe it or not, were born in

India. Of course, they met many years later in England. But what they had in common—sometimes I think it was *all* they had in common—was a longing for the past and a sense of dislocation. A type of postcolonial disease, I suppose. Whatever it is, I seem to be afflicted, too."

"The symptoms?"

"Hard to pin down, at least in my case. Of course, the London riots didn't help. Our part of town wasn't spared by the violence. A white bobby was stabbed in our neighborhood, and my best friend's elder brother, Vinit, a chess champ—I had a bit of a crush on him—was attacked by a gang. His skull got fractured by a cricket bat. Growing up was confusing enough without all that."

The restaurant had become busier, waiters zigzagging between tables, carrying flaming kebabs, vegetable dishes, dals, puris, plates of rice. Tiger seemed to be everywhere: greeting customers at the entrance, refilling glasses of water, inspecting desserts as they emerged from the kitchen, tallying bills.

"This place is pretty far from London," said Sonny.

"That may be, but a flight between here and London doesn't take that much longer than one to L.A. . . . Anyway, there were other reasons why I had to leave."

He waited for her to elaborate. She didn't.

Sonny poured more wine into Gwen's glass. "I used to think everyone had a perfect place," he said.

"A perfect place? What do you mean?"

"I believed everybody had an optimal longitude, latitude, altitude. Most just accept the coordinates where they were born—or go wherever they can make enough to live decently. Nothing wrong with that, if it doesn't bother you. But it's not so straightforward for certain people. The locations of the cities, states, sometimes even the countries they happened to be born in aren't right. And those people feel a *need* to do something about it. After all, if you've got no family to speak of, no close friends no religion, either—all you've got is place, right?"

Gwen took a sip of her wine. "You said you *used to* think everybody had a perfect place. Does that mean you don't think so anymore?"

"If that place kept eluding you, wouldn't you question your theory?"

She made no comment. He thought his theory must sound quite silly to her. Maybe he should just drop the subject. But then he looked into her eyes. This morning's harshness was gone; her blue eyes were still, intelligent, wistful—uncertain. He wanted her to understand.

"There are different ways of looking at it," he went on. "Millions of years ago, India was an island—'drifting,' as they say—searching for a continent to fuse with. Of course, it eventually found Asia, and that great crash resulted in the Himalayas. But was it preordained? What if the internal engine of the earth had been in a different mode—or a different *mood*? Maybe the island that was to become India could have crashed into any continent: North or South America, Europe. Wherever."

"Your point?"

He smiled. "There is one, actually. What if India had been destined to keep colliding with different continents, never completely fusing, leaving pieces of itself everywhere—and taking bits of each place it bumped into along with it to its next destination? After all, they say the Himalayas are fairly new, geologically speaking. Who knows if that Himalayan seam is so tight?"

"I don't quite see what—"

"Think of it as human, rather than continental, drift. Maybe we're all like that island that keeps bumping into different continents, taking bits and pieces with us. For the moment, we're here. But only for the moment."

Gwen tapped her index finger against the stem of her wineglass. "That means there *isn't* any perfect place. There never can be. They are all temporary destinations. Have you considered that?"

"Many times."

• •

AT QUARTER PAST TEN, Gwen and Sonny stood before the entrance to her apartment building, a six-story redbrick edifice one block from Esmoor Street.

Gwen wanted to invite Sonny in—for a cup of tea, nothing more—but she feared her overactive drives would gain the upper hand. From prior experience she knew that entry into her apartment could easily become entry into her body and, temporarily, into her life. She hadn't expected much from their dinner date, but over the past two hours she'd come to like Sonny. Without realizing it she had abandoned the guise of cultivated indifference—the only way to avoid a mistake whenever she was in this state. Best to part quickly, wait till her instincts cooled down, then see where this went.

"I guess it's sort of late," she said.

"I'll see you at work."

Her eyes softened. "Would you like to come up for tea and chocolate cake? I'm still a bit hungry."

"After all you ate? . . . Sorry, I didn't mean it like *that*."

"Don't worry."

"I'll pass on the cake," he said. "I wouldn't mind some tea, though."

Gwen was quiet for a moment. "Do you read much?"

He gave her a quizzical look and said, "I barely even have time to read medical stuff these days. To wind down, I listen to jazz and the blues."

"On second thought, tea isn't a good idea."

Sonny shrugged. "Fine, whatever. Good night."

He started to turn away.

"Maybe you'd like to check out the view from the roof?"

"What?"

"The view from the roof—"

"That's what I thought you said."

They took the old elevator to the rooftop. All the way up Gwen cursed herself. When the elevator doors opened, her finger reached for the Door Close button. But Sonny was already stepping onto the rooftop. Gwen trailed, reminding herself that the roof wasn't her apartment—didn't need to imply it, either.

The warm September night was full of city shrieks and rumbles. Sonny walked to the railing and leaned over. Gwen followed, at once anxious and excited. She positioned herself about a foot from him, her hand on the railing. His hand, also on the railing, inched toward hers. Their fingers touched. Soon she was looking into his eyes. Never before had she been able to walk away when things had gone this far. . . . Damn these absurd courtship rituals! Just look at him! Well, it *is* an interesting expression, an interesting face—his eyes so deeply set, dark and gentle. And yet there's a restlessness. A wildness? . . . He's too young, Gwen! Mr. Perfect Spot, indeed! Has he read Thoreau? Probably just the ant passage everyone *had* to read in school. . . . Ah, he's making his "move." Why can't it ever be like Jane Austen—like Elizabeth and Darcy, or Emma and Knightley—slow and incremental? Why do I always have to fuck first?

• •

GWEN AWOKE WITH HER usual postorgasmic headache. She was still sleepy, but the constant throbbing kept her eyes from closing again. She glanced at the alarm clock, which she'd forgotten to set last night. Seven-o-eight! She was supposed to work the early morning shift; her phone would be ringing any second, her supervisor's rasp on the other end. She carefully lifted Sonny's hand off her breast. His fingers grazed her nipple. It became firm; she was tempted to stay in bed. She set his arm down on the pillow, sat up, and shook a couple of aspirins from a bottle on her bedside table. Then she slipped into her robe and headed for the fridge. She swallowed the tablets with a glass of apple juice, then searched the fridge, stuffing herself with chocolate cake and milk.

She went to the bathroom and took a hurried shower. While toweling off before the mirror, she noticed the narrow, reddish lines on her skin—extending from both her jaws, going down her neck, and ending at the depression just below her larynx. There they connected at acute angles to similar lines extending along her collarbone and all the way to both shoulders, also red. An anatomy specimen marked for dissection? What an eerie thought! But then she remembered how good it felt as Sonny nibbled down her neck. She powdered the red lines, then slipped into her nurse's uniform and buttoned it to the very top. She turned her head from side to side to make sure no other marks were visible.

Just as she was leaving, she remembered the books that the Transplanted Man had asked for. She tiptoed around the room and managed to locate *Emma*, *The Mayor of Casterbridge*, and *Moby-Dick* but couldn't find *Adam Bede*. Instead of *Adam Bede*, she considered taking *Walden*. She owned four copies, but the only edition she found right away was her personally annotated one, which she would lend to nobody. She shut her apartment door gently.

While Gwen walked to the hospital, the books bulging in her handbag, she chided herself for allowing Sonny into her apartment last night. This wouldn't have happened under a different phase of the moon, or whatever it was that triggered her disease. And why hadn't she shown the sense to boot the stranger out in the morning? Well, she could probably trust him not to rummage through her apartment, and in any case he had to be at the hospital soon. Okay, the real reason she'd let him stay was that she liked him. But she needed to think through the events of last night, carefully consider their implications. What a peculiar guy! Troubled? True, he had a reputation as a clinical wizard, but people also said he was an odd one. Some of the senior physicians even referred to him as "the rogue resident." Still, after that conversation last night at Tiger's, maybe she saw something the others didn't. Medicine doesn't forgive unconventionality. Both as a nursing student and as a licensed nurse, she'd seen interns just out of medical school arrive on the wards every year full of life; within a few months they'd become automatons.

No question, Sonny *was* an exception. How much of an exception? That was the real question.

And adding to her perplexity was a strange feeling that he'd left the apartment in the middle of the night.

• •

SONNY LAY IN GWEN's bed, staring at the ceiling. He didn't feel like rolling out of bed. Or even leaving the apartment. He glanced around the room. Last night he had noticed the bookshelves, but his mind had been elsewhere, and the lights had gone out seconds after Gwen and he entered the apartment. Now he saw how many volumes there really were. Apart from minimal furnishings there were *only* books, thousands of them, neatly arrayed on tall shelves. Even the bedside table was stacked high. On the very top was something by Sappho, whoever he was.

As a child Sonny had suffered mild dyslexia, and even though he later overcame this limitation, he remained uncomfortable with the printed word. Of course, he scanned medical journals to keep up with advances, but words had always seemed to him inadequate substitutes for an intuitive knowledge that couldn't be conveyed by sequences of letters. As he moved further along in his medical training, he came to trust his nonvisual senses more and more. When his fingertips gauged a pulse, they also fathomed something deeper about the patient. He knew the smells of syndromes and with his stethoscope often heard heart murmurs missed by specialists. Like those of someone with a neurological defect affecting only a specific kind of sensory processing, his other senses had not only expanded their range but become exquisitely tuned.

His need for coffee drove him from the bed to the kitchen. Though tiny, it was well stocked, everything arranged to utilize space efficiently. On the counter were four types of black tea, three different greens, and half a dozen herbals—a tea for every mood, it seemed. No sign of coffee, though. But the presence of an automatic coffeemaker gave him hope. He opened a few cabinets, finally located a can of coffee. While the coffee brewed he thought about Gwen. He couldn't figure out this cynical, lustful, obsessively neat, tea-drinking, book fiend who dressed in battle fatigues. Already he sensed problems. For one, she'd snuck out before he woke up. Maybe she was just being considerate. But pleasurable as last night was, something about the way everything had unfolded bothered him.

He'd never been particularly good at figuring out women in his life. He had loved two, both Indian. Marilyn was a Navajo law student intent on recovering tribal lands back in Arizona. Alka he met while traveling through India one summer during his college years. With both women he had felt there could be no one else. Both relationships ended because he wasn't Indian enough.

Since he'd moved here, there had been no one to speak of. For a while he felt so lonely he even considered an arranged marriage, though what he had in mind wasn't much more "arranged" than a personal ad. In fact, he sent one to an Indian American newspaper:

> Average-looking, above average height, Indian American doctor living in New York City area seeks to meet intelligent, unconventional woman (Indian, Indian American, or Indophilic American) in mid to late twenties without strong religious beliefs.

Not a single response. When he called the newspaper to continue the ad for another week, the woman in charge of "Matrimonials" said it was the first time in the eight years she'd been with the paper that no one had replied to a doctor's ad. Nosy, though in a pleasant way, she suggested radical revisions. "Everybody lies," she said. "'Pretty' means plain; 'tall' means average height; age, especially in women who admit to being over twenty-five, means nothing."

"So eleven inches means nine?"

"If it's really nine, then my name's Renu."

They spoke flirtatiously for a while until she disclosed that she was forty-one with three kids. Since that could mean sixty-two with five kids, he reverted to his original plan.

His new ad was put together by Renu—or whoever she was. He asked her to write it, and he didn't want to know what it said. All he knew was that he'd paid for thirty-seven words.

He received 348 replies, most with photos, from all over the world: Cape Town, Port of Spain, London, Lagos, Delhi, Madras, Bombay, Dallas, Philadelphia, San Jose, Boston, Phoenix, Vancouver, Hong Kong, Singapore, Djakarta—and almost every town in New Jersey.

By then he had concluded this wasn't for him. He spent his free evenings slipping the 348 photographs into envelopes and appending handwritten notes, one version of which read, "Your daughter is very attractive, and I'm flattered, but this whole business is crazy, and you don't want a son-in-law like me. I'm extremely sorry for your trouble."

He didn't expect any replies to his 348 notes, but there was one. It came from the woman herself, a Sonya Sehgal in New Delhi. He remembered her photograph, the one that had made him think twice about not pursuing matters further. Even in black and white, her eyes sparkled with intelligence and playfulness. She was a painter, the daughter of a high government official. "Although my parents now couldn't care less about you," wrote Sonya, "suddenly I'm quite interested."

That had been a year and a half ago. Sonny never wrote back. But in his mind Sonya Sehgal became an almost palpable fantasy of uncomplicated happiness in a different world.

5

In the Room Across the Hall

AT 9:42 ONE MORNING A WOMAN IN HER EARLY FORTIES WENT OVER TO the information desk to inquire which room her husband had been transferred to.

"Go down the corridor, turn right."

Four minutes later a woman who could have passed for the first woman's sister stepped up to the information desk and asked for the room number of her lover. She, too, was told to go down the corridor and turn right.

Both women were looking for the same man.

That man remained in a coma. Yet by ICU criteria he had improved. Extensive neurological tests had confirmed that the comatose man's brain was still functioning, if at a rudimentary level. His endotracheal tube had been pulled out, and he was able to breathe on his own. His heart was beating regularly, and the temporary pacemaker inserted by Sonny had been removed. His blood pressure was normal, as were all his blood tests. As a matter of fact the comatose man looked so good that someone unfamiliar with his case might have wondered what this patient was doing in the ICU: a healthy, middle-aged man in a deep, restful sleep. So when a pregnant woman with internal bleeding needed an ICU bed, the comatose man was transferred to the room across the hall from the Transplanted Man.

Now that the comatose man was out of the ICU, Sonny insisted on being his doctor. Although the slight improvements had given Sonny hope that the comatose man might recover, the more contact he had with his imperturbable patient, the more he felt that what he'd done that night in the ER had been rash, maybe even criminal. Rushed at the time, exhausted too, he hadn't thought things through. How does anyone ever know in this business? What kind of existence was this, trapped in a limbo that was neither life nor death? Of course, eventually it could only be death. At least it would be a quiet one, free from agonizing contortions. Still, this man's ghost would haunt him forever.

When Sonny emerged from the Transplanted Man's room around ten-thirty that morning, he heard a commotion across the hall. He darted over to the comatose man's room. All noise ceased as soon as he entered. At first glance the comatose man looked no different. His respiratory rate was regular, and the portable cardiac monitor displayed a normal wave pattern.

Sonny turned his attention to the source of the commotion: the two women on opposite sides of his patient's bed. He stared at them for a few seconds, trying to assess the situation. Eventually he said, "What's all the racket over?"

The comatose man's wife pointed her index finger at the other woman. "That whore won't leave!"

The eyes of the comatose man's mistress flashed with rage. "Look who's calling who a whore!"

"Yes, look!"

"Please!" said Sonny. "This . . . This . . ."

The two women waited for him to complete his sentence. With all the doctorly authority he could muster, he finally said, "This is a hospital. This is a very ill patient. This—"

"*This* man loves me," interrupted the comatose man's mistress.

"I'm his wife!"

The mistress chuckled sarcastically. "His wife! What does that mean? The man scarcely knew you when he mumbled a few words in front of a fire twenty years ago. That doesn't mean he *loves* you, which is all that matters. What proof do you have? *Show me.* I don't mean some piece of paper like a marriage certificate, though maybe you don't even have that. Hah! You don't! I can tell from your face. You can't even prove that you're married to him, much less that he loves you."

"What proof do you have that he loves *you?*"

A smile stole across the face of the mistress. "Can you read faces? Then look at me. Care-ful-ly."

The wife scrutinized the other woman for a long time. The wife's face reddened, and bit by bit her eyes filled with humiliation. Her eyebrows, smoothly curved a moment ago, had twisted into an expression of doubt and anger, waves of flesh jutting out between the furrows on her forehead. Meanwhile, the features of the mistress's face sharpened as she watched the wife's face transform.

"There are different kinds of love," mumbled the wife.

It sounded like a retraction, as the wife seemed to realize. Suddenly her dark eyes widened and started to shine again. "You're deluded! For all I know, you believe we're on the moon, but that doesn't make it true. Syphilis rots the brain, doesn't it, Doctor?"

Both women stared at Sonny.

"Listen, ladies," he began. "The poor man almost died. No, he actually *did* die. For a few minutes he fulfilled many definitions of death. And now, he's like this." Sonny gestured with his open hand toward the comatose man and then, for added effect, at the portable cardiac monitor and intravenous infusions. "The chances are slim that he'll snap out of it. Very slim. A ninety-nine-point-nine-percent chance of death. And you two are fighting over—"

He stopped short: This really wasn't his business. Yet he felt he had to protect his patient from the two women who claimed to be loved by him. At last he said, "Doesn't anyone care whether he lives or dies?"

"Only if the bastard can talk!" snapped the wife. "He has some explaining to do."

"As far as I'm concerned, there's only one issue," said the mistress silkily.

The wife reflected for a moment, then looked the mistress in the eye. "You're right."

The women sat down on opposite sides of the bed, folded their arms, and stared at each other with gazes intended to ignite.

· ·

MANNY ROLLED A WHEELCHAIR up to the Transplanted Man's bed. "Dialysis time."

The Transplanted Man groaned.

"Hey, it's better than no dialysis, right?"

The Transplanted Man placed a bookmark between the pages he was reading, and Manny helped him into the wheelchair. "Ready?" asked Manny.

"Please go slower this time."

"Be a sport! Think of poor me, wheeling people around all day. I'd die of boredom if I didn't go for a new record. We'll try to break two and a half minutes this time. Come on, please?"

The Transplanted Man's hands clenched the armrests of the wheelchair. "All right."

A harrowing two minutes and twenty-eight seconds later, the Transplanted Man passed through the doors of the dialysis unit. Five of the seven beds were occupied. The drone of dialysis machines competed with other sounds in the room: radios, TV sets, voices of nurses and doctors.

Soon the Transplanted Man was shifted into an empty bed. Then he was connected to a dialysis machine, which cleansed his thinned blood of waste products—a job once done by his own kidneys.

The first few times he was dialyzed, the Transplanted Man had felt dazed and suffered terrible headaches. For hours after he couldn't eat because of nausea. But each dialysis session bothered him less, and by now he was used to being hooked to the machine three times a week, four hours at a time. He passed the hours reading novels supplied by Gwen. His appetite for fiction, once whetted, had fed on itself—grown into a monstrous hunger that could be satisfied only by thick nineteenth-century English classics. So he read and read.

An old-style patriot, the Transplanted Man was aware of the irony of his deriving solace from novels penned by accomplices to the imperial agenda, their exquisitely nuanced portraits of a world that had no place for his kind. This morning, however, he was reading something different, a book by the most renowned Indian writer of the day. When the Transplanted Man came to one passage, he laughed out loud. In what at first appeared to be a parody of an ancient myth, the writer compared parts of India to human body parts. For over a minute the Transplanted Man couldn't control his laughter—despite half a dozen pains from his own body parts. Other patients undergoing dialysis stared with concern, as though he were going mad from the treatment.

Suddenly the Transplanted Man stopped laughing. Had he been the inspiration for the sentences before his eyes? He was a well-known figure, in the news for decades. This writer must have heard about him and his much-transplanted body. Suddenly he was certain the writer had used him. He burned. He didn't particularly mind that he might have been the writer's muse, but the politician in him wanted credit. Millions must have bought this book! All he could think of was the lost publicity. And another thing. Someday these paragraphs might be all that was left of him in this world. Books outlast people—or some do. This might have been his only chance at immortality . . .

A buzzer went off, sending a shudder through him. A nurse hurried over to the dialysis machine and adjusted the controls. The buzzer stopped. The Transplanted Man sighed.

Immortality? He had no right to be so greedy. All he really wanted was a little more life.

• •

THE COMATOSE MAN'S NEUROLOGICAL status still hadn't changed. But the patient continued to appear robust and, to Sonny's eye, younger. His wrinkles had vanished, and his skin possessed a ruddy glow. That striking contradiction between the comatose man's youthful appearance and the absence of higher brain function made Sonny brood over the strangeness of it all. Whenever he went into his patient's room, he left depressed.

Then, one afternoon while Sonny was routinely testing his patient's knee jerks, the comatose man opened his eyes.

Sonny froze. For a minute the whole hospital went silent. No beeping machines, no relatives chattering in the hallway—no noise at all.

Sonny had always assumed that his patient would gradually slip closer and closer toward death until one day he quietly lost his pulse, fading out for good. The comatose man obviously had other plans. Sonny didn't know yet whether his patient could speak and, if so, how well. In all likelihood he had suffered damage to parts of the brain where speech centers were located. If not, at most Sonny expected a Where am I? kind of question.

Having finally recovered from his initial shock, Sonny gently squeezed his patient's hand. Suddenly he was filled with terrible anxiety. What if the comatose man's brain remained severely damaged? *Permanently.*

The comatose man was staring at him. Not a blank stare, but Sonny could discern no meaning in it. He was about to utter some standard words of reassurance when the comatose man's brow furrowed.

"My wife knows, doesn't she?"

It was as if he and Sonny had been in the midst of a conversation—interrupted by the unfortunate matter of his temporary death and coma—and now the comatose man was continuing that exchange, responding to some remark Sonny had made.

Sonny stammered, "Knows what?"

"My . . . er, girlfriend. She and my wife have met, haven't they?"

Sonny's face filled with pity. "Yes."

The comatose man appeared to age two decades in thirty seconds, his face almost as pale as when his heart had stopped. "It didn't go well, did it?"

"No."

The comatose man shrank into his bed as though withdrawing from this world all over again. Finally, in slow, deliberate words, he said, "Doctor, don't tell them I can talk, okay? Promise you won't tell *anyone.*"

Sonny didn't feel he could promise such a thing. At the very least, he'd have to make a note in the comatose man's chart, and then, the story being what it was, it would spread through the hospital in no time. Perhaps the comatose man's wife and mistress could be kept in the dark for a day or two—after all, that could be construed as protecting a patient's privacy—but they'd find out sooner or later.

"Please, Doctor. You *must* promise—at least until I figure out what to do."

The comatose man's face was so full of anguish that Sonny replied, "I'll do what I can."

The comatose man sighed, then shut his eyes. A few seconds later he reopened them. "There's no way those two can ever get along. They are such opposites! Shanta's front might as well be Gayatri's back, and vice versa."

"Their fronts look pretty similar to me," said Sonny.

A mischievous smile made its way across the comatose man's face. "Come to think of it, so do their backs."

• •

AT QUARTER TO FIVE the next morning, Sonny lay in bed wondering if the comatose man's recovery had been a dream. Still groggy, he tried to fall back to sleep but couldn't.

He yawned and stared into the dark. Last night he'd been out with Gwen: their fourth date. Their second and third outings had been very tentative; she seemed to be backtracking to the point before they'd slept together. But last night they'd finally returned to that point—and then moved forward. He didn't leave her place until well past midnight.

His thoughts returned to the comatose man. Very clearly he remembered that night in the ER when the comatose man had lost his heartbeat and everybody else had given him up for dead. He would have, too, were it not for . . . How to describe it? The feeling was so subtle, an echo of an echo, a call from a distant world—yet unmistakable for anything else.

Was that *it?* The difference between life and death?

Once again he began to doubt whether his patient had, in actuality, recovered. So just before six Sonny rolled out of bed and, without drinking coffee or even brushing his teeth, rushed to the hospital.

Forty minutes later he had finished examining the comatose man. "You're doing great!" said Sonny, putting his stethoscope back in his pocket. "I still can't believe it. If all goes well, you'll be out of here in a week or two."

"Doctor, do you have a few minutes to talk?"

"A few minutes" usually meant half an hour or more, one reason why doctors ended conversations abruptly. But the comatose man's voice was so shrill, his expression so distraught—the very opposite of that peaceful look he'd had when he was in a deep coma—that Sonny pulled up a chair. "What's on your mind?"

"I'm usually a sound sleeper, Doctor, but I've been awake all night, thinking a great deal about my—oh, how to put it?—predicament. As best as I can tell, there are only two options. You can either make two of me or say I died suddenly."

"I can't tell them you died."

"Why not?"

"I'm a doctor. If I say someone is dead, that person had better be dead."

The comatose man gave Sonny an utterly pathetic look. "It may come to that."

"Don't be silly! You've done the miraculous. You've returned from the dead!"

"That miracle would seem like nothing if I could figure a way out of this pickle."

Sonny had to admit there was some validity to the argument. All he could do was offer encouragement. "I know it'll be difficult, but you're made of strong stuff."

"They're made of *stronger* stuff. When they found out yesterday that I'd emerged from the coma, they hovered over me like angry goddesses. And after I'd fooled them into believing that I couldn't understand anything, you should have heard the way they talked about me! Like a pair of shoes that could only be worn by one of them. Why must each woman have both? Let Shanta take one, let Gayatri take the other. One shoe is good; after all, it covers one foot. You can cover the other foot with a different shoe, right? Besides, I'm such worn-out pair, I wish they'd just toss me out."

"There's an idea."

"Not a realistic option, Doctor. They're determined to take me back, no matter what. Everything has become so twisted, like one of those silly Hindi film plots. But I know it won't turn out well. The whole time Shanta and Gayatri were in my room yesterday, I stared blankly at the ceiling—as if my brain had been permanently damaged. I really didn't need to act. I was dumb with fear!"

Sonny nodded sympathetically. For a second he wondered what the consequences of falsely declaring a man dead might be. Illegal, yes, loss of his medical license for sure—if he was caught—but perhaps it fell into the category of a noble lie . . .

"What about the other option?" asked the comatose man.

"Which is?"

"Make two of me."

"Funny."

"I once saw a thriller in which they took a snippet of a man's skin and grew his evil twin. It was one of those fifties black-and-white sci-fi movies. But that kind of thing is possible now. So why not me?"

Sonny pursed his lips. "Unfortunately—"

"I'm desperate! There *has* to be a solution! Help me think this through, Doctor. Maybe I'm missing a good idea because my mind hasn't fully re-covered yet."

Sonny found himself weighing possibilities.

After a while, the comatose man asked, "Any ideas, Doctor?"

"Yours were better."

The comatose man grimaced.

"I'm afraid you're going to have to come clean on this."

The comatose man closed his eyes. "I know."

· ·

UPON LEAVING THE COMATOSE man's room, Sonny crossed the hall to check on the Transplanted Man. His patient was on his side, curled up, head sand-wiched between two pillows. Rather than disturb him, Sonny went down to the cafeteria for coffee.

Shortly after Sonny left, a tall spectacled man with a deferential hunch qui-etly entered the Transplanted Man's room. He held a briefcase in one hand. For twenty minutes he stood at the foot of the bed, listening to the loud snores. At last the Transplanted Man opened his eyes and yawned.

"No need to stand, Verma."

The minister's right-hand man bowed slightly and sat in the chair beside the bed. "I hope you are getting better, sir."

"I am better only until I get worse."

"What do the doctors say?"

The Transplanted Man yawned again. "What they think and what they tell their patients are different. They lie as much as politicians."

"Sir, if you're unhappy with your care—"

"No, these doctors are better than most. One of them, the youngest, may be the best I've ever had. Now tell me about the ministry. Is everything all right?"

"Not to worry, sir. With all due respect, we've had new ministers so often that we've learned to run things ourselves. Of course, it runs much better with you there."

"You're a silver-tongued toady, Verma."

"In the Indian government, sycophancy pays handsomely."

The Transplanted Man raised his eyebrows.

"A joke, sir."

"Look, my friend, I don't know when I'll be back—if I'll be back. From your perspective, the point may be moot. It won't be long before the prime minister is forced to replace me."

Verma shook his head from side to side. "All this actually works out quite well for the PM. Your name remains associated with the government, but meetings end early, since you're not there to interfere with their agenda."

The Transplanted Man smiled wryly. "They have an agenda?"

"A good question, sir."

"They may need my name now, but one day they won't. The political situation can change in a blink. Until then, though, you realize that *you* are the minister."

"Even after, sir."

"Cocky bastard."

"Yes, sir."

The Transplanted Man coughed, then drank from a glass of water on his bedside table.

"Though you're not here in an official capacity, sir, I was wondering if you've had any contact with the American government."

"What's the point?" said the Transplanted Man. "It's humiliating how little we've mattered to the Americans all these years. If we had gone communist like China, or if we were ruled by an insane, ruthless despot, we would have held their interest."

"Being ruled by an insane, ruthless despot is not entirely out of the question, sir."

"Enough nonsense," said the Transplanted Man, propping himself up. "Listen to me, Verma. Keep a close eye on details. Be sure that all the village health centers have adequate supplies of antituberculosis medicines and that the health workers are trained to perform AFB smears of sputum specimens. Make certain the funds to educate prostitutes and truck drivers about condoms are dispersed as planned. Every one of them must know it's a death sentence otherwise! Make sure the pediatric oral rehydration programs are in full force in the villages during the next diarrhea season . . ."

"I'll take care of everything, sir."

The Transplanted Man's eyes narrowed. "You'd better! If infant mortality isn't down this year, I'll have you transferred to a remote district in the desert where you'll have to ride a camel to work. Understand?"

Verma smiled faintly. "I want to discuss security. Here, sir. There are many who hope you do not survive this time. As far as I can tell, there is no security at this hospital. Anyone can walk into your room—just as I did."

The Transplanted Man lay back in his bed again. For a long time he stared across the room. Then, in a soft voice, he said, "Let them."

"But—"

"You may not see it this way, Verma. But a man whose own body keeps threatening him with death can't worry about less probable threats."

"Sir—"

"Don't argue. Now go back to New Delhi and do both our jobs."

Verma rose. "Sir, I would like to say something else, if you don't mind."

"Go ahead."

"I went into this profession for all the right reasons," began Verma. "I didn't care much for money. I wanted to serve my country. Now, as I approach retirement, I find myself dwelling on how everything might have turned out if we'd gone about it the right way. There was greatness in our body, but, through either idiocy or masochism, we chopped off our limbs. I would like to believe it is still possible for them to grow back. But lately I've become even more anxious because, now that you are ailing, many think that, when this government falls, someone like Ronny Chanchal will end up in the PM's residence. After all, he's one of the few big names still untouched by scandal."

The Transplanted Man clenched his jaw.

"Excuse my boldness, sir, but when you were appointed our minister, I expected very little. I knew your hands weren't clean. I was aware of what you had done to serve your ambition . . . *Kher, woh purani baat hai.* It is, after all, a very long road from an unknown MLA representing a rural district in the center of the country to a contender for PM."

The Transplanted Man stared coldly at Verma.

"Please don't misunderstand, sir. Because what I'm really trying to say is that working with you has been the greatest privilege of my career. Look at my face, sir. You will see that I mean what I say."

The Transplanted Man continued to stare but said nothing.

"Whatever you may have been in the past is irrelevant, sir. Perhaps it was even necessary to become the man you are today. But you are exactly who we now need. So please, sir, do not die."

· ·

LONG AFTER VERMA LEFT the Transplanted Man continued to ponder his associate's words. While he lay in his bed, brooding, Gwen entered his room. In one hand she held a bottle of pills, in the other a book upon which was balanced a paper cup half-filled with water.

"Great Expectations!"

"Sounds like you've read it."

"Long ago—too long ago. One reads Dickens in youth and forgets that he needs to be read throughout life. Hopefully this will take my mind off what I have no control over: whatever is going on inside me, whatever is happening ten thousand miles away. I'll just immerse myself in this book and . . . Say, have you ever been to Dickens House in London?"

"Several times."

"I went there once. I was *so* ill that day. But it was worth it. What a feeling to imagine him writing at his desk whenever he could find a spare moment—day or night, weekday or weekend, somehow stitching chapters together—surrounded by screaming children, saddled with huge debts, sickness all around, afflicted by a thousand fears. And he just kept at it, one installment after the next. *Nicholas Nickleby, Oliver Twist, Barnaby Rudge.* I felt so much better when I left Dickens House that day, and even now, whenever I'm on the verge of losing hope, I think of how he went on, no matter what."

The Transplanted Man held out his hand, and Gwen passed him the book. "This will do more for me than all that medicine," he said.

As Gwen watched the Transplanted Man eagerly flip through the pages, her eyes became deep blue wells. Here was a man who believed in the power of stories. Not in the abstract but for healing his own body. Could literature possibly inject new life into this man's tortured organs? How much suffering must he have gone through! Suddenly she felt drawn to him in a way that she thought was inappropriate between a nurse and a patient—and also, perhaps, between a man and a woman born three decades apart. Then again, in his eighties Goethe had developed a passion for an eighteen-year-old. What was she thinking? And just when her relationship with Sonny was starting to develop into . . . well, something. Was her disease about to act up again? But a moment's reflection led her to conclude that her feelings for this man fell into an altogether different category; they were much more like the genuine affection that nieces felt for their favorite uncles in those great English novels the Transplanted Man so admired. Nobody quite knew what to do with those feelings these days. That was why she had, a minute ago, confused them with other feelings, which, come to think of it, no one knew what to do with, either.

· ·

THE NEXT MORNING the comatose man's wife and mistress leaned over his bed. They had encroached on him so much that he saw little more of the world than when he'd been in a deep coma. Excited by his improvement but uncertain as to its extent, the two women were so absorbed in trying to interrogate him that neither noticed Sonny enter the room.

"Well," said the wife, "who is it?"

"Tell us," urged the mistress. "Whom do you really love?"

"Point—if you can't speak."

"Or just wink with your right eye if it's me, with your left if it's her."

The wife looked across the bed at the mistress. "Do you really believe he doesn't understand?"

"He couldn't have pretended for two whole days!"

"Don't be so sure. He's a wily bastard. King of the Loopholes, they used to call him. Everyone said he was one of the best tax lawyers in town."

"Maybe he'll recover fully."

"What if he doesn't?" said the wife in a doleful voice.

The two women became lost in thought.

"On the other hand," said the wife in a completely different tone, "it might not be such a bad thing, if he stays just like this."

"And maybe he could still do what we *both* need."

"Oh, *that!*" The wife blushed. "Yes, perhaps he could, though I've almost forgotten what it's like. But you said 'both.' You don't propose—"

"Why not? Look, we've suffered the same ups and downs. All those fretful days on opposite sides of his bed, waiting for His Highness to awaken. Just to find out he has no brain left! If it weren't for him, I'd have to admit I rather like you, Gayatri. And who'd have guessed that you're an opera buff, too?"

The wife took a moment to reply. "Shanta, did he ever take *you* to the opera?"

The mistress laughed. "Him? You'd never catch him anywhere near Lincoln Center. He's strictly the lowest-common-denominator type, a drone good only for one thing. And even at that he was too quick and conventional. Sometimes I wonder why I . . . Well, anyway . . . Now tell me, what do you think about my proposal?"

"Is it really workable?"

"If he can't talk, he can't tell us who he loves, right? That might be for the best."

"Perhaps one day he'll be able to write," said the wife.

The mistress nodded slowly. "That's a real possibility, seeing how much progress he has made. Ah well, so much for that idea."

"We could break his fingers."

"There's a thought," said the mistress. "Who would know? And if he can't talk or write, it would be virtually impossible for him to communicate."

"Then I could do the one thing I've been wanting to do since all this began," said the wife, giggling.

"What?"

"Depilate his deceitful testicles, hair by hair."

"You wouldn't!"

"Nothing would give me more joy."

At this Sonny cleared his throat. "Good afternoon, ladies."

The two women turned their heads quickly.

"Did you just get here, Doctor?" the wife asked suspiciously.

"Just."

"We're so pleased he has come out of the coma! Aren't we, Shanta?"

"Yes, very!" said the mistress. "Has he said anything at all, Doctor?"

Sonny gave his patient a probing look. The comatose man had shrunk deep into his hospital gown, his eyes glazed. He looked as if he might slip back into a coma from sheer desperation.

"He hasn't uttered a sound," said Sonny.

"Do you think he'll *ever* speak again?" asked the mistress.

Sonny glanced at the comatose man for a hint. There was none.

"These things are very hard to predict," said Sonny. "It's amazing he has come back this far. Now, if you'll excuse me, I need a few minutes to examine him."

The two women simultaneously bent over the comatose man's face, their foreheads almost touching, as each kissed one cheek. Then they left. Sonny

could hear them laughing in the hallway. So, evidently, could the comatose man.

"Doctor," he said in a feeble voice, "can you spare fifty dollars?"

Sonny didn't reply.

"My whole life depends on what I do next," said the comatose man, his
voice gaining strength. "I can't play a deaf-mute forever! Please oblige me,
Doctor. I promise you'll get the money back, though it may take some time. I
don't want to tell you exactly what's on my mind, because I'd rather not put
you in an awkward position."

Sonny fished into his pocket for his wallet. Only yesterday he'd made a
withdrawal at the cash machine in the hospital lobby. He had eighty-six dollars, forty-seven cents, and two subway tokens. He handed all except the
tokens to the comatose man.

"A subway token would help, too."

"Take them both," said Sonny. "I'll walk home."

The comatose man raised his hands, then kissed each of his fingers. "Break
my fingers! Did you hear that, Doctor? And my balls! They want to pull the
hairs out of my balls! When I heard that, it made me shudder."

"Me, too."

The comatose man shook his head disbelievingly. "Thanks for everything,
Doctor. I hope you understand. Maybe you think I'm a coward. Maybe you
think only a scoundrel would abandon his children. I guess it has already been
established that I'm something of a scoundrel. But you've heard those two.
Together, they will destroy me. What good will I then be to my children?
Luckily, my wife is a resourceful woman. I know she will raise my kids well.
It's probably better to be fatherless than to witness your father's decimation.
How I'll miss rubbing my beard against my children's soft skin in the morning, miss reading to them at night, miss seeing them in school plays, miss slipping dollar bills under their pillows whenever they lose a tooth. Miss watching
them grow! It's such an incredible thing: how a few minutes of sex leads to a
baby, how a baby rolls over and babbles one day, then walks and talks the
next—and in no time, they're adding and subtracting, riding a bike, shooting
baskets and . . ." The comatose man wiped a tear. "I may have been a rotten
husband, but not a bad father. I hope Gayatri doesn't poison their memories
of me. That's my biggest fear."

"Maybe you'll be back one day."

"I hope so, Doctor. But you know how things are, these major intersections in life. You turn once, maybe twice, and you could be speeding down the

highway to who knows where, with the next exit a hundred miles away. By then the ride is so thrilling, you go further and further, and the route you finally take leads to a whole new life."

• •

THE FOLLOWING MORNING the comatose man was reported missing from the hospital.

A brouhaha followed. Along with other members of the hospital staff, Sonny was questioned by a police detective. He could honestly say he had no idea what had become of the missing patient.

At home that night Sonny sipped from a glass of red wine and thought about the way the comatose man had, like a reptile, shed his old skin and fled. Those thoughts rekindled his own longing for escape to a different world. In a way that longing had been the basis for all major decisions in his life. Even for college, he had chosen the university farthest from home that offered an in-state tuition discount. During those four years he spent more time exploring the rugged terrain of northern Arizona than in class. He hiked through high-walled canyons, where the only sounds were of startled lizards, desert birds, an occasional rattler, and wind rushing down corridors of sandstone. His tamarind skin blended with the rocks, and at times he thought of himself as a lost Sinagua looking for his people, unwilling to accept the fact that he was the last surviving member of an extinct civilization. Searching for old ruins, he trekked along obscure trails, crawled through dark caves, leaped between massive boulders formed millions of years ago.

But that was the past. Now, lying on a sofa in a second-floor apartment at the other end of the continent, it too seemed millions of years ago.

STATES OF AWARENESS

6

Dreams of Sleep

DURING THE WEEKS SINCE SONNY FIRST ENCOUNTERED HIM ON THE subway, the hypokinetic man had been inching along local sidewalks. The city hadn't been hospitable. People had no time for the slow. If they couldn't understand someone in ten seconds, they simply could not understand. At night the parks filled with bandits, and teenagers with guns roamed the streets in loose packs. Finding safe places wasn't easy. The hypokinetic man had been harassed many, many times.

On the day he got stuck between subway doors, the hypokinetic man had stepped off the train in Little Vietnam. Today he passed through the southeastern corner of Little Korea on a course that would, if held at his current speed, have landed him in Little India within a week. In undertaking this voyage, was the hypokinetic man rejecting the world of his birth for newer visions of an older world? A likelier explanation was physical rather than metaphysical: As he continued through Little Asia, people seemed to bother him less and less. So he kept following the gradient of gentleness.

In reality people in these neighborhoods were no nobler than those from where the hypokinetic man had fled. They were simply different. At first they watched the hypokinetic man's extremely slow movements with curiosity. But soon they got bored and went their own ways. The precinct police officer was initially concerned about the nonmotile human on her beat, but when someone told her that the stranger might be suffering from a mental illness, she placed the hypokinetic man in that category of homeless people she wasn't required to deal with unless they posed a threat.

Schoolboys had their fun. They made faces at the odd man in a gray sweatshirt and thinning jeans, called him names. But his lack of a response limited the laughs that could be had, and soon they, like their elders, paid him little attention. Dogs, however, always went out of their way, since they were fond of his odor and quiet manner. And when the hypokinetic man stood still for half a day at a time, a butterfly sometimes hovered over him. Every now and then sparrows alighted on his dark, wavy hair, perhaps confusing it for dry foliage. Or did they sense something else in this very different human? On occasion a bird stayed for a whole hour, chirping merrily. This would cause the hypokinetic man to blink with gratitude. Once he even smiled.

And so, at his own faltering pace, the hypokinetic man wandered through neighborhoods in search of a suitable street corner on which to park his body until his mind returned from wherever it had gone. How he would choose that corner was anyone's guess.

· ·

PSYCHIATRIC DISEASES WERE NOT among those that occupied medical researchers at the hospital. But neither were those researchers working on any of the diseases that hospital administrators claimed, during fund-raising drives, were being studied by its "internationally renowned" scientists in "state-of-the-art" research facilities. The picture painted was unabashedly romantic: Surrounded by effervescing test tubes, bald geniuses wearing wire-rimmed glasses with the thickest lenses worked deep into the night, stripping away life's mysteries to cure cancer, heart ailments, debilitating genetic defects, diseases caused by wicked viruses. Chintu Paudha, the hospital's CEO, was fond of telling potential benefactors, "Nobel Prize quality work goes on here."

In truth, the research "wing" of the hospital—really just a small laboratory and animal room on the eleventh floor—was singularly unimpressive. Much the same was said in scientific circles about research performed there, which reputable journals refused to publish. The single problem under attack—insomnia—was so intractable that few scientists had dared to tackle it head-on. The burden of this quest rested upon the slender shoulders of Dr. Nirdosh S. Ranjan and his longtime technician, Alvin Quimby. Dr. Ranjan's interest in sleeplessness wasn't only academic. He hadn't slept much himself. Sometimes he felt as if he'd never slept at all.

If insomnia was a nearly impossible riddle, it was less so than the topic of Dr. Ranjan's previous fascination: love. He had tried to divine a scientific theory for a phenomenon long held to be the domain of poets. One morning seven years ago, while watching his wife nurse his daughter, Dr. Ranjan experienced what he judged to be a profound insight. He conjectured that the same processes that operate between mother and child must apply to man and woman. Maybe all kinds of love—maternal, sexual, fraternal, and every other kind—were essentially the same! Which meant that they must have the same physiological basis. Thus Dr. Ranjan formulated his grand hypothesis, explaining how emotional stimulation between people initiated a cascade of signals that collectively resulted in the bond known as love.

Because of Dr. Ranjan's conviction that his hypothesis explained all love, at first he called it the Unified Theory of Love. But a colleague commented that the theory's name sounded grandiose at best, hippieish at worst. Someone else pointed out that it couldn't explain *all* love. What about love of gardening and philately? Dr. Ranjan could have rebutted with valid arguments, but he thought his theory would already be controversial enough without bringing orchids and stamps into it. So after further thought he renamed it A Self-amplifying Signaling Theory of Interpersonal Attraction. He tried to publish some intriguing experimental findings that supported, but did not prove, his theory. At the end of eighteen months all he had was a thick file of rejection letters.

Frustration kept Dr. Ranjan more sleepless than usual. One wintry night—while he sipped hot chocolate and gazed out the window at snow glistening on moonlit branches—Dr. Ranjan arrived at a new hypothesis. A theory of insomnia. In short, he believed that insomniacs had a substance circulating in their blood that inhibited sleep.

Only upon convincing himself of the theory's soundness did Dr. Ranjan begin to read scientific papers in the field. Sleep turned out to be even more fascinating than he'd hoped. After carefully digesting the latest research on sleep and sleeplessness, Dr. Ranjan concluded, in the manner of great scientists, that an entire field of brilliant researchers was wrong. Who had a unifying hypothesis? No one—except him. His own suffering from chronic insomnia made him even more certain of his theory. It *had* to be correct. This affliction had chosen him! In no time he and Alvin were conducting experiments designed to identify a sleep inhibitor responsible for insomnia.

Colleagues dismissed his notions as ridiculous. But Dr. Ranjan understood insomnia almost mystically, and a scientist matched with a perfect problem can become a man possessed. Dr. Ranjan knew that some said he was too possessed—that he was crazy. So what? That was what they'd once said about Darwin, Kepler, and Semmelweis. A little madness was just what was needed to crack a prodigiously difficult problem.

• •

ALMOST EVERY WEEKDAY MORNING for the past seven years, after swallowing a second cup of sugarless, black coffee in his office down the hall, Dr. Ranjan entered the laboratory to go over the previous day's experiments with Alvin. This morning was no different. Under the flicker of fluorescent ceiling lights, and with a hopeful glint in his eyes, Dr. Ranjan asked, "Any progress?"

"Still getting nowhere," muttered Alvin.

The expression on Dr. Ranjan's face changed abruptly. Alvin could almost see his boss plunge into a dark, bottomless chasm. After seven fruitless years of experimentation on love and sleep, Alvin had glimpsed that chasm, too. What he saw made the Grand Canyon look like a rabbit hole. He had no idea how to climb out of an abyss like that. Thank God, Ranjy did. And now, as on other mornings, Alvin watched Dr. Ranjan crawl out of that hellish pit of uncertainty. Suddenly the scientist's face looked refreshed, younger. His eyes gleamed again. With renewed faith in the power of scientific method, he was ready to redouble the effort, court failure for many more years.

After this morning's journey to the netherworld and back, Dr. Ranjan knit his brow and said, "Let's troubleshoot."

Thus began their daily ritual, a discussion of mundane technical issues that could get in the way of discovering the sleep inhibitor. Alvin was a gifted experimentalist—he'd been working toward a Ph.D. at Berkeley before dropping out to join the dwindling counterculture movement of the early seventies—and Dr. Ranjan treated him like a junior colleague.

"Did you check the pH of your buffers?" asked Dr. Ranjan.

"Of course."

"The conductivity of the fractions?"

"Yeah."

They considered impurities in solvents used for cleaning glassware, freeze-thaw cycles of the deep freezer, problems with the chromatography columns. Soon they moved on to the art of protein purification, with Alvin recapitulating his recent work in minute detail and Dr. Ranjan suggesting this or that modification in the experimental protocol.

"Details—it's all in the details," said Dr. Ranjan. "I'm sure we're overlooking something."

Alvin shrugged. "Sometimes I wonder if we'll ever purify the sleep inhibitor from mice. Maybe we should work with another species. Sharks, for instance—they don't seem to sleep much. If we're ever to have a chance—"

"Chance showers blessings upon the trained mind," interrupted Dr. Ranjan, slightly misquoting Pasteur.

Alvin already knew where this conversation was heading. Watching Dr. Ranjan climb onto his imaginary dais, he didn't have to wait long for the lecture to begin.

"Anything as complex as sleep," said Dr. Ranjan, "with all those neurotransmitters coordinating electrical activity in the brain during cycles of sleep and wakefulness, has to be very simply regulated. Has to be! That's the way Nature works. Nature figures out a simple mechanism—that can work in flies, fish, worms, mice, and men—then keeps changing and complicating it, like a Bach variation. Which is why there are, in fact, flies, fish, worms, mice, and men. But the themes are the same. Wake up, eat, move, reproduce. Sleep! How can there not be a single substance managing such a basic operation? A switch! The switch to alter consciousness! What discovery could be more important? Just think how people suffer from sleep disorders! At least some of those disorders could be due to a malfunctioning switch—and I am certain that switch is a single protein. Don't you see, Alvin? It could be the most significant advance in medical science since . . . since . . . since . . . My God, it's so important I can't even think of a since!"

"Penicillin?" offered Alvin.

Dr. Ranjan pondered the comparison.

"Yes. *Pen-i-cil-lin!*" declared Dr. Ranjan, like a stunned Dr. Frankenstein announcing, "It's alive!"

Alvin was struck by how incongruous, almost comical, this lunatic enthusiasm seemed on the small, awkward, balding, bespectacled man standing before him. Was he a genius or a self-deluded fool?

In the end Dr. Ranjan's pronouncements had their customary effect on Alvin, providing a modicum of inspiration to one who'd searched far and wide. Still, it was only enough for Alvin to get through one more day of tedious experiments that were doomed to fail. Alvin knew that the time would eventually come when Dr. Ranjan's exhortations wouldn't be enough. Even though he was quite sure Dr. Ranjan would never abandon the mission, he didn't think *he* could keep at it another seven years.

Alvin was starting to itch. A good feeling, all things considered—one he hadn't experienced in years. Decades? But that feeling was also associated with unpleasant memories from his hippie days. Back then he'd been not your routine flower child but a serious aspirant. Three times he had traveled to India; each time he was forced to cut his visit short. While his mind sought that region of higher consciousness between earth and heaven, his bowels reacted with diarrhea. On his last visit he was stricken by cholera outside Calcutta. He nearly died. Enough was enough, he decided. Nirvana might be a worthy goal, but worth all this suffering? And did it have to be discovered in India? That was why he had moved to this neighborhood in New York City, where he thought it might be possible to have it both ways. In time he realized there was no nirvana here, but there wasn't much diarrhea, either. It seemed a reasonable trade-off: India Lite.

Lately, though, things had changed. Old hopes were stirring within him, confronting his fear-ridden past. Should he refuse to scratch the itch? After all, he liked this neighborhood, his job, his boss. There was a lot to be said for sticking around here, at least long enough to determine whether Dr. Ranjan was a genius or a fool. If Ranjy found what he was looking for—if he turned out to be a Pasteur, a Fleming, a Salk—Alvin knew the itch would become uncontrollable. With new faith in impossible dreams, the scientist's assistant would resume his abandoned quest. There could be only one destination.

India. Again.

• •

SATISFIED HE'D TRANSFUSED ALVIN with enough courage to go on with yet another set of dubious experiments, Dr. Ranjan returned to his office in search of his own courage.

He leaned back in his chair, took off his glasses, and rubbed his eyes. He stared myopically out the window at the graffiti-adorned buildings, their broken windowpanes. Everything looked dirty and gray. How many years had he gone without success? That depended on how you counted. Seven years with Alvin, six with his previous technician, nine years of doctoral and post-doctoral training before that. Over two decades of failure! How long should a man try to climb out of an icy gorge before giving up and accepting the inevitable slide back down? Didn't they say freezing is a pleasant way to die?

But it wasn't in Dr. Ranjan's nature to think like that for long. The product of a zany family of closet magicians and wishful thinkers, Dr. Ranjan had inherited his forebears' distaste for the sharp-edged world of black and white. His favorite uncle used to dabble in alchemy, and as a teen back in Lucknow, he'd spent the summers in his uncle's study poring over ancient Tantric treatises. Even after years of rigorous Western-style scientific training, Dr. Ranjan still had a bit of the alchemist in him. He had faith in the possibility of the impossible. So, as he gazed out the partly open window, it wasn't long before the soft world of his ancestral past beckoned, transforming the decrepit buildings. The gray resolved, and the black graffiti contrasted nicely with the redbrick wall. He heard the shrill songs of birds hopping between telephone wires. And while listening to those birdsongs, Dr. Ranjan had an idea. He jumped out of his chair and rushed back into the lab to tell Alvin that, if the chemical composition of a key solution was changed, he was certain— absolutely certain!—the experiment would work.

• •

HAVING JUST TOLD ALVIN to add 2 millimolar calcium to his buffers (a suggestion that would ultimately prove useless), Dr. Ranjan walked toward the elevator. He pushed the Down button, then put his hand in his pocket, absentmindedly fiddling with loose change. The elevator doors screeched open, and a delivery man got out. Dr. Ranjan squeezed into the crowded metal box, only to realize it was going the wrong way.

"Sorry," he said, quickly stepping back out.

As the elevator doors closed, he caught a glimpse of Dr. Menaka Bhushan, who flashed him a friendly, possibly affectionate smile.

Dr. Ranjan's heart skipped a beat. Forgetting why he'd been waiting for the elevator, he strolled back to his office, lost in thoughts of Menaka.

She always did that to him. For most of his tenure at the hospital, he'd been starved for scientific interaction. It was a strange kind of loneliness: being on a voyage of discovery with no one to appreciate it. Then he met Menaka, a neurologist and the new director of the Sleep Studies Lab. A petite, energetic woman with wide eyes and shoulder-length hair, Menaka had recently moved to New York City from somewhere in the Northwest. Although Menaka was a clinician, Dr. Ranjan had always been impressed by her grasp of scientific principles. He liked hearing about her patients with various insomnias, hypersomnias, and parasomnias. He liked listening to her describe the complex nerve pathways that underlie eye movements during REM sleep.

He also liked her.

Of course, romance was out of the question. He'd heard that Menaka had been recently divorced and, to his knowledge, was available. But he wasn't. He loved Bhavana and his two children.

Yet there was no denying his feelings for Menaka.

Other than his wife, Dr. Ranjan had no romantic experience with women. So these feelings for Menaka were incredibly confusing. His prior insights into the biochemical basis of love provided no guidance whatsoever, once more confirming in his mind the perils of extrapolating from the test tube to the living being. Equally perplexing was the way Menaka made a habit of patting his shoulder whenever they parted after coffee or lunch. Collegially? Tenderly? He spent a lot of time wondering. Even the way she addressed him—the particular manner in which she said Nirdosh—sounded a lot more affectionate than his wife's Nirdosh.

• •

LOOKING FOR ALVIN, Sonny opened the door of the laboratory. Right away his nostrils reacted to the strong phenolic odor. In an age of sophisticated biotechnology, this room always reminded Sonny of something out of the past. The gray paint inside had cracked everywhere. Shelves were stacked high with chemicals, beakers, flasks, graduated cylinders, racks of test tubes. Multicolored charts were stuck to the walls with tape that had yellowed. To Sonny's right was a huge periodic table of the elements; to his left, a diagram of a cell and its myriad organelles. Next to it was a chart of metabolic pathways with crisscrossing arrows, detailing how chemical reactions between oxygen, carbon dioxide, water, and nitrogen, together with dashes of sulfur and phosphorus, create the molecules of life.

As a first-year medical student, Sonny had known nearly everything on those charts—and much more. But the subsequent bombardment of clinical facts, the practicalities of patient care, the hundreds of drug doses and their thousands of side effects had managed to erase nearly all he'd once known. Standing here, he found it almost painful to contemplate the bright medical student he'd once been. It seemed as if he'd grown more stupid with every passing year. He'd seen blood and suffering—hell, too much!—but was he any wiser for it? The wise doctor, witness to the infinite pain of the species, seemed just another myth.

In the far corner of the lab, Sonny spotted Alvin leaning back in a chair, feet crossed on the desktop, his sandy hair peeking over the outstretched pages of the newspaper. As Sonny approached, Alvin lowered the headlines.

"Hey," said Alvin, folding the paper and laying it on the desk. "What brings you this way?"

Sonny glanced around suspiciously, then whispered, "I need something."

"Yeah?"

Sonny hesitated. Couldn't he do without the stuff? He didn't really *need* pot. Could he walk away, though? Most of the time. But these days his head was throbbing with thoughts and images, disturbing in their incoherence. Some of it was familiar: a rehashing of his teens in Arizona, when he was constantly fighting with his mother and still had hopes of locating his father. Until recently Sonny had thought most of that was behind him. Why were those memories chasing him again? At the hospital he was too focused on his patients for the thoughts to trouble him much. Home was another matter. One solution—a solution he had considered half seriously—was simply to live in the hospital. But that seemed too close to being institutionalized. Eighty hours a week was enough. Perhaps there was a psychiatric diagnosis, DSM something or other, for a person overly attached to the hospital. *Hospitophilia.*

"You know what I want," said Sonny.

Alvin ran his fingers over the graying stubble on his chin. "I thought you were trying to stop. Didn't you say wine was doing it for you?"

Sonny had said that. A couple of glasses of red wine certainly helped settle his ricocheting mind. Wine diminished the noise, the troubling thoughts. It was as if the alcohol sealed the memories in a bubble that could float away. There was no friction, no ambiguity—just a shiny, delicate, flawless bubble. Unfortunately, the effect of the wine was short-lived. The bubble popped.

Pot was different. Those jumbled thoughts became more vivid, churning themselves vigorously, like water at the base of a waterfall. A subtle reshaping occurred. Sonny sensed a larger, deeper world out there. After every high he felt as if he'd seen a little more. More coherence, clarity. The innumerable jagged pieces of a massive 3-D puzzle only he could solve seemed to be gravitating toward one another. The forces of attraction weren't strong, but little by little the fragments were assembling into tiny islands. So he kept smoking marijuana, searching for better and better quality, in the hope that the missing pieces would materialize, form new islands or attach to existing ones.

"I was wrong," said Sonny, pulling out his wallet.

"Keep your money," said Alvin. "What's a few bucks in the scheme of things? I'm doing this because you're different, and I like you—can't say that about too many people."

"Me neither."

Alvin took out a set of keys and opened a locked drawer in his desk. He tossed a small packet at Sonny, who caught it with his left hand.

"That should last you awhile."

7

That #### Butterfly!

At Sonny's afternoon clinic, Sonali lay facedown on the examining table while he inspected the wound on her left buttock. "You can get dressed now," said Sonny. He stepped out of the room to write a note in Sonali's chart.

Sonali pulled up her panties, retied her petticoat, and began to wrap her sari. For the thousand and somethingth time, she went over Nishad's possible motives for biting her buttock. Her engineer's mind required a reasonable explanation, but now that she and Nishad had separated and were no longer speaking, there was little chance of new facts coming to light. That made her thoughts spin even more.

Sonny came back into the room. "Now that everything is completely healed, you don't need to make another appointment—unless some problem arises."

"What about the scars, Doctor? Will they *ever* go away?"

"They should fade with time. Of course, given where they are, I don't think they'll be very visible, even on the beach."

"But *I* know they are there! I've been marked for life by my deranged husband's jaws!"

Sonny knit his brow. All along he'd had doubts about Nishad's "temporary amnesia" story, but he didn't see the point in voicing them. "I'm sure it was an accident," he said.

"Accident, my foot! Do you know of another instance like this?"

Sonny appeared to ponder the question, though in truth he was searching for a way out of this discussion. At last he said, "In hospitals, you see strange things all the time."

"If strange things happen *all* the time, then something like this should have happened, too. Simple probability theory. Doesn't that make sense, Doctor?"

Sonny thought the point could be argued. Both this case and the comatose man's seemed to defy simple probabilities. The confounding factor seemed to be marriage, capable of turning everything on its head . . .

"You see, Doctor, this is *so* strange it has never happened in all human history! It is *so* improbable that it is impossible. It was no accident."

Sonny remained quiet.

Sonali started to pace back and forth. "You don't know Nishad as I do. Beneath that innocent exterior is a man with a devious mind who has been turned into a perverse maniac by Hollywood and Madison Avenue!"

"Perhaps you're making too much of this."

Sonali shook her head vigorously. "Doctor, it may *look* as if my husband bit my buttock, but in reality he bit my brain! Instead of debilitating me, though, it has energized me—given me a new perspective on life. My eyes see new things. My ears hear songs I've never heard before."

"It sounds like you've been listening to Ms. Evans-Puri's song."

"That social worker is a brilliant woman! I've never met anyone quite like her."

"Most people haven't."

· ·

LATER THAT AFTERNOON Nishad sat down in a chair for his second appointment with Dr. Giri. This time he'd come not because Sonali had forced him but rather because he needed sound advice. And Guruji seemed wise in the complexities of life.

After a calculated silence, Dr. Giri spoke. "How are things between you and your wife?"

"Not well, Guruji."

Dr. Giri had slept in an awkward position, and his back was acting up. He shifted in his ergonomic recliner. Comfortable for the moment, he said, "Tell me about it."

"You must have heard of the butterfly effect, Guruji. It explains how as trivial an event as a butterfly flapping its wings in Zambia can cause a tidal wave in Japan."

Dr. Giri stroked his chin. "So the butterfly is not so trivial after all."

"It's a *very* mischievous insect, Guruji. You see the parallel, don't you?"

"Not quite."

"Let me explain," said Nishad. "A perverse impulse led to my biting Sonali while I was admiring her body. This crime of passion resulted in her hospitalization, which placed her in the care of that oddball Dr. Seth, who connived with that wicked Ms. Evans-Puri, who turned Sonali into a radical who referred to me as 'a pawn of neoimperialists' the last time we spoke. Now do you get what I'm saying? And the real tragedy is that, angry as I am at Sonali, I lust for her body exactly the way it is. Strange how all this tension only increases my desire."

"Is your wife still thinking about returning to India?"

"If she chooses to go back, I don't know what I'll do. My mind is *so* unsettled these days. When your whole life is unraveling, all kinds of thoughts enter your head."

"Just because certain thoughts enter your head doesn't mean they have to stay there."

Nishad massaged his temples with his fingers. "I guess I'll go now."

"There's still some time," said Dr. Giri, glancing at his watch.

"Let's hope," replied Nishad, rising.

After Nishad left Dr. Giri lay flat on the floor of his office and performed a series of exercises designed to stretch the muscles of his lower back. His spine let out little crackles as it partially realigned. While he stared at the ceiling, he thought about the absurd sequence of events that was, indeed, unraveling Nishad's life. A butterfly effect? Maybe. But so much can be explained away in that fashion, seemingly trivial events leading to huge consequences that change lives. If that was how it really was, then you had no power over your own life. Though quite the opposite of an all-controlling Fate, in a practical sense it amounted to the same thing. Most people who went to therapists—or gurus, for that matter—felt either that life had spun out of control or that some external force was driving it against their wishes. Wasn't the role of the therapist or guru to impose meaning on what seemed incomprehensible? And did it make much difference whether one invoked Freud or the stars?

◆ ◆

AT LEAST TWICE A DAY Sonali would stand before a full-length mirror in her bathroom, examining the semicircular scars on her left buttock. Dr. Seth had said the marks left by Nishad's jaws would fade, but to her eye they appeared to be darkening. Were the changes real or in her head? Every time she examined the scars, she asked herself why she had married Nishad. All arranged marriages didn't turn out this way. As far as she knew none turned out this *particular* way. Who'd have guessed that coming to America would lead to such insanity?

Then again, it *was* Nishad. The idiot! Of course, she'd been foolish in her own way, always following his preferences: where to live, which job to take, what car to drive, which movies to see. Thank God she had so far resisted his wish to have children—by which he meant as many pregnancies as it took to have a son, his heir as he called the hypothetical child. Now it was time to wrest back control of her life. The events of recent weeks had opened her eyes. She was tired of working for a company day after day. Where was it going? Was she doing anything she genuinely cared about? Just making a little money for herself and Nishad—and a lot for the company.

Was this why they had crossed oceans and struggled to build a life in this country? For automatic transmissions and central air-conditioning they had bartered their souls—Nishad more obviously than she, but it was only a matter of degree. Bit by bit America had peeled away their Indianness; soon nothing would be left. Already so little remained in Nishad. Oh, how it maddened her when she thought of his teeth clenched on her buttock! What really happened that night? Nishad was hiding something, and that belief, fueled by speculations placed in her head by Ms. Evans-Puri, continued to enrage her.

Before she could change her life, though, she had to change Nishad. If that failed, could she take the next step? Well, first she had to *try* to fix her lunatic husband. But how? Their views had surely grown even further apart since they'd separated. She knew she had changed. She wore only saris and had even visited the local temple—the first time she'd set foot in a place of worship since leaving India six years ago. In her spare time she read feminist literature and rented Hindi film videos, an unlikely combination that sowed a new conflict between her mind and heart. But that conflict was nipped in the bud when she viewed the latest Ronny Chanchal release. After that she vowed never to see another Hindi film, concluding that they perpetuated the very entitled Indian male syndrome that was behind this whole mess.

• •

EVENINGS WERE PARTICULARLY HARD for Nishad, who was now living in a fully furnished apartment he'd sublet from a professor on sabbatical. His social life had been entirely a function of Sonali's once gregarious nature, and he had no real friends of his own. At first he killed time at the movies. After he'd seen all the new releases, he started frequenting bars. But he didn't know how to talk sports with the men or flirt with the women, so the bar experience proved more disappointing than the most tedious movies. Depressed and bored, he ventured into seedier parts of the city, where curiosity led him to sample the local pornography.

One evening he emerged from a porn shop with a bag of videos, giddily anticipating the nubile bodies soon to appear on the TV screen. As he hurried toward the subway station, he heard heels clomping on the sidewalk, gaining on him. He turned around and stared at a woman standing only two feet away.

She stepped up so close that, despite the breeze, he could smell her perfume.

"Would you like to buy me a drink?"

In all the bars Nishad had been in, no woman had ever said anything like that to him. But he understood what was implied. He debated. His sole sexual experience had been with Sonali, and he had actually given less serious thought to infidelity than most married men. Yet having just inspected some of the world's most memorable smut, he was in a mood that could tempt even the best man to sin.

Nishad looked the woman over. Her face was pretty enough, her thick lips heavily reddened. She had a long neck and was very slim, attractive in a way that was at once sexual and sterile.

"What's your name?" she asked.

"Ni-Nishad."

"Hi, I'm Bertha."

"I've never met anyone with that name."

She laughed.

Without thinking it through, Nishad asked, "Safe sex?"

Bertha pondered the question. "A better way to put it is that I'm virus-free."

• •

STARK NAKED, GAGGED, and handcuffed to a bedpost, Nishad groaned in pain. From this compromising position, he gazed at the blurry, fiendish woman circling him like a lioness guarding her dead prey. Or was he experiencing vertigo? Since the ceiling was circling, too, he concluded it must be the latter. His eyes focused on a leather whip lying on the floor, one of several instruments Bertha had employed during his flagellation.

The world stopped spinning. Bertha's face became clear. Her eyes were lit with rage.

Nishad had the most horrendous headache of his life. He moaned for sympathy.

"You're the goddamn worst I've ever had!" she shrieked. "And I've had lots. But you're the pits!"

Standing there in a tight leather outfit, her gloved hands on her hips, her shiny black boots with metal heels twenty inches apart, she looked like the Catwoman ready to pounce upon Batman. "What do you have to say for yourself?"

Nishad was afraid to say anything. At last he muttered, "I'm just an engineer . . ."

"An engineer, are you? You have besmirched the reputation of every Indian male engineer—and that's hell of a lot of guys. I should know!"

"I'm sorry," he said meekly.

"Louder!"

"Sorry! I'm so, so, *so* sorry."

"That's not good enough." She picked up her whip.

"No! Please! I'm sorry for everything I've ever done."

She threw the whip on the floor. "Oh, what's the use! You have all the defiance of a gnat. You're no fun at all. Just get out!"

She pulled the key from her black leather pants and unlocked the handcuffs.

Slowly, painfully, Nishad got off the floor.

He couldn't locate his socks, so he left without them. In the hallway he thought he wasn't walking straight. He wondered if he'd suffered permanent brain damage. He came to a staircase. A long, long way down. He sat on the top step for a moment. Even sitting hurt. Finally he descended, one treacherous step at a time. When he reached the bottom, his balance seemed better and his head hurt less. Maybe his brain was okay after all.

• •

"SONALI," PLEADED NISHAD. "Please come back."

Draped in her Varanasi sari, sindoor on her forehead, she sat there, utterly implacable.

"Sonali, I love you! I love you *exactly* as you are!"

She squinted at him. *"Achanak ye mohabat kahan say agayee?"*

"You don't understand," he said. "People have warped your mind."

For the first time in weeks she spoke to him in English. "Excuse me, whose mind did you say is warped?"

He wasn't sure what else to say or do, so he tried the truth. "All right, Sonali. I confess. I never had temporary amnesia. It was all a lie . . ."

He stopped. Her cool gaze unnerved him. How could he explain that he'd been secretly admiring her on that fateful night? Would she understand the ecstasy he'd experienced before he lost all control and bit her? What new questions would it raise in her suspicious mind?

"Sonali," he continued, his eyes averted, "I did it out of deep-seated hostility. Not toward you, but . . . oh, it's all so complicated, Sonali. It has to do with my childhood, my upbringing. But I've been getting help. I'm seeing Guruji regularly. Soon I will be cured of my perversity."

"The only cure is to leave this country where women have no flesh, and men have semiautomatic rifles."

Nishad kept silent, for after last night he really couldn't argue—except to add that there were also fleshless women with semiautomatic rifles.

"Nishad, I love you too, but . . . We *must* go back home." She said it with such conviction that there was no room for discussion.

"India has changed since we left," she went on. "Incredible opportunities exist for people with our technical expertise. As a matter of fact, there always were. We were drawn abroad because everyone else was, that's all. Now is such an exciting time back home! The new India of computers, satellites and test-tube babies is going to be at the center of a huge explosion in the global economy. One day every village will be connected to cyberspace: Think of the change that will be driven by that! A revolution greater than any Marx could have hoped for!"

He just listened, intimidated by her growing fervor. She said she always knew he'd come to his senses. Then she revealed her plan. Upon returning to India the two of them would join an engineering firm—just to get reacclimated. Eventually they'd start a company of their own. The exchange rate being so favorable these days, between them they'd probably saved enough to finance the initial outlay for the company. She had started to give him a breakdown of what it would cost when she stopped in midsentence and pointed at his arm. "Nishad, you have a *huge* bruise!"

He swallowed. "A bruise?"

"Don't you know? Look at your right elbow."

Bertha had beaten him so horribly he was surprised only a single bruise showed. Every part of him, outside and in, felt bruised.

"What happened?"

His head was hurting again. "I was beaten last night."

"Beaten?"

"I mean mugged, Sonali. Yes, mugged. Two guys, maybe three. It was dark."

Sonali embraced him. "Poor, poor Nishad. I'm sorry you had to suffer all this. But there were other issues so much more important than why you bit me. You understand now, don't you?"

He nodded.

Over and over Sonali kissed his face, which had been smacked at least three dozen times last night. Sonali's kisses felt good, but they hurt, too. Nishad was filled with terrible guilt; he hadn't even bathed yet.

She pointed to the bruise again. "*This* is why we must return to India, Nishad. These villains on the streets who hurt decent people."

He shut his eyes.

"Don't worry," she said. "When we get back to India, everything will be all right. We can move in with Mummy and Daddy, and . . ."

His head was really throbbing now. He had little desire to return to India to begin with, and none whatsoever under those conditions. He could already imagine life with his mother-in-law, who'd be holed up in the bathroom for two hours every morning, drinking tea the rest of the day, inflating the merits of her side of the family, always implying he wasn't good enough for her daughter, nagging him about household chores . . .

Suddenly he felt every lash and blow inflicted upon him last night. And he feared the pain would never go away.

8

Performances

AMONG THE MONGRELS THAT TRAILED SONNY WHEN HE SLEEPWALKED was a mutt, part poodle, part cocker spaniel, and many parts who knows what. Despite his mixed pedigree and unkempt look, the best features of various breeds had combined to create a handsome beast with a noble snout and incomparable deep brown eyes. Somehow the dog knew when Sonny was going to sleepwalk. Those nights he'd wait outside the apartment building and trail Sonny through the neighborhood.

Soon the homeless dog was sitting outside the building in the morning, too. He'd then follow Sonny to the subway station or, on those days that Sonny walked the eighteen blocks to work, the dog would accompany him part of the way to the hospital. Sonny started to feed the collarless animal.

Day after day Sonny looked forward to seeing the dog when he headed off to the hospital and when he returned in the evening. The dog didn't understand Sonny's on-call schedule and always looked hurt when Sonny finally came home a whole day later. On those days Sonny would let the dog into the apartment for an hour or two. It was a trial of sorts, and both creatures seemed aware of the implications.

The third weekend of the month, Sonny was off, his first completely free weekend in months. That Saturday morning he let the dog inside. The two lay on the couch, watching one insipid TV program after another. When nothing was left to watch but a *M*A*S*H* rerun, Sonny turned off the television. A few years ago the show had been his favorite, but now he found it impossible to watch fake doctors on TV. He called Gwen to ask if she wanted to go into town for a movie, but she was engrossed in a book and sounded lukewarm to each of the movies he proposed. After he hung up he thought it was just as well they hadn't planned anything. He was beginning to learn that whenever she was in a mood to read, it was best to leave her alone.

The dog stayed all morning, all afternoon. It was nice to have another presence in the apartment, and the hours went by just like that. The dog ought to have a name, thought Sonny, as he gently stroked the animal's burgundy fur. He stared at the dog's face for a long time. What was his past? Why was such a good-looking animal roaming the streets? The dog seemed tough, proud, defiant. Again Sonny attempted to come up with a name. After he'd tried several, one stuck: Tandoori. Soon the dog was responding to his new sobriquet.

Early the next morning Sonny allowed Tandoori onto his bed and stroked him affectionately. After a while he addressed the dog with words he'd never uttered before: "Do you want to live with me?"

Tandoori didn't seem to object.

Two hours later, at a veterinary clinic that was open on weekends, Sonny did his best to hold down the furious dog for his vaccinations.

• •

ONE OF THE NURSES in the ICU had offered Gwen tickets to a classical dance school's annual recital, so on Sunday afternoon she dragged Sonny along. As Sonny strolled down the aisle of the auditorium holding Gwen's hand, he became aware of the disapproving gazes of older Indian women. For once he was glad that Gwen dressed in dull, baggy clothes that hid her figure. Another time he would have sneered at these staring women clad in silk saris and gold necklaces. But right now he felt some vague guilt. And even more guilt for feeling that guilt: as if he'd somehow capitulated. An uneasy feeling gradually concentrated in the center of his chest.

As Sonny sat down he caught sight of Dr. Ranjan's balding scalp two rows ahead. While waiting for the show to start, Sonny flipped through the program. It gave a brief history of the dance school and expanded upon its mission "to help foster a sense of Indian identity in the next generation, to increase understanding of Indian culture in the non-Indian community, to cultivate an ancient art form that is being forgotten . . ."

The first half of the program consisted of a series of solo dances, with performers arranged youngest to eldest. Slated for the opening dance, an offering of flowers to the Goddess, was Archana Ranjan.

A lovely and tiny girl of seven, Archana kept dropping her flowers as she struggled to keep pace with the music. Sonny glanced at Dr. Ranjan, who was putting his arm around his wife. She, in turn, rested her head on his shoulder. The small boy beside them laughed hysterically at his sister, now on the verge of tears. Fortunately for Archana, the dance lasted only three minutes, and the Goddess, well-known for her violent temper, had not reacted badly to receiving only two of the dozen flowers in the original bouquet, the other ten being dispersed over the stage. Sincere effort seemed to count for something after all.

Dr. Ranjan stood to applaud. Sonny barely knew Dr. Ranjan, but at that moment he envied the scientist. He took Gwen's hand.

Dance followed dance, one brightly colored costume succeeding another. With every dance the girls were older, more poised. It was like watching the same girl grow up over a span of hours. As the girls of high school age performed, a polished Indian step occasionally gave hints of an American skip, briefly breaking the spell as the dance lost a bit of its ancient grace.

After the show Sonny and Gwen left the auditorium hand in hand. The occasional stares didn't bother Sonny anymore. There were other mixed couples, but he felt different. Mixed or unmixed had little to do with it. He simply wasn't one of them. He remembered a time when he desperately wanted to be one of them and realized that the uneasiness he'd felt when he first stepped into the auditorium had to do with that youthful longing. During his teens he had imagined *their* lives to be very different. *They* had close-knit families, suburban bliss, America and India mixed together just right. *Their* parents were brown versions of the parents in sixties TV shows: professional dads and stay-at-home moms who raised their kids in affluent, upper-middle-class neighborhoods and spent summer vacations at Yellowstone or Cape Cod. Of course, he now knew it hadn't been that way for most of them. Yet even now they gave the impression that it had been exactly that way. All too comfortable diasporics: If they felt dislocated, they hid it well.

• •

IN ANOTHER PART OF TOWN, Nishad and Sonali stood in a long line of economy passengers waiting to board a jumbo jet bound for New Delhi via Heathrow. Over the past ten minutes the line had barely moved. With people finding friends and cutting in, they were actually farther from the plane than when they'd joined the line.

"How do they manage to make getting on a plane so difficult?" asked Sonali.

Nishad took her question as rhetorical, but an elderly man standing in front of them turned around and said, "It was always difficult, but now it has become so much worse. And does all this so-called security make a difference? I've been taking tranquilizers the whole day. Why do we go back anyway? Guilt, that's why. Over abandoning the mother country. But does the mother country care? Only for our dollars—only if we invest in their silly Not-Real-Indian schemes."

"That's very interesting," said Sonali.

"We can still turn back," whispered Nishad. "Are you absolutely sure about this?"

"Excuse me," Sonali said to the elderly man, who had just swallowed a capsule of something. "Could you hold our place for a moment?"

The man put the pill bottle back in his pocket. "Sure. Go sort it out."

Sonali grabbed Nishad's shirtsleeve and tugged him over to the pay phone at the opposite side of the boarding area. There she faced her husband, whose back was, quite literally, against the wall.

"Listen to me," she said. "We are past the point of discussion. *I certainly am.* It is natural to be nervous about change. One never knows for sure how things will turn out. But you must stop this irksome questioning and requestioning. Do you understand?"

Nishad's expression became frantic. "I don't understand at all! Why are we doing this? Wait! Don't answer. Let *me* tell *you. The truth!* We're doing this because, one night, while I was admiring your body—while I was admiring *my wife's* body, thinking that she looked like a voluptuous apsara—I became overwhelmed with a passion so uncontrollable that I took a bite. I know it was crazy, but that's how it was. And you understand what happened afterwards even better than I. I've endured so much humiliation! It might as well have been on the evening news! And what has come of it all? This! You and I have places in a line to go back to India. For good! But for no good reason—as far as I'm concerned. The India we're returning to is more crowded, more polluted, more intolerant, more dangerous. You keep talking about the cyber-revolution in India; if you're so interested, why not move to the *real* Silicon Valley? Several of my IIT batchmates have their own start-up companies. I'm sure they'd help us find suitable jobs. Sonali, I know we've 'discussed' this dozens of times, but what we're doing—what you're *forcing* me to do—makes no sense at all. None!"

"Are you finished?"

"Yes!"

"Then get back in line."

· ·

SIX HOURS EARLIER Ronny Chanchal had flown in from New Delhi on the very same plane Nishad and Sonali were about to board. The actor-politician had spent the previous week trying quietly to muster parliamentary support for a no-confidence vote against the prime minister. The effort had failed. Ronny Chanchal was depressed, not to mention exhausted and jet-lagged. To make matters worse, later today he had to fly off to catch up with his song-and-dance troupe for a series of performances in Detroit, Minneapolis, and Milwaukee. Then back to India again: another twenty-hour journey, another ten-hour time change, more jet lag.

One consequence of the time changes and jet lag was that Ronny Chanchal—who'd frequently been accused of possessing no imagination at all—had been experiencing extraordinarily vivid dreams. Often, nightmares. Some were so scary he woke up shaking, gasping, soaked in sweat. His grandmother had taught him to believe in dreams and, though he used to dismiss this as mere superstition, he was now at an age when superstition mattered again. He'd begun to dread sleeping and had started swallowing short-acting sedatives every night, which added a whole new dimension to his dreams.

Tonight Ronny Chanchal awoke from another dream. Not a nightmare but an enjoyable dream. He had visualized a scene from his next movie, an East-West film he'd been wanting to make all these years but had only the vaguest hint of until now. The first masala film that would appeal to highbrow tastes around the globe and turn him into an international sensation. The film that would sweep the awards at Cannes and Venice, garner an Oscar for Best Foreign Film. The film that would erase all the cheesy work he'd done in the past.

A master of sentimentality, he'd become famous making old-fashioned tearjerkers crossed to the modern Bollywood style. In an India stirred by Levi's jeans, computer games, and beauty pageants, Ronny Chanchal had managed to find a mix of old and new that struck a chord throughout the country. But Ronny Chanchal was no longer satisfied with being the idol of rikshawalas, or the imaginary lover of frustrated housewives. Although the realization had come to him late, he finally understood the difference between kitsch and art. Before completely giving up the cinema for politics, he longed to create one film that was an enduring work of art. His East-West film would be it. Even so, he didn't want to abandon the familiar Bollywood formula: the melodrama dosed with slapstick, the stock characters and contortions of plot, the implausible combined with the realistic, the catchy songs and kung-fu fight scenes. There was some kind of magic in that mix, a magic that transcended languages, cultures, continents.

He knew this could very well be his last chance to make a great film. In a year or two no amount of makeup could keep him from looking old beside those tall, lean, twentyish man-boys with innocent eyes, mischievous grins, and resilient knees. Many were children of film stars, who, like children of politicians, believed mass adulation to be their birthright. Never married—with no children—he had little sympathy. So far he had outlasted them all—the Kapoors and sons of Kapoors. But grandchildren of Kapoors? That was too much to expect. At some point even Amitabh had started playing the father-uncle type. Ronny Chanchal detested the idea of taking on such roles. He would make his East-West film, then retire from the industry.

After that, politics. With an unstable coalition governing the country, with the Transplanted Man ailing—and few other credible contenders for the throne—the next election, whenever it was called, would be the perfect opportunity. To him the attractions of Bollywood and national politics were remarkably similar. If the janata couldn't see his face on the marquees of cinema halls, they'd see it on campaign posters, television screens, and the front pages of newspapers.

• •

THE NEXT DAY, while Ronny Chanchal sat in the hospital cafeteria drinking a cup of milky, sugary tea, vainly attempting to formulate unformulaic plotlines for his East-West film—trying to decide whom to cast as his heroine, who ought to compose the score, who should direct the fight scenes—he felt someone's gaze. He glanced first to his right, then to his left, where a young man dressed in hospital garb stood staring at him. Ronny Chanchal went out of his way to ignore the gawking man, a mere orderly. He did this by virtually looking through him, as only an idol of millions can do. Then his attention returned to the plot of his film.

But Manny was not so easily rebuffed. He was doing some plotting of his own. Opportunities like this didn't wander along every day. Back home in Trinidad his voice had been compared with Kishore Kumar's, especially his rendition of "Roop Tera Mastana." That was how Manny had learned Hindi—by memorizing as many Kishore Kumar songs as he could, writing them out first in English script, then, as he mastered the language, in Hindi. To Manny, Hindi films were India, but an India he'd never been to. He was desperate to return to the land of his ancestors—and sing up a storm in Bollywood.

Three feet away sat a man with the power to make his dream come true. Already Manny could hear his own voice broadcast via All India Radio to remote villages throughout the subcontinent, played on Indian radio stations in London, Singapore, Toronto, Johannesburg, not to mention New York City and his native Port of Spain. Ronny Chanchal could make it all happen. With exactly this in mind Manny approached the film star, who was still puzzling over the plot of his East-West film. "Excuse me, Mr. Chanchal."

Ronny Chanchal flashed a look of disdain. "Autograph? . . . Pen?"

"That would be great, sir, but I was really wondering if I could audition."

Ronny Chanchal smiled patronizingly and took a sip of his tea. "Kindly contact me in Mumbai."

"I'm a singer—quite good, really. Some say as good as Kishore."

"Ah, Kishore. Wonderful voice. A terrible loss."

"Yes, it was," said Manny. "But what I meant was that nobody has been able to step into Kishore's shoes yet, and lots of people think my voice is just as good."

"Yes, yes, I'm certain it is. Now please, I'm quite busy."

Seeing that he was getting nowhere, Manny made a quick cost-benefit calculation, subtracting the likelihood of humiliation in the hospital cafeteria—and the loss of his job if his antics got back to his supervisor—from the remote possibility of instant stardom. The answer was clear. A whole life can depend on a single moment; Manny thought this might be it.

So he began singing. Accompanied by sundry cafeteria noises, he sang at the top of his voice, better than ever.

Divinely.

Unfortunately for Manny, Ronny Chanchal didn't have an ear for music; he would have had a hard time telling how good the real Kishore Kumar was. So the only effect Manny's singing had on the actor was to provoke irritation. Manny could see this, but it was too late to back down. He started another song: *"Hum Bewafa."* By then a crowd had gathered. They applauded loudly when he finished. Manny hoped the crowd's enthusiasm would impress Ronny Chanchal, so he kept singing. But Ronny Chanchal felt upstaged by this amateur's tamasha, since no one in the crowd had recognized him.

Finally Manny stopped. "What do you think, Mr. Chanchal?"

Now the people in the crowd took a closer look at the man sitting at the table. As soon as they realized that Ronny Chanchal was before them, they swarmed the actor. Manny's supervisor, a man of no small mass, climbed on top of the table and begged for an autograph. Though Ronny Chanchal was in no mood for such nonsense, the star turned politician knew the value of a nice-guy image. He signed autographs on paper napkins until lightning pains shot through his fingers.

Manny was still standing there when the last autograph seeker left. "Well, Mr. Chanchal," he asked, "how was I?"

"I'll see you in Mumbai," replied Ronny Chanchal with a sly grin. He then pulled out his wallet and handed Manny the card he gave everyone who pestered him. On it was printed a fake studio address and bogus phone number.

"Wow!" was all Manny could say.

So he said it again: "Wow!"

And a third time: "Wow!" Then he walked away, dreams intact.

9

Johny Walker

DR. RANJAN HAD PLANNED TO SPEND SUNDAY WORKING IN THE LAB. But that morning, while he lay in bed thinking about an experiment, his wife suggested a family outing at the beach. Dr. Ranjan found himself unable to say no. Raised in the heat of Rajasthan, Bhavana had never gotten used to the East Coast climate. From past experience Dr. Ranjan knew that, as the days shortened, her mood would sink deeper every week until spring came. That was why she marveled at another warm weekend, perhaps the last of the season.

But there was another reason he couldn't refuse. Lately Bhavana had been complaining more than usual about his being an "absent husband." The complaint had validity. She was the one who had built the pillars of their family; when he was immersed in experiments for weeks at a time, he would, upon finally emerging from that intense activity, feel like a relative visiting after many years. And yesterday evening when she said that, in addition to being an absent husband, he'd become an "absent father"—loud enough for Archana and Neel to overhear—he couldn't think of an honest way to refute her. Besides, he and Alvin were getting nowhere in their quest for the sleep inhibitor.

So that Sunday they went to the beach. Half of New Jersey seemed to have the same idea, and it took some time before they found a suitable spot. Dr. Ranjan took off his shirt and screwed an umbrella into the sand. Then, while Bhavana went for a swim, he played catch with the children.

Eventually Bhavana emerged from the ocean. "The water's wonderful," she said, still dripping. "Why don't you go in, Nirdosh?"

He smiled and quietly headed for the surf.

His body gradually adjusted to the cool water. Buoyed by the ocean, he stretched his arms and legs, then floated on his back, staring at a small cloud in the otherwise clear sky. A strand of seaweed became tangled between his toes. He wiggled them and set it free. His submerged ears perceived rhythms from the deep. Didn't it all start there? Somewhere on the ocean floor, perhaps in a black smoker or underwater volcano, it had happened. Life! He closed his eyes and watched an abbreviated version of evolution replay itself on the screen of his eyelids: archaebacteria to slime molds to trilobites to who knows what. And a couple of billion years later, Nirdosh Sonaperkash Ranjan, descendant of a female humanoid ape that once roamed Africa, was floating on the surface of that ocean in which life had originated, contemplating the whole of creation. Incredible!

He watched a lone gull passing over him and followed its flight until the bird was lost in the sun. It made him think of Icarus.

He turned his head toward the shore and located his family. He swam over. Bhavana, shining in her own quiet way, stood between the two children, her gaze more in the direction of Archana, who was closer to the water. The scene seemed perfect for a moment—pure, sincere, unattainable in any context other than the young family. If scenes from your life really flitted through your mind before death, this was what he wanted to remember.

When he came out of the water, he felt like hugging his whole family in one huge embrace.

Just then he glimpsed a woman walking a few yards behind his wife. She wore a two-piece swimsuit and dark sunglasses, and held a can of cream soda in each hand. Her chocolate body was polished by lotion and sweat. She looked Indian. Could she be. . . ? *She was!* Dr. Menaka Bhushan! Here? How? His scientific eyes took it all in, etching the image of Menaka's slim body into his memory as if he'd been peering at a fascinating histological specimen through the microscope. He also imagined what could not be seen. Only then did he become aware of the depth of his lust.

Another thought intruded. A jealous thought. To whom was she planning to hand that second can of cream soda? He tried to convince himself it didn't matter; after all, he was married, and Menaka had a right to her own life.

But suddenly it mattered a great deal.

Now he heard his children's voices. They were fighting over something, his wife trying to mediate.

"Buttface!" shouted Archana.

Neel immediately began to wail. Bhavana scolded Archana. Soon the girl was crying, too.

Although he was aware of the shame growing within him, Dr. Ranjan's eyes remained fixed on Menaka. His gaze was no longer lascivious but instead stern and inquisitive. He had to know who had accompanied Menaka to the beach. Which of these men sprawled on the sand shared her bed?

At last Menaka stopped at a candy-striped umbrella under which lay a female surgeon he recognized from the hospital. She handed her a can of soda.

Dr. Ranjan's chest deflated, and his fists unclenched. He smiled as the oblivious Menaka settled under the umbrella, opened her own soda can, and began to sip.

"Nirdosh!" shouted Bhavana. "Help me with these two! Even on the one day we try to have a nice time, your mind is on your silly experiments!"

• •

ANOTHER WEEK WENT BY, and still no evidence for a circulating factor that inhibited sleep. Fearing that his theory might be wrong, Dr. Ranjan barely slept. Of course, this was nothing new. Something in his physiology made it possible for him to exist for months on two or three hours of sleep a night. He knew that Thomas Edison used to sleep no more than this, and he hoped the similarities between himself and Edison didn't end there.

Night was the only time he could think deeply. At work there were too many distractions. The creative lobes of his brain performed best outside hospital walls, where he wasn't reminded of so many years of failure. The trouble was, it wasn't easy to find an opportunity to think outside. At home there was hardly a spare moment. Here he was in his mid-forties, chained to a pedestrian existence of self-perpetuating routine, time pecking away at the rest of his life. Three minutes into mulling over a new idea, the kids would begin shouting at each other, or Bhavana would ask him to go buy laundry detergent at the drugstore or remind him that the car needed to be taken in for an oil change and the lawn had to be mowed and, by the way, the Aggarwals were coming for tea and pakoras.

In spite of it all, he knew he was meant for domestic life as much as science. But he worried that the two lives might be incompatible. When he first heard that Einstein wrote his article on the theory of relativity while sitting at the kitchen table with a baby in one arm, he thought there might be some hope. Later he learned that Einstein's wife left with the kids shortly thereafter. Was that how it had to be? Would he one day be forced to choose between his two lives?

He was contemplating that very question as he shaved this morning, his sense of frustration growing with each stroke of the razor. While he lay awake in darkness for much of last night, his mind had been darting from idea to idea, and before sunrise he'd had scores of exciting notions. But by the time Neel and Archana had woken and he'd served them warm chocolate milk, together with the brand of cereal that happened to strike their fancy, he was unable to retrace key connections between his thoughts. Somewhere had been lost that gem of an idea that just might have changed the world.

"Daddy!"

Thinking the children were fighting, he rushed out of the bathroom and into the family room. To his surprise, Neel and Archana lay on the couch, each wrapped cozily in a quilt, trying to postpone the realization that today was, in fact, another school day.

"What's the matter?"

"Daddy, can you fix those lines on the TV?" asked Archana.

Dr. Ranjan adjusted the picture.

"Now it's worse!" said Neel.

Dr. Ranjan fiddled with the knobs again. "That's the best I can do."

Even though the picture was no better, neither child complained. He went back to the bathroom, finished shaving, and dressed.

As on other Thursdays, it was his wife's turn to take the kids to school. At 7:20 A.M. he kissed his family and left for work. A dark, cloudy morning. Thunder clapped somewhere in the distance. As he backed out of the driveway, he set his car radio to his favorite classical music station. Then he zigzagged through the side streets to avoid congested intersections. Soon he was on the highway. It was a long drive to the hospital. Still, he liked the idea (at least in the abstract) of an existence that alternated suburban calm with metropolitan frenzy. Eventually the morning's erosions healed. While he listened to Mozart's *Turkish Concerto*, it occurred to him that family life had its own music. Of course, it wasn't Mozart. But even Mozart's compositions were artificial; what was missing was the background noise of life. Admittedly, there was too much noise in his life.

While Dr. Ranjan drove over the George Washington Bridge, it started to rain. The rainstorm quickly gathered intensity, and the radio reception became erratic. Traffic slowed in the middle of the bridge, stalled. Suspended over the Hudson River, Dr. Ranjan turned off the radio. He listened to the rain pounding the windshield and became lost in complicated reflections about the meaning of it all. What was life in this cosmic drama of exploding stars and collapsing galaxies? How special was man, if evolution had resulted in a hundred thousand distinct species of beetles? Was the genus *Homo* an accident out of control? Or the reason for it all? If so, did that mean someone who advanced mankind's vision—say, a scientist or an artist—was doing the bidding of the whole universe?

Startled from his ruminations by the sounds of a dozen honking cars behind him, he looked ahead. The bridge had cleared. His foot pressed the accelerator.

• •

"ANYTHING NEW?" ASKED Dr. Ranjan, when he entered the laboratory.

Alvin stood behind the far lab bench, mixing a solution in an Erlenmeyer flask. "Not a thing."

Dr. Ranjan's shoulders slumped. He was about to turn away when Alvin added, "By the way, you know those mice you injected with the new sedative last night? You missed one."

Dr. Ranjan shook his head vigorously. "I'm sure I did not."

"You definitely missed one. I got here at seven-thirty this morning, and all the mice were asleep except one."

"That's strange."

"Go look at them. They should still be sleeping."

Dr. Ranjan possessed a characteristic common to inventors and idiots: His mind seized upon the improbable. He ran down the hall to the animal room. There he found the cage full of mice he'd injected last night with a long-acting sedative that was available only for experimental use. The drug was so potent it would never find its way into the clinic. Just before going home yesterday evening, he had administered a high dose of the drug to the mice; it should have kept them asleep until the late afternoon. Now, as he looked over the mice in the cage, his eyes confirmed Alvin's report. All were asleep but one: a male mouse with reddish eyes, greenish ears, and an uncanny stare that seemed directed right at Dr. Ranjan.

It *had* to be a careless mistake, though he didn't make such mistakes often. So Dr. Ranjan drew up more sedative into a hypodermic syringe and injected a double dose. The mouse squealed. Dr. Ranjan watched closely. In minutes a normal mouse should have become groggy; within half an hour the animal should have entered an imperturbable slumber. Dr. Ranjan waited and waited, but the sedative had no effect on the red-eyed, green-eared male. Dr. Ranjan quadrupled the dose—lethal for an ordinary mouse. An hour later the mouse was rubbing himself indecently against the cage. Unaffected by the stench of mouse urine in the animal room, Dr. Ranjan sat down to ponder the matter.

Hours passed. The mice he'd sedated last night started to wake up. But this sedative-resistant mouse made him forget to perform the rest of the experiment.

It made no sense. But then Dr. Ranjan happened to glance at an adjacent cage of mice where a very different experiment was being carried out. That cage contained mice on which the effects of a new organic compound (proposed for use as an artificial flavoring) were being studied. To provide funds for Dr. Ranjan's work on the sleep inhibitor, the hospital had contracted a fraction of the research effort to a company that needed data on the long-term consequences of new compounds before considering them for human use. This was just one of those mindless experiments Alvin performed as part of the contract. Now, as Dr. Ranjan observed those mice, he wondered if one of them had gotten mixed up with the sedated mice, perhaps during cage cleaning.

Had the organic compound caused the mouse to undergo a mutation? Possibly—and, of course, he needed to alert the company to a potential problem with their compound. But right now Dr. Ranjan's deeper interest lay in the mouse itself. However it happened, it had happened. Before him was a mutant mouse that couldn't be put to sleep, probably the first such creature in the planet's history.

"It all started with a mouse," Dr. Ranjan muttered cautiously.

"It all started with a mouse," he said again, less cautiously.

Soon he was repeating the words more clearly, words he envisioned as the first sentence of his plenary lecture before an international congress of neurobiologists.

His vindication!

He pulled the mouse with reddish eyes and greenish ears from its cage and placed it in a smaller cage. Then he carried the small cage into his office and observed the mouse. For three days and three nights.

. .

By Saturday, Dr. Ranjan's shirt was covered with coffee stains as he stared through bloodshot eyes at the mouse he'd been awake with for three days and three nights. He would have tried to stay awake for another night had Bhavana not threatened divorce if he didn't show up for dinner.

Dr. Ranjan still couldn't quite accept it. But there, eleven inches from his nose, was the incredible creature with absolute insomnia he'd whimsically named Johny Walker—in honor of the old Hindi film comedian who'd named himself after a bottle of whiskey. With much more confidence than three days ago, Dr. Ranjan repeated, "It all started with a mouse."

Johny Walker seemed to smile.

Although Dr. Ranjan had a more open mind than most scientists, even he refused to believe certain things—like Johny Walker's mousy grin. Smile or not, though, the mouse's expression moved him. He took Johny Walker out of the cage and gave him a gentle kiss on the snout. Then he carried the mouse back to the animal room. He added two handfuls of sawdust to make the cage more comfortable, since it didn't look like Johny Walker would be getting much rest. For nearly an hour Dr. Ranjan carefully examined the other thirty-six mice. At last he chose one—the animal he deemed the sexiest, most voluptuous female of all. He placed her in Johny Walker's cage.

For the time being Dr. Ranjan decided not to tell anyone about the insomniac red-eyed, green-eared mouse. He knew no one—with the possible exception of Alvin—would believe him. But Dr. Ranjan considered Alvin's mind so warped by drugs and counterculture ideas that he could be convinced of anything. Besides, he didn't want word to leak out. Immortality was at stake—his own. And he felt uncomfortable not knowing exactly how it had happened. Could some kind of mutation have led to overproduction of a circulating sleep inhibitor? Scientific glory would go to whoever figured out what really had happened. But mutants often turned out to be dead ends. Frequently they didn't reproduce. A single red-eyed, green-eared mouse wouldn't convince anyone.

Dr. Ranjan needed junior Johny Walkers.

10

Fusion

Tandoori lay on the couch between Gwen and Sonny. Gwen gently stroked the dog's belly while Sonny scratched him behind the ears. Feminine principles, masculine principles: Tandoori was experiencing the canine equivalent of that state of fusion sought by mystics and ascetics alike.

While Sonny and Gwen pampered the blissful dog, their eyes were focused on the TV screen across the room. Their fingers grazed, linked, lingered awhile. Gwen felt the tenderness in Sonny's touch. She cast a sidelong glance at him and, for a split second, wondered what it would be like to have his baby.

Sonny was fully aware of Gwen's fingers as they fluttered against his own, but he stared at the TV and pretended to be absorbed in the details of tomorrow's weather forecast. He felt the huge reservoir of gentleness in her touch; it reminded him of something he hadn't had enough of in life. Those thoughts, inevitably linked to his mother, he quickly chased away.

The news was over. Commercials followed. He reached for the remote and turned off the TV. "Want some wine?"

Gwen shook her head no.

An awkward silence: Something meaningful needed to be said. What? And who was to say it?

"It's supposed to be a fine Cabernet," he finally added.

"I'll pass."

He headed for the kitchen to get a glass of wine. She picked up the phone to have Chinese food delivered for dinner. Tandoori hopped off the couch and sauntered over to his favorite spot beneath the window, curling up on the rug Sonny had bought for him.

Forty-five minutes later they finished their dinner of hot-and-sour soup, steamed dumplings, cold sesame noodles, and chicken lo mein. Gwen helped Sonny clear the table. Then she said, "I'd better be going."

"Why don't you stay over?"

"I would, but I'm working a lot of hours this week, and there's laundry to do, and I still haven't paid my bills, and . . ."

Her words grew distant. He suddenly became aware of his apartment's spare furnishings: the bed without a proper cover, the blank off-white walls in need of a coat of paint, the dusty wood floors that somehow looked even more bare with Tandoori's small rug, the lamp without a shade, the two forks, two knives, and three spoons that were his cutlery. Again he thought of asking her to stay. But Gwen had already put on her shoes and slipped into her sweater. At the door he kissed her on the cheek. Gone was the ease they had felt while sitting on the couch with Tandoori.

After he shut the door he asked himself what it was that drew him to Gwen. In the beginning much of it was, frankly, physical. He liked the unpredictability of her desire, the way her body felt, her frenzied immersion in the acts of love. And, to his surprise, he liked quietly whiling away weekends with her. But he couldn't help wondering about the logic of their being together. Then again, what kind of woman might be his logical match? Maybe they weren't such an unlikely couple after all. She was a misfit, too, and, like him, hovering at the cultural border zone. The language of that zone, his language, wasn't foreign to her, even if she wasn't as fluent as he. How many people had he met who *really* understood it? But while he derived a thrill from straddling that border, she seemed to shrink from it. She seemed exhausted by something he didn't understand, eager to withdraw into her books—for solace or protection, he was never quite sure. And when he thought of the future, as he increasingly did, logic continued to build its relentless case. Not against Gwen, but against anybody. He had no business entangling his life with someone else's—not right now, not for a long time to come.

• •

THE REAL REASON GWEN had refused to stay over at Sonny's was that she had an appointment early in the morning on the other side of town with her endocrinologist, Dr. Bates. Since Sonny already knew that she was working the night shift, if she had stayed over she would have had to explain why she was leaving so early. She wasn't ready to tell him about her disease.

Gwen was alarmed. Those periods when her appetite and libido went wild had been recurring with greater frequency. Would it only get worse?

Just after eight that Monday morning, Dr. Bates walked into the examining room. A tall woman in her late forties, she had shoulder-length hair so silvery it could have been made of fine wire. Gwen liked Dr. Bates's businesslike manner, the cool tone in which she spoke. It had a way of making her clinical opinion sound objective and easier to digest.

"Any improvement since I last saw you?"

Gwen shook her head from side to side. "Whenever I go into a fit, I become like someone who's just discovered the fun of sex. I want more and more and more. Same with food, especially chocolate. I don't think of consequences. Of course, there *are* consequences, serious ones that keep messing up my life. And I can gain five pounds in a couple of days—unless there's lots of sex to burn up the calories. It's horrible. Well, it's horrible *after.* In the midst of it, there are some damn good moments."

"Do you want to try medication again?"

"Not unless there's something new. Nothing we've tried has worked so far. Those last pills made me feel weird even when I wasn't in the middle of a fit."

Dr. Bates quietly flipped through Gwen's chart.

"I'm worried things will get worse," added Gwen.

Dr. Bates leaned back in her chair. "Since your symptoms and blood tests overlap with several syndromes, it's hard to predict how things will go in your case. But these diseases usually pass through peaks and valleys. Within a few months, the attacks should diminish."

"And until then?"

It was a plea, and Dr. Bates's face softened into an expression of genuine sympathy. "I wish I knew what to tell you. Somehow you'll have to learn to tame your instincts. I suppose it requires the willpower certain hermits and monks are said to possess. But hermits have their forests, and monks have their monasteries. To do it in the real world, and that, too, with your instincts so determinedly working against you, won't be easy."

"But *how* might I go about it?"

Dr. Bates pursed her lips. "As I said, I really don't know. Meditation, maybe? Regular mental exercises are thought to cause lasting biochemical changes in the brain. Some experts even hypothesize that the brain gets rewired. In your case, the idea would be to use meditation to short-circuit the overactive connections that make you go into a fit. Of course, you can't expect to get rid of the disease, but maybe you can attenuate it."

"That's staking a lot on someone's hypothesis."

"As an ICU nurse, I'm sure you know there's a huge gray zone in medicine—some days it seems in most of medicine—where we never quite know how to treat a patient because the illness doesn't fit what's described in textbooks. That's where the art comes in."

Gwen nodded slowly.

"Look, it's up to you," said Dr. Bates, her tone suddenly formal, as if she'd been too candid a moment ago. "At the very least, you must learn what circumstances prevent you from getting into trouble."

"When I suffer several fits over a short time," said Gwen, "it helps to be in a long-term relationship with a decent, sane guy. Otherwise, I can end up with almost anyone. Believe me, it's happened."

"Are you in such a relationship now?"

"It has potential."

"A decent, sane guy?"

Gwen took a while to answer. "Decent, yes. Maybe even more than I think."

"And sane?"

"That I'm less sure of."

• •

LATER THAT DAY Gwen called the East-West Practical Metacognition Institute, which had a small ad in the yellow pages. Over the phone she enrolled in "Beginning Meditation," held two evenings a week from six to seven.

Gwen arrived early for the first class. While waiting for the instructor to show up, some students tried to impress the others with how well versed they were in matters Indian. A few had traveled to India and spoke of their experiences in hyperbolic terms.

The group hushed when the instructor entered. A lithe man of about sixty, he flashed a disarming smile and asked his students to call him Mike. He said he'd once been a Peace Corps volunteer and, during the early seventies, lived in a Bengali village where he taught farmers new methods of cultivation. He left when local politicians began accusing the volunteers of being CIA agents. "The trouble was," he added, "some probably were."

That remark tempered Gwen's skepticism.

Following one-by-one introductions, Mike walked over to a wall on which was hung a schematic of an androgynous body inscribed with the seven chakras. Using a pointer, he explained the nature of each chakra, giving examples of how their aberrancies lead to distortions of the soul. "You must free the kundalini energy," he said, "so it can climb from the base of your spine through your brain and beyond, pushing out the undigested karma that complicates your life . . ."

Gwen's skepticism returned. What was she doing in a place called the East-West Practical Metacognition Institute?

"Now shut your eyes," said Mike in a soft, mellifluous voice. "Take slow, deep breaths. Re-lax. Unclench those fists and jaws and toes. That's it. Slow, *deep* breaths. Slow-er, deep-er. Good—you're getting the hang of it. Unburden your mind of the cares of the day, the week, the month, the year. Enter a world without those problems. Do you see the door?"

Gwen saw nothing.

"I know that most of you can't see it yet," said Mike. "Don't worry. You *will*. Everything important takes time, and this does, too. Here, on the third floor of a building on the West Side, we are far from the source of everything. Just knowing this is the first step. We've been living wrong lives. The universe is not ambivalent, and neither should you be. Gradually, with lots of practice, the chakras will loosen and the energy will flow again . . ."

Gwen opened her eyes. Did she need to listen to this watered-down philosophy? The only thing preventing her from leaving was the fact that the exit was on the other side of the room, and she felt it wasn't fair to disturb all the spellbound students who thought they were going to get something out of this.

"Visualize a tranquil pond," said Mike. "Any size, any depth, any place, Central Park or Central America."

What the hell, thought Gwen. Desperation had brought her here, and she was still desperate. She closed her eyes again and tried to imagine a pond.

"Do you see the gentle surface of the pond? It is very still, isn't it? Don't be fooled. So much is going on below! Peer into its depths. Concentrate on the bubbles."

Gwen saw no pond, no bubbles. Every now and then, though, a couple of round things flitted across the amber screen of her eyelids. But mostly the screen stayed blank. Even so, the band of tightness around her forehead began to loosen. Gradually the rest of her body relaxed, too.

"Can you see the bubbles? Some are big, some are small. Where are they coming from? Where are they going?"

Gwen couldn't see any bubbles, but she was able make out dim patterns forming here and there. Sometimes they linked up; other times they separated. Eventually the patterns went away and the round things appeared again. Still not bubbles, but this time they didn't vanish. Of different sizes, they swirled all around.

"Keep your attention on the bubbles. Only the bubbles. Watch the bubbles rise to the pond's surface. What happens when the bubbles fuse? Can you hear them pop?"

Gwen's whole body felt light, as if it might float away. Soon the screen of her eyelids had changed from amber to blue-green. And those round things were no longer swirling. Instead, they were moving in an orderly fashion, slowly upward, gradually becoming more shiny—transparent. Like . . .

Bubbles!

Delicate, shimmering bubbles!

"Now," said Mike, "very gently, enter a bubble. Careful. Don't let the bubble pop. There, that's it. You're inside now, just going along for the ride . . ."

Gwen couldn't believe it! She was inside a bubble slowly floating upward, her body caressed by its clear, sticky sides.

"Let yourself *ex-hi-la-rate*."

She felt secure, whole. An entire universe was within the bubble, another outside. Were they the same universe, or different? Looking around, she saw rays of sunlight penetrating the blue-green water, their refracted beams giving off a diffuse glow that allowed her to peer deep and far . . . "The water is so transparent . . . like molten glass, cool but not congealed. . . . I see the sandy bottom and detect how shallow it is. Its thin current slides away, but eternity remains."

Walden?

Her bubble continued its journey. She could see the blurry world above. Red-brown leaves twirled down from overhanging branches and joined others floating on the pond's surface. Gwen's heart pounded—she could hear it! *lub-dub, lub-dub, lub-dub*—as the bubble drifted closer and closer to the surface. Nothing seemed more important than the moment of fusion. Then, at long last, the bubble fused, and she slipped into another realm.

11

Questions

IN RECENT YEARS THE TRANSPLANTED MAN'S LIFE HAD BECOME A BLUR of events, with little time to reflect or derive the kind of satisfaction that one finds in a good story. So he kept devouring all the books Gwen supplied—for the sheer pleasure of absorption in another world. But sometimes even literature couldn't alleviate the tedium of the hospital, the loneliness. Three bland meals were interrupted by brief visits of the hospital staff: doctors to perform examinations, nurses to monitor vital signs and dole out pills, technicians to draw blood. Which meant that, on the four days of the week when no dialysis session was scheduled, the Transplanted Man spent roughly 1,400 of the day's 1,440 minutes alone. His room's minimal furnishings and gray walls didn't help matters. Sometimes he woke up feeling like he was locked in a high-security prison.

Luckily, he had a view. He spent a lot of time staring out his ninth-floor window at the neighborhood below. He soaked it all in, acutely aware of how the scene changed with the passage of the day. From airplanes he had seen New York City several times—and on those clear nights when the pilot flew straight over the length of Manhattan, he had marveled at the city's sparkling, rectilinear beauty. But at the more modest height of his hospital window, the jagged silhouette of skyscrapers was nowhere in sight. Did it even have to be America? You could easily be fooled by those streets below lined with Indian groceries, sari and video shops, homeopathic pharmacies, one-room "computer colleges," henna parlors, marriage bureaus, restaurants.

Today he noticed a new element in the local landscape. On the sidewalk— at the periphery of his view—was a white man, very still. The Transplanted Man observed for more than fifteen minutes, but the man did not move. What was wrong with him? At last the hypokinetic man's left foot crept forward: the initiation of a step that would take nine and a half minutes to complete.

The Transplanted Man's concentration was interrupted by the sound of his door squeaking open. He turned around. It was a young woman, tall, pretty, with an unwavering gaze. He half-expected her to pull a gun from her handbag and fire.

"I didn't think it would be so easy," she said in a hard-palated American accent. "I thought there would be guards."

"Who are you?"

"Reena Roshan."

"I don't know that name."

"You aren't alone, unfortunately. I'm a reporter."

The Transplanted Man sighed. "A reporter."

"I have a few questions."

"No questions."

Reena Roshan took a step forward. "You're as big a story as I'll ever get."

"Perhaps not. Ronny Chanchal is in town these days for his show. He's a big story—a big film star, a big politician. And he *loves* to give interviews."

"I've already interviewed that windbag."

The Transplanted Man couldn't keep himself from smiling as he walked over to his bed and settled into it. "Sit down," he finally said, motioning to the chair beside his bed.

"You must, of course, do what you feel is right," said the Transplanted Man. "But what will you accomplish by announcing that I am here? You will confirm what some already suspect, but you'll also place me in danger. Is that what you want?"

Reena Roshan looked thoughtful. At last she said, "You're a very manipulative old man."

The Transplanted Man couldn't suppress a mischievous grin. "Did it work?"

"One condition. You must promise not to grant an interview to anyone else: Indian, American, Indian American—"

"Agreed."

"And you must give me one," she said, sitting down again. "Right now. It won't be published until after your discharge. Do we have a deal?"

The Transplanted Man studied the woman before him. He decided she was one of those principled youngsters who often went into journalism but would never make the compromises necessary to survive at a major paper. He could trust her. "I'll give you half an hour," he said. "Not a second more."

There was a knock at the door. Gwen entered with the Transplanted Man's medications. "I didn't know you had a visitor," she said.

"Ms. Roshan dropped in unexpectedly."

Gwen eyed Reena Roshan carefully, then turned to the Transplanted Man. "Is everything all right?"

"I believe so."

Gwen handed him a glass of water and nine pills. The Transplanted Man made a face.

"Swallow, and I'll vanish."

As soon as Gwen left, Reena Roshan pulled a small tape recorder from her handbag. "So tell me, how long can the Ministry of Health and Family Welfare function with an absentee minister?"

"You don't waste words."

"You only gave me thirty minutes, and that nurse used up two."

"The ministry is functioning smoothly thanks to senior bureaucrats with whom I'm in regular contact," said the Transplanted Man in a formal tone. He pointed to a folder on his bedside table containing recent faxes and couriered documents.

"There must come a time when—"

"If the need should arise, the prime minister can replace me."

Reena Roshan continued with a series of difficult questions. The artillery barrage quickly exhausted the Transplanted Man. He was a patient right now, an old man with failed kidneys, other organs on the verge of rejection, his mind clouded by medications. He didn't have it in him to dodge the truth with the finely nuanced answers of a seasoned politician. Already he'd been too loose-lipped. No telling what he'd say if this reporter managed to draw him out.

Reena Roshan didn't give up. Soon the Transplanted Man's replies had dwindled to two or three words. He felt a headache coming on, worried that his blood pressure had shot up.

"I can see that I'm tiring you," said Reena Roshan. "All right. It's unfair to badger you in your current condition. I think I can work with this. But I'd like to ask one last question."

"Ask."

"First, I'd like to inject a personal note."

"Inject."

She crossed her legs, then readjusted her skirt. "As you've surely guessed from my accent, I grew up here. When I was in grade school, our textbook— a dozen years old even then—portrayed India as a poor, backward, overcrowded land. I felt ashamed—and guilty for feeling ashamed. In reaction, I guess, I got more interested in India as I grew older. Maybe it even explains why I'm here interviewing you."

The Transplanted Man stroked the gray stubble on his chin but said nothing.

"I went to India recently—my first visit in years. Of course, things have changed a great deal. But as I traveled around, I began to realize that the country is still ensnared in problems that should have been solved decades ago— problems soluble back then but perhaps insoluble now. And it made me wonder if the country had missed its chance to take off."

"We took off long ago!" said the Transplanted Man. "We build our own fighter jets, satellites, missiles, computers. No matter how you look at it—cars, radios, TVs, literacy, life expectancy—things are much better. Hyderabad, Bangalore, and Chennai will soon be the software capitals of the—"

"But how much better off are the people who can't log on to the Internet? That's what I want to know. Maybe no one starves anymore, but the poor remain poor—and there are more of them, according to recent statistics."

"Statistics," the Transplanted Man repeated in a mocking voice. "For half a century statistics have been saying India will fall off the face of the earth. Has it? Of course not! The problem is that you look at India through the eyes of a foreigner."

Reena Roshan grimaced.

"Do not be offended. It was an observation, not a criticism. The slums of Kolkata, snake charmers, the sweet aroma of mangoes—that type of thing. You see India as either an impoverished, spent civilization or an exotic land. Maybe you see both simultaneously. Perhaps you find the juxtaposition fascinating. I don't deny that there is something in it. The trouble is that the modernization of India interferes with that fantasy. And such a powerful fantasy it is! So why not forget the modern India and indulge in the fantasy? Do you know what I mean? But to me—and most other Indians—India is what it is, the only place in the world we want to live. The pull of one's homeland— there's nothing like it. Whenever I go abroad, I am struck by the fact that Indians fight so hard against assimilation. On the one hand, they are superficially quite good at it, but there is also a deeper resistance."

"You didn't answer my question."

"I thought I did."

"No. You gave me a patronizing answer, basically saying that I, being an Indian American, see India the same way as a foreigner with no Indian heritage."

"That is not what I meant."

"Sure," said Reena Roshan, her face expressionless. "Now let's get back to my question. You can go on forever about the 'modern India,' but that doesn't erase the 'other India,' the embarrassing one—which is still, by the way, the vast majority of the country. Most Indians get very defensive about this. They seem to view it as dirty linen, or a family secret—and, of course, one shows only one's best face to the West, right? Nobody denies that there has been progress on many fronts, but it's sad, if not downright painful, to contemplate how everything might have turned out. India had so much going for it: highly educated talent, natural resources, strong institutions. What happened?"

The Transplanted Man stared at Reena Roshan for a long time. "It's complicated," he finally said. "Many factors—"

"Spare me the long sociopolitical analysis that, in the end, says nothing. Look, I'm asking *you* because you're supposed to be the leader of the other India, its great hope. At least that's how you portray yourself."

The Transplanted Man ran his hand through his hair. "Stop your tape recorder."

"But—"

"Stop it, *please.*"

"Done."

"Off the record, agreed?"

Reena Roshan nodded.

"It's because of certain people."

"*Certain* people?"

"People who have been irresponsible, selfish, sometimes corrupt, often lacking vision."

Reena Roshan raised her eyebrows. "Like whom?"

The Transplanted Man gazed straight into her eyes. "Like me."

12

The Show

Even though Ronny Chanchal had slept with many women, he'd never known sexual ecstasy with a woman who genuinely loved him. Never married, his sex life had been limited to calculated seductions and bargains for parts in his films, prostitution of a sort, and he'd always known it. With little hope of discovering love so late in life, his only option was to imagine it—which he could do only with visual aids.

Ronny Chanchal had a passion for porn. At one time or another he had roamed the underbellies of great metropolises around the globe in his quest for exciting videos. And now he happened to be in one of the most sex-obsessed cities of all, where pornography could be bought to suit any fantasy. So the night before his big show, the actor-politician took a taxi to a seedy part of lower Manhattan in search of additions to his already substantial collection.

For ten minutes he strolled up and down the street, scanning storefronts: here a dildo store, there a bottomless bar, here a triple-X movie theater. In between were porn shops, each packed with enough hard-core videos to give a whole high school terminal acne. Eventually Ronny Chanchal ducked into one of those shops. He was dismayed to find that the fortyish salesperson at the cash register was Indian. The man tried not to stare, but Ronny Chanchal knew he'd been recognized. At such moments it helped to be an actor. He went up to the salesperson and looked him in the eye. "Excuse me, but where do you stock aspirin? I have an excruciating headache."

"Go to the pharmacy in the next block, sir."

"Thank you."

Ronny Chanchal rushed to the other end of the street and slipped into another adult video store. Here, too, the man behind the cash register was Indian, though this fellow was much younger, twenty-two at most, and didn't seem to recognize him. Ronny Chanchal was relieved but also slightly disappointed. This was yet more evidence of his declining popularity among the youth. As he headed toward a corner of the store where his face couldn't easily be seen by other browsers, he wondered why so many Indians worked in these places. Then again, was it all that surprising? Having observed Indians abroad for many years, he'd noticed that some of them—even those with advanced but unmarketable degrees from Indian universities—could be found wherever money was to be made, even at the cost of respectability. There was something to admire in these people. They sold X-rated videos for a few years, then moved to the suburbs and sent their children to Harvard.

Ronny Chanchal searched the shelves for what he liked most: the rare video that promised very traditional sex. For him the experience depended on believing the actors and actresses were making authentic love. Given the quality of acting in porn films, this was a tall order, which continued to inspire his quest for the perfect video.

He took two videos to the cash register. When he pulled out his wallet, the salesman said in a thick Brooklyn accent, "You look a lot like that film actor. . . . What's his name? My mother is always watching his films, secretly hoping I'll turn out like the heroes he plays. That guy who has a show tomorrow—I wish I could remember his name . . ."

Ronny Chanchal was prepared. "A lot of people say I look like him. Of course, he's much younger than me. Bigger, too. Besides," he added with a sly grin, "you wouldn't expect to find *him* in a place like this. Would you?"

The young man squinted suspiciously. "My mother would certainly be upset if he came here."

"Don't worry, I'm not him. See?"

Ronny Chanchal turned his head in profile, a view he never let any camera shoot, since his nose was hooked.

After scrutinizing his profile the salesman said, "On the other hand, you'd be surprised who turns up here. Are you sure you're not—"

"*I'm not.* Don't even wonder. And don't suggest it to your mother. It would ruin her world."

The young man nodded solemnly as he took three twenty-dollar bills from Ronny Chanchal's hand.

• •

THE ORCHESTRA TRILLED AND trumpeted a medley of fast-paced tunes while hawkers with colas, kulfis, and samosas navigated the packed stands.

The stage lighting changed from white to green to purple. Cheers erupted in the crowd and then wild screams as the stage flooded with dancers in skimpy outfits, dozens of legs and arms moving in synchrony. And somewhere there was an instant—a point between when Hindi film music was being driven by a Western beat and rock and roll was tamed by Indian rhythms—when the stadium, packed with seventy-six thousand people who, in one way or another, considered themselves Indian, suddenly fell silent. In that almost religious moment, whole lives made sense. Then the moment was swallowed by hubbub and lost forever.

Suddenly the stage lights went out, and loud booms sounded above. Everyone's attention was directed toward the display of fireworks crisscrossing the night sky. The crowd oohed and aahed at the bright red, green, and blue streaks of light that appeared to stretch to the edges of the universe.

The stage lights came back on. At the center of the stage had been placed a large blue box tied with a golden ribbon; it looked like a giant birthday present. A chorus in the far left corner of the stage started to sing, *"Dilruba, oh meri dilruba, chalo mere saath, dilruba. . . ."* Everyone recognized the song. In no time the amplified lyrics were drowned out by the roaring crowd, which had worked itself into a frenzy befitting the resurrection of Elvis.

A dancer skipped up to the blue box and pulled the gold ribbon. The box fell apart, and out jumped a small man in a glittering mauve tuxedo. Seventy-six thousand people seemed to shout at once as the man began to gyrate— very stiffly—and completely out of sync with the music and dancers.

No one seemed bothered by the rigidity of his movements. Feet pounded the aisles. Elbows bumped and jewelry jingled as young jostled with old to improve their views. Dozens of bouquets landed at the man's feet as security personnel fended off the madly screaming women in saris and jeans who tried to climb onto the stage.

Ronny Chanchal felt like a god.

· ·

MANNY HAD TRIED TO get out of the midnight-to-eight shift in order to party with friends after the performance. But he couldn't find anyone to cover for him since everybody had gone to see Ronny Chanchal. And so, just before the show let out, Manny reluctantly left the pulsating stadium and rode the subway to work.

It was a slow night at the hospital. Around 12:45 A.M. Manny's meanderings took him by the Transplanted Man's room.

The Transplanted Man was sitting on the edge of his bed, hunched over. Imagining Ronny Chanchal, a man almost of his generation, prancing around like a twenty-year-old before a delirious crowd incited more than a little jealousy in him. It seemed cosmically unjust that Ronny Chanchal should be allowed multiple extensions of youth while his own life was always a question mark.

"What are you doing up so late?" asked Manny.

"Only thinking—wondering."

"About what?"

"Ronny Chanchal's show."

"Stop wondering."

The Transplanted Man's face brightened. "You were there? How was it?"

"That Ronny Chanchal is a fine dude. Did you know he said he'd get me an audition to sing in Hindi films? I performed for him in the cafeteria."

"Tell me about the show," said the Transplanted Man.

"What would you like to know?"

The Transplanted Man wanted to hear every detail. How many people were in the audience? How many minutes of fireworks? How big was the stage? How many dancers and musicians? What did Ronny Chanchal wear? How long did people clap? A standing ovation? Really? How long did they stand? It took Manny over an hour to satisfy the Transplanted Man's curiosity about a three-hour show.

"How good was he?" the Transplanted Man finally asked. "I'm sure you know he's my friend, but please tell the truth. After all, Ronny is getting old. He isn't what he once was. A fifty-two-year-old man dancing like a teenager must look ridiculous. So tell me, did the show live up to your expectations? Was it worth the ticket price—how much did you say, seventy-two dollars for your seat? Be honest."

"I could sit through that show ten more times."

It was nearly two o'clock. The Transplanted Man felt sick. With envy.

• •

HALF AN HOUR LATER Sonny got out of bed. He walked in circles for more than a minute. The creaking wooden floors woke Gwen.

"What's the matter?"

Sonny gave no reply.

"Sonny? . . . Hey, Sonny!"

Still he didn't answer.

Baffled, she watched him somehow put on his jogging shoes. Then, naked but for underwear and shoes, he opened the apartment door. As if all this were quite routine, Tandoori ran up to the threshold and followed Sonny out the door.

Gwen had no experience with sleepwalkers. All she remembered from nursing school was that sudden awakening could provoke a hostile reaction. That was the kind of thing you remembered. As she watched Sonny from the window—sleepwalking down the desolate street, Tandoori at his heels—she considered calling the police. After all, violent gangs roamed the area. She dialed the local precinct number from memory. As soon as someone answered she hung up. What if Sonny overreacted when the cops woke him? The police could be brutal, especially with nonwhites. Given Sonny's general direction, he was probably about to enter a relatively safe, working-class Korean neighborhood. Why risk it? Gwen now recalled how, after their first night together, she'd had an eerie feeling that he'd left the apartment in the middle of the night. That night Sonny had obviously returned intact. And tonight he had Tandoori with him. Even so, Gwen paced the wooden floors, much to the dismay of the tenant below, who kept banging his ceiling with something.

Sonny wasn't in the Korean district. He had turned toward the Indian neighborhood, the only neighborhood without a violent gang, a matter of embarrassment at the local high school. It was a crisp night, though Sonny didn't take note of the weather. Nor did he see the bright aura that hovered above the sleeping neighborhood, the result of city lights reflecting off low clouds. Which was a pity. For, devoid of human traffic and noise—the film songs blaring from every third shop, the paanwalas in their sidewalk stalls shaking peppermint crystals onto betel leaves, the out-of-towners hunting for rare spices—Little India's essential character had resurfaced.

Sonny went past the home of Dr. Giri, who, sleepless that night, happened to be gazing out the window. Then Sonny turned a corner on which was located a matrimonial agency, which analyzed biodata and horoscopes from around the globe in order to "guarantee a perfect match using the latest software." He passed two movie halls, one that screened Hindi movies and another that showed triple X–rated films. Then he went by an immigration lawyer's office that promised "no charges billed until visa approved." Half a block from Tiger's restaurant, he nearly collided with the hypokinetic man, who, thin and rigid, stood like a lamppost erroneously placed in the center of the sidewalk.

Sonny's mind wasn't blank. He was dreaming that he was somewhere in Delhi—standing at the end of a long line at a cinema waiting for a matinee ticket. Ahead of him in the line were men, hundreds of them, all in their early sixties, all glancing back at him, smiling benevolently. Only men. Sonny knew it was hopeless; he'd never get a ticket. He stepped out of line and tried to convince one smiling man after the next that he was his long-lost son, and the least a father could do was take his son out for a film.

He asked every man. But no one wanted a son that day.

13

Double Takes

GWEN SAT AT THE BAR OF AN UPTOWN HOTEL WITH HER OLD GRADUATE school roommate, now a lecturer in literary criticism at a college outside London. Joan was in town to present a paper at a conference called "Deconstruction or Decimation?: A Critical Reassessment." Virtually inseparable in grad school, the two hadn't kept in touch, other than yearly Christmas cards, since Gwen moved to the States.

"How was the first day of the conference?" asked Gwen, stirring her margarita.

"All decimators."

"All they've ever been."

"You never were much for any school of criticism."

"You once said I had a Disney aesthetic."

"Surely I was joking. Seriously, though, you wouldn't have had such a rough time if you'd committed to one of the critical theories fashionable in the department."

"I'd have done just fine if a certain visiting fellow had kept his hands to himself one afternoon when my instincts had spun out of control."

"Blame your disease, but you were flirting with Santino long before it happened. I remember how you went out of your way to be at the library whenever he was there."

"I went to the library to read, that's all."

"Oh, that's right—I forgot all about your sudden fascination with Boccaccio."

"It wasn't like that, Joan. I never intended to sleep with a married man!"

In the silence that followed Gwen wondered, possibly for the thousandth time, whether her disease had simply provided a convenient excuse for getting involved with Santino—for not weighing consequences. To make matters worse, Santino's wife had been a visiting fellow in the Music Department. The scandal had consumed all.

"More drinks, ladies?"

"Another margarita," said Gwen. "Equally tepid."

"Got the point. This round's on me."

Soon the bartender placed two potent concoctions before them.

"How's the battle with your disease going?" asked Joan. "Still life-threatening?"

"Potentially. I'm trying meditation."

"And?"

"Too early to tell."

They listened to the pianist at the far end of the room.

"You know," said Joan, "London is *so* different from when you left. *Revenge of the Colonized, Part 3.* It's certainly made the place more interesting. You should visit. You might decide to stay."

"Every now and then I think about going back. Let's see how things turn out."

"What things?"

Gwen didn't reply. They sipped their drinks quietly.

At last Gwen said, "You've scarcely said a word about yourself."

Joan's lips tightened. "What's to say? I'm married to a man who works a lot, smokes a lot. We don't talk much anymore—or make love. We have two kids, who are gradually getting messed up by our messed-up marriage. I'm about to be denied tenure, and since there are no jobs in academia, I don't know what I'll do after. Sounds mundane, but it hurts."

Gwen rested her fingers on Joan's wrist.

After a while Joan asked, "Are you with anyone these days?"

"A resident at the hospital."

"I thought there might be someone. You're not in your standard factory worker uniform. As a matter of fact, that skirt could creep down closer to your knee. Or is this the American Gwen?"

"I still have a closet full of drab factory worker uniforms. I only bought this outfit last week. You really think it shows too much thigh?"

"This guy is obviously doing something for you."

Gwen kept quiet.

"If you don't want to talk about it . . ."

Gwen sighed, then took another sip of her drink. "It's too convenient for doctors and nurses. You don't think enough about it, where it might lead."

"So what draws you to this guy?"

"Complementary inadequacies."

"What's wrong with him?"

"For starters, Sonny is four years younger than me. He just isn't there yet."

"Where?"

"*There.*"

"Not the right guy to take to Walden Pond? Remember how you used to fantasize—"

"Still do."

"Going from a married man with three kids to a young resident doctor is a big leap."

"A leap or a dive? Only now do I realize how far apart those two phases of life are. I'm somewhere in between, I guess. But I feel myself gradually moving closer to Santino's phase—"

"You want three kids?"

"Heavens no! But I wouldn't mind having one—someday."

"With Sonny?"

Gwen didn't reply.

"Well, Gwendolyn?"

"If only he were more like the Transplanted Man."

"The who?"

"A patient of mine—*the* Indian health minister, believe it or not. . . . Hey, keep this confidential, okay?"

"Like I know anyone who gives a hoot."

Gwen nodded slowly. "The Transplanted Man is the exact opposite of all my preconceptions of politicians. Literate, wise, sensitive—"

"You aren't infatuated, are you?"

Gwen blushed. "Don't be silly! He's in his sixties!"

"Older men, younger women: It's a tradition. Rubens, Wagner, Picasso—"

"Henry the Eighth," added Gwen, sipping her drink. "If Sonny and the Transplanted Man could somehow be fused, you'd have one incredible guy."

"What's Sonny like?"

"Holden Caulfield at twenty-nine."

"One of them, eh?"

"Not one of anybody. Even at the hospital, he's different. But there, his warped lenses help him see—and do—what no one else can. Just a couple of weeks ago, a patient of his, someone who *should* have died, came out of a coma."

Joan swirled her margarita. "You can waste a lot of time attempting to convince yourself a screwed-up younger guy has a profound basis for his immaturity."

"Maybe you're right."

"On the other hand, a younger man's body could tip the balance."

Gwen couldn't help smiling.

Joan's eyebrows arched. "That good?"

"Better."

• •

WHILE WALKING TO WORK the next morning, Sonny spotted the hypokinetic man inching down Esmoor Street between Forty-fifth and Forty-fourth. It was the first time he'd seen the hypokinetic man since that morning he got stuck between the subway doors. Sonny still felt guilty about not coming to his aid quickly enough.

Sonny stopped in front of the hypokinetic man. "Remember me, pal? Maybe you don't. Frankly, I wouldn't remember me, either, after what happened that morning. Just remember that I work at the hospital down the street. Way over there—that ugly brick building. Whenever you feel up to it, come by and see me. Ask for Doc-tor Seth, okay?"

The hypokinetic man gave no hint of comprehension. Sonny patted him gently on the shoulder and started to walk away. But after a few steps he was seized by a sudden panic. Looking back at the hypokinetic man, he felt as if he'd left part of himself behind. He shrugged off the thought and hurried away. Half a block later the feeling reasserted itself, much stronger now. He spun around and stared at the hypokinetic man again. Had the hypokinetic man even moved? Against the dark buildings he looked lonely, beyond rescue. And yet there was a defiance in his stolidity that seemed to question whether it was he who was irrelevant to the scene, or just the opposite. The longer Sonny stared, the more he felt like he was over there, standing beside the hypokinetic man.

As he rushed off to work, he tried to dismiss what had just happened. After all, it wasn't *really* mind-body dissociation. Or was it? He thought about the dreams he'd been having lately. Some of them had been awfully strange. Perhaps he should consult a psychotherapist. But he feared it wouldn't be kept secret if he went to someone at the hospital. He knew of only one other psychotherapist nearby, the man they called Guruji. Although the hospital shrinks considered Dr. Giri a charlatan, Sonny had heard praise on the outside.

As soon as Sonny got to the hospital, he called for an appointment. Dr. Giri offered to see him that very afternoon at two-thirty.

• •

SONNY PRESSED THE BUZZER twice before Dr. Giri came to the door. After brief introductions Dr. Giri guided Sonny into his sparsely furnished office and asked him to take a seat.

Dr. Giri carefully settled into his ergonomic recliner and adjusted the knobs. Over the weekend he had helped his daughter rearrange furniture in her bedroom, and his back was in spasm. The pain went from a point between his shoulder blades down the length of his spine all the way to his sacrum. Just before Sonny arrived he had applied a deep-heating ointment with a winter-green odor. He wondered if Sonny, sitting four feet away, could smell it.

"They call you Guruji."

"I don't encourage it."

"You don't discourage it."

Dr. Giri's lips curled into a wry smile. "With every patient I have to decide whether to don the guru's robes or the psychologist's white coat."

"What do you usually wear?"

"Robes."

"What are you going to wear for this appointment?"

"The sarcasm is unnecessary. I'm not particularly proud of the compromise."

A long silence passed. In the beauty shop next door, a track from an Ananda Shankar album could be heard.

Sonny glanced at his wristwatch. "I've got to be back at the hospital in half an hour, so I might as well spit it out. I'm worried that I might be going crazy—schizophrenia or something. I'm the right age, you know. As if life isn't complicated enough."

Dr. Giri knit his brow. "Why schizophrenia?"

"You can't guess what thoughts run through my head. I've been having weird dreams, too. Sometimes I find myself swimming to a tropical island or lost in the desert. And there's a really bizarre dream in which something keeps calling out my name."

"Some*thing*?"

"I think it's a cactus. A saguaro."

"Hmmm," said Dr. Giri, shifting in his recliner. "I once dreamed that a mango spoke to me. Actually, it was a man with a mango for a head."

"Huh."

"Surely you've seen the paintings of Dalí? You know, melting watches, other fantastic images that sometimes seem more real than the view from your window. Do you get my point?"

"No."

"We dream all kinds of things, and the power of dreams, those that occur during our sleep *and* the ones that we have when awake—the ones that propel our lives—is that they can seem more real than anything that happened today or yesterday."

"The dreams must *mean* something."

"A slippery matter. Some dreams mean something, but one must be careful not to overinterpret. Certainly it's not schizophrenia."

"Then there's that guy inching down Esmoor Street."

"The homeless fellow? What does this have to do with him?"

"I feel an affinity for him."

Dr. Giri raised his eyebrows. "An affinity, you say?"

"When I saw him this morning, I felt like . . . Well, it's hard to describe. And sometimes I have an urge to drop everything—as if I'm being called to a far-off place."

"Every voice one hears isn't necessarily delusional."

Sonny took a deep breath and sighed. "It's good to hear that from a person like you. I've ignored all this because I've been so busy at the hospital, especially with the Transplanted . . . uh . . . a patient of mine. There's something about him, I don't know what it is, but, well, I've never quite felt this way about a patient. He seems more like an uncle, or . . ."

"A father?"

Sonny didn't answer.

"You might benefit from talking on a regular basis," said Dr. Giri. "A residency has to be one of the most stressful experiences for a young person to go through short of war. So maybe we could talk about that. Or we could start with the usual things: your parents, your childhood, your home . . ."

Sonny abruptly got up.

"What's the matter?"

"I need to get back to work."

• •

As SONNY WALKED BACK to the hospital, he couldn't keep his mind off the topics that Dr. Giri had broached. *The usual things:* his parents, his childhood, his home. What could he say? He and his parents had always been an unconnected triangle. Literally. There had never been a line from him to his father— he had no memory of the man—and his mother had revealed next to nothing, as if she was guarding some secret. He didn't even know if his father was still alive. Perhaps his mother didn't know, either. And his relationship with her, always stormy, had grown so tenuous it was now virtually nonexistent. She called every so often—a three- or four-minute telegraphic conversation, full of bitter silences, ending in numbness. That was all that was left of his parents, his childhood, his home: "the usual things." As far as he was concerned, even that was too much.

His parents? Call him an orphan.

His childhood? Something he wanted to forget.

His home? He had none.

HIGHS AND LOWS

14

Epiphanies

PERHAPS BECAUSE HE DIDN'T SLEEP, JOHNY WALKER WAS REMARKABLY prolific. And since his many mates produced unusually large litters, soon the cages were full of insomniac mice with reddish eyes and greenish ears. Dr. Ranjan's mind shivered with excitement about new scientific frontiers. A crucial experiment had yet to be performed. Did the insomniac mice produce a sleep-inhibiting factor that could be transferred to normal mice?

He'd find out soon enough. Today he was going to begin *the* experiment that might change how humanity viewed one-third of its existence.

But first he wanted to clear it with his wife.

He telephoned her at work. "Bhavana, I'm sorry, but I'm stuck at the lab again. I need to be here for the next three days . . . uh . . . and nights."

She reminded him of his responsibilities as a father. From her tone of voice he knew that the corners of her mouth had tightened into that rigid expression he'd seen so much of lately.

"Yes, Bhavana, I know I was supposed to pick the kids up from school today, but the mice are ready *now*. Can't you pick them up?"

His wife, usually soft-spoken, yelled.

"Listen, Bhavana darling, I don't like it any more than you—"

She scolded him in Hindi and hung up. A recorded voice came on the line and told Dr. Ranjan either to put down the phone or to redial the number.

Dr. Ranjan sighed as he replaced the receiver. Not that he had second thoughts. If it was necessary to suffer a little marital strife for the cause of science, so be it. Yet it bothered him that Bhavana had no sense of the importance of his research—or his passion for it. And it briefly crossed his mind that they no longer shared much passion of any sort.

He took a tiny hypodermic syringe out of the fridge. The syringe contained serum that had been drawn from one of Johny Walker's offspring earlier in the day. Then he went back to his office, where he'd already placed a cage containing a normal mouse. He injected the serum from the insomniac mouse into the normal mouse. The mouse squealed.

Dr. Ranjan sat down and waited.

For three days and three nights he waited. Dr. Ranjan dozed off several times, but the injected mouse did not: The factor was transferable.

"Eureka!" he cried on the fourth morning—not once but half a dozen times. All his life he'd been waiting for his "Eureka!" moment, and now it had come.

He phoned Bhavana to inform her of his triumph, but she hung up as soon as she heard his voice.

• •

DR. RANJAN REPEATED the experiment again and again. In the hope of devising a way to avoid three-night vigils, he tried to monitor the mice with video equipment. But it was hard to distinguish a resting from a sleeping mouse on videotape. Other methods required more sophisticated equipment. He wrote a letter to the hospital administration asking for funds, but the request was denied. So he kept staying up with the mice. After each seventy-two-hour stretch Dr. Ranjan's eyes were red and, although his ears didn't turn green, he bore an uncanny resemblance to Johny Walker. And yet, despite the enforced sleep deprivation, the aches in his lower back and cricks in his neck, he found something deeply gratifying in his quest.

At home things could have been better. Whenever he returned after three nights in the lab, he got into a quarrel with Bhavana or, more accurately, resumed a quarrel that never ended. As usual, it was over being an "absent husband and father," but more bitter than it had ever been. He did all he could to make up for the absent father part, and whenever Bhavana was near he put on a contrite look that he had practiced before a mirror. But that look didn't appease her for long. Soon he was sleeping on the living room sofa and, much to his surprise, he slept quite well. On the days that he wasn't responsible for dropping off the kids, he'd leave early—before Bhavana woke up and growled at him—to begin a new set of experiments.

After seven years of failure these experiments were pure joy. The basic experiment always worked: Injecting the serum from the insomniac mice kept the normal mice awake for days.

At last Dr. Ranjan was fully convinced. He had proved the existence of a circulating sleep inhibitor.

His theory.

"I've got to see this myself," said Alvin one Friday morning. "I'll spend the weekend here."

Dr. Ranjan was pleased, since Alvin's willingness to stay awake with the mice for a whole weekend demonstrated genuine commitment. Also, it was convenient. All the seventy-two-hour sleepless stretches were taking their toll on Dr. Ranjan. Forty-three was different from thirty-three: He wasn't young anymore. And then there was the tension at home. It had gone so far that Bhavana threatened to change all the locks if he didn't start coming home at a reasonable hour. "I don't care if you win a Nobel Prize!" she shouted once. When he replied, only half-jokingly, that he might, Bhavana was neither impressed nor amused.

That weekend Dr. Ranjan did his best to make amends at home: playing one board game after another with his children, watching old Audrey Hepburn videos with Bhavana late into the night, moving back into the master bedroom for the first time in weeks, making love to Bhavana for the first time in much longer.

Meanwhile Alvin spent Friday, Saturday, and Sunday with the mice. By Monday morning he was desperate for sleep. The mice were not.

As Alvin rubbed his eyes and yawned, the far-reaching implications of the experiment dawned upon him. He, too, wanted to yell, "Eureka! Eureka!" all the way down the hall. But Dr. Ranjan had already done that, and Alvin always tried to avoid being derivative. It wasn't quite five yet. Alvin wanted to celebrate before Ranjy's arrival, so he lit a joint in the lulling hours of dawn. He savored the fumes.

Then he lit another.

And another.

Although he'd smoked marijuana countless times before, this morning it was an altogether different experience. He had never done it after being so sleepless, so exhausted. As his brain absorbed the cannabis smoke, he became aware of an extreme looseness in his joints. After a few minutes his limbs seemed to take to the air; he felt as if he had levitated to the ceiling. He'd never experienced a high like this, even during his hippie days, when he smoked pot more often than he ate.

Somewhere near the peak of his high, Alvin caught a vivid glimpse of how the world might look from a Himalayan mountaintop. He saw a porcelain sky, bright blue and endless. Jagged, icy mountain peaks reflected sunlight in novel ways; the snow was shaded purple and green. It was freezing though windless. Time slowed down so that Alvin was able to consider a thousand things in a single thought. The universe was infinite and manifold, yet—and there could be no mistake about this—it was one.

One!

This marvelous impression stayed with Alvin long after he had landed back in Dr. Ranjan's chair.

• •

On Monday morning Dr. Ranjan was glad to learn that the experiment had gone as expected. But his nostrils reacted to the acrid odor in his office. Didn't Alvin realize it was all right to take a shower in the staff locker room during these experiments? Still, Dr. Ranjan was pleased to find Alvin in such a halcyon mood after seventy-two sleepless hours. Quite remarkable, really. At the same time Alvin seemed more remote than usual.

"Are you all right?" asked Dr. Ranjan.

"Fine, just fine."

"You seem a trifle preoccupied."

"I've been doing a little wondering, that's all. Three days without sleep makes everything look different."

"Go home," said Dr. Ranjan, patting Alvin's shoulder. "Don't come back until Wednesday."

Alvin was gone in thirty seconds.

An hour later Sonny came to the lab after a long call night, looking for Alvin. Partly a friendly visit, but he was also running low on pot. Over the phone last week Alvin had said he was expecting some high-quality weed, the efficacy of which he had confirmed a short while ago.

Sonny went over to Dr. Ranjan, who was seated at a desk, writing in a laboratory notebook. "Is Alvin around?" asked Sonny.

"He's off for a couple of days," replied Dr. Ranjan. "He was up with the mice all night."

"Why?"

"Surely you are aware that we are searching for the cause of insomnia?"

"That's one way to cause it."

Dr. Ranjan smiled as he closed the laboratory notebook. "You know, I never hear much about the rest of the hospital. The lab is rather remote from the main show."

"These days the main show seems to be heart disease," said Sonny. "At three this morning I was paged to the ER to see a forty-four-year-old man with severe chest pain. That makes five Indian men in their forties admitted this week with heart attacks. It's an epidemic. Scary."

Dr. Ranjan's face became grim. "Even scarier if you're an Indian man in your forties. Just last month the father of a girl in my daughter's Bharatnatyam class died of a heart attack. One day he was at the peak of his career, the next day a six-year-old was fatherless."

"I can't figure it out," said Sonny. "There's got to be more to it than samosas."

"The *real* reason must be a mismatch between our genes and the environment," said Dr. Ranjan. "*This* environment. We didn't evolve for this lifestyle. Our clocks tick to a different rhythm."

Sonny nodded slowly.

A deliveryman entered the lab with a package. While Dr. Ranjan signed for it, Sonny glanced around at the beakers, flasks, bottles of chemicals, chromatography columns, centrifuges, and other equipment.

Noticing Sonny's curiosity, Dr. Ranjan asked, "Do you have an inclination toward science? We've made a *tre-men-dous* discovery. We've found a circulating sleep inhibitor!"

As he said this Dr. Ranjan's eyes sparkled, and his lips started to quiver. Until that moment he'd never communicated his discovery to anyone with a doctoral degree. Now, with revolutionary ardor, he added, "We're about to alter the way mankind views sleep!"

At first Sonny was spellbound by the excitement in the scientist's face, the tiny haloes of reflected light on Dr. Ranjan's glistening irises. But while Sonny was tantalized by the scientific quest to fix the soft, slippery universe into hard reality, that vision ultimately couldn't take. The world as Sonny saw it *was* mushy, everything tentative. Firm realities seemed artificial; they made him uncomfortable. "That's really great," said Sonny. "Sometimes, though, I think there's too much science going around."

Dr. Ranjan frowned. "Would you rather be ignorant?"

"I was talking about medicine—the *art* of doctoring. That's just as important as the science."

"I'm not sure what you mean."

"The off-the-cuff stuff that can sometimes save a patient when nothing else works. It's hard to explain—like trying to explain Charlie Parker's improvisations. You know, the way Bird's saxophone spontaneously tickled notes, flipped them upside down, always managing to come up with just the right note. He was so good the orchestrated stuff wasn't good enough. Tell me, how does one explain that?"

· ·

RELENTLESSLY, DR. RANJAN and Alvin worked to purify the sleep inhibitor. Day after day they took blood from Johny Walker's sleepless offspring, isolated the red blood cells from the serum, then separated components within the serum using standard purification techniques: extractions, precipitations, microscale chromatography, electrophoresis. Then they injected the partly purified components into normal mice. Those components that produced sleeplessness underwent further purification. More extractions, more precipitations, more chromatography, more electrophoresis. More, more, more. Endless drudgery—or so it often seemed. Would the sleep inhibitor ever be purified?

Now it was Alvin who usually stayed up with the mice. He didn't mind. Alone in the research wing all night, the arduous work felt something like an ascetic's penance. And at the end of it all, an interlude of bliss: that cannabinolic splendor the morning after the third sleepless night. He always waited till the end of the experiment before lighting a joint, so that his high wouldn't compromise the scientific data.

After extensive negotiations Dr. Ranjan and his wife arrived at an agreement that would allow him to spend nights with the mice, though no more than one stretch every ten days. "Only because I'm feeling guilty that so much of the burden is falling upon poor Alvin," said Bhavana, who liked Alvin for the gentle way he played with the children whenever he came to dinner. "And don't forget you've agreed to drop the kids off at school *every* morning you're home *and* pick them up two afternoons a week."

More than ever Dr. Ranjan valued those nights alone in the laboratory: his refuge. He especially relished the long periods peering at the cells of insomniac mice through a microscope. One Thursday night, after spending hours intently gazing through high-power lenses at some particularly interesting microscope slides, Dr. Ranjan felt as if he had entered a cell and was embarking on a journey through a world that he had, until then, known only in the abstract. Now within the cell's membrane, he waded through the gooey cytoplasm, then fingered the spidery endoplasmic reticulum, the tubular lysosomes, the biscuit-shaped mitochondria, the jungle of actin filaments. Smack in the middle, round and confident as the sun, sat the nucleus, its thick envelope protecting the cell's DNA.

The key to the mystery! What was going on in there that made these mice sleepless? As Dr. Ranjan pondered this question, complex interactions were revealed to him; he was thrilled by their subtle connections, their resonances. A symphony, an opera—Wagner! For the first time, he began to see—*really see*—how life worked. Any second now it would come to him—a great answer that had eluded everyone else . . .

The phone rang.

He did his best to ignore it. Nine rings, ten, eleven . . .

"Hello?"

"Hi, Daddy."

Dr. Ranjan smiled. "How's my *bitya?*"

"I called to say good night, Daddy."

"Good night, honeybunch. Give me a kiss."

Archana made a kiss sound.

Neel came on the line. "Daddy?"

"Yes, Neelu *beta?*"

"Archana stole my gum!"

In the background he heard Archana shout, "I didn't!"

"You did!"

"Don't fight," said Dr. Ranjan in a stern voice.

He heard a loud clunk as the receiver on the other end fell to the floor. The *I didn'ts* and *you dids* continued for another twenty seconds. Then the crying started. Soon he heard Bhavana yelling at the kids. The crying got louder. So did Bhavana's shouts.

The phone disconnected.

• •

ALAS, THE PURIFICATION was going slowly. At times it didn't seem to be going anywhere at all. As the work threatened to drag on for months, even years, Dr. Ranjan couldn't help but notice that Johny Walker was looking sad, frail. The mouse's declining health greatly disturbed Dr. Ranjan. Was it due to Johny Walker's terminal insomnia or anxiety over his offspring?

Dr. Ranjan decided to place the tiny patriarch in a different room. Still, he doubted the mouse could be fooled. He was certain that Johny Walker, wise beyond his species, possessed the enigmatic sapience of the human insomniac.

Separated from his progeny, Johny Walker appeared even more morose. He became slower, frailer. Dr. Ranjan tried to justify the experiments to the sagely mouse.

"Johny," he begged, "you *must* understand. This is what I've spent my whole life waiting for—my great discovery! Don't you see, Johny?"

Unmoved by Dr. Ranjan's plea, Johny Walker stopped eating. The mouse's hunger strike further upset Dr. Ranjan, whose own appetite also diminished. Sometimes he felt angry at the passive-aggressive rodent. Mostly, though, he felt anguish.

"Johny, please listen," implored Dr. Ranjan one day. "What we're doing is *so* important! The secret of sleep—half a mouse's life! A third of a man's life. A third of my life! Okay, maybe just a sixth. But I sleep less than the rest of them. Like you, Johny, like you!"

The mouse looked away.

· ·

DR. RANJAN WAS CLOSING in on the cause of insomnia, at least in a particular strain of mice, and he certainly believed his experimental results. Yet his own insomnia worsened. It had as much to do with the inherent ambiguities of experimental work as with Johny Walker's declining health. The excitement of discovery had taken on a chronic aspect; it could no longer provide a jump start when he got stuck in the valleys of anxiety. Multiplying valleys, turning into bottomless gorges.

Dr. Ranjan would awaken at night in a panic, assaulted by doubts, his face sweaty. Had he interpreted the data correctly? Certainly he'd discovered *something*, but was it as important as he believed? Had he really found evidence for a factor that prevented sleep? His mind filled with bitter recollections of the scientists who had laughed in his face, dismissed him altogether. There had been so many! His reputation had been sullied by prior unproven claims, particularly related to his theory of love. Those same scientists—and others—would scoff at his latest results. It would be difficult, maybe impossible, to publish his work in any good scientific journal. More alchemy, they'd say, and titter among themselves. He could already hear them!

Dr. Ranjan continued to fret through the nights, torn between his desire to reveal his findings to an astonished world and fear of ridicule. At times the renown that would surely greet his announcement seemed unimportant. For he realized he'd become comfortable with obscurity. There was something wonderful about a caterpillar in its cocoon: Was metamorphosis really so great from the butterfly's standpoint? Under the present circumstances he was able to pursue his passion unhurried, unfettered, unperturbed. Anonymously.

Wasn't that what he loved most about science? Once he and Alvin had purified the factor that caused insomnia, everything would change.

Was it worth it?

• •

BHAVANA'S INSISTENCE THAT HE spend more time at home made Dr. Ranjan's days at the office feel like a videotape on fast-forward. He took only one coffee break and usually skipped lunch. This afternoon, however, his exhaustion caught up with him. So when Menaka Bhushan called about lunch, he agreed to meet her at Tiger's restaurant.

While Dr. Ranjan ate his mutton biryani, he debated whether to inform Menaka of his discovery. He'd been wanting to tell her for days, but he didn't want it to be just in passing. He wished to relish the moment of disclosure. This discovery was the most important thing that had ever happened in his scientific life, and he felt that Menaka, being a specialist in sleep disorders, was the one person he could happily share it with. Dr. Ranjan had his own fantasy of what the right time and place might be, but a candlelit dinner at a posh restaurant overlooking Central Park was thoroughly incompatible with the rest of his life. Lunch at Tiger's was as close as it would get.

"How are your wife and children?" asked Menaka.

"Fine."

"Good."

They ate quietly for two minutes.

Menaka's tongue swept over her upper lip to remove a grain of basmati rice. "And your research?"

His mouth full of mutton and rice, he blurted it out. "We found it! A factor that regulates, maybe even controls, sleep. We found it, Menaka!"

"Oh my!" was all Menaka said.

But it was the way she said it that had a profound effect on Dr. Ranjan. It sounded like a moment of surrender.

Dr. Ranjan did his best to control the surge of emotion he felt for Menaka, not to mention the urge that accompanied the surge.

Tiger came by with a jug of ice water. "How is your meal? The spicy-spicy dishes are tasty today, don't you think?"

Menaka's and Dr. Ranjan's faces flushed, and they nodded for a long time before they found words of praise, justly deserved, to mutter about the spicy-spicy dishes. Tiger smiled toothily, filled their glasses with water, and left. Both of them swallowed the ice-cold liquid in a continuous series of gulps. Their temperatures lowered. Menaka fiddled with her bangles for an inordinately long time.

Dr. Ranjan decided it was best to switch topics. "Enough about my work. How is yours going?"

"All right, I suppose. A clinical report I'd submitted was just accepted by the *North American Journal of Sleep Disorders.*"

"Wonderful!"

"Oh, it's only a small paper—nothing like what you've accomplished—just some data on a group of patients with hypersomnia. We've become quite a referral center, surprisingly."

"Given your reputation, Dr. Bhushan, it's no surprise at all."

"I haven't been in the field long enough to develop much of a reputation. But it's lovely of you to say so."

"I would love to—"

"Me, too."

"Oh?"

"I would love to collaborate with you, Nirdosh. What I mean is, with your expertise in biochemistry and all my patients with sleep disorders, we could do many interesting things together. And now you've found a factor that might regulate sleep!"

"An excellent idea, but it's premature to talk about involving patients."

"In the meantime, I'm sure there are other ways we could collaborate together on sleep."

"It would be great to sleep together."

"Pardon?"

"Collaborate—scientifically, of course."

· ·

AT TWO IN THE MORNING Menaka was doing her best to fall asleep. Which made it even harder. She was as normal a sleeper as they come, but she couldn't stop thinking about her lunch with Dr. Ranjan—his astounding discovery. If, indeed, the substance that he'd found regulated human sleep, why, the implications were. . . ! Not just for the field of sleep research but also for people suffering from sleep disorders. She knew the field as well as anybody—better than anybody, she'd often told herself. An admirer of William James, she had for many years been contemplating the similarities and differences between states of awareness: various kinds of ecstasy, catatonia, schizophrenia, hypersomnias, insomnia, dream states, trances. Unlike Dr. Ranjan's, her thinking wasn't biochemical in nature; it had gone beyond the clinical as well. The questions she pondered bordered on the metaphysical. She understood that there is a great wisdom to be gleaned from ministering to the sufferings of others, if the ministers but reflect—and she was among the few who did.

As she lay with her hands folded behind her head, Menaka's eager mind was connecting ideas that might otherwise have been dispersed by the night. Her vast technical knowledge, her years of clinical experience, and Dr. Ranjan's recent experimental findings all coalesced into something like a revelation. She fully appreciated his alchemical cum scientific approach to questions like sleep and love. Her thoughts drifted from the research to the man himself. Was he a genius? In the ensuing moments she might have arrived more firmly at some conclusion had she not, much to her amazement, experienced back-to-back orgasms. She had never thought—just *thought*—her way to an orgasm, never had them sequentially, either. As she stared into the dark, her mind lingered on Dr. Ranjan. Sleep . . . love . . . sleep . . .

Love?

15

At the Movies

ON THE MOVIE SCREEN THE SCAMPS VEERU AND JAI, PLAYED BY THE actors Dharmendra and Amitabh, were tearing down a dirt road somewhere in rural India on a stolen motorcycle. The two were really doing up the rapscallion routine, making rooster and crowlike noises that bordered on the obscene. Although both actors were middle-aged, they were having good adolescent fun. A catchy melody began, and Dharmendra burst into the song *"Yeh Dosti"*—in Kishore Kumar's voice. Then Amitabh sang his reply—in Manna Dey's voice.

As their motorcycle raised dust across the Indian plains, the two lovable rakes continued their duet about eternal friendship. Soon half the audience was singing, too. It was one of those epiphanous Hindi film moments.

A quarter century old, *Sholay* was Bollywood's *Casablanca*, arguably the best commercial Hindi film ever made. Alvin thought so. Manny thought so. And so did Sonny, as he sat in Golden Jubilee Cinema with his arm around Gwen, who after two hours was finding the experience extremely trying. She'd seen a few Hindi films back in England and felt only contempt for their stereotypical characters, their incurable soppiness, their absurd twists of plot, their love stories aimed at satisfying the silly fantasies of your average rikshawala. Even though she had to admit that this film was better than the others, ultimately it boiled down to the same old kitsch.

The lights came on. Manny offered what was left of his popcorn to Gwen first, then to Sonny and Alvin. "What a movie!" said Manny, wiping his buttery fingers on his jeans.

"Damn right," replied Alvin.

"Love that song," said Manny. *"Yeh Dosti."*

"You know," said Sonny, "after *Sholay* came out young men all over India rode together on motorcycles imitating Veeru and Jai. The whole country was taken by the film. Someone once told me that you aren't a *real* Indian until you've seen *Sholay* seven times."

"Hardly," said Gwen. "Anyway, what's the big deal? It's just your standard buddy-buddy, little boy's movie—*Butch Cassidy and the Sundance Kid* crossed with the usual Bollywood campiness."

"Excuse me, Ms. Highbrow," said Sonny. "The *rest* of us liked it."

Gwen flashed him the nastiest look in her repertoire.

"I saw *Let It Be* seven times," said Alvin.

"I don't think I've seen anything that many times," said Manny. "Wait—maybe *Guide.* But that was because I was working on a couple of songs for a concert back home in Port of Spain. Practicing with the video helped me get the songs right."

"I've probably seen *Debbie Does Dallas* seven times," said Sonny.

Gwen frowned. "I'm waiting outside."

"I was fourteen," Sonny added feebly.

"Was?" She headed for the exit.

"I have an idea," said Alvin. "The movie's playing for a month, right? What do you say we go for seven times?"

"Sure, why not?" replied Manny.

"Why?" asked Sonny.

"*Real* Indians . . . what you said."

"Oh, that was just a joke. Besides, the hospital has been hectic. And then there's this patient of mine, the Transplanted Man . . ."

"He's a really good guy," said Manny. "I wheel him over to the dialysis unit a few times a week. Even though he's a big shot, you feel like you're chatting with your favorite uncle. How are things looking for him, anyway?"

"Not great."

"Damn."

Nobody spoke for a moment.

At last Manny said, "I need to hit the men's room."

While they waited for Manny, Sonny and Alvin began talking about *Sholay* again. "Think about it, Sonny. If you let us know your on-call schedule, we can go on your off nights."

"It's a fine movie, but seven times is a lot."

"I'll make it worth your while," said Alvin. "A serious gift. The most heavenly *indica* known to mankind."

Sonny smiled. "I can be bribed."

When the three met up with Gwen outside, she asked, "Why do all of you have those ridiculous smirks?"

Manny winked at Alvin, who then winked at Sonny, who winked back.

Gwen felt like disemboweling the whole winking lot. "Are we going over to Tiger's for dinner or not?"

· ·

But Tiger's restaurant was closed. A red poster in the window read, QUARANTINED. BY ORDER OF THE HEALTH DEPARTMENT.

Puzzled, they went to the video shop next door to get the scoop from Manny's friend, a fellow Trinidadian. "Some of yesterday's customers started vomiting," said Manny's friend. "Others got diarrhea. The Health Department says it's one of the worst cases of food poisoning this year."

"I'm surprised," said Sonny. "Tiger runs a shipshape outfit."

"He offered a special early in the week—all the Tiger kebabs you can eat for five ninety-nine. The kebabs were delicious, and people just ate and ate. The demand was so great that Tiger ran out of sauce. And since he didn't want his customers to know that he couldn't meet the demand, he ordered extra sauce from another restaurant. Tiger claims that they gave him contaminated sauce. He thinks they did it on purpose."

"What does the owner of the other restaurant say?" asked Manny.

"He told Tiger to wash his hands with soap."

"To his face?"

Manny's friend nodded. "It got nasty. Poor Tiger, the restaurant was everything to him. I don't know if he'll ever recover."

"Oh, Tiger will recover," said Manny. "That royal blood is probably all heated up right now. He'll be back."

Just as Manny finished saying this, Tiger, who lived in a second-floor apartment on the other side of the street, ran out of the building. "Thank you!" he yelled as he darted across the street without looking and was almost hit by a truck. "Thank you so much for coming! My true friends! The rest are but the fair-weather variety. Perhaps it's important for a man to go through this, just to know who his real friends are."

"Tiger, we're very sorry," said Gwen.

"We are *so* careful! My kitchen is the cleanest in town!"

"And the best," said Alvin.

"Yes, the best!" shouted Tiger. Suddenly his eyes narrowed. "But there is jealousy. I come from royalty, and I have always tried to rise above subcontinental pettiness."

"I'm sure it's not what you think," said Sonny.

"Yes, yes. You must be right. My mind is awhirl with suspicions, fears. I have done my best, worked so hard, and now . . ."

"It will pass," said Manny.

Tears began to roll down Tiger's cheeks. He couldn't speak, just pointed to the large black letters on the red poster: QUARANTINED. Tiger looked like it was he, not the restaurant, who'd been condemned. His neck bent forward as if to allow a hangman to slip a noose over it.

• •

BACK AT HIS APARTMENT, Sonny put on a Billie Holiday recording, then poured a glass of red wine. While listening to "I've Got It Bad and That Ain't Good," he finished the glass and poured another. Billie Holiday receded as he dissolved into the cozy world of mild inebriation. His peacefulness was interrupted by the ringing phone. Too relaxed to answer, he let it ring, hoping the caller would give up soon. But the ringing didn't stop, and the answering machine was off. Each ring got louder, more insistent. His mellow state was rapidly evaporating. On the twelfth ring he reached for the phone. He fumbled the receiver, then placed it against his ear.

"Sonny?"

The ringing was still reverberating in his head. "Uh-huh?"

"Don't sound so excited."

He took a deep breath and pressed the remote to turn off the stereo.

"A bad time?"

He said nothing.

"How are things?"

"Fine."

An uncomfortable silence.

At last she said, "Are you sleeping well?"

"You know me."

"Better than you think."

"Right."

"You're okay?"

"Yup."

"As usual, not very communicative."

"Isn't much to say, is there?"

"You can ask about me. We haven't spoken in a while."

He was rapidly falling into the depression that follows intoxication. "No, we haven't."

"I'm the only one who calls, Sonny. Can't you call *just once?*"

It was true. He hadn't called in years.

"Sonny?"

A meanness entered his voice as he said, "How's Stepfather Number Three?"

"The way you say *step!*"

"What do you want me to say? *Real?*"

"Please don't start—"

"You didn't even invite me to the wedding!"

"I wanted to, but you're so . . . unpredictable."

"Look who's talking!"

"How can you blame me after what happened the last time you visited me and my ex?"

"Number Two was a jerk."

"He wasn't the only one that day."

Another silence—chilly, perhaps terminal. But he wasn't going to be the one that hung up.

Half a minute passed before she said, "Take care, Sonny. I . . . I . . ."

He hung up.

He lay down on the sofa and did his best to get his mind off her. That only made him think about her all the more. Ever since that night two years ago when he and Stepfather Number 2 nearly came to blows—the night she'd made him leave her Tucson home—she'd been doing what little she could to make reparations: phone calls, New Year's cards, birthday gifts. He couldn't honestly blame her for not inviting him to her latest wedding. He had always created rifts in her marriages and relationships. In his youth he purposely came between her and her men, resenting the attention she gave them. Later—when he no longer cared much—it just seemed to happen.

Staying away was the only solution.

16

The Pose for the Ism

DURING THE FEW DAYS SINCE SONNY HAD LAST CROSSED PATHS WITH him, the hypokinetic man had continued to inch down Esmoor Street in his quest for a place to rest safely until his mind recovered. Eventually he made it to the corner at Forty-third, the location of Tiger's quarantined restaurant. As if waiting for a perpetually red traffic light to change, the hypokinetic man stood motionless at the corner for hours. At last he sat down in front of Tiger's restaurant. That attracted the attention of two truant boys, who began to pester him. Frustrated by the stranger's immobility, enticed by it as well, one of the boys pushed him from behind. The hypokinetic man's entire torso bent forward at a forty-five-degree angle and stayed in that awkward position for not one or even ten minutes but half an hour. Atul, who happened to be Tiger's son and was the more sensitive of the two boys, said, "Jay, do you think we killed him?"

Jay—who also went by Jason or Jayaprakash depending on whether he favored his non-Indian father or his Indian mother—was worried, too. A sharp if devious thinker, Jay briefly wondered whether the courts tried fifteen-year-olds as adults in homicide cases. He began to formulate an alibi for the police. Then he noticed the slow, rhythmic movements of the hypokinetic man's chest. "I think he's still alive," said Jay. "He's breathing very slowly, though. Better check his pulse."

Atul wasn't quite sure how to check a pulse. From watching doctor shows on TV, he knew it had something to do with the wrist. So he grasped the hypokinetic man's hand, incidentally raising his whole arm, and tried to locate a pulse.

"That's not how!" said Jay. "Here, let me."

Atul let go of the hypokinetic man's hand. Both boys stared in amazement when the stranger's arm remained raised, almost perpendicular to the ground.

"Man, this is really weird," said Jay.

"I'll say. We'd better get out of here."

"We need to know if we killed him or not," said Jay, who had the presence of mind to keep searching for the hypokinetic man's pulse.

"Well?" asked Atul. "Is he dead?"

"No, he's alive. About fifty beats a minute alive. It's as if . . . Hey, I've got an idea."

"What?"

"Watch." Jay folded the hypokinetic man's legs, repositioned his hands, and tilted his head forward. "How's that?"

"What an awesome pose!" said Atul. "He looks kind of, well . . . mystical."

"He does, doesn't he? You know, before my sister got married, she studied philosophy. And when our home computer crashed last summer, I started flipping through her old books, reading about this and that ism."

Atul chuckled. "Sure did you a lot of good."

"My sister used to talk about how nice it would be if there were just one ism for everybody."

"What do you mean?"

"An ism that has nothing to do with any other ism, but that's the same whether you're brown or white or green. My sister used to say that, if something like that really caught on, people would stop fighting. But I think the real reason she talked that way was because my dad and mom fought so much over what us kids ought to believe in. They almost broke up over it." Jay shook his head. "Messed up my sister in a big way."

"If there's an ism for everyone," said Atul, "maybe there's a pose that's right for everyone, too."

"Maybe."

Atul's face brightened. "If we could find the right pose—the *pose for the ism*—maybe everybody would do it, and people would stop fighting!"

Jay thought of his parents again. "Doubt it."

"What if your sister is right? My dad says pretty much the same thing. My dad thinks—"

"Your dad thinks he's a king."

Atul was used to being teased about Tiger's regal claims and ignored the comment. "Jay, it could be *real* important."

"Yeah, sure. Let's leave him like this for tonight, see if he stays that way. We can change him tomorrow if he's still here."

..

THE HYPOKINETIC MAN did not alter his pose. All through the next day passersby, struck by his nondenominational piety, tossed coins in his lap. Some even left dollar bills. After school let out Jay and Atul went to see how the hypokinetic man had fared. Not only were they pleased that he'd maintained his position but they were delighted by the small fortune that had accumulated in his lap.

Late at night the boys returned to collect the money.

"Thirty-six dollars!" said Jay, after he finished counting.

"You think it's okay, don't you?" asked Atul.

"Sure it is. If we hadn't set this pose, there'd be no money, right? That means it's partly ours. And how do you know he isn't really some kind of mystic? Those guys don't care for money. So the rest is ours, too."

"No Indian would believe he's a mystic."

Jay felt that his multiethnic background gave him a certain authority on this topic. "You've got a point. This money probably didn't come from Indians. We'd make more if he were in a white neighborhood."

"I'm not so sure," said Atul. "They might not pay attention then. He'd just be another homeless guy on a street corner. In our neighborhood they probably think it's something cool. Like when the Beatles went to India."

"Whatever. We're lucky he picked a street with lots of restaurants. That's the main reason the rest of the city comes here. Too bad your dad's place is closed down."

"Jay, we shouldn't forget why we're doing this."

"Why's that?"

"The ism for everyone!" said Atul in a passionate voice. "To find the *pose for the ism,* so people will stop fighting."

"Right. Here's your eighteen bucks. Good money for no work. What everyone wants out of life."

"Do you think we ought to feed him?" said Atul. "Poor guy, he's *so* skinny. Who knows when he last ate?"

"I don't think he chews."

"What about apple juice or ginger ale? Maybe he drinks."

"Maybe."

"Well, are we going to feed him or not?"

"Okay!" said Jay. "Go to that twenty-four-hour convenience store down the street and get some milk. Bring a cup with a straw, too."

"Do you think he goes to the bathroom? We'll probably need to change him, too."

"You're overdoing it, Atul."

"Look, if he's working for us, then we need to take care of him."

"All right, all right. We'll deal with that tomorrow. I'll swipe a few diapers from my sister's kid. You bring underwear. Who knows, maybe he'll be gone by then."

"Jay, quiet! I hear someone."

Jay squinted into the dark. "It's just that crazy guy sleepwalking in his boxers again. Lately a dog has been trailing him."

"He's a doctor," said Atul.

"No kidding?"

"He comes to my dad's restaurant with his girlfriend. She's pretty."

"Cute girls always go for weirdos."

"Then you'll have no problem, Jay."

• •

GWEN WAS WORRIED. She couldn't just let Sonny go on sleepwalking through streets full of maniacal taxi drivers and hoodlums. And yet she didn't know what to do. In search of answers she went to the hospital library, where she read about cases of sleepwalking much more bizarre than anything Sonny did. In one neurological textbook she found ideas on how to minimize the risk of injury. But most of them were useful only if the sleepwalker lived with someone. Almost nothing was relevant to the sleepwalker who lived alone. The psychiatric textbooks were also of little practical help. One cautioned against directly confronting adult sleepwalkers who, like Sonny, were unaware of their nocturnal behavior, arguing that some forms of sleepwalking might be due to an internal conflict so painful that it could be resolved only outside the bounds of consciousness. In an older book Gwen found a description of a fuguelike syndrome that wasn't true sleepwalking but nonetheless sounded a lot like Sonny's problem. The author went so far as to suggest that certain patients possessed an inner gyroscope that prevented them from coming to harm. That sounded suspect to Gwen. Besides, even if *some* people with the syndrome had an inner gyroscope, what was Sonny if not a man with a misaligned gyroscope?

Gwen needed to have a serious talk with Sonny—to inform him about his sleepwalking and, more important, convince him to seek help. But since she didn't think he'd be particularly receptive, she wanted to wait for the just the right time: one of those rare moments when Sonny opened up a bit. In the meantime she hoped that there was something to the "inner gyroscope" theory—though of course she'd do whatever she could to reduce his chances of hurting himself. To this end she found excuses to spend the night at his apartment.

The first night was uneventful.

He did, however, sleepwalk on Wednesday—but Gwen didn't realize it until Sonny was long gone.

On Thursday night she lay next to him in the dark with her eyes open wide. When his snores became slow and regular, she quietly slipped out of bed and hunted around the apartment. Eventually she located a belt, a towel, a necktie, and her own stockings. Hands full, she tiptoed back to the bed and carefully tied Sonny's wrists and ankles to the bed frame and posts, making certain to leave enough slack for him to move from side to side. After she finished securing him she realized she'd have some explaining to do if he awoke to find himself tied up. She hoped to wake first and untie him before he realized anything. If not, she'd improvise. Right now she was too tired to think it through.

A voice broke the midnight silence. "In another kinky mood?"

Gwen gasped. She squinted into the darkness and was barely able to discern the outlines of Sonny's head.

"What do you have in mind?" he asked.

"Nothing."

"Tell me."

"Oh, what the hell! Sonny, sometimes in the middle of the night, you sleep . . ."

"So do most people."

"How about that."

"Out with it, Gwen! What's really going on?"

She decided that this wasn't the right moment. So she said, "Sometimes in the middle of the night, you really turn me on. I want to take you to the edge, baby."

"Yeah?"

"Not all the way," she added in a fiendish voice. "I want to keep you there for as long as possible, until you beg, Sonny. Cry! And I'll just keep you there, all tied up, and you'll do anything—anything!—to make it happen. But no, I won't let it happen, just keep you going."

"How long?"

"Till dawn. It will transform you, Sonny. You'll be a new man."

"You really want that?"

"Most definitely."

"Why?"

"Does everything have to have a why?"

He didn't reply.

Relieved that that was the end of it, Gwen began to untie his right arm.

"Wait! I'm game."

Surely he was joking! And yet she couldn't tell from his voice or, in the dark, from his expression. So she allowed her fingers to graze his pajamas gently.

He was game, all right.

17

Dirge for an Insomniac

On Wednesday afternoon Dr. Ranjan knocked on the door of Menaka Bhushan's office. No answer, though he heard opera inside. The recitative sounded familiar. Puccini? Yes, *Madama Butterfly*. He opened the door. Menaka sat hunched over her desk, staring at patterns of brain waves on an EEG. He debated whether or not to disturb her. Finally he stepped up and cleared his throat loudly.

"Oh, Nirdosh!" she said, startled. She turned off the music.

"Sorry."

"It's all right," said Menaka, smiling. Her bangles jingled as she pointed to a jaggedy line on the EEG. "Look at this recording from a sleep study. A ninety-two-year-old patient who used to work as a volunteer at the information desk in the main lobby. These K-complexes and delta wave periodicities are highly unusual, don't you think?"

Dr. Ranjan leaned over the desk to take a closer look at the EEG. "I've been thinking of getting a sleep study myself, Menaka. My insomnia is getting worse."

"Any time, Nirdosh. Just make an appointment, and we can spend the night together."

"Excuse me?"

"I meant, you can get your sleep study. Normally the sleep technician would preside, but I thought, with you being a colleague and all, I'd perform the study myself. Unless you prefer—"

"Of course not. I'll definitely take you up on it. But, Menaka, I came about something else. It's Johny. I'm very worried. Do you know of any comparable human illness?"

"What exactly are the mouse's symptoms?"

"Poor Johny, he doesn't sleep. *At all.* His eyes are redder than ever. He's slower than usual and . . ."

Dr. Ranjan went on and on, describing Johny Walker's condition in loving detail: his food preferences, his resting posture, his favorite corner of the cage, his bowel habits . . .

At last he finished.

"I don't think there's any human disease quite like it," said Menaka. "The closest thing is an extremely rare fatal insomnia syndrome."

Dr. Ranjan gulped. "Fatal?"

"When the insomnia is intractable—when the patient can no longer sleep at all—death follows in about nine months. At autopsy there is degeneration of the thalamus—"

Dr. Ranjan breathed a sigh of relief. "What Johny has must be entirely different. We've examined the thalamus in his offspring, and it appears completely normal."

"So it's probably a unique syndrome," said Menaka. "On the other hand, intractable insomnia is intractable insomnia and likely to have similar consequences in men and mice."

That wasn't what Dr. Ranjan wanted to hear.

• •

MENAKA WAS RIGHT. Absolute insomnia continued to take its toll on Johny Walker. Every day the mouse looked older. He developed crow's-feet around his little eyes, his skin got baggier, and his movements became slower. Although he still had some teeth, his rare grin appeared toothless, resembling that of Rembrandt in late self-portraits. He started to dribble urine, perhaps because of prostate trouble, or simply because that is what old males do.

Dr. Ranjan watched with alarm. Day after day he doted over the ailing mouse. Eventually Johny Walker was unable to get up. Dr. Ranjan couldn't bear to watch. Yet watch he did, hoping it would end soon.

Finally, it happened. Johny Walker fell asleep.

It was exactly three days after they had purified the sleep inhibitor, the single protein that just might prevent a mouse—and maybe even a human—from sleeping.

Alvin, who'd been in the lab all night, found the mouse dead in his cage. He called Dr. Ranjan at home just before 5:00 A.M.

"Johny's dead," said Alvin in a quiet monotone.

Dr. Ranjan hung up without a word.

"What is it?" asked Bhavana, half asleep.

"I have to go in," he replied in a choked voice.

"So early?"

He took a minute to rein in his emotions. When he was finally ready to explain, she'd already fallen back to sleep.

He stepped into the lab forty minutes later, unshaven, ungroomed, his nightshirt beneath his coat. He said nothing to Alvin, just went down the hall to the animal room. He sat before Johny Walker's cage, staring at the dead mouse.

After some time Alvin entered. "You all right?"

Dr. Ranjan nodded—barely.

"I know it's a tough moment, but I'd like to tell you about the experiment I just completed."

Dr. Ranjan didn't want to hear if Alvin's experiment had worked—whether the normal mouse that had been injected with the now-purified sleep inhibitor was still awake. If so, it would be cause for a jubilation he was in no mood for. If not, there was lots of work ahead, retracing steps, the renewed possibility of absolute failure—despair. He wasn't sure if he could bear any more right now. But the result of the experiment was written all over Alvin's face even before he blurted out, "It worked!"

Dr. Ranjan shrugged.

"I thought you'd be more excited."

Dr. Ranjan took a while to reply. "You know, it's just Johny."

"I'm very sorry," said Alvin. "But the poor mouse had gotten so feeble, it was probably for the—"

Dr. Ranjan held his hand up, and Alvin didn't finish.

"I won't be in for the rest of the day," said Dr. Ranjan.

After Alvin left the room Dr. Ranjan caressed the lifeless mouse for a long time. He thought back to that day when he first found this red-eyed, green-eared creature, guardian of the answer upon which he'd staked nearly everything. He recalled the deep solitude of all those three-nighters in the lab, the subtle thrill in the tedium of the purification, the inexpressible joy of watching his own hunch transform into scientific truth . . .

At last he put the mouse down and crossed the room to get a sheet of plastic wrap. After carefully covering Johny Walker with the wrap, he placed the mouse in his coat pocket. Johny Walker needed a proper cremation, and Dr. Ranjan decided the best place for that was his own home.

• •

THE DAY WAS BRIGHT but cool. While Dr. Ranjan drove across the George Washington Bridge, he glanced at the polluted waters below, sparkling with unholy energy. A smoggy blur of foliage lined the other side of the river. Dr. Ranjan felt sad yet serene. Life was so fragile, he thought, but that very fragility made it all the more beautiful. Life's secrets would always remain mysterious, no matter how hard men like him tried to unravel them. Then he had what was for him a heretical thought: *That was how it should be.*

He got off the freeway and drove slowly through his small town. He halted nearly five minutes at a stop sign and stared at an old church steeple peeking over a tall birch. The bronze spire gleamed magnificently against the blue sky, clear but for a few wispy clouds. While he drove down his street, Dr. Ranjan became mesmerized by the patterns of alternating light and shade created by trees arching high over the road. He nearly missed his own house. When he stepped from his red Honda sedan onto the driveway, he smelled a fresh suburban scent. He took a few deep breaths. It was *so* quiet. For a couple of minutes he watched leaves drop—the slow melting of trees.

He unlocked the front door. Inside he headed straight for the living room fireplace. He opened the grill, tossed in an artificial log. It didn't seem right. Johny Walker deserved a *real* pyre with real logs, unadulterated by chemicals.

Dr. Ranjan went to the garage where the firewood was kept. No real logs anywhere—only more fake ones "guaranteed to burn five times as long." He went to the toolshed in the backyard and grabbed the electric saw. He attached a hundred-foot extension cord, plugged it into an outlet on the back porch. Then he strode over to a willow tree from which long leaves twirled down, one by one. It had a low, dying branch that hovered over the fence, crossing into Mr. Richardson's yard. He owed a favor to Mr. Richardson, a kindly optician who regularly trimmed both sides of the bushes that separated their properties. But the main reason behind his choice of the branch was that the tree was Bhavana's favorite. He resented the fact that she'd kept him from spending more time with Johny. Also that she, like everyone else, dismissed him as a silly dreamer.

He turned on the saw. The branch crashed to the ground. He sliced it into four equal pieces, then gathered some dry reddish brown leaves and went back inside.

He spent a few moments contemplating how best to position the four pieces of wood in the fireplace. Then he made a tiny bed of dry willow leaves atop the wood. He carefully unwrapped Johny Walker, whose eyes were still open—and redder than ever. Very gently, he kissed Johny on the snout. A tear fell on the mouse's green ear. He laid Johny on the bed, meticulously placing several other leaves over the mouse's face and body.

He whispered a line of Mirza Ghalib that his uncle back in Lucknow loved to recite. He remembered how he and his uncle used to sit on the veranda in wicker chairs during hot summer afternoons, drinking nimbu-pani— conversing about alchemy, science, mysticism, and metaphysics as if they were all one and the same. His uncle had no children, and when he'd passed away a few years ago, Dr. Ranjan had felt that, as the eldest male relative, it was his duty to go back to India to perform the rites. But Bhavana was expecting Neel any day, so he couldn't go. He didn't know who, in the end, lit his uncle's pyre.

He struck a match. The dry wood ignited. Soon Johny Walker was turning into smoke. Dr. Ranjan listened to the dirge of crackling noises, his eyes remaining fixed on the fireplace until the last spark went out.

18

A Tale of Three Kidneys

WHEN THE TRANSPLANTED MAN FIRST ARRIVED, IN ADDITION TO SUF-
fering from kidney failure his body had been on the verge of rejecting several
of his transplanted organs. Now, after many weeks in the hospital, the rejection of those other organs had been nearly thwarted. His kidneys were
another matter. Out-of-control blood pressure, toxicity from medications,
and his underlying disease had, over time, caused the two kidneys to lose their
normal earthy color, harden and shrink, distorting the delicate architecture of
tightly arrayed tubules with the deposition of fibrous tissue. Blood no longer
flowed through the shriveled tuft of tiny vessels in each scarred glomerulus;
the kidneys could not regulate the body's balance of water, acids, and miner-
als. There hadn't been a drop of urine in weeks. The Transplanted Man's kidneys were damaged forever, yet another set of failed organs in a body that had
witnessed so much failure.

Sonny was taking this failure personally. That was unusual for him. He'd
done his very best. Sometimes, no matter what you did, the patient got worse.
But in the case of the Transplanted Man, it was hard for him to accept.

During the morning dialysis session Sonny went up to the Transplanted
Man's bed and pretended to study the bedside chart. Then he stared at the
many dials and indicators on the dialysis machine. When he finally turned to
his patient he was unable to look the Transplanted Man in the eye. The
oppressive buzz of the dialysis machine almost made him decide not to
broach the subject. But he felt the Transplanted Man's questioning gaze.

"I'm afraid your kidneys won't recover."

At first the Transplanted Man's face became a panicky web of wrinkles.
Gradually a resigned look settled on his face. "I suppose I already knew that,"
he said. "But it sounds so much worse to hear *you* say it. So what does this
mean?"

"It means your kidneys have permanently failed."

"Yes, yes, I understand that. But what does it *mean*?"

"Your body won't magically make new kidneys."

"Which means?"

"Dialysis. Four hours a session, three sessions a week."

"This?" said the Transplanted Man, pointing to the dialysis machine. "Impossible! I know what J.P. and V.P. went through. It would restrict me to big cities forever, where the modern hospitals are. My people are in the villages, and there are no dialysis machines there. That is where I must campaign when the next elections are called. Dialysis won't do. I'd have to give up politics—everything I've worked for. I'd rather die."

"You will, without dialysis. . . . Listen, people can go decades on dialysis."

The Transplanted Man shook his head. "There must be something else."

"All your previous abdominal surgery really limits us to only one other option."

"Which is?"

Sonny peered into his patient's anxious eyes. The Transplanted Man's pupils dilated, and the light in the room was such that Sonny could see the circular rims of another man's transplanted corneas. "A kidney transplant," said Sonny.

The Transplanted Man massaged the inner corners of his eyes for a long time. "I thought you would say that."

"You see, you're better off—"

"No, if a transplant, so be it."

"Listen," said Sonny, "who am I to say, but maybe the time has come for you to leave politics. Your life is at stake."

The buzz of the dialysis machine turned into an intolerable roar.

"You are no one to say! Politics is all the life I have. Arrange for a transplant."

"To be honest, I don't know if you can survive another transplant. You're older now, frailer. Your heart—"

"A transplant!"

Sonny pursed his lips. "We'll have to see about that. First, I want to order a few tests to further evaluate your heart and lung function—determine if you can tolerate a big operation. Then we'll need to consult other doctors. One of them will, of course, be Dr. Sangam, the transplant surgeon. Didn't he do one of your earlier transplants?"

The Transplanted Man nodded.

"In your case, the posttransplant care will probably be what matters most."

"Will you be involved in my care after the transplant?"

"Once again, I'm not ready to recommend a transplant."

"But if you did?"

"I'll do my best to be with you for as long as necessary."

"I want that."

"So do I."

• •

BACK IN HIS ROOM the Transplanted Man stared out the window at the neighborhood below, the city beyond. He hadn't been outside hospital walls since the night he was admitted, and with another transplant potentially looming, he felt like spending a few hours in the city. Alone. But he knew that, given his condition, the hospital would probably require someone to accompany him. So he abandoned the idea, consoling himself with the thought that it didn't matter much. He'd seen a great deal of America on previous visits, and it was not a place he could feel at home in. There was too much geometry here—rectangles and squares, right angles everywhere. Everything was repainted, embellished, glowing in neon. Even so, he knew that, more than any other city in America, this one had the kind of character he valued. The layers of paint had peeled, revealing the otherwise hidden residue of a less synthetic era, sometimes even raw wood and bare cement. The bricks were chipped, the walls cracked. Mysterious shadows hovered here and there.

Suddenly he felt homesick. He had already been away for much too long, and now it might be months before he went home.

If at all.

He walked back to his bed, then lay down and stared at the ceiling. He had no illusions about the risks involved in another transplant, and he was afraid. The fact that he had gone through all this before didn't make it any easier. He knew his body—or, rather, this patchwork of many individuals that passed for his body. For years he'd existed in a limbo that kept him in and out of intensive care units and operating rooms. And now, more limbo.

He had never been a man of deep faith and could not summon it now. He admired people with such faith. His mother, for instance. She used to wake up before dawn, bathe, then sit for two hours in front of an assembly of tiny idols on her puja table. He remembered the tranquillity in her face as she gently rocked back and forth in the incense-filled room, counting beads, then putting on her bifocals to read verses from the Gita. That kind of devotion had to be nurtured day after day, year after year. But as much as he longed for it—as much as he hungered for its sustaining vitality and redemptive power— he knew he hadn't earned it: True conviction ultimately had to be built from sacrifice and suffering.

And yet . . .

Hadn't he had his share of suffering? Well then, he ought to have earned something, after all. If not based in religion, what was it? Certainly not political ideology—a revolutionary manifesto brazenly announced to the rest of the world. But wait! Hadn't he been doing exactly that for years? Hadn't he— through the circumstances of his disease, the force of his personality, and considerable skill in the Kautilyan games of politics—*become* a manifesto? And hadn't millions accepted his claim to special status?

He, *only he*, was the Transplanted Man.

His renewed belief in himself lifted his spirits. He would get through this, and everything else that Fate hurled at him.

Someone knocked on the door. Slowly, it opened. A nurse.

"Time to go for your cardiac imaging test," the nurse said. "An orderly will be here in a minute to wheel you over."

Suddenly the Transplanted Man's strength evaporated. Maybe not so special, he thought. Just an old man surviving off the organs of people already dead.

And now, no kidneys.

• •

THE RESULTS OF THE TESTS Sonny had ordered were equivocal, and senior doctors were divided over the idea of a kidney transplant. Dr. Rajchand was vehemently opposed, Dr. Sangam in favor, most others on the fence. After considerable debate and many more tests, there was still no consensus on whether a man so frail and aged, with his other organs functioning so precariously, could survive another major transplant. It was agreed, however, that the potential risks should be candidly presented to the patient.

That afternoon Sonny explained all the ifs, ands, and buts of the matter.

"One must do what one must do," replied the Transplanted Man.

Sonny nodded slowly, having by then become resigned to the Transplanted Man's choice to proceed despite the risk.

Once the go-ahead was given, the powers that be stacked the waiting list for transplantable kidneys in favor of the VIP patient. While someone else might have had to wait months, the Transplanted Man was scheduled to receive the next available kidney that matched his blood and tissue type.

It came sooner than anyone expected.

• •

SONNY HAD TOLD Dr. Sangam that he wanted to be present for the operation. The phone rang at 2:53 A.M. Sonny hurriedly slipped into his clothes. Outside there was no taxi in sight. He ran. Seven minutes later he arrived at the hospital, and a few minutes after that he stepped into the operating room garbed in surgical scrubs, gloves, and a mask.

The anesthesiologist was already inducing general anesthesia. Crisscrossed with scars from previous surgeries, the Transplanted Man's belly looked like an exotic board game. Nurses carefully cleansed his skin with a dark iodine solution, then used sterile green towels linked by clamps to create a square operating window.

Gloved and masked, Dr. Sangam entered the operating room. He raised his eyebrows at Sonny, who raised his in return. A tall, angular man, Dr. Sangam had the confident manner common among surgeons who helped give new lives to patients, sometimes five or six times a day. To boot, he was a transplant surgeon, and among them one of the most aggressive and versatile. He didn't just fix broken hearts or lop off cancerous liver lobes; he replaced whole organs. His success rate was astonishing—it was in large part responsible for the hospital's international reputation as a transplant center.

Dr. Sangam was a no-nonsense man: no wisecracks in the operating room, almost no words. When he was ready to start he simply held out his hand for the scalpel. The nurse passed over the instrument. Then Dr. Sangam and the assisting surgeon, a woman in her late thirties named Dr. Smith-Kaul, went to work.

A series of swift scalpel strokes slit through layers of skin, subcutaneous fat, and muscle. Severe distortions in the Transplanted Man's internal anatomy from prior operations meant that his entire belly would have to be opened up. As Dr. Sangam explored the viscera, ligating and cauterizing bleeding vessels, Sonny glimpsed the shiny liver, the amorphous pancreas. When he finally saw the shivering aorta, he realized this was one of the few tissues in the Transplanted Man that had been in the original blueprint. Like some deity, the Transplanted Man could be seen as one or many. And now he was absorbing yet one more identity.

Sonny watched the surgeon's performance with envy. He had never felt this way before; he'd always had an aversion to the crude approaches of surgery. Now he, too, wanted to slip his hands into the Transplanted Man's belly, run his fingers over the lobes of his liver, slide them along his shimmering intestine. Hidden somewhere was a secret, a philosophers' stone masquerading as an organ, or a precious elixir disguised as blood or lymph. It had to be an incredible substance, whatever it was, for it had survived so much. It couldn't be intrinsic to one of the transplanted organs, or among those currently diseased. Right there, much of the Transplanted Man's body was eliminated. So how hard would it be to find?

Having at last cleared the way for the donor kidney, Dr. Sangam examined the organ to be transplanted. He shrugged. The shrug appeared to be one of resignation rather than indifference, and it sent shudders through Sonny.

One by one the surgeons clamped blood vessels. In less than an hour they had attached the veins and arteries of the donor kidney to the Transplanted Man's own vessels, and the donor ureter had been stitched into the bladder. The blood vessels were unclamped. Scarcely breathing, Sonny stared intently at the pale kidney. Sluggishly the newly transplanted organ regained its natural color as blood seeped in.

Even Dr. Sangam sighed. Then he gazed at Sonny. "Soon he'll be all yours. I expect the postoperative course is going to be rough."

COMPLICATIONS

19

Hoopla

THE DIFFICULTIES DR. RANJAN HAD ENCOUNTERED WHILE TRYING TO publish his theory of love were still vivid in his mind. Those years were gone now, wasted, nothing to show for them. And more and more he feared that the same fate awaited his efforts to publish his findings on the sleep inhibitor. His detractors were now the arbiters of the field—and thus likely to be the first to review his data. Not only might they reject his manuscript for publication but the unscrupulous might use the information it contained to advance their own research, while he sought in vain to report his discovery. Even though it was *his* hypothesis, *his* discovery, he'd be robbed of the credit! The sheer unfairness of this possibility led Dr. Ranjan to seek an appointment with Chintu Paudha, the hospital's chief executive officer.

While Dr. Ranjan sat outside Paudha's office, however, he had second thoughts; Paudha was feared throughout the hospital—exactly the type of person Dr. Ranjan usually sought to avoid.

"Mr. Paudha can see you now," said the CEO's secretary in a cheerful voice.

Paudha wore a black suit and thin red tie. For a man so slight he squeezed Dr. Ranjan's hand with unexpected strength. Even before Paudha released his hand, Dr. Ranjan was losing nerve.

"How's the research going, Ranjan?"

"Quite well. Actually, that's what I wished to discuss with you."

"I'm no scientist, mind you. Just an MBA who tries to keep this place running. No small job."

Dr. Ranjan smiled sympathetically. "I'm sure you must be very busy. But I think my recent work has broad implications."

Paudha folded his hands and swiveled in his leather-upholstered chair. "What do you mean by 'broad implications'?"

"It's hard to say, actually. I myself am not quite sure what the implications are. Possibly commercial. . . . Perhaps all this can wait, though. My results are, after all, very preliminary. This discussion is premature. Sorry for wasting your time."

Glad he hadn't revealed more, Dr. Ranjan rose.

"Sit down!"

Dr. Ranjan sat.

"Commercial, you say? I like that."

"Oh, I was just talking nonsense," said Dr. Ranjan. "Actually . . . I didn't mean commercial. I meant comical. Yes, my research is quite comical—hah, hah!—always has been, actually."

"Stop beating around the bush, for God's sake! What are these results that have gotten you so wound up? Don't worry. If you want them kept confidential, just say so. *Trust me.*"

"Actually . . ."

· ·

WHEN SONNY APPROACHED the hospital the next morning, he saw trucks from local TV stations parked in a lot normally reserved for ambulances. In the lobby a crowd of employees, visitors, and reporters had gathered. All eyes and cameras were focused on the group sitting next to the podium. Beside Paudha and other top administrators sat the hospital's most generous benefactor, U. U. Bhimdas, the much-gossiped-about businessman reputed to have ties to arms merchants on the subcontinent. Squeezed in the middle of the group, sitting erect and looking particularly lilliputian today, was Dr. Ranjan.

Sonny turned to the man standing next to him. "What's the fuss about?"

The man was about to reply when Mr. Dhar, the hospital's vice president, stepped up to the microphone. "May I have your attention?"

The crowd quieted abruptly.

"Our hospital," began Mr. Dhar, "has a long history of contributing to the advancement of medical science. Our research effort is, in turn, indebted to philanthropists like Mr. Bhimdas, who have given vast sums to the hospital." Mr. Dhar turned to his left and bowed slightly toward Mr. Bhimdas, who beamed a self-satisfied smile. "I am sure everyone is aware that our director of research, Dr. Ranjan, is held in high esteem in the scientific community. After today, however, he may have no peer. I know that word of Dr. Ranjan's *in-cre-di-ble* discovery has leaked out. We can hardly contain our own . . . Well, let me allow Dr. Ranjan to elaborate. Friends, colleagues, I give you Dr. Nirdosh Sonaperkash Ranjan!"

Everyone, including the corpulent Mr. Bhimdas, rose to applaud.

Dr. Ranjan inched toward the microphone. For a moment he appeared dumbstruck. "Thank you," he said, almost whispering. He closed his eyes, then slowly reopened them. "Thank you very much," he added, his voice a little louder. "Actually, the results of our work have yet to be published. Naturally, I am hesitant to reveal our findings, but the process of scientific peer review can be extremely slow, and if I did not consider this so important, I wouldn't be before you. Still I am hesitant. In fact, I did not actually want to do it this way, with so much fanfare. For the matter is complex, actually, and now I am forced to simplify—even before the data have been fully analyzed. But I feel justified in communicating the results to you today because . . ."

Paudha leaned over and said something to Mr. Dhar, who in turn got up and whispered in Dr. Ranjan's ear.

"He wants me to get on with it," said Dr. Ranjan with a faint grin.

Many in the crowd chuckled.

"This is what I am afraid of, but get on with it I shall. We have discovered a factor—a sleep inhibitor—that causes a very rare type of *rodent* insomnia. Of course, it's too early to say what role, if any, it plays in human sleep . . ."

A loud murmur ran through the crowd. Mr. Dhar seized the microphone. "Dr. Ranjan, on behalf of the entire hospital, the entire community . . . No, on behalf of everyone who has risen exhausted after a sleepless night—and I suppose that *is* everyone—I thank and congratulate you . . ."

Applause drowned out the rest of Mr. Dhar's brief speech. The flurry of flashes created a supernatural glow around Dr. Ranjan—and also Mr. Bhimdas, who wouldn't stop shaking Dr. Ranjan's right hand. Dr. Ranjan appeared keen to answer reporters' questions, to elaborate, but instead kept cupping his ear or shrugging his shoulders, unable to hear the questions through the commotion, or to speak over it.

Dr. Ranjan was the talk of the hospital all that day, and his announcement was featured on the TV news. A pharmaceutical company spokeswoman described the discovery as a boon to all humankind and, yes, they had already started negotiating with the hospital in the hope of bringing the fruits of this research to the marketplace. Had the spokeswoman said *marketplace?* What she really meant was the public good, all those poor, sleepless people who were the company's primary concern, and she only meant that there was, incidentally, a huge market, which her company intended to exploit. Well, she didn't quite mean *exploit* . . .

Other scientists offered their opinions. Those who didn't know Dr. Ranjan were optimistic, but the ones who did were far from laudatory. "To the layman," commented one Harvard professor in a radio interview, "scientists a whole lap behind in the race can appear to lead the pack. Let's see it in print first. Remember cold fusion?"

. .

DR. RANJAN LEFT the hospital just before seven that evening. He had been unprepared for so much hype, and the morning's press conference had completely unnerved him. All day he'd been closeted in his office in a state of virtual paralysis. He'd kept his phone disconnected and hadn't answered the many knocks on the door. But as he drove home he couldn't resist the impulse to tune the car radio to the seven o'clock news. After reporting the national headlines, followed by local murders, thefts, and arsons, the newscaster said, "A scientist in the Big Apple has discovered the cause of insomnia . . ." The categorical nature of that statement made Dr. Ranjan cringe. Then, even more to his consternation, he heard himself quoted entirely out of context: The sound bites made it seem as though he was claiming that he'd discovered a *cure* for *human* insomnia! An uneasiness that had been inside him throughout the day metamorphosed into a tight knot in his stomach. He switched off the radio and inserted a cassette tape containing melancholy songs sung by Kishore Kumar. Tunes from *Safar, Anand,* and *Amar Prem* kindled memories of a different time.

When he entered his home Dr. Ranjan still felt slightly nauseated. But his wife and children, who had seen him on the evening news, were so thrilled that his spirits rose. Topping it off was Bhavana's apology for being difficult about his nights in the laboratory; she confessed that only today had she appreciated the importance of his research.

"Forgive me, Nirdosh."

That was definitely the high point of his day.

In the two and a half hours since she'd been home from work, Bhavana had managed to prepare the kind of huge meal she cooked only on the children's birthdays and festivals like Diwali and Holi. The dining table was neatly arranged with four stainless steel thalis surrounded by samosas, shammi kebabs, aloo-matar, rotis stuffed with spiced potatoes, saffron-flavored rice, raita.

"I've made gulab jamuns for dessert," she said. "I thought we'd have them while we watch the eleven o'clock news on TV."

That remark brought Dr. Ranjan's nausea back in full force. The shudder in his stomach threatened to recruit his bowels; stabs of fear quickly became searing thrusts. Lacking the habit of serious discussion with Bhavana, he was unable to articulate his feelings of impending doom. He himself didn't quite understand them. He may have jumped the gun by announcing his discovery, but he was certain of his claim. Unfortunately, the matter had gotten inflated, twisted. That was the nature of publicity, of course—the very intention of hospital administrators seeking to increase the market value of his discovery and enhance the hospital's reputation. Nothing really wrong with that. And once he published his results, everything would be placed in proper perspective. There was a politics to science, which in the past had always worked against him. Now, for the first time, it might work in his favor. Even if skeptical, other scientists would have to evaluate his claim seriously and offer concrete reasons for dismissing it, if that was to be the case. Then he could challenge them publicly—prove them wrong. Science was on his side.

As he contemplated various scenarios, none of which seemed headed for disaster, he began to feel better. Though he was still nauseated, he couldn't hurt his wife's feelings by refusing to eat. There was too much devotion in this meal. He filled his thali.

Fifteen minutes later he darted to the bathroom and shut the door. He took off his glasses, retched twice, then threw up in the toilet. Even after the retching stopped, the cramps in his stomach didn't abate. He flushed the toilet, flipped down the cover, and washed up. In the mirror he glimpsed the face of a man much older than himself. The rings around his eyes had darkened; new furrows snaked over his glistening brow. The tiny indentations on his cheeks—old acne scars—appeared to have deepened. Even his sideburns looked grayer. He locked the bathroom door and turned off the light. Then he made his way back to the covered toilet, sat down, and pressed his palms against his forehead to stabilize his ricocheting thoughts.

Bhavana knocked. "Are you all right, Nirdosh?"

"I'll be okay. I just need a moment alone."

He sat in darkness, taking slow, deep breaths. His thoughts hovered around some catastrophe he couldn't quite visualize. Suddenly he jumped up, lifted the toilet cover, and threw up again.

When he finally emerged from the bathroom twenty minutes later, Bhavana's face was full of concern. "What is wrong, Nirdosh?"

"A stomach virus, I think. A lot of people who ate at Tiger Raj's restaurant have gotten sick lately. The Health Department shut him down, you know."

In truth, the last time he had eaten there was a month ago—with Menaka Bhushan. He realized he'd lately been telling his wife little lies for no reason.

No reason?

Bhavana went into the kitchen, mixed a home remedy containing clove, cardamom, and fennel extracts with carbonated water, and poured it into a glass with a straw. While he sipped she put a kettle on the stove for a hot-water bottle. Then she helped him get comfortable in bed. Archana and Neel came upstairs, snuggled next to him. With the hot-water bottle on his belly, he read the children a story about a baby brontosaurus who wished he were a *T. rex.* Soon both children were sleeping, their heads nestled in his armpits. His shuddering viscera calmed down.

He fell asleep.

. .

RUMOR BEGOT RUMOR. Soon scientists on advisory boards of pharmaceutical companies were paying more attention to the rumors than to biomedical journals. Though they hadn't seen any data, a bandwagon mentality had usurped their otherwise acute skepticism, the result of years of rigorous scientific training and fruitless experiments. Likewise, the businessmen who paid those scientists their fat consulting fees—themselves schooled in probability, cost-benefit analysis, the fickle nature of profit and loss—suddenly seemed robbed of their entrepreneurial good sense. Sleep dysfunction was so widespread that the potential demand for an effective treatment dwarfed that of almost every other ailment. A multibillion-dollar market for sure, but who knew, with a genuinely useful drug it could turn into a trillion-dollar market. In the minds of excited investors, a hypothetical drug that neutralized the mouse sleep inhibitor—itself discovered only a short while ago—was already a saccharine-coated orange pill available at the corner pharmacy. One financial analyst went so far as to suggest that the sleep inhibitor might be an addition to the required childhood vaccination schedule. Immunized against the sleep inhibitor, toddlers wouldn't wake their parents at night. What working parent wouldn't pay thousands for that?

Perhaps it was due to the uncertain times—and the unrealistic hopes of investors who no longer knew where to put their money—but price quickly divorced from value. Every other day the hospital added another zero to the end of the asking price for exclusive commercial rights. With so much at stake, Dr. Ranjan began to fear for Johny Walker's descendants. After all, security at the hospital was lax. Custodial workers who mopped the floors at night often left the doors unlocked. Anyone could just ride the elevator up to the eleventh floor, go down the hall to the door labeled ANIMAL ROOM, and run off with the mutant mice. No mice, no sleep inhibitor.

Dr. Ranjan expressed his concerns to Paudha.

The CEO just laughed. "Who'd steal those filthy rodents? The whole world knows *we* made the discovery."

Discovered what, though? The more Dr. Ranjan thought about it, the more puzzled he was. An inhibitor of sleep, yes, but where in the body was it made? Where did it act? How did it act? Lots of experimental work was still needed. And even after all that, it would be a long time before anyone could really say how important it was in *human* insomnia. Despite the excitement Dr. Ranjan knew that the best that could be hoped for was one percent of what everyone hoped.

Even that was a lot.

• •

ON FRIDAY, PAUDHA'S SECRETARY phoned Dr. Ranjan to tell him that he was expected for a meeting in the CEO's office at exactly one o'clock. Dr. Ranjan asked what it was about.

"Hold for a moment," said the secretary. "I'll check."

Fifteen seconds later she came on the line again. "Just talk. That's what he says—just talk."

When Dr. Ranjan stepped into the CEO's office that afternoon, he found Paudha chatting amiably with a man in an expensive-looking dark gray suit.

"Ah, Ranjan," said Paudha. "Meet Mr. Shalsoe of Univelta Biopharm."

Dr. Ranjan nodded politely.

"Mr. Shalsoe is interested in the rights to your protein. Univelta aims to corner the sleep market."

Dr. Ranjan eyed the other two men with suspicion. Finally he said, "The protein may not have the same effect in humans. And even if it does, it will keep people awake, not put them to sleep. Who knows if it will ever be clinically useful?"

"There are lots of ways to bring it into the clinic," replied Mr. Shalsoe. "We can design a drug that acts against it for a short time, say, seven hours— the perfect sleeping pill. Of course, some folks will *want* to stay awake. They could take it straight. College students during exams, for instance."

"Interns at the hospital," said Paudha. "The possibilities are staggering."

Dr. Ranjan rolled his eyes in disbelief. "You're talking about the sleep inhibitor as if it's ice cream!"

"You can't patent ice cream," replied Mr. Shalsoe. "Public domain."

"That's not the point!"

"That *is* the point," said Mr. Shalsoe. "My research people tell me that if we have enough protein, we can grow crystals. If we can grow crystals, we can bombard them with X rays and determine the protein's structure. If we have a structure, we can model it on a computer and try to understand what kind of molecule may bind to it—inactivate it. Our organic chemists can then synthesize the molecule. If the molecule really inactivates the protein, and if it gets past animal and human testing, then it will be the most physiological of sleeping pills . . ."

At first Dr. Ranjan thought there might be some sense in Mr. Shalsoe's argument. But years of criticism had done wonders for Dr. Ranjan's own critical faculties. As he listened more closely, he detected a rehearsed quality in Mr. Shalsoe's words. The man must have uttered variations of these sentences many times before—to stockholders, venture capitalists, board members, mutual fund managers. By the time Mr. Shalsoe had finished, Dr. Ranjan realized the pharmaceutical executive understood just enough to give other executives like Paudha the impression he had a profound knowledge of biochemistry and pharmacology.

"Those are a lot of ifs," said Dr. Ranjan, smiling patronizingly. "The probability of it all happening is infinitesimal."

Now it was Mr. Shalsoe whose smile was patronizing. "If it's at all possible, *we* can do it. We're a hundred-billion-dollar company! We'll put every resource behind it. My friend, do you have any idea what it's like to go sleepless? Let me tell you. It is the most miserable, wretched, stupid, exhausting feeling. Do you know what percentage of humanity experiences this feeling on some occasion? One hundred percent. And they'll do anything to sleep at that point. Anything! The drug we make against your sleep inhibitor could solve their problems forever!"

Dr. Ranjan was still shaking his head. "Do you know how difficult it is to grow a protein crystal?"

"If a million monkeys . . ."

Paudha snickered.

"I don't get your meaning," said Dr. Ranjan.

"We have thousands of scientists," said Mr. Shalsoe. "We can hire thousands more."

Suddenly Dr. Ranjan understood how unimportant his views were to these two men. As his appreciation of his own position changed from that of a giant among intellectual philistines to that of a blabbering fool among amoral despots, he shrank into his chair.

"Any side effects?" asked Mr. Shalsoe.

"I don't know," said Dr. Ranjan. "Perhaps red eyes. Oh, and green ears."

"That's a joke, right?"

"Actually—"

"Of course it is!" interrupted Paudha. "Dr. Ranjan has quite a sense of humor."

"Does the protein have a name?"

Dr. Ranjan adjusted his glasses. "I call it p-forty-six, based on its relative molecular mass."

"Not good. It's got no pizzazz. The name's gotta have pizzazz."

"How about insomnin?" said Paudha.

"In-som-nin. I like that. I'll have our advertising people do some surveys, test it on focus groups. Insomnin. Not bad, not bad at all. Now, about the contract."

Dr. Ranjan stared incredulously at Paudha. "You didn't tell me things had gone *so* far—that you were about to make a deal with them! Actually, you said you wanted to talk—just talk—that's what you asked your secretary to tell me: just talk!"

"Can we have a moment in private?" said Paudha.

"Of course," replied Mr. Shalsoe, winking.

"We'll just step outside my office—won't be but a minute. Dr. Ranjan, do you mind?"

Dr. Ranjan rose obediently and followed Paudha out of the office. The CEO gently shut the door, then turned to Dr. Ranjan. "What the hell were you doing in there? You'll undermine the whole deal!"

"All this is happening too fast! Much more basic laboratory work is required, then carefully controlled studies—"

"Look here! You announced this discovery of yours, and now you must ride the bronco with all you've got. Broncos don't wait."

"I didn't want to announce! I did it only after you begged me to, and in any case what you are saying is illogical: There is no bronco!"

"I have *never* begged in my life!" said Paudha, shaking his forefinger at Dr. Ranjan. "And don't try to tell me what a bronco is. I used to spend my summers on a ranch."

"That might be the problem."

"Listen, you! Don't forget who pays your salary—who funds your laboratory. When was the last time you were awarded a research grant? Anywhere else you'd be expected to bring in money to support your research. You've never had any! No other place would have allowed you to stay so long. Don't feign astonishment. I know your reputation. I hear things. You owe this hospital, and the time has come to pay up. Understand?"

"I will not permit—"

"We don't need your permission. It's just a formality, and it will certainly make your life easier if you go along. *Much easier.* You forget that the hospital owns the rights to your discoveries—all of them. It owns your lab, your equipment, your supplies, your data. Everything!"

"Perhaps. But, actually, the hospital does not own me."

"*Actually,* we might."

The humiliation crept all the way down into Dr. Ranjan's toes. Paudha went back into the office. Dr. Ranjan followed, hunched, his step slow.

"Everything all right?" asked Mr. Shalsoe.

"Just fine," answered the CEO.

"We want world rights."

"Mmmmm," said Paudha.

Dr. Ranjan looked away.

"We are prepared to offer a hundred and fifty million plus royalties."

Almost simultaneously, Dr. Ranjan's and Paudha's jaws dropped. For once, Paudha appeared at a loss for words. Finally he said, "What?"

Mr. Shalsoe misinterpreted. "All right. Two hundred million. No more."

20

The Perfect Pose

THE LOCAL TELEVISION CREW ARRANGED THEIR EQUIPMENT ON THE corner of Esmoor and Forty-third Streets. Just as they began to shoot, clouds that had been threatening all day erupted into a thunderstorm. Televised images of a lonely ascetic, illuminated by flashes of lightning and unperturbed by vicious winds, seemed apocalyptic. The reporter said that the stoic white man who refused to move or speak was drawing visitors from all over. "A true phenomenon," commented the reporter.

All the people who came to see the hypokinetic man needed a place to eat. Tiger's restaurant, literally steps away, had recently reopened because the Health Department could not prove his negligence. So as the crowds grew, Tiger's business did, too. But many neighborhood residents still had visceral memories of that fateful Tiger kebab special. Only a handful of Tiger's old customers returned—Sonny, Gwen, Manny, and Alvin among them. Because the quarantine had left Tiger without enough cash to pay a full staff, his wife, Sushma, acted as hostess, while their daughter, Rohini, handled the cash register, and Atul waited tables. Tiger himself supervised the kitchen.

Tiger relished the opportunity to work side by side with his children. "The blood of royalty is thick," he proudly told his wife one evening as he watched Atul jot down a customer's order.

His wife flashed a stern look. "Don't we have higher hopes for our children? Besides, do we really need their help anymore? The restaurant is fuller than ever."

Tiger stroked his graying mustache with his index finger. "You're right, Sushma. If business continues like this, we'll need to rehire not only the old staff but others as well."

Then Tiger marched across the room and snatched the order pad from Atul's hand. "A crown prince should not be waiting tables," he told the stunned boy. "Now go, my son. Study to be worthy of your ancestry."

· ·

JAY AND ATUL'S BUSINESS was growing, too. One night after the boys had collected the coins and dollar bills from the hypokinetic man's lap, Jay said, "That algebra is good for something, after all."

"What do you mean?" asked Atul.

Jay pulled a folded sheet of paper out of his shirt pocket and flicked on his flashlight. "Look here," he said, unfolding the sheet. "I've graphed every day's profit on semilog paper. See? It's growing exponentially. All you have to do is extrapolate. In three years we'll split a cool million."

"You sure?"

"Who won the ninth grade math test?"

"You were smarter then."

"No, I'm smarter now."

"Jay, doesn't this whole thing bug you sometimes? Maybe we should give the money to charity."

Jay rolled his eyes. "That's easy for you to say! Your dad is making a bundle off this."

Atul kept quiet.

But when Atul got home, he couldn't sleep. It was clear to him that Jay was interested in the pose-for-the-ism only as a moneymaking gimmick. While his own motivation was purer, Atul knew it had become tainted. The hypokinetic man was a treasure; it was impossible to be oblivious to this fact. Atul felt he owed the hypokinetic man an explanation. So at 3:20 A.M., Atul slipped out to visit him again. He brought along a glass of mango lassi. The hypokinetic man noiselessly sipped his favorite drink through a plastic straw. During the two and a half hours it took him to finish the glass, Atul tried to explain.

"I've decided to donate my share to UNICEF," said Atul. "All of it. So you see, you're going to help a lot of poor kids. But remember, it's bigger than that. Once we find the pose-for-the-ism, the whole world could change. That's why what we're doing—what you are doing—is so important. My dad always says, 'The greatest things begin very simply.' . . . I guess that brings us to my father. You must be wondering about him. He's a good man, really. It was awful hard on him when they shut the restaurant down; it brought back memories of his family losing everything in Uganda when he was a teenager. He's a proud man, descends from a line of great kings, you know . . ."

So went the first of many middle-of-the-night conversations between Atul and the hypokinetic man. Although the hypokinetic man never gave any reply, Atul believed his words were being heard. And all the mango lassis put flesh on the hypokinetic man. He also developed a hint of a smile. The smile was so subtle, so enigmatic, only Leonardo could have done it justice. But it was real. In nearly a decade of painful homelessness and isolation, no one in the city had given the hypokinetic man even a fraction of the attention he was getting from his young friends.

Soon the hypokinetic man's new smile created excitement among tourists. The crowds grew.

So did the boys' revenues.

. .

TANDOORI INITIALLY MISTOOK the hypokinetic man for a fire hydrant. After that inauspicious beginning, they developed an intimate friendship. Slipping out the occasionally open window of Sonny's apartment (and then climbing down the fire escape), Tandoori would visit the hypokinetic man to share the solitude of the night for those two or three hours when this part of the city was quiet. The dog found comfortable places on the hypokinetic man's body to nestle into, relishing human interaction without being bothered by human whims. Here was a person, redolent of exactly the odor dogs like, who allowed his face to be thoroughly licked without any fuss. So, unleashing affection as only a canine can, Tandoori licked. And licked. The hypokinetic man's pupils dilated, and sometimes he shut his eyes—very slowly—to savor the experience.

In daylight more lasting changes were evident on the hypokinetic man's face. Under the strong autumn sun, he had acquired a healthy tan. His bronze tint wasn't dark enough to be confused for Indian, but his complexion no longer looked particularly foreign, either. In fact, when the afternoon light hit him a certain way, he bore an uncanny resemblance to an ancient North Indian statue of the Alexandrian period.

The hypokinetic man's derangement had to do with interpretation, not vision. From the corner of Esmoor and Forty-third, he observed thin old men with virility problems slip in and out of the homeopathic pharmacy. He watched middle-aged women dressed in saris rushing in and out of video shops, younger women in colorful salwar-kameezes strolling alongside their husbands, teenage girls in snug blue jeans flirting with boys wearing leather jackets. Of course, the hypokinetic man didn't experience his surroundings exactly that way but rather in a fuzzier, more intense version. Neither the old men's faces nor the saris had wrinkles. The gold on women's necks glittered more brightly. The heavenly aromas emanating from Tiger's grill had a more profound effect on him than upon the customers before whom the sizzling dishes were set. And his ears picked up the full gamut of neighborhood sounds: screeching delivery vans, boisterous children heading home from school, film songs, angry taxi horns, cackling telephone-wire birds, buzzing insects. The hypokinetic man's fractured mind somehow separated all the components of the cacophony and recombined them. He was the only one in the neighborhood who really heard its music.

• •

WEDNESDAY EVENING, SONNY and Gwen held hands in the long queue outside Tiger's restaurant. Like everyone else's, their eyes focused on the main attraction.

"Sonny, some scoundrel is exploiting that poor man."

"That may be, but it's good to see him anchored, not wandering here and there."

"You talk like you know him."

"We're old friends."

Gwen's eyes widened. "Oh?"

"It's hard to explain—hard to understand."

"Not hard for me to understand."

Sonny ignored the insinuation.

"He's catatonic, right?"

"I used to think so," said Sonny. "I'm not sure anymore."

"What else could he be?"

"Sometimes I see him as a lone protester."

Gwen's eyebrows arched. "Protesting what?"

"That's the question."

"We need to get to the bottom of this."

"I won't deny that I'm curious," said Sonny. "I've even thought of staking out the corner to discover what's really going on. But maybe it isn't necessary. After all, he's safer here than on the subway or in the shelters. At the moment, this may be as good as his life gets. Why not let him be?"

"Do you think he will snap out of it?"

Sonny thought for a moment. "I don't know if he'll ever fully recover. He'll probably get better, though. Someday."

"We should do something to prevent him from being used by all these shopkeepers and restaurant owners."

Sonny put his arm around her. "Believe it or not, in his own way, he likes it here."

"How do *you* know?"

• •

UNSATISFIED BY SONNY'S ASSURANCES, Gwen phoned the local mental health authorities as soon as she got home. "Half the neighborhood is exploiting the poor fellow!" she told the man on the phone.

"We're aware of the guy," he replied in a thick Brooklyn accent. "We've already had lots of calls, and one of our people even went out to take a look the other day. The report is lying around somewhere."

"What are you going to do?"

"Nothing, ma'am. We can't take him in unless he's harmful to himself or others."

"He's catatonic!"

"Whatever he is, he isn't doing badly, all things considered. Hygiene impeccable, nourishment good "

"Your definitions are awful technical."

"Extreme slowness is not a crime, ma'am. Nor is sitting in one place. These people have rights, too. Let's just say the rest of the world thought you were crazy—doesn't really matter whether or not you were. Tell me, would you want to be dragged off to an institution? For electroshock, no less—because that's the main treatment for severe catatonia."

"But—"

"And what if he isn't catatonic? I'm not saying he isn't, mind you, but it's possible."

"Don't tell me you also think he might be a mystic!"

"I didn't say that. Though now that you bring it up, explain to me how you'd exclude that possibility. There's no foolproof way to differentiate a catatonic from a mystic—"

"I can't believe this!"

"Imagine yourself undergoing electroshock treatment just because some nice woman with a British accent called this office. *Bzzzz, bzzzz, bzzzz!*—your body convulsing—you know what I mean? How'd you like someone else making that decision for you? Remember, you might not be catatonic in the first place."

"This is insane!"

"Since you mention it, you wouldn't believe the amount of insanity in this town. Our funds have been cut, and we have no place to put people who *are* dangerous. This guy on Esmoor and Forty-third is no more dangerous than a butterfly. Before we take him in, we'd have to pick up countless others. Some days it seems like the whole city should be—"

Gwen slammed down the phone so hard the receiver cracked.

• •

AFTER THE STREETS HAD EMPTIED, Gwen paid the hypokinetic man a visit. In one hand she held a flashlight, in the other, a volume of Tagore. Choosing Tagore over Thoreau was difficult, but for the purpose at hand, verse seemed most apt. She shone the flashlight on the hypokinetic man's face. His expression gave her a jolt. With the flashlight held at an angle, he bore a faint resemblance to, of all people . . . No—her imagination. And yet the longer she stared, the less sick he looked. She gently placed her hand on his neck, absorbing the warmth of his skin and listening to the quiet of the neighborhood.

At last she took a step back and read from the first bookmarked page of *Gitanjali:*

> *If thou speakest not,*
> *I will fill my heart with thy silence and endure it.*
> *I will keep still and wait like the night with starry vigil*
> *And its head bent low with patience.*
> *The morning will surely come,*
> *The morning will vanish,*
> *And thy voice pour down in golden streams*
> *Breaking through the sky . . .*

Gwen read six more passages. Were her words penetrating the hypokinetic man's mind before dissolving into darkness? She considered turning the flashlight on his face to check for a change of expression. But then she thought that it might be too jarring and neutralize the effect of the verse. Besides, the words needed time to percolate through his mind—tickle this, rearrange that—before their true power became manifest.

Gwen would have kept on reading had she not been startled by a man stepping out of the shadows.

Then came a dog.

She almost yelled, "Stop, Sonny!" But she swallowed her words at the last second.

Tandoori ran up to her, licked her hand—and also the hypokinetic man's face. Then he chased after Sonny.

Gwen followed at a distance. How did Sonny manage to stay on the sidewalk, avoiding fire hydrants and lampposts? He even crossed at intersections! It was as if he was in some kind of fugue state—only half asleep. Half awake?

Sonny and Tandoori turned down a dark street. Gwen's flashlight wasn't powerful enough, and she soon lost sight of man and dog. She dropped *Gitanjali* and ran ahead but was unable to locate Sonny or Tandoori. They must have gone down an alley, she thought. She took a few steps down one alley, then stopped. All around her were sinister-looking buildings. She began to feel vulnerable. Wasn't this gang territory? Her flashlight still on, she retraced her steps until she found *Gitanjali*. She picked up the volume, dusted it off on her jeans, then hurried back to her apartment.

• •

SHORTLY AFTER GWEN REACHED home, Jay and Atul visited the hypokinetic man. Jay had a small paper bag in his hand.

"Let's go for it this time," said Jay. "I think I've got it."

"Really? The pose-for-the-ism?"

"This pose has something for everybody," said Jay. "Look, it's like this."

Jay put the paper bag aside and sat down on the pavement beside the hypokinetic man. First, he folded his legs. Then he placed his left elbow on his left knee, keeping his wrist gently bent, with the fingers partly extended and resting pensively against his cheek. His neck had a slight forward tilt; his lower back was straight. Jay winked at Atul, then rolled his shoulders and took a deep breath. Everything fell naturally into place.

"Hey, that's pretty good," said Atul. "You're right—it's got a bit for everyone, though you can't say it's this or that."

"Very comfortable, too. I could sit like this forever."

"You know, Jay, I think you really might have it."

"Go ahead and say it: I'm a genius."

"If this catches on, it could solve the world's problems."

"Sometimes you talk like a kid, Atul. You're almost fifteen!"

"Do you believe in an ism, Jay?"

"Sort of."

"What's that mean?"

"Well, I think there is Something, only it isn't worth fighting over the way most people do, since there's probably only one Something, and it's the same for everyone, no matter where you live or what name you give it, and it doesn't think much about us, because it's so busy spinning galaxies at the edge of the universe and doing who knows what else."

"That sounds deep."

"I may be a delinquent, but I can think for myself."

"Maybe I've been wrong about you."

Jay pointed to the hypokinetic man. "We've got to shave his head."

"Absolutely not!"

"Be quiet, will you? His hair's getting long anyway. With this pose, he'll be a gold mine if we shave his head."

"He's already a gold mine!"

"A diamond mine, then," said Jay, opening the paper bag. "Look, I've got scissors, a can of shaving cream, and a razor. Now hold the flashlight and keep watch."

Jay pulled out the scissors.

"Wait, Jay! Let's think about this."

"Nothing to think about."

But just as Jay started to snip, the hypokinetic man stood up. And without a sound he shuffled—very slowly—into the darkness.

After a long silence, Atul whispered, "I nearly died."

"I guess it's all over."

"I wonder if he really is a mystic."

"Doubt it. But it looks like he makes his own plans."

· ·

ALTHOUGH THE HYPOKINETIC MAN was on the move, he wasn't moving fast. And his thoughts were extremely disorganized. Even so, he felt better than he had in a long time. He associated this well-being with the fuzzy-cheeked faces of Jay and Atul. Especially Atul.

His quarter-mile-a-day pace, phenomenal by his standards, added novel dimensions to his world. He seemed to be in a foreign land; yet it was strangely familiar, too. After a while he couldn't tell if he was heading home or away. Most surprising was the fact that, although he'd traveled a seemingly immense distance, no one had harassed him.

Of course, there was nobody on the street at this time of night to harass the hypokinetic man. Eventually he spotted someone: a man walking toward him. Soon the man had sped by. The hypokinetic man had seen this man before, but he couldn't remember where or when. That sense of familiarity increased when Tandoori gently pawed his shin a few times before catching up with Sonny again. Nevertheless, the shock of this brush with a reckless man, who traveled orders of magnitude faster than *he* could go, led the hypokinetic man to reconsider his recent actions. The world was unpredictable, complicated. Dangerous. The youthful faces of Atul and Jay flashed through his mind. He missed them. The emotion turned on a switch—or, perhaps, turned it off. Suddenly the hypokinetic man was slowing down with every step. A cockroach passed him.

By dawn he had retraced his steps and was back at the corner of Esmoor and Forty-third.

21

Beeps and Buzzers

THE TRANSPLANTED MAN PROPPED HIMSELF UP IN HIS ICU BED. WITH so many beeps and buzzers going off around him tonight, he hadn't been able to sleep. Now he cleared his throat. All night he'd been clearing it. He felt something clutching in his chest.

He motioned to Gwen as she passed by.

"Everything okay?"

"I'm worried something is brewing in here," he said, pointing to his chest. "I've been through so many complications, I get concerned over the slightest thing."

Gwen looked at his bedside chart. "Your temperature and pulse are fine. Let me listen to your lungs." She helped him sit up, then laid her stethoscope on his back. "Take a few slow, deep breaths, please."

The Transplanted Man inhaled deeply, then exhaled.

"Your chest sounds all right, but it's best to be vigilant. I'll page the resident on call to see if she wants a chest X ray. The problem is that they can only get a good-quality X ray at the radiology department in the basement. The portable X rays done up here usually don't reveal subtle abnormalities, and if you have anything, it'll be subtle. Since they're planning to move you out of the ICU tomorrow morning, I see no reason why you can't go down. But let me check with the doctor to make sure it's okay."

Half an hour later an orderly wheeled the Transplanted Man's stretcher into the basement of the hospital, where a radiology technician snapped front and side views of his chest. The radiologist on call read the X rays as "No active disease" and reassured the Transplanted Man that he needn't worry. Soon the Transplanted Man was worried about something else, though. He had a sneaking suspicion that someone had forgotten to pick him up.

He was right. The radiologist and the X-ray technician had rushed off to the ER to take portable X rays of a hit-and-run victim, so the Transplanted Man lay alone in the basement for three-quarters of an hour. He was about to yell for help when Manny happened to walk by.

"What are you doing in this dungeon?"

The Transplanted Man coughed into his fist. "Would you mind taking me back to the ICU?"

"No problem. I push people around all the time."

Manny wheeled the Transplanted Man into an elevator. The elevator rose but then got stuck on the fourth floor. The doors refused to open.

"These things happen," said Manny. "This hospital is old—in case you hadn't noticed—and so are its elevators. We'll get going in a few minutes. Like to hear a song?"

The Transplanted Man didn't object, so Manny entertained the nervous patient.

"You have a wonderful voice," said the Transplanted Man after Manny finished. "Like Kishore Kumar."

"You really think my voice is like Kishore's?"

"Indistinguishable."

"Did I ever tell you I sang for Ronny Chanchal once? In the cafeteria, of all places. He gave me his card."

"Probably the card with the fake number he gives everyone."

Manny's heart sank. He had believed that card was the passport to his dream. As soon as he set foot in Bombay—whenever that was—he had planned to flash the card all the way to a recording contract. Stardom—immortality.

"That's a nasty thing to do," said Manny. "You think Ronny Chanchal would do that?"

"I *know* he would. Don't worry. I'll give you his real number at the studio and also his three home numbers, including the private line in his bedroom. I know other filmi people, too. . . . May I listen to something else?"

"I don't care much for the new songs," said Manny. "Most of my favorites are from before I was born—the late sixties and early seventies."

"Mine, too."

Manny began to sing.

As the Transplanted Man listened, he forgot his worries. He was transported back to a time and place when he was happy, vigorous. Manny's voice was astounding in its range and texture. There were echoes of pain and longing, yet at the same time it seemed like nothing could suppress its natural verve.

"Now that really was Kishore!" said the Transplanted Man when Manny finished. "You could go on All India Radio, and *no one* would know the difference!"

Manny beamed.

The elevator started to move again. On the ninth floor the doors opened.

"There you are!" said Gwen. "I've been calling all over the hospital. God, you really scared me! We're more than an hour late for your medications." She gave Manny a severe look.

"Don't glare at me. This is volunteer work."

"I'm genuinely grateful," the Transplanted Man told Manny.

"Remember my voice to your friends in Bombay."

"Mumbai."

"Right," said Manny as he walked away, humming.

Gwen placed her hand on the Transplanted Man's forehead. "Let's take your temperature."

· ·

BY THE NEXT MORNING, the Transplanted Man's cough had worsened, and his joints ached. His temperature was 102.4 and climbing. Throughout the night Gwen had been checking on him every half hour. But the Transplanted Man feared abandonment when she came to say good-bye. Six A.M.: Her shift was over. She looked tired.

Gwen held the Transplanted Man's hand affectionately. "I've been in touch with Sonny. He'll be in around eight and remain till tomorrow. I'll be back tonight."

The Transplanted Man was touched by the concern in her eyes, and knowing that Sonny would soon be in the hospital gave him a measure of comfort. "He reminds me of my son."

"From the way he talks about you, I think he'd like your saying that. But I didn't know you had a—"

"Arvind is dead," said the Transplanted Man. Then he went into a fit of coughing.

Gwen handed him a tissue. He spat up thick, yellow-green sputum tinged with tiny specks of blood.

"Maybe I should page Sonny now," said Gwen. "I'll order another chest X ray, too. This time it'll have to be a portable one—here in the ICU."

After Gwen left his bedside, the Transplanted Man stared at the kaleidoscopic sputum smeared on the white tissue. How many times had he been through this? Two dozen? More? He could come up with the exact number if he tried. But he didn't want to remember all those doctors and nurses, all those X rays and blood tests, all those tubes and injections, all those intensive care units with alarms going off right and left, signaling death or simply a disconnected wire. Each time he went through a crisis he feared it would be the last. No, he wouldn't count them all. Luck is a rare commodity, and he'd had more than his share. Counting might prejudice the outcome.

· ·

"You have pneumonia," said Sonny, after examining the Transplanted Man.

"I thought as much."

"I hope it won't be difficult to treat. The problem is that your heart isn't pumping as well as it should. And your immunity is suppressed by the drugs we're giving to prevent your kidney transplant from being rejected."

"How is the kidney doing, anyway?"

"Unfortunately, not great—according to your latest blood tests."

"And how bad does this morning's X ray look?"

"There's a haziness that wasn't present last night. The pattern is a bit strange, too."

"Everything that happens to my body is strange."

"Let's hope this is just a routine pneumonia, and a few days of antibiotics does the trick."

"I've had many pneumonias. Not one was routine."

Sonny looked the Transplanted Man in the eyes. "I'll be frank, then. You're right, it may be rough—as rough as it's ever been. But I promise you . . ."

Sonny clasped the Transplanted Man's right hand between his palms. He opened his mouth but was at a loss for words. He cast his eyes downward, aware of the Transplanted Man's gaze locked upon his face. Then he shook his head, overcome with emotion. This had never happened before with a patient. He wanted to comfort the Transplanted Man, yet something prevented him. Not any sense of professionalism; he'd be the last to hold back on that account. But along with the overwhelming affection he felt, he experienced echoes of a remote pain—which, for reasons he didn't understand, he partly blamed on the Transplanted Man.

Sonny let go of the Transplanted Man's hand. "I promise you," he said—and left.

· ·

It was no routine pneumonia. Despite huge doses of this cillin and that mycin, within two days bacteria had crawled into the furthest interstices of the Transplanted Man's lungs. Soon he was gasping for breath. Every time he inhaled he felt horrible stabs in his chest that traveled into his shoulders and spine. Eventually the pain became so great that tears were streaming down his face. The Transplanted Man didn't want to breathe anymore.

It almost came to that. His lungs, smothered by pus and inflammatory fluid, were no longer able to supply oxygen to the rest of his body. The Transplanted Man's blood turned from red to purple, and in the middle of the night Gwen noticed that his fingers had a bluish hue. Sonny wasn't on call, but it was he that she phoned.

He fumbled the receiver and groggily listened to Gwen's report.

"Keep him on one hundred percent oxygen. I'll be there soon."

Sonny slipped into his sweatpants and running shoes. In no time he was out the door, racing down the street. At this time of night there was almost no traffic, and he arrived at the hospital in six and a half minutes. In another minute he'd climbed the nine flights to the ICU. He stood before Gwen, panting.

"That was fast!"

Without replying he examined his patient. The Transplanted Man appeared confused. Spit bubbled at the corners of his mouth.

Sonny turned to Gwen. "Get me his lab results, his X rays, have an endo-tracheal tube ready, and call the respiratory technician. Stat!"

A few minutes later Sonny inserted a plastic tube into the Transplanted Man's windpipe and connected it to a mechanical ventilator that would, for the time being, take care of his breathing.

Sonny stayed in the hospital all night. It made no difference. By morning, lung and kidney failure weren't the Transplanted Man's only problems. The entire federation of organs, native and foreign, was deconstructing. His heart could no longer pump with enough force to maintain his blood pressure, and its beat was erratic. His liver refused to produce clotting factors. His intestines were oozing blood. A new bruise appeared on his skin hourly. Most alarming was how his mental state had gone from confusion to stupor to near coma.

The Transplanted Man had never been sicker.

• •

As if a world war had broken out, every one of the foreign organs in the Transplanted Man was being rejected. Even his corneal transplants—

normally not susceptible to immune attack—were now riddled with microscopic deposits containing white blood cells that were gnawing at the rims of corneas that had once belonged to other men. Faring worst of all was his new kidney. Originally no bigger than a child's fist, it had swollen to twice that size as it became colonized by enraged white blood cells. With all the bruises and pale blotches on its surface, its usual earthy brown color, still evident in tiny patches, seemed incongruous, although it was, in fact, the only healthy tissue left.

Deep inside the transplanted kidney, a slow massacre was occurring. Normally tall and proud, the tamarind-hued cells lining the kidney tubules were being pummeled by invading white blood cells intent on destroying the organ. Gradually, the tubules capitulated. The white blood cells kept coming, thousands at a time, spitting out their weight in degradative enzymes, chewing up tubules that were heroically trying to detoxify the Transplanted Man's blood—maintain the delicate chemical balance necessary for life.

The blood vessels that fed into those wretched tubules weren't faring much better. On the outside they were assaulted by one battalion of white blood cells; from within, by another. The river of blood coursing through the vessels turned into a stream, the stream into a trickle. Soon the blood stopped flowing altogether. The Transplanted Man's new kidney wasn't functioning at all.

Once again he was hooked up to a dialysis machine.

• •

SONNY WENT SLEEPWALKING on every one of his nights off. And tonight— the only night of the week that neither he nor Gwen happened to be in the hospital—he did it again.

Gwen woke shortly after Sonny left. She ran to the window, from where she watched him cross the street in his underwear, trailed by Tandoori. A truck was speeding down the road, heading straight for them. The dog hopped out of the way, but Sonny was still in the street. The truck didn't slow down. Tandoori leaped back into the street, barking madly.

Gwen slid open the window and screamed, "Sonny, the truck! The truck!"

At the last second Tandoori jumped to the side. The truck missed Sonny by inches.

Half an hour later Sonny reentered the apartment, still asleep. Gwen watched him lie down in bed. Slowly she counted to one hundred. Then she whispered, "Sonny?"

He remained asleep.

She switched on the light and gently shook him until he opened his eyes.

"What's going on?" he asked, squinting. "Turn off the light, would you?"

"The light needs to be on."

"Why?"

Gwen was brief.

"Sleepwalking? No way!"

"*Way.* Tonight you were nearly run over by a truck. One of these days you won't be so lucky."

"Are you sure I was sleepwalking?"

"Absolutely."

It was 2:56 A.M. Sonny got up and quietly paced back and forth. When Gwen awoke four hours later, he was still pacing.

22

Of Calls and Callings

WORD HAD FINALLY LEAKED OUT. THE TRANSPLANTED MAN, REPORTED a major news service, was in a New York City hospital, dying. Within hours after the story broke, the hospital fielded over a hundred inquiries about his condition. As before the hospital denied that the Transplanted Man had been admitted. Nobody believed a word. Reporters snooped through the corridors. When armed police officers were stationed outside the ICU, everyone knew exactly where the famous patient was struggling for his life.

Back in India, leaders of the Opposition—quietly urged on by Sharad Kakkar—demanded that the Transplanted Man be replaced as minister of Health and Family Welfare. How could the ministry operate with its head so ill and so far away? When the prime minister pointed out that during the Transplanted Man's tenure the ministry had been functioning more efficiently than ever, the Opposition changed tactics. They joked that it really made no difference whether or not the ministry had a head, since all the other ministries effectively had no heads, either. Antigovernment political cartoonists began depicting the ministers themselves—including the prime minister—as headless men and women. Owing to recent defections and scandals, the ruling coalition had already weakened. The prime minister was forced to give in. The Transplanted Man was sacked.

After that the hospital received fewer and fewer inquiries about the Transplanted Man. Soon there were only two or three a day. Security was loosened, since the threat to a former minister already on the verge of death seemed minimal. Gone were reporters trying to snap a photograph of the gravely ill patient, or pestering hospital personnel for information. As recent subcontinental history had demonstrated, the only way to remain interesting to the very end was to get assassinated. The Transplanted Man was just another old leader fading away. After J.P., Vinoba Bhave, and so many others since, everyone was used to this.

The next story about the Transplanted Man would be his death.

· ·

EAGERLY AWAITING NEWS of his condition was Ronny Chanchal. Sitting in his New Delhi office this morning, he gazed out the window at a plane piercing the clouds. A jumbo jet, it looked like. He was *so* tired of flying! Making matters worse, the flight from New York via London he'd recently arrived on had landed at an ungodly hour. From all the transoceanic back-and-forth for his U.S. tour, he felt as if his mind and body had separated 35,000 feet above the Atlantic, some pieces flying eastward, others westward—perhaps never to unite again. All he could think of was sleep. He picked up the morning paper, scanned the headlines for news of the Transplanted Man's condition.

Nothing.

Ronny Chanchal put down the paper and glanced at the day's itinerary. Every minute was filled: strategy meetings with senior officials from his own party, lunch with members of a splinter party to further discuss toppling the government, an afternoon parliamentary session, a cocktail reception at the Russian embassy and, finally, a late dinner with the man he hoped would agree to serve as codirector of his East-West film. Although Ronny Chanchal had been thinking a lot about the film in recent weeks, he hadn't gotten beyond a nebulous vision that would lift the Bollywood masala style to a new level. Of course, his mind had spun many potential plots. For a while he'd been toying with the idea of a Silicon Valley multimillionaire returning to India for an arranged marriage to a beautiful software developer. At first he thought he finally had something promising. But his mind quickly turned it into another campy Bollywood story and, like every other idea he'd had, it fell far short of his ambition. Might he be forced to resort to mere permutations and combinations of the old? He'd made a career of imitation and repetition, and he feared that his only attempt at real art would prove to be more of the same.

He turned his attention to the files stacked upon his desk—letters to read and reply to, papers to initial or sign. So much to do in one week! Then back to America for three more shows: Philadelphia, St. Louis, Chicago. He picked up a document that spelled out his own party's position on a variety of national issues. He grimaced as he skimmed the pages. Democracy! As far as he was concerned, the parliamentary system hadn't worked. At Independence it was mob rule by millions; now, more than a half century later, it was mob rule by a billion. He enjoyed from afar the adulation of the masses, but he despised their greasy hands, which he had to shake wherever he went. Once he'd privately debated the virtues and vices of democracy with the Transplanted Man. From the Transplanted Man's casual remarks about Charu Mazumdar and Sanjay Gandhi, it was clear that the *neta* was equally frustrated by Indian-style democracy—except he believed that, imperfect as it was, there was no other option. The Transplanted Man didn't trust any leader, not even himself.

As he pondered this, a smile crawled across Ronny Chanchal's face.

• •

OUT OF DESPERATION GWEN had been slipping different books between the Transplanted Man's mattresses, hoping that one of them would somehow heal the man who believed in the healing power of literature. The Transplanted Man liked nineteenth-century English writers, and he got the very best: Austen, Eliot, Dickens, Trollope, every Brontë. When all those books produced no improvement, Gwen switched to Eastern literature, including *Shakuntala,* the haiku of Basho, the devotional poems of Kabir, and *The Tale of Genji*—which, owing to its bulk, had to be opened to the middle pages before being inserted, facedown. After even that failed she tried pairing a nineteenth-century English classic with the work of a living Asian writer, hoping that some combination of West and East, colonial and postcolonial, dead and alive, might do the trick. At home the yellow bulb of her bedside lamp burned deep into the night as she desperately searched for just the right passage— the perfect sequence of words that would forestall the death of the Transplanted Man.

Meanwhile, Sonny spent every spare minute scavenging medical textbooks and journals for insights into the Transplanted Man's deteriorating condition. Had he not paid sufficient attention to a test result that, if correctly interpreted, could change everything? He consulted senior physicians whose judgment he respected. But to their eyes the Transplanted Man was no different from other ICU patients with multiorgan failure. When Sonny responded that the Transplanted Man had recovered from dire predicaments in the past, no one could explain his failure to do so this time. All agreed that one could only pretend to treat the chaotic physiology of a body so determined to die.

Sonny refused to accept this reasoning. He kept telling himself that the usual logic did not apply. There had never been a patient even remotely like the Transplanted Man.

The case was discussed at the citywide Transplantation Conference held every Tuesday evening. Among those present was one of the foremost authorities in the field, Dr. Camilla Winkel. Sonny described the Transplanted Man's case to the group of surgeons, hepatologists, nephrologists, cardiologists, pulmonologists, and infectious disease specialists. He was asked many questions: Were the blood levels of immunosuppressant drugs monitored closely? Was the patient tested for cytomegalovirus? Had he undergone transbronchial biopsy?

Sonny answered patiently: Yes, they'd done all that—and much more.

A highfalutin academic discussion ensued. Everyone thought the Transplanted Man was fascinating; they all wanted more details of his medical history. Sonny, who by now knew all twenty-nine volumes of that history (the original twenty-five plus the four generated during this hospitalization), described everything at length. After hearing the whole story, one specialist went so far as to suggest that the patient had a completely new syndrome. This led to a heated debate that split the group. A nauseating feeling invaded Sonny as he heard the Transplanted Man's struggle abstracted into polysyllabic Latinate terms that seemed to get more entangled every second.

Toward the end of the discussion, one doctor, also an ordained minister, asked, "Why has so much suffering been inflicted upon a single person? There *must* be a reason! Why has God chosen to take this man to the very brink of death time after time, then bring him back to life?" The deep concern in the man's voice touched Sonny. But the doctor-minister's comments elicited only patronizing smiles.

The physician moderating the discussion asked Dr. Winkel to offer a concluding comment. She gazed straight at Sonny and said, "This is as difficult a case as they come. His heart is failing. You can't give any more drugs without wiping out his last bit of immunity, and his body is already crawling with microbes. True, he has made it before, but you can stretch a rubber band only so many times. Then one day, all the elasticity is gone. Instead of rebounding, it snaps."

• •

WHEN SONNY GOT HOME that night, he found a single envelope in his mailbox. As soon as he entered the apartment, he tore it open. A photograph fell to the floor. He read the unsigned typewritten note, to which was stapled an eighty-six-dollar bank check.

I still owe you two subway tokens, Doctor. I'd like to tell you everything that has happened since I last saw you, but the lawyer in me knows it's best to say nothing at all. I feel a bit like Odysseus roaming the world, though one day I too will find my way home. Then we'll have a beer, and I'll give you those tokens. Thanks again for another life. This one is even better than the last, which was, I might add, damn good— despite the part you witnessed.

Sonny examined the postmark on the envelope: Tobago. He bent down and picked up the photograph of a sandy beach, turquoise water, and a spotless blue sky. In the distance he noticed a faint, blurry shadow at the junction of water and sky; he wondered if that might be Trinidad. He imagined the comatose man lying on a beach under the shade of palms, sipping daiquiris with his new girlfriend, listening to calypso on headphones plugged into a radio.

Sonny smiled—very slowly—for the first time in three days.

He turned on the stereo: *Parker's Mood.* His mind followed the twists and turns of Bird's saxophone, but when the piece finished, his thoughts returned to the Transplanted Man. He paced around for a while, then kicked off his shoes and fell into bed without changing. He couldn't sleep. He turned on the light again and sat down on the couch with half a bottle of red wine. He drank it all, then took out the bag of joints that Alvin had recently given him. He smoked until he dozed off.

He dreamed he was on an island of peaceful lagoons and lush greenery, a place enveloped by lavender skies spotted with pink clouds. Butterflies everywhere. On the beaches were wild pigs roaming freely, strong, dark men building canoes, beautiful women with tamarind skin and long, black hair adorned with tropical flowers.

One of the women ran up to him. "Go away!" she shouted. "It's not time yet!"

Suddenly he was surrounded by the men, all holding spears and daggers.

He woke in terror.

• •

DR. GIRI WAS PLEASED to see Sonny at his door, despite the early hour. He tied his nightgown and led Sonny into his office.

Since Sonny's last visit, only five people had come to see Dr. Giri—all for the guru, not the psychotherapist. He'd been asked to tell fortunes, suggest names for babies, broker marriages, even pick horses for offtrack betting. The family's finances were so precarious that he had little choice but to glance at life lines, shuffle cards, and mutter fortune-cookie truisms. It was a bitter compromise for a man who took pride in his academic credentials—whose greatest fear was turning into a stereotype. So frustrated had he become that he'd altered his signboard to remind people that he had not one but two doctorates: It now read, SHAUNAK U. Y. GIRI, PH.D. (INDIA), PH.D. (U.S.).

"I'm glad you decided to come back," said Dr. Giri. "I believe I can help you."

"You can help *me* another day."

"Who are we helping, then?"

"The Transplanted Man."

"I read in last week's paper that he wasn't doing well."

Sonny glanced away. "He's dying. Fast."

"You seem quite attached to him. Sometimes that doesn't help either the patient or the doctor. Why are you so emotionally tied to this case?"

"I just am."

"There's always a reason."

"I like the guy. And . . ."

"Go ahead."

"I have no time for this! The Transplanted Man won't make it through the night. I'll try anything—experimental drugs, prayer, poultices, medicine dances . . ."

"I hope you're not abandoning scientific medicine."

Sonny shook his head from side to side. "I can't remember when I last spent so much time reading textbooks and journals. Unfortunately, the important things aren't written down."

"*Some* important things aren't written down, but you shouldn't forget what is."

"Whatever works."

"What *works* is scientific medicine."

Sonny shrugged. "Sometimes it does, sometimes it doesn't. After more than two years of sticking people with needles, giving them all sorts of medications, putting them through scans that require engineering more sophisticated than it took to put a man on the moon, I realize that the most important thing is a talent for healing. *Talent.* I've got it—maybe the only talent I have. And now is the time to test it."

"You are fortunate to have identified your talent. So few ever find their true calling."

"It's more a call than a calling."

Dr. Giri's brow wrinkled. "Call? What kind of call?"

Sonny didn't reply right away. Dr. Giri shifted uneasily in his ergonomic recliner, his back crackling like a bad connection. Outside in the street a group of boys could be heard laughing on their way to school. Soon their voices faded.

At last Sonny said, "According to my girlfriend, I sleepwalk through the streets in my boxers."

"I know."

Sonny's jaw dropped.

"I don't sleep so well myself, and occasionally I gaze out our upstairs window in the middle of the night. I've seen you."

"Someone my age, sleepwalking like that—it has to be rare."

"Being rare does not make something a call. Besides, how do you know it isn't a wrong number?"

"Funny."

Dr. Giri's face remained serious. "Well?"

"It's about vision."

"You have trouble with your eyes?"

"You know what I mean! No vision, no life."

Dr. Giri fidgeted with his hands but remained silent.

"Maybe we need the guru's take on this."

The sarcasm in Sonny's voice made Dr. Giri flinch. He stared at Sonny for a long time, but as usual Sonny's expression was hard to read.

"We both know I'm not a guru."

"If you were?"

Dr. Giri was uncomfortable with the direction this conversation had taken. What was really on Sonny's mind?

"Until you find your vision," said Dr. Giri, "I suggest you stick with scientific medicine. I don't want you to make a terrible mistake."

"He's dying! Look, I have to come through for him. I've got to try everything I can think of. Everything! Conventional, unconventional, whatever it takes. The Transplanted Man isn't just any patient. He's like . . ."

"Yes?"

An image flashed before Sonny—a photograph that he'd found in his mother's old suitcase fifteen years ago. His mother would never tell him who it was, but even now, he did a double take on anyone who resembled that man.

· ·

AFTER SONNY LEFT Dr. Giri felt he ought to do something. Urgently. What? He couldn't just stand by while Sonny went ahead with . . . well, whatever. Dr. Giri considered calling the hospital authorities. But since he didn't know exactly what Sonny intended to do, he wasn't sure what to tell them. He was also held back by his professional ethic—the pact of confidentiality between himself and his patient. Then again, Sonny hadn't really come as a patient— not this time—but as a colleague, a fellow healer. Wasn't it his duty to report another healer's unprofessional actions?

Yet Dr. Giri couldn't bring himself to pick up the phone. From all Sonny had told him, he was quite sure the Transplanted Man was going to die no matter what. Maybe whatever desperate measures Sonny was considering could be justified under such circumstances. But what really kept Dr. Giri from picking up the phone was something else. Something about Sonny. Not what he said, or even the anguish in his face, but an authentic quality that one healer can detect in another. He'd read somewhere that initiates in ancient tra- ditions often developed peculiar symptoms prior to becoming full-fledged healers. Usually it was a seizure or an experience of mind-body dissociation. This sleepwalking business, this "call" . . . What to make of it? Was it like Schweitzer's call to Africa? Van Gogh's call to paint? What constituted a call? He thought about all those students back in India—bright, idealistic young men who, in the late sixties and early seventies, quit college to become communist guerrillas intent on fomenting a peasant revolt. Some had been his seniors in school. They, too, had heard calls, and followed them—only to be mowed down by police bullets or rot in filthy prisons. Now, over thirty years later, did those who survived believe they had been right in heed- ing the call? To every call was attached a high price. True calls, false calls, ambiguous calls.

Were they all ambiguous?

23

A Weird Night

THE TRANSPLANTED MAN'S MATTRESSES WERE LUMPY TONIGHT. BETWEEN them Gwen had inserted *One Hundred Years of Solitude, Godan,* and *Walden,* each book open to a passage that she had selected after much reflection.

As soon as Gwen went on her break, Sonny and Manny entered the ICU and quietly wheeled the Transplanted Man's bed down the hall to the procedure suite, where emergency heart catheterizations were usually performed. The suite, with its huge, bright central light, resembled an operating room. Above the corner sink were stacked sterile latex gloves, green gowns, blue plastic masks, and paper shoe covers. In another corner a stainless steel cart held sterile scalpel blades, suture material, and needles.

"You sure this is okay?" said Manny, a slight quiver in his voice. "Your eyes are *so* red, Sonny. Are you stoned?"

"Hey, you ought to be a doctor."

"Shit. You sure this is——?"

"You'd better leave, Manny."

"But——"

"Get out!"

Manny left—hesitantly. Sonny locked the door and returned to the Transplanted Man's bed. In the pocket of his white coat were four 10 cc syringes full of medication. Of what? The cannabis had erased their long multisyllabic names from his brain. He hadn't intended to smoke up—certainly not this much. He'd only been trying to calm his nerves, soothe his despair, gather courage for . . . *This.* But his nerves had been too edgy, his despair too great, his courage too weak. So he'd smoked one joint after another, and before he knew it he was so stoned he could barely rise from the floor of his apartment. Some of it had worn off, but his mind was still clouded—and there was no time to wait for it to clear up. Either he did something now or the Transplanted Man died. He had to trust the fact that he'd thought this through—*before*—and that the use of these medications, though perhaps unorthodox, made sense based on what he understood of the Transplanted Man's complex physiology, to the extent it could be understood at all. As far as he was concerned, the medications in his coat pocket were the Transplanted Man's last hope. Serially? As a cocktail? In what proportion? He had figured it all out only hours ago, but now he couldn't remember: The doses had burned up with the weed.

A voice inside him kept saying that he shouldn't be here—in this state. He did his best to silence the voice as he reached into his pocket. He felt the four syringes but he couldn't tell whether or not he was pulling them out. His fingers seemed to be grasping for a syringe even as his hand slipped out of his pocket and uncapped one of them. How could that be? Either the syringe was in his hand or it wasn't. Had he lost his mind? If not, he was losing it now. Eerie images passed through his head. He saw bodies he'd dissected in the anatomy lab as a medical student reassemble themselves, roll off the table, walk away. People he'd seen die in ERs and ICUs came alive, went back to wherever they'd come from. A clenched fist slowly approached his right eye, got bigger and bigger until it hit. He couldn't feel the pain in his socket—just the humiliation of falling to the ground. Someone said, "Get up!" Instead, he sank. Deeper and deeper he sank—until his head was under the dry earth of the Arizona desert, his gravestone marked, INJUN SHOT FOR BEING AN INJUN. Yet six feet underground he could see all the stars. The Milky Way seemed like a rope he could reach for—and climb to a new universe. Morning came, and he saw the sunrise above a tamarind ridge of desert mountains. It was almost holy.

His thoughts caromed off the walls of the procedure room and vanished into another realm. His breathing slowed, deepened. After a while all he could hear was the sound of air rushing in and out of his chest. His fingers and toes felt cold. Soon the chill penetrated his whole body. A minute later the colors in the room changed, turning first subtly green, then purple. The Transplanted Man's body gleamed, iridescent. His skin slowly thinned, clarified. Sonny could see the muscles, bones, and tendons underneath. Then they also lost color, and he saw faint shadows of organs in the chest and belly. Soon the Transplanted Man had become entirely transparent except for his pulsating viscera. The bluish gray lungs expanded and contracted. Between them peeked out a rapidly beating heart. The dark liver sat above a shiny tangle of intestine. Gradually all that became transparent, too. The only thing left was the transplanted kidney: purple, blotched, swollen to the size of a fetus.

Sonny's fingers felt as though they would spark if they touched. Now his electric hands seemed to separate from the rest of him and enter the Transplanted Man's body. He could feel the erratic pulsations of the Transplanted Man's blood vessels, the slowing heartbeat that, after a few seconds, synchronized with his own. Then his hands moved deeper, gently caressing the inflamed kidney. He could feel its warmth. Yes—alive, if barely.

Suddenly he was seized by the greatest anxiety he'd ever known. Here he was with his hands inside the Transplanted Man—perhaps in a position to save him—and yet he didn't know what to do! He abruptly let go of the kidney, stepped back. The Transplanted Man became opaque again. A profound sadness invaded Sonny.

Pounding.

In his head?

No, the door. The pounding of fists—loud, painful.

He wanted the pounding to stop. He went to the door, unlocked it.

"What the hell is happening in here?" asked Gwen as she entered, Manny trailing close behind.

"Nothing," muttered Sonny. "Nothing at all."

He walked back over to the Transplanted Man's bed. A vague memory of music flitted through his mind. Maybe music . . . ? It couldn't hurt. He turned to Manny. "You say you can sing. Sing something."

"It's not the right time," said Manny, staring at the Transplanted Man.

"It's the only time this man has," insisted Sonny. "I know him. He'll like it."

"I can't think of anything appropriate."

"That song from *Sholay*, 'Yeh Dosti.'"

Manny was silent.

"Go on!"

Manny hummed a few lines, then stopped. "It isn't right, Sonny."

"It *is* right," Sonny replied, anger creeping into his voice.

Gwen came to Manny's defense. "If he doesn't want to—"

"Sing!"

Glancing around nervously, Manny began to sing.

The ventilator continued to blow oxygen in and out of the Transplanted Man's lungs; the cardiac monitor beeped with every heartbeat; assorted bells and buzzers went off as pressures changed and drugs infused.

Somehow it all turned into an orchestra, accompanying Manny perfectly.

• •

SHORTLY AFTER MIDNIGHT GWEN and Manny wheeled the Transplanted Man's bed over to his corner of the ICU. While Gwen reconnected the patient to various tubes and wires, the nurse who was supposed to relieve her walked up. "I can take over," she said. "By the way, what were you guys doing in the procedure suite?"

"Oh . . . Just Dr. Seth's usual hocus-pocus."

Gwen reconfirmed the machine settings, then went over to Sonny, who had been observing from a distance, his hand in the pocket of his doctor's coat. The four syringes were still there, his pocket fully soaked: easily 40 ccs of liquid. His mind was a blank. Had the *entire* contents of those four 10 cc syringes leaked into his pocket while he'd been fumbling with them? Had he injected *nothing at all* into the Transplanted Man?

"Maybe we should stay here tonight," said Gwen.

Sonny didn't reply.

Gwen rested her hand on his shoulder. "Stay, then?"

"Let's get out of here."

"Your place?"

It occurred to him that his apartment must still be reeking of pot. "No, yours."

"Why?"

He didn't answer.

She didn't push him. She had more important questions. Like: What had he been doing in there with the Transplanted Man?

· ·

IT WAS JUST PAST 1:00 A.M. when they stepped into Gwen's apartment.

"I'm going to take a quick shower," said Sonny.

Gwen had been hungry all day. She hadn't thought much of it until she watched Sonny undo his shirt. Now she understood. As usual, understanding made no difference. With so much going on in the ICU these past few days, she hadn't been meditating—the only thing that seemed to mute her instincts. But she really had no reason to control herself right now. The strange events of the night had created tremendous tension in her. It required release. She grabbed Sonny's half-unbuttoned shirt, almost ripping it, and they fell into bed.

Gwen tried to wrest control of their lovemaking, as she'd always been able to do during her hypersexed states, no matter who the man was. For the first time this was impossible. She wrapped her legs around Sonny's hips tightly, squeezed with all her might. Men much stronger had submitted, but he went on as if the vise her thighs gripped him with was elastic. There was a gentle rhythm in the way he was making love to her tonight. After a while it began to get boring; her current mood demanded more acrobatics. She kept changing positions, using all her ingenuity. He didn't fight, just kept rocking her with that same steady rhythm: It was like screwing a metronome! Out of frustration, and just to get it over with, she yielded. Then something happened. She grew *so* relaxed—seemed to levitate. Higher and higher she floated. She'd never experienced anything like this before, a feeling of tranquillity deeper than her deepest meditative trances. Somehow Sonny had calmed her wild brain; she wanted it to last forever. Then, as she approached her climax, she got a long look at something inside Sonny—uncharted, turbulent. Could its power ever be harnessed? Or would he—*they*—forever be at its mercy?

Soon the pleasure was so intense she forgot her questions.

· ·

AFTERWARD SHE LIT a cigarette, took a puff, and passed it over to Sonny.

"Why do you do this Hollywood thing with cigarettes?" he asked.

"Hollywood?"

"You know, smoke after sex. It's the only time I see you with a cigarette."

"There are moments when I like the idea of breathing smoke and fire. It makes me feel less vulnerable, I guess. It makes me feel like—"

"A dragon lady?"

"I'd prefer calling it the George Sand look."

"Who's he?"

"Forget it."

"Do you still feel the need to breathe smoke and fire with me?"

After everything that had happened tonight, she didn't know what to think. "It's an old habit," she finally said. "Comes back sometimes."

"You didn't answer."

"Some questions shouldn't be answered."

They heard the feet of the man upstairs shuffle across the ceiling. A minute later the toilet flushed. The man's footsteps retraced their path across the ceiling. Then, a soft thud as he dropped into bed.

"Do you think the Transplanted Man is going to make it?" asked Gwen.

"God, I hope that kidney opens up! A few drops of urine will change two lives."

"Two?"

Sonny didn't reply. Still naked, he got out of bed and slowly paced in the dark. When he looked through the window, he saw more stars than he'd ever seen hovering over the city. One star in the handle of the Dipper seemed unnaturally bright, like a beacon of some sort, inviting him. Where? For what? He tried to gather his thoughts, scattered like all those stars. Finally he got back into bed with Gwen. He took the last few puffs of her cigarette and watched the glowing embers extinguish.

Suddenly he sat up and switched on the light. He needed to know the Transplanted Man's blood pressure, heart rate, arterial oxygen level, pulmonary capillary wedge pressure, latest EKG tracing, complete blood count, serum creatinine and electrolyte measurements, and—most important—his urine output.

He reached for the phone to call the ICU.

24

Liquid Gold

IT WAS A STERILE VINYL BAG HOOKED ONTO THE BEDSIDE RAILING. To the bag was connected a long plastic tube that coursed under the bedsheet, snaked over the Transplanted Man's thin, hairy, brown thigh, and fed into a soft rubber urinary catheter, which had been inserted into his penis with the aid of lubricant jelly. The catheter traveled up the Transplanted Man's urethra and into his bladder, where it remained, tethered by a deflatable balloon. All eyes were on the vinyl bag that morning. To everybody's disappointment, not a single drop of urine was in it.

"More Lasix?" Gwen asked Sonny.

"His kidneys stopped responding to diuretics long ago."

"It won't hurt."

"Okay, go ahead. Two hundred forty milligrams, IV push. And turn on the dopamine again—four a minute. If he doesn't piss soon, it'll be all over."

Sonny stared at the vinyl bag as though he might be able somehow to coax the Transplanted Man's kidney into producing urine by an act of will. He stared five useless minutes. As he walked away, he cursed himself for what he did last night.

He fretted the rest of the morning, returning every fifteen minutes to check the empty vinyl bag. What else to do? Nothing. Just as there had been nothing to do last night—which was what had led him to try . . . well, whatever it was.

Then came a drop.

Gwen saw it first: a tiny bead of yellow liquid hiding at the junction of the clear vinyl bag and the plastic tubing.

"Sonny!" she yelled across the intensive care unit.

Heads turned. She flushed as Sonny raced across the room with so much force that he almost knocked her onto the Transplanted Man's bed.

"Urine?"

"Just a drop."

"Really? Where?"

Gwen pointed.

"Shake it, squeeze it!"

"What?"

"The tube, Gwen, the tube! Manipulate it."

Gwen gently shook the plastic tubing.

"Here, let me try."

He jiggled the tubing every which way.

Another drop, larger and yellower, rolled down, coalesced with the drop already in the corner of the vinyl bag. Sonny reached for Gwen's hand. She squeezed his fingers when another drop rolled down. Then came another. And another. Soon there was a thimbleful. Sonny and Gwen continued to hold hands, their eyes fixed on the bag, as the drops turned into a trickle, the trickle into a stream. In half an hour the stream had become a river.

"It's a fucking flood!" said Manny when he walked up to the bed around eleven o'clock.

"I never realized how marvelous a color urine is," said Sonny, smiling broadly.

Gwen's eyes were moist. "It really *is* beautiful."

"Beautiful or not," said Manny, "someone ought to change that bag full of piss before it bursts and they make a poor orderly clean it up."

Gwen left to get a new bag.

Manny turned to Sonny. "Guess whatever you did last night accomplished something after all—what d'ya think?"

Sonny watched the fluorescent wave pattern on the screen of the cardiac monitor for a few seconds. He wanted to say yes—that *something* he did last night had affected the Transplanted Man's kidney, and maybe the rest of the patient as well. But what? His mind, which had been hallucinating then, was now fully aware of the complex technology keeping the Transplanted Man alive. In the light of day the connection between what, if anything, he did last night and the Transplanted Man's improvement seemed purely coincidental: God *does* play dice with the universe, and sometimes He throws snake eyes.

"Well?" said Manny. "Did you do this?"

"Can't say."

"So you think what you did had nothing to do with it?"

"Haven't a clue."

Manny pointed to the solutions dripping into the Transplanted Man's veins. "Then you think it was all these medicines?"

"No idea."

Manny's expression became thoughtful. "Hey, do you think my song helped?"

Sonny smiled. "Maybe."

• •

To CELEBRATE, SONNY and Manny went over to Tiger's for lunch. The place was packed with tourists who had come to see the hypokinetic man.

Tiger was truly apologetic. "You, my most prized customers, stuck with me through terrible times. Yet now I must make you wait because of the spectacle outside!"

"It's all right," said Manny. "Your bank account needs to recover from those weeks you were shut down."

Tiger grinned, his double chin forming a tiny third chin. "I have to admit that fellow out there has been a boon for business. But I must warn you about today's menu. You see, for some of my newer customers, it's their first encounter with Indian cuisine; I've altered the seasonings because they can't tolerate my spicy-spicy dishes. A trace of hot pepper makes most white people turn red. The other reason is that I'm trying to develop an Indo-American style—something tasty yet convenient."

"Indian fast food?" asked Sonny.

"Not exactly. But nobody has done Indian food right yet—for the American palate. The Chinese and Mexicans have done it so well that what they eat has become almost as standard as hamburgers and pizza. All supermarkets carry frozen Mexican and Chinese dinners. Why not Indian? So I study leftovers on every plate. Each day I make slight changes in the menu. That way, my new customers get what they want. Almost no hot pepper, bland by your standards, but I tell them it's 'a subtle mix of Oriental spices.' They like hearing that. And everything is dished out separately—no mixing. The way we usually prepare Indian food is too chaotic for the average American eye and palate. It saturates the senses. Of course, that's exactly its beauty—for us. Here, though, they have a different concept of beauty. But I'd trade any Hollywood heroine for Rekha."

Manny grinned.

Tiger's expression became serious. "Not so funny, really. Though you fight against their standards, you too are trapped by them. Atul, my son, faces the same predicament. It's even worse for my daughter. She's so beautiful, my little Rohini, yet her beauty goes unappreciated. And now her father panders . . ." Tiger bit his lower lip.

"It's just business," said Manny.

"Maybe," said Tiger. "But I have chosen this. In the past, I had been very much against the current 'fusion' fashion that turns all of Asia into a single sweet and tangy dish. Now I must take back my words. A man makes all kinds of decisions in life without a clue as to where they will lead. In the end, though, whatever I earn is for my children. . . . I've gotten sidetracked. Again I apologize for today's lunch. It's on me."

"Not necessary," said Sonny.

"I insist. That statue outside has more than made up for my earlier losses."

Sonny and Manny waited another twenty minutes before Tiger was finally able to seat them at the table in the far corner of the restaurant.

"Say, Manny, I've been meaning to ask you something. The other day I got a letter from an ex-patient. Postmarked Tobago. He sent a photograph, too— mainly of a sandy beach and turquoise water, but in the distance was a small blurry mass of something, maybe land. So, I was wondering. Can you see Trinidad from Tobago?"

"I don't remember ever looking from Tobago. But there's a spot in Trinidad from where you can see Tobago on a clear day. Why are you so interested?"

"It's just that Trinidad seems like—I don't really know if it's true, which is why I'm asking—a place for everyone, where everybody has come from somewhere else, where the cultures are all mixed, unencumbered by ancestral echoes."

"Sounds like Trinidad—except for that unencumbered part. Everyone's pretty encumbered. Those ancestral echoes can get real loud. Take my dad, for instance."

"Yeah?"

"It's like this. My dad used to be a batsman for the West Indies cricket team. Once they played the Indian team in Port of Spain. Though my dad's side of the family had migrated over a century ago, my dad had always been proud of his Indian ancestry. Playing his fellow Indians in Trinidad was an honor, or so he said to everyone. But after the Indians lost the match—my dad played brilliantly, by the way—one Indian player told a reporter that

Trinidadian Indians weren't genuine Indians. In fairness, it was never quite clear what the Indian player was trying to say. But the remark was taken as the insult it was probably meant to be and, needless to say, created a huge outcry. The Indian embassy even issued a public apology. I think the whole affair hurt my dad more than anyone else. After that he never claimed to be Indian again. 'We're different,' he kept telling me, 'and that's that.' So when I started to talk about going to Bombay to sing in films, my dad and I had lots of fights. 'There's so much here in Trinidad,' my dad said, 'the whole world—India, China, Africa, Central and South America—all on one tiny Caribbean island. Why do you want to go to a place where they'll think you're a fake? Stop dreaming! India is nothing like what those silly films make it out to be. It's a poor country full of narrow-minded people. Trinidad's your homeland and a thousand times better!' My dad just went on and on like that, day after day. It's sad. Me and my dad used to be very close." Manny slowly shook his head. "So you see, neither me nor my dad has gotten rid of India, even though my family has to go back four generations before you find anyone who's even set foot there. The shadow of India still hangs over us like hurricane clouds."

"That shadow hangs over all of us," said Sonny. "You can't get rid of it; you can't come to terms with it, either. It's like one of those impossible problems mathematicians try to solve their whole lives and die thinking about."

Manny pursed his lips. "That's pretty depressing. Must be different for people in India, don't you think?"

"I'm not so sure. Between my sophomore and junior years in college, I spent a summer traveling through India. The whole country was pulling its own hairs out then. The central government teetering, states trying to secede, riots, bombings. Maybe things are better now, but one wonders for how long. I don't pretend to understand the ins and outs of Indian politics, but I'd bet that it's the shadow of that same albatross, just a different part."

"That bird has quite a wingspan."

Sonny took a sip of ice water. "Hey, do they need doctors in Trinidad?"

"No. People never get sick in paradise."

"What do you think, could it work for me?"

"Trinidad might be too much for you. For me, it's home—and, frankly, if I wasn't so desperate to try my luck in Bollywood, I'd ultimately go back. But, Sonny, you might find yourself jumping into the ocean and swimming to Tobago, which is the way tropical islands are supposed to be. Trinidad casts pretty huge shadows of its own for such a small island. The place has got a whole different kind of power."

"That's what I want."

"You sure you don't just want to head off to Shangri-la?"

"No, I want someplace *real*."

"Shangri-la *is* real. Ask Alvin."

Sonny couldn't help chuckling.

"From the way you talk about the Arizona desert," said Manny, "I'd have thought you'd want to go back there."

"Believe me, I've thought about it. Some of my happiest hours have been spent wandering through the desert. But it's the past—and a very mixed one at that."

Manny sipped his water. "Sometimes I think that the part of Trinidad where I come from isn't so different from here—the hospital, this neighborhood."

"You think it might work for me?"

"Does this place work for you?"

"Sometimes. Not enough."

"Then there's your answer."

SLINGS AND ARROWS

25

Kismet

A STORM ORIGINATING OFF AN UNINHABITED ATLANTIC ATOLL SWEPT through the Caribbean as a full-fledged hurricane. Then it crawled up the eastern coast of the United States with almost no dissipation of its ninety-mile-an-hour winds. One by one, coastal towns succumbed. Power lines fell. Streets flooded, and beachfront homes were destroyed.

Forecasters up and down the coast predicted that the angry gale would bypass New York City. It would head back to the ocean, they said, miss the city by seventy miles. At most, heavy rains would give the streets a much-needed wash. But at the last minute the storm turned the other way. When it arrived at two that night, the sleeping inhabitants of the metropolis were caught unprepared. Huge windowpanes in skyscrapers shattered. The lights of the most brilliant city in the world hadn't flickered so tenuously in four decades.

The power to the research wing of the hospital went out. The old emergency generator should have kicked in, but it had aged too much. All the freezers in Dr. Ranjan's lab stopped. Inside one was a tube containing the world's supply of insomnin. While the frozen material thawed, molecules of the protein underwent contortions and distortions. As the hours passed and the tube warmed up, the protein molecules began to degrade, losing their sleep-depriving efficacy. By the time Dr. Ranjan stepped into the lab the next morning—having spent over four hours in gridlocked traffic fretting over this very possibility—the protein, purified from Johny Walker's descendants, was dead.

"Oh, no!"

"Shit!" was all Alvin could say when he arrived a few minutes later. "Shit! Shit! Shit!"

"All the work gone—just like that!"

"What now?" asked Alvin, hoping Ranjy would find a ray of sunlight somewhere.

Head bent and shoulders sunken, Dr. Ranjan slowly walked away.

. .

AN HOUR LATER Dr. Ranjan entered Paudha's office. The CEO was standing with his back to the door, gazing out the window at the rain. Dr. Ranjan cleared his throat. Paudha turned suddenly, like a gunslinger ready to fire. "What's this about an urgent matter, Ranjan?"

"Very urgent—extremely urgent, actually—*so* urgent—"

"Well? I have exactly one minute for you. The storm has caused the hospital a lot of problems."

"That's it! A *ter-ri-ble* tragedy!"

"What happened? Spit it out!"

Dr. Ranjan spat—or, rather, sprayed Paudha's face with saliva—as he blurted, "The insomnin! It's gone!"

Paudha scowled, pulled out a handkerchief, and wiped his face. "What do you mean, *gone?* How can it be gone?"

"The power to the freezer went out during the hurricane, the emergency generator failed, and the protein thawed!"

"Then freeze it back up! What's the big deal?"

"It's a very big deal, actually. You see, when you isolate most proteins, they retain their structural and functional properties over extended periods only when frozen—"

"So?"

"When they thaw out—and if they remain thawed—proteins can lose their activity. Forever."

"Which means?"

Dr. Ranjan closed his eyes. "The insomnin no longer works, actually."

"I was afraid you were going to say that. Now, look here . . . Look, I said! Open your goddamn eyes!"

Dr. Ranjan looked at Paudha. In the CEO's narrowing eyes, Dr. Ranjan saw only menace.

"Make more!"

"But it requires lots of work, lots of time, and lots of luck. Actually, I don't know if—"

"Listen to me, Ranjan. Do you know how much two hundred million dollars is?"

Dr. Ranjan's face turned pale. "Actually . . ."

Paudha lifted a sheet of white paper from his desk and held it eight inches from Dr. Ranjan's nose. The creamy sheet bore the letterhead of a law firm, Diamond and Heeralal. Dr. Ranjan realized it was a letter of intent—a preliminary agreement between the hospital and Univelta Biopharm.

"*Actually,*" said Paudha, "it's two hundred thousand thousand dollars: a dollar sign followed by two and seven zeros."

"Eight, actually—eight zeros."

"Make more, godammit!"

• •

"Such a mess!" Dr. Ranjan told Menaka Bhushan half an hour later in her office. "I had no idea, Menaka, not a single clue, that it would turn out like this. Kismet has never been kind to me, but now it is clear: She has made it her mission to ruin me. A knockout punch! Everyone will think I'm a liar. I was foolish to make these claims before publication—in front of TV cameras, too!—but Paudha twisted my arm. Somehow everything got exaggerated and oversimplified, and . . . and . . . just see my predicament! You believe me, don't you, Menaka? You understand the difficulties of experimental research, the subtleties of science, the complex nature of sleep?"

"Yes, Nirdosh, I believe you."

He gave her a grateful smile. "Menaka, I knew you'd understand. Important things are hard, and a sleepless man has only so much energy. I can't afford to be diverted by all this. Life goes by *so* fast in your forties. Soon a whole decade will have slipped by, and then retirement will come, and I will have done nothing with my life. Nothing at all! This was my one chance—and now it's gone!"

"I know it has been difficult," said Menaka.

Dr. Ranjan gazed out her office window at a break in the clouds. "I always wanted to fly toward the sun. Like Icarus. Everybody said I was a fool, that my wings would melt. I still kept trying—had to. These past weeks, I've flown very close to the sun, Menaka. *Very* close. My wings seemed forged from a special alloy that couldn't melt. But I turned out to be the fool everyone said I was. My wings were wax, always had been."

Menaka played with her bangs. "Nirdosh, you're a wimp."

"Pardon?"

"Wimp. Milksop. A gutless wonder. You let people push you around. You don't take control of matters. If you did, you might be able to fix this mess, as you call it. And I'm not talking about what happened after last night's storm. That's Kismet, as you say, and no one has control over *him.* The whole thing is so pathetic! You've made such an amazing discovery, the kind that should place you in contention for a Lasker or Nobel. Bad luck, yes—a mean trick of Fate, I grant you—but you've made everything worse by letting others dictate to you. The CEO is right, though. *You have to make more.* I'm sure you can. Nirdosh, you're an extraordinary scientist, perhaps an even more extraordinary person. You're also a wimp."

Dr. Ranjan looked at the floor. "You're right, Menaka. I *am* a wimp."

"Damn!" shouted Menaka. "You infuriate me!"

Dr. Ranjan removed his glasses and wiped his eyes with his handkerchief.

Menaka rose, walked to her office door, peeked outside, then shut and locked it. She glanced at her watch and began to unbutton her blouse.

"Menaka, I . . . I don't understand."

"I'm busy as hell this afternoon," she said. "Eleven more patients. The next appointment is at two—a new patient with hypersomnia. Which gives me exactly twenty-three minutes to make a man out of you."

• •

CALAMITY HAD PILED ON CALAMITY, imbroglio upon imbroglio. First, the insomnin fiasco—then this! So thought Dr. Ranjan as he sat in his office after the most ecstatic twenty-three minutes of his life. Eventually, though, the music of Menaka's bangles that had been playing in his head was replaced by the music of a uniformed band at his wedding ten years ago. He remembered how he rode a thin white horse to the entrance of Ashoka Hotel, surrounded by dancing baaratis; the uniformed band playing *"Mere Sapno Ki Rani";* the congratulations from people he didn't know; the sly winks from his friends and cousins; sweets and colas everywhere; the silly antics of the family pundit during the endless wedding ceremony; the ghee sprinkled over the fire, its sweet suffocating smoke; his kurta knotted to her sari, silk to silk, while he led her around the flames; the night of lying awake beside each other, inches apart, but not touching—until Bhavana finally squeezed his hand just before dawn.

The montage of memories wouldn't stop. In no time, his mind was a tempest rivaling the one that had swept through New York City last night. Not only had he betrayed his wife—that was horrible enough—but his quest for the secrets of Nature had been undone by the secrets of Menaka's body. So much had been lost in twenty-three minutes! He hadn't a shred of integrity left.

The man who often felt guilty for insignificant reasons was now tormented by a genuine one. The pile of guilt quickly grew to Himalayan proportions. His conscience kept slapping him—harder, harder. His crime required punishment. He performed his standard penance: standing upon one leg and biting his tongue. But this was no standard sin, and he didn't stop at his usual pain threshold. Instead, he kept biting long after blood started trickling down his lips, long after he was crying from both pain in his body and pain in his soul. The room began to swirl, at first slowly, then with great rapidity. He was forced to put his leg down. He staggered, on the verge of collapse. As he sank into the cushioned chair behind his desk, his only thought was that his sin demanded more penance. He rose once more, stood on one leg, and started biting his tongue again.

••

MENAKA BHUSHAN WAS GLAD she didn't have time to think about what had happened. She'd been married once—to a man unhealthily devoted to his mother. Having finally gotten over that disaster, she had vowed to proceed cautiously before becoming involved again.

Now this!

She did her best to concentrate on her new patient, a sixty-six-year-old man suffering from chronic sleepiness. His heavily lined face was still handsome, and when he smiled there was a roguish glint in his eyes.

"How long have you been like this?"

"Ever since I went on a worldwide tour a couple of years ago—although I don't know if there's a real connection."

"Ever had a sleep study?"

"Several. My old doctor said he'd forward my records. I guess they haven't arrived yet. I've had EEGs, CAT scans, MRIs, lots more."

"We'll track down your records," said Menaka. "Now why don't I examine you? Strip down to your underpants."

"I'm not wearing any, Doctor. My washer is broken and, well, I'm sorry . . ."

"There's a clean gown on the examining table. I'll step out for a moment while you change."

Just as Menaka reached for the doorknob, the door swung open.

Dr. Ranjan stood before her. "Menaka, we must talk!"

"Can't you see that I'm with a patient? The receptionist shouldn't have—Oh, Nirdosh! What happened to your mouth? It's bloody!"

"I bit my tongue—slightly, actually."

"Let me take a look."

Touched by Menaka's concern, Dr. Ranjan opened his mouth.

"Nirdosh, you didn't *slightly* bite your tongue; you nearly bit it off! How did you do this? Oh, never mind—I don't want to know. Listen to me. Go to the emergency room. Ask for Dr. Sonny Seth, if he's still around. I spoke with him an hour ago about one of my other patients. He's a little odd, but he definitely knows what he's doing. You know him? Good. After he sews up your tongue, go home. We'll talk about all this later."

Without a further word, Dr. Ranjan left.

Menaka stared at the closed door, lost in thoughts of Dr. Ranjan—fearful that his shredded tongue was only the first of many consequences.

After a while her patient asked, "Is everything okay?"

Menaka had completely forgotten about him. "Uh . . . yes . . . Nothing to get concerned about. I'm very sorry. He shouldn't have barged in like that."

"Your boyfriend?"

"No!"

• •

BY THE TIME DR. RANJAN got to the emergency room, his partially severed tongue had swollen. At that moment the ER wasn't too hectic, so Sonny attended to him quickly. After fourteen stitches Dr. Ranjan's tongue was sewn back together—though numb from local anesthetic and even more swollen.

Sonny snipped the ends of the last suture. "Do you want to talk about this?"

Even though Dr. Ranjan couldn't talk about *this*, he was desperate to utter a few words, however unimportant, to a sympathetic ear. He nodded.

"Go ahead, my friend."

"Baa, baa, baa, baa, baa . . ."

Dr. Ranjan frowned. He tried again. "Baa, baa, baa . . ."

"Your tongue must be incredibly swollen," said Sonny. "Make sure you suck on some ice when you get home. You can write, if you'd like."

A solitary tear rolled down Dr. Ranjan's cheek as he shook his head from side to side. It was best not to communicate at all until he'd thought over everything.

He left the hospital and drove home slowly, taking the longest route.

When he stepped into his house, he conveyed what had happened to his worried wife through pen and paper. "I was assaulted by a hoodlum in the parking lot," he wrote.

Bhavana read the note to the kids, who were full of questions.

"But, Daddy," asked Neel, "how come the robber only beat up your tongue?"

Dr. Ranjan gave his son a painful, pleading look.

"Let Daddy rest," said Bhavana. "Can't you see how much this has hurt him?"

· ·

DR. RANJAN COULDN'T SLEEP. That was nothing new, but tonight there was more to it. As usual he heard every noise in the house: innocent creaks in the attic, a drippy faucet downstairs, the periodic hum of the heating system, the leaves rustling outside, the groans of cars passing by. To these irritations was added the growing discomfort from his swollen tongue now that the anesthetic had worn off. He could feel the pain from every one of the fourteen stitches that Sonny had put in.

He did his utmost to avoid thinking about the events that had led to the pain. All his years of solitary research had built a monkish element into his character, and his powers of concentration, when invoked, were formidable. So great were they that on occasion he had actually managed to will himself to sleep. This is exactly what he now attempted. He meditated on the word *the*—the letters *T*, *H*, and *E*. He was so spent that it worked.

Forty minutes later he woke up—sweating, heart racing fast, mind racing faster. What if he was wrong about the sleep inhibitor? A man who desperately seeks something will find it—even if it doesn't exist! He had announced his discovery prematurely, and there was no longer any proof. Not a single molecule of active insomnin! Who knew if he and Alvin would be able to purify more? If not, he'd never be able to vindicate himself. They'd say what they had always said—that he was a deluded nut. Or worse! That he had lied. A world full of liars is quick to believe such accusations.

Maybe he really was a liar! A man who cheats on his wife can easily lie to the rest of the world. Had he lied to himself, too? Insomnin was his dream. Had he fooled himself into perpetrating a hoax? The more he thought about it, the more plausible it seemed. Of what value are good intentions if they go astray? How different are they from evil intentions when they produce the same result? Just look what had happened today with Menaka!

He worried that his heart might not be able to withstand so much stress. He rested his hand on his belly. Soft, a little flabby. His panic grew. He didn't exercise enough. Nor did he eat right. He was a prime candidate for a heart attack!

He rolled out of bed, tiptoed down the hall. As he passed the children's room, he overheard Archana whispering to Neel in the dark.

"I got a new Barbie."

"A white one or a brown one?"

"Brown."

"Can I see her naked?"

"Tomorrow. I'll take off her clothes, and you can spank her bum."

Dr. Ranjan fought off an urge to intervene, deciding that a six- and a seven-year-old could have an innocent late-night conversation on this topic, even in America.

Downstairs he placed two ice cubes in a glass. Bhavana always kept fresh lassi waiting for him in the fridge, believing an old tale about its hypnotic properties. The ice-cold concoction soothed his tongue. He went into the family room, slipped on the stereo headphones. He chose to listen to the *Goldberg Variations*, originally written for an insomniac prince. Dr. Ranjan had heard the recording so often he liked to think that Bach had composed the music just for him.

He yawned, decided to attempt sleep again. After stubbing his little toe on the leg of the coffee table—and yelping louder than warranted by the injury—he limped back upstairs and lay in bed, where he listened to Bhavana's faint snores. Again his mind became occupied with the insomnin fiasco. What was the probability that . . . ? Oh, it was so improbable it could only have happened to him! Whatever higher power was in charge of individual fates had singled him out for extra doses of rotten luck. And yet, despite the circumstances, it was against his nature to remain trapped in despair for long. There were always more experiments, and with every new experiment the universe had the potential to be reinvented. So did his life.

He realized he had an erection. Very clearly he visualized Menaka's round chocolate breasts, her cinnamon nipples. Yet painful thoughts kept intruding. Infidelity, dishonor—and the fear that he might lose the only thing he valued more than science. His family.

No longer in a panic, he saw in all this a certain complication that wasn't without appeal—the perverse satisfaction even a decent man derives from intrigue. His life until now hadn't been entirely devoid of complications, but nothing like this. In an odd way he'd always viewed the lack of such complications as a major deficiency. Now there were complications everywhere. Would he lose what mattered most because of his lapse today?

He went limp and began to sob silently. Had Bhavana woken, he would have confessed right there.

• •

WHEN BHAVANA CAME DOWNSTAIRS the next morning, she kissed his forehead. "How is your tongue, Nirdosh?"

Sitting at the kitchen table, he couldn't look her in the eye. Nor could he look at the small bronze statue of Shiva Nataraja in the far corner of the room. Bhavana took an egg from the fridge, and he focused his attention on its smooth, unblemished surface. She cracked the egg. Yolk and white fell into the hot skillet, sizzled. He turned the other way and gazed out the window at the willow tree, whose branch he'd cut for Johny Walker's cremation. He became lost in fond memories of Johny.

Bhavana poured him a glass of orange juice. "Are you sure you don't want to stay home today?"

If he was sure of nothing else, he was sure of that.

"I can take the kids to school."

He shook his head no.

"Sure?"

He nodded and again stared out the window at the willow tree. He had always liked looking at trees: If he were a philosopher, or a scientist lucky enough to study a purely abstract question for its own sake, he'd try to formulate a theory of trees. Not just the kind in his backyard but also the ductal trees of lungs and kidneys, and countless other treelike structures: corals, blood vessels, lightning, river deltas . . . Might trees harbor a great secret that transcended the animate and inanimate? As his mind drifted, Dr. Ranjan imagined an infinite tree that he could climb and climb, following its endlessly bifurcating branches until he reached a fluffy cloud that would forever hide him from the rest of the world.

The chatter of his children brought him back. Bhavana buttoned Archana's sweater, then tied Neel's shoes. She was a good wife and mother, he thought, but she was so preoccupied with the family that they rarely spoke about anything other than this or that bill, calling someone to clean out the chimney before the first snowfall, dentist appointments for everyone, parent-teacher meetings, swimming lessons. It went on and on, nibbling away at the day, the week, the month, the year. There was hardly any time for dreaming. And he was, above all, a dreamer.

"Nirdosh, the children are ready!"

Dr. Ranjan hadn't touched his orange juice yet. Now he gulped it in a rush. The acid set his tongue on fire. He rushed to the sink, where he rinsed his mouth until most of the sting was gone. He went to the freezer for an ice cube to suck on. Then he gathered the children's lunch bags.

Just before the three of them stepped out the door, Bhavana hugged the kids and planted a gentle kiss on Dr. Ranjan's cheek. "I hope you feel better, Nirdosh. Be careful in the parking lot tonight!"

So great was his guilt that he hurried away without even attempting to say good-bye. He helped the children into the car, fastened their seat belts, and drove them to school.

Six minutes later he parallel-parked, got the kids out, and crossed the street when the gray-haired crossing guard allowed them to proceed. He squeezed the children's hands. Their soft, innocent fingers, tense over the prospect of another school day, soothed his own anxieties. He felt a deep communion with his scions: the three of them against the world.

Near the school's entrance, he hugged the children until Neel whispered angrily, "Stop it, Daddy! Everyone's looking!"

"Do you know how much I love both of you?" he said in barely comprehensible speech.

Archana laughed. "Daddy, you sound funny."

Dr. Ranjan tried to laugh with his daughter but couldn't.

The school bell rang, and the children ran off.

It was a pleasant morning. He drove to work listening to Mahler on the car radio. It started to feel warm. He turned down the heat. The reception of the classical station gradually weakened, and he switched to an oldies rock station: the Supremes. One catchy love song followed another. His spirits lifted. By the time he took a left turn into the hospital parking lot, his only thoughts were of Menaka.

26

Making Sense of It All

A VIRTUAL CORPSE ONLY TWO WEEKS AGO, THE TRANSPLANTED MAN had, to the amazement of all, regained consciousness. But he remained groggy, confused. Sometimes he thought he was still in India. Once he launched into a parliamentary speech on religious tolerance, national unity, and inflation. For eleven hours he ranted in a hybrid of English and Hindi, banging his fist on the bedrail—especially when he got to the subject of cooking oil prices—until, much to the relief of ICU patients and staff alike, he fell asleep, exhausted.

Although the Transplanted Man's brain was still in a muddled state—and his heart, always problematic, beat erratically—his other organs were racing toward full recovery. The transplanted kidney led the way. Autumn was waning on the streets of Little India, but in the Transplanted Man's new kidney, half a million glomeruli were in full bloom. The tree of the kidney's collecting system stood tall and sturdy, its branches proudly supporting their monumental physiological burden. The white blood cells that had only recently been attacking the kidney's slender tubules—viciously spitting out degradative enzymes and cytotoxins—had been vanquished. Freed from foreign invaders, the tubule cells regained their natural earthy color. The intricate geometry inside the kidney became reestablished: Standing side by side, the tamarind-hued tubule cells looked like the Midtown skyline on a clear day.

For days Sonny had been trying to convince himself that there was no connection between whatever he had done that night in the ICU and the Transplanted Man's remarkable recovery. Over and over his mind replayed the events of that night, trying to pin down details. Nothing would stay pinned. Might it simply have been chance? Two random events that had nothing to do with each other? That made the most sense. "Correlation does not mean cause," he kept telling himself, repeating a favorite line of his college statistics professor. Yes, everything could be explained rationally. Quasi-rationally? But not irrationally! Just because he'd seen *something* in a drugged state—just because he *thought* he'd done *something* in that state—didn't mean anything had *really* happened outside the confines of his mind. To believe otherwise was a delusion, right? How many patients on the psychiatry ward thought they were Gandhi or Tipu Sultan? Lots. And when he doubled their dose of antipsychotic medication, they once more became whoever they, in reality, were.

He knew that Gwen was bothered by his moodiness, but she said nothing and he didn't explain. How could he explain what he didn't understand? The Transplanted Man's recovery *had* to be just another example of the incredible resilience programmed into the human body. After all, if not the Transplanted Man, someone who'd come back from the dead many times, then who? And yet, there was no denying *something* had happened. Sonny himself felt transformed. Even his past acquired a new veneer. The troubles of his youth seemed part of a natural design to ensure that he turned out differently from everyone else. Had the world changed? Or had he? Lying in bed at night, he did his best to undo the tangled thoughts of the day. But the tangle was back the next morning.

• •

DR. GIRI HAD GOTTEN used to experiencing the world vicariously: through the words of his patients. People revealed their innermost secrets to him, then disappeared—sometimes for weeks, sometimes forever. Rarely did he learn the end of a story. What, for instance, had become of that man, Nishad Something-or-the-other, who bit his wife's buttock in a moment of passion? Last he knew, the couple had separated, and the wife wanted to return to India. Had they reunited? And if so, had they gone back?

Incompleteness was, of course, the nature of his trade. But because his practice was limited to these few blocks of New York City, occasionally stories intersected. Unexpectedly he'd glean tidbits about one patient from another. Although he was generally good at keeping his curiosity at bay, he was human, too. Ever since Sonny's last visit, he'd been wondering what had become of the Transplanted Man. Alive or dead? He'd neither heard nor read anything, which suggested to him that the Transplanted Man had survived his ordeal. That made Dr. Giri all the more curious, and he battled a temptation to go to the hospital and find out what he could. Ultimately, though, his sense of professionalism prevailed. He could only hope to learn more about this puzzle in pieces.

Wednesday morning, another piece entered his office.

"I'm upset," said Gwen. "Over a man."

"Why does he upset you?"

"Because he's an odd man, and he doesn't read, and . . . oh, there are so many other things!"

"Why did you choose to become involved with an odd man who doesn't read?"

Gwen shook her head sideways. "My goddamn disease! You see, once in a while—not for long, thank goodness!—I eat like crazy and become a nymphomaniac. Have you ever heard of anything like this?"

Dr. Giri scanned his memory of the many textbooks he'd read in the process of earning his two Ph.D.s but came up blank. He admonished himself for doing too much guru, not enough Giri. He resolved to spend more time perusing professional journals. "I don't believe I've heard of it," he finally replied.

"I'm practicing meditation to subdue my drives."

Dr. Giri himself had once flirted with yoga and meditation, but sitting cross-legged for so long put unbearable strain on his lower back, forcing him to give it up. "Is it helping?" he asked.

"I think so," said Gwen. "The deepest trances give me such an expansive feeling—as if I can go anywhere."

"Where do you go?"

"Sometimes Walden—you know, Thoreau's pond. Other times, nowhere. Or everywhere. It's like there's an endless space within me. After I come out of it, that sense of something larger stays with me."

An old Lata-Mukesh duet could be heard in the beauty parlor next door.

"Tell me more about your relationship with this man."

"I happened to be in the midst of a fit the day he asked me out."

"But now you're not in the midst of one. What prevents you from leaving him now?"

"Some days, not much. More and more, it bugs the hell out of me that pathology played such a big role in how our relationship started. Of course, there's a lot in him to admire. When you watch him in the hospital, it isn't hard to conclude that this man possesses a gift."

Dr. Giri shifted in his ergonomic recliner. "You've developed strong, if complicated, feelings for this man. Would you call it love?"

"A dangerous word. In ten years, I might call it love. Or I might not. At the moment, all I can say is that I don't want it to end."

"What do you want, then?"

"That he were different."

"What is he like to be with?"

"Sometimes Kutuzov, mostly Pierre."

"Again, please?"

"At his best, he reminds me of Kutuzov, the Russian general in *War and Peace*, but also Pierre. Have you read the book?"

"Years ago. Pierre, I remember. I'm afraid I skipped the battle scenes."

"Those were some of the best parts! Kutuzov makes the decisions that defeat Napoleon not because of any organized application of military theory but because he trusts something deep within himself. Kutuzov scarcely listens to what others say, and he speaks mainly in grunts."

"Maybe this man you're involved with could be more verbal—"

"I said that's him *at his best*, which is mainly in the hospital."

"At his worst?"

"Childish!"

"How?"

"Well, it's not your standard immaturity. Lots of genuine angst is mixed in. Not to mention a seditious streak. He has to settle—inside. But he thinks finding where he needs to be *in*side depends on finding where he needs to be *out*side. He has developed a whole theory about it, a theory of a 'perfect place.' Oh, maybe it *is* standard immaturity. After all, he's four years younger than me. Some days it seems like a whole generation! You see, the only other man with whom I've ever been so intimate was eight years older than me."

"Hmmm."

"That's not all. He does some pretty strange stuff."

"Eccentric?"

"Beyond eccentric. He gets up in the middle of the night and walks outside in his sleep."

"Followed by a dog?"

"You've seen him?"

"Some nights when I can't sleep, I look out our upstairs window. From what I've observed, this is no ordinary sleepwalking. There's more to it."

"What?"

"I don't know."

"Ever since he cured the Transplanted Man—God only knows what he did!—we've become more distant. It's a very uneasy feeling, like something *needs* to be resolved."

"He *cured* the Transplanted Man?"

Gwen's eyes narrowed. "You sound like you know something about this already."

Caught off guard, Dr. Giri did his best to recover. "Oh, just those news reports saying that he was at the hospital on the verge of death. So I was surprised to hear—"

"Since then Sonny has been sleepwalking less—which is good, I guess—but I hardly know him anymore. I don't like the change. . . . Maybe I'm more attracted to the sleepwalker! What a thought!"

Dr. Giri took a moment to digest this news about Sonny and the Transplanted Man. "You say *he* cured the Transplanted Man. Are you sure it wasn't simply outstanding medical care?"

"I'd like to believe that, too. Sonny did everything he could have done—which means everything any doctor could have done. And I've never cared more attentively for a patient. It was as though the beeps and buzzers of the machines the Transplanted Man was hooked to were going off inside my head. And I stuck books between the Transplanted Man's mattresses, their pages open to the most powerful passages. The healing power of art. For me, that's easier to accept than . . . well . . . whatever."

"So," said Dr. Giri, barely suppressing a smile. "The Transplanted Man received the very best care. 'Whatever' was simply coincidental."

"I'm not so sure. Everything is suddenly different. It's as if Sonny's strangeness—the sleepwalking and everything else—is guiding him somewhere. Could that be why he sleepwalks? Because he's trying to get somewhere that doesn't exist in the light of day? Could it be that his perfect place exists only outside the bounds of consciousness?"

Dr. Giri kept quiet.

Finally Gwen said, "Maybe he's just screwed up. Or ill."

"If he is ill—mind you, I'm not saying he is—it's the type of illness only he can cure. And if he's the kind of person I think he is, he'll try to cure himself. But it will take time."

"You talk like you know him."

Dr. Giri shook his head as innocently as he could.

"There's also a parent thing," said Gwen, "though he refuses to talk about it. Sometimes I think he's like an orphan who never had the satisfaction of knowing he was orphaned. People try to compensate in peculiar ways. Like me and my disease. Whatever helps you go on, right? Pretty soon, it's hard to tell the real from the compensation."

"Maybe the real *is* the compensation."

27

Bad Dreams

RONNY CHANCHAL PEEKED INSIDE THE TRANSPLANTED MAN'S ROOM. The patient was sitting up in bed, facing the other way, his attention directed at a physical therapist, who was demonstrating arm exercises. Following the therapist's instructions, the Transplanted Man raised his arms, then moved them this way and that.

Preferring to stay unnoticed for the moment, Ronny Chanchal tiptoed away, troubled by what he'd seen. Not only was the Transplanted Man alive, he looked well! Ronny Chanchal suddenly felt the exhaustion from months of travel. Only last night the actor-politician had, at long last, completed his American tour with a performance in L.A., then flown here on the red eye. And in his coat pocket was a first-class ticket on tonight's flight from JFK to New Delhi. He was in no mood to get on another plane.

It was approaching lunchtime, so Ronny Chanchal went down to the cafeteria. The room was already half filled; people were giving him second looks. He wouldn't be able to eat here in peace. As he was about to leave, he noticed Sonny sitting alone at a corner table, sipping from a large styrofoam cup, a sandwich in his other hand. Ronny Chanchal walked over and sat down without asking. "Doctor, it is truly incredible! My dear friend looks well again!"

Sonny flashed an automatic smile.

"I know you must be busy, Doctor. Please indulge me for just a moment. When do you expect to discharge him?"

"I really can't discuss that. I'm sure you understand."

"Of course. With such an important patient, privacy must be closely guarded. Believe me, I know. Those filmi gossip magazines print everything! It goes with the business, I suppose."

Sonny took a bite of his sandwich.

"I'll let you in on a secret," said Ronny Chanchal, leaning forward. "I'm going to make a Hindi film about East and West, and it *will* say something. On the other hand, one has to be careful about saying too much. The critics don't like that, either. But my film will definitely say *something*. It will be the film of all films, greater than *Pakeezah*, greater than *Sahib, Bibi Aur Ghulam*, greater than *Casablanca*, greater than *Citizen Kane*, greater than *The Godfather*! It will be fully translatable, and whether subtitled or dubbed, the translation will seem perfectly natural. East will meet West, and the two will waltz to sitar music, dance the Bharatnatyam to rock and roll, rap with the tabla. People's lives will be changed. It will be a film about India, about America—about everything in between—with the masala just right: beautiful songs, thrilling fight scenes, a story that grips your heart and enlightens your mind!"

"Sounds like quite a movie. What's it about?"

"I just told you."

"I mean, what is this story that 'grips your heart and enlightens your mind'?"

Ronny Chanchal's mouth tightened. "I never divulge details until just before the film is released. I'm sure you understand."

Sonny glanced at his watch. "I'd better get back to the wards."

Sonny got up, leaving Ronny Chanchal to ponder his East-West film. But in truth there was little to ponder. All the back-and-forth between India and America still hadn't provided the inspiration necessary to flesh out his grandiose idea. He didn't understand why it was proving so hard. Could it be because the true interfaces of East and West were not the frictionless juxta-positions he'd considered but, rather, raw, festering abrasions? Was the syn-thesis he sought a philosophical impossibility? Maybe that was the real problem. Or was he just making excuses for his own creative limitations? He was beginning to doubt whether the Bollywood masala style, the only way he knew how to make films, was capable of doing justice to his lofty vision.

After leaving the cafeteria Ronny Chanchal lurked around the hospital for another twenty minutes, debating whether to go back to the Transplanted Man's room to get a clearer fix on the patient's condition—and also, perhaps, his political plans. But in the end he decided that seeing the return of color to the old man's face, not to mention new vigor in his limbs, would only depress him more.

Hungry and tired, he left the hospital and slowly walked down the street with his hands in his pockets. He stopped in front of Tiger's restaurant.

Tiger recognized Ronny Chanchal at once and ushered him to what had become the most requested table in the restaurant—the one with the best view of the hypokinetic man (whose enigmatic pose had recently been further refined by Jay and Atul). In complete awe of the film star, Tiger could barely speak. He simply handed Ronny Chanchal a menu and retreated. From the peephole in the kitchen door, Tiger watched his famous customer study the menu. At last Ronny Chanchal set the menu on the table. Tiger rushed out.

Even hungrier now, Ronny Chanchal ordered two appetizers, a main course, a side dish, tea, and a mango lassi.

Still tongue-tied, Tiger jotted it all down, though it really didn't matter what Ronny Chanchal ordered, because Tiger had already decided what to serve. But since he couldn't feed his special guest the bland Indo-American fare that had become the restaurant's signature, he had to ask one question. "Spicy?" he blurted. "Or spicy-spicy?"

Ronny Chanchal couldn't bring himself to utter "spicy-spicy." So he said, "As hot as you can make it."

Tiger shuffled away to the kitchen, where he donned an apron, much to the cook's surprise. As if for the first time, Tiger's eyes scanned the room's contents. Stacked against the decaying wall was a pile of ten-pound sacks of flour and another of twenty-pound sacks of basmati rice. Both piles almost reached the unpainted ceiling. On shelves throughout the kitchen stood glass jars filled with yellow-green lentils, garam masala, fennel seeds, ground coriander, desiccated tamarind, fine powders colored yellow, orange, and brown. The way business had been lately, they would go through nearly all of it before the weekend was over. Only the jars containing red pepper, which had been moved to the topmost shelves, would remain virtually untouched.

"What are you doing?" asked the cook as Tiger mounted a stepladder and reached for the ground cayenne pepper.

"Preparing a spicy-spicy feast."

"Why?"

"Look."

The cook squinted through the peephole. "All I see are tourists gawking, as usual, at that crazy fellow outside. At least they're starting to leave. About time! We should place a limit on how long people can sit after receiving their check."

"There's an Indian, too."

"Ronny Chanchal!"

"A special guest needs a special meal prepared by a special chef," said Tiger. "With all the spiceless food you've been cooking, you're probably out of touch with the 'spicy-spicy' dishes."

The cook didn't take offense. He'd been playing cards all night and had slept less than an hour. He wasn't enthusiastic about preparing a feast for just one customer, whoever he happened to be. Even so, the cook couldn't help muttering back, "You're in touch?"

A big grin crept across Tiger's fleshy face, revealing his uneven teeth. "Great kings are always in touch."

The cook who, like everyone else, had serious doubts about Tiger's royal ancestry, raised his eyebrows but had the sense to keep his thoughts to himself.

Tiger sliced tomatoes, cut cauliflower, and diced onions while the cook stepped back and watched. Despite his considerable bulk, Tiger moved gracefully, sautéing this, frying that, sprinkling this, mixing that. Then he began to cook. He metamorphosed into an artist, a conjurer in communion with another world. More than ever the divine logic of food flowed effortlessly from his fingertips into pots on the stove as he instinctively balanced hot with sour, sweet with bitter, salty with sweet. He added dashes of this, pinches of that: cumin, turmeric, coriander, tamarind, cloves, cardamom, mustard seeds, ginger, garlic.

Pepper!

Tiger's mouth watered at the sight of his own glistening creations bathed in rich sauces colored various shades of brown. He sampled each dish. Perfect! Tiger was certain he'd never prepared such tasty food. As far as he was concerned, that meant no one had.

The cook was dazzled.

"Don't stand around like a cauliflower!" said Tiger. "Stir the soup! Drain the rice!"

One by one the dishes were ready. And just in time: Ronny Chanchal was about to leave.

Tiger first brought out a bowl of mulligatawny soup and a plate of samosas with tamarind chutney. After Ronny Chanchal finished, Tiger cleared the table, only to crowd it with more dishes: saffron rice, onion khulchas, two kinds of dal, okra curry, kheema biryani, paneer with spinach, raita—and a sizzling plate of Tiger kebabs. When everything had been served, Tiger stepped back to evaluate the arrangement. The spectacular display of food, together with the elemental experience of cooking it, had given him the nerve to speak. "I prepared it with my own hands, sir. Such a guest deserves only the finest."

Ronny Chanchal, whose palate was no more discriminating than his other senses, nodded indifferently. Tiger lingered, waiting for some compliment about the food's appearance or aroma. But Ronny Chanchal said nothing.

"Sir, I do not boast when I say I am the best. Just as you are the best at what you do, so am I. My food will fill your stomach, massage your soul!"

Again Ronny Chanchal nodded.

"Sir, if you don't mind my saying, you seem rather preoccupied. I would very much like for you to have a pleasant experience in my restaurant. If you'd like to unburden yourself . . ."

Ronny Chanchal sneered.

Tiger stepped back. "Forgive me, sir. Of course, it is none of my business—unless you choose to make it so. A king needs time for reflection."

Ronny Chanchal examined Tiger's face and decided the man was not being sarcastic, simply obsequious. And since he had a weakness for toadies, he finally said, with world-weary importance, "It has been a hectic few weeks."

"Don't hesitate to ask me for advice," said Tiger. "I too am a king—heir to a great kingdom."

"Ah," said Ronny Chanchal. He had no time for this nonsense.

"Sir, I have seen nearly all your films. I wish I could express what they have meant to me—"

"I understand. They are your substitute for India. You miss home, and I am able to soothe your pangs of nostalgia."

"Not exactly, sir. I have never been to India. I am from Uganda."

"Oh, you're one of them."

"I beg your pardon, sir?"

"A doubly foreign Indian. You are even more desperate for glimpses of India."

"Desperate?"

"Because you have no real home. You were a foreigner in Uganda and are foreign here. I understand why you are unhappy—why I mean so much to you."

"I was talking about the films, not you. Having met you, the films suddenly seem less important."

"Thank you."

"I was happy in Uganda before we were forced to leave, and I still miss it. I've never wanted to make India my home. At most I wished to visit—briefly. Now, perhaps even that is unnecessary. I have never been as comfortable with my abdication as at this moment. Besides, what is royalty in India these days? This is my home, and I like it very much."

"Of course, of course."

Ronny Chanchal's patronizing tone only fueled Tiger's irritation. "We don't *need* India here. We don't have to carry three thousand years of baggage with us. We can live in the modern world and refashion the old world as it suits us."

"It's not the real thing," said Ronny Chanchal, suddenly interested in the conversation. "It is artificial, fake."

"*This* isn't fake! Your films are fake. They are successful because they simplify everything. You satisfy the uncultivated tastes of the man in the street, just as I've lately begun to satisfy the tastes of tourists who come to see that fellow outside." Tiger pointed to the hypokinetic man. "But this place—this neighborhood where I live—satisfies me in a much deeper way. Unlike your films, it is original. It exists on its own. On a lesser scale than India, but it exists no less."

Ronny Chanchal wiped his hands with a napkin. "I've always felt that Americans have a taste for cheap imitation because they have no history— because nothing old lasts here. Indians in America seem to suffer the same affliction."

"Of all people, you should be one to talk about cheap imitation!"

Ronny Chanchal got up and coolly said, "I can see I hit a raw nerve. It's understandable. It is unnatural to lead a eunuch's existence."

"Eunuch?" screamed Tiger. "How dare you!"

Ronny Chanchal gave the most condescending smile in his repertoire to the growling Tiger.

Then he left without paying.

• •

LATE THAT NIGHT—while Ronny Chanchal was downing a glass of Scotch high above the Atlantic in the first-class cabin of an Air India jumbo jet— Tiger awoke from a nightmare, gasping. He'd dreamed that he and his army were fighting off invaders, but now, after days of relentless assault, all his men were dead. He alone was left. He rode his stallion, swinging his sword blindly. The foreign enemy fell right and left. But they were too many. He was surrounded. The fate of his kingdom, his race, depended upon him. The enemy leader galloped up.

It was Ronny Chanchal.

Ronny Chanchal waved his sword. "Don't worry," he said, laughing wickedly. "We won't finish you off. We'll just complete the process you've already begun. A swift stroke—two if they're as big as you claim. Of course, I've always been sure they were quite small, shriveled and droopy. Anyway, now we'll see. They'll just roll away. They're already so useless you won't even miss them."

This wasn't the first time Tiger had dreamed this particular dream. But it was the first time he'd visualized the enemy leader's face—and heard him speak. Tiger broke into a sweat and began to tremble. He'd always been a poor sleeper, but these past few nights he'd been fearing that something terrible would happen in his sleep—that he might never wake up. What was going on?

• •

TIGER'S GENERAL PRACTITIONER REFERRED him to the local sleep specialist, Dr. Menaka Bhushan. Owing to a sudden cancellation, Menaka's secretary offered Tiger an appointment the same day he called.

"I manage to fall asleep," Tiger told Menaka that afternoon, "but I don't get much rest. And I have such bad nightmares! I wake up thinking that Ronny . . . er, someone is trying to kill me. My wife won't sleep in the same bed with me anymore. She says I toss around too much and scream in the middle of the night."

"Is this new?" asked Menaka.

"My wife rarely complained before. But she has been complaining about a lot of things lately. Menopause, I think."

"Have you been under a great deal of stress or put on weight recently?"

Tiger patted his belly. "Both, Doctor Madame. I became terribly upset when my restaurant was quarantined. And when I'm upset, I eat. Jalebis, samosas, gulab jamuns, aloo tikis, pakoras, burfis—the deeper fried, the better. I chewed so much supari that my teeth cracked: My dentist had to put in three new crowns! Reopening the restaurant was nerve-racking, too. At first no one came, and I thought we'd go bankrupt. But thanks to that human statue on the corner, business is better than ever. So I've been celebrating—eating! You see, I eat when I'm happy, too. My weight is more or less stable when I'm neither happy nor sad—which, except for these recent topsy-turvy months, had been most of the time."

"How much coffee do you drink?"

"Five or six cups in the morning. After all, even when one doesn't sleep, one still has to wake up, right? And since the restaurant stays open late, I also drink a cup or two in the early evening. Otherwise, it would be very hard to keep smiling at customers."

"What about your libido?"

"My what?"

"Your sex drive."

"These are not things for a woman to ask a man, though I know you are more modern than most."

Menaka's face tightened. "Look, if you want my medical opinion—"

Tiger was irked, too. "I come from a long line of great warrior-kings. Our sexual prowess is legendary!"

"That's not what I asked."

Tiger looked away. Neither he nor Menaka spoke for a while. At last he mumbled, "It is down a bit."

"I see."

"But my wife, once an attractive woman, is not what she used to be. I'm sure you have heard the expression that a woman's beauty is like a rose?"

"Too many times, I'm afraid."

"What do you think, Doctor Madame?"

"Many things. About your sleep problem, though, it's hard to say whether your symptoms are mainly due to everything you've gone through recently or whether you have a mild sleep disorder. Then again, it could just be all that coffee."

"What to do, Doctor Madame?"

Menaka jotted down some notes in Tiger's chart, then set her pen on the table. "Many doctors would put you through a lot of expensive tests, including a sleep study. That means you'd have to stay in the Sleep Studies Lab for at least one night—during which we would monitor your heart rate, blood oxygen level, leg motion, airflow through your nostrils. We would also videotape your sleep and analyze your brain waves on an EEG machine. Or you can just try to reduce the stress in your life, lose some pounds, stop drinking coffee, and see if that solves things. Frankly, I'd rather not put you through all those tests right now. I'm beginning to believe, more and more, that a little common sense can easily substitute for many of the high-tech tests we doctors order."

• •

AFTER TIGER LEFT, MENAKA looked out the window of her office at the busy street below and asked herself why so many people around here suffered from disturbed sleep. It was as though, after moving halfway around the globe, their biological clocks had never reset. Would careful statistical analysis reveal a disproportionate prevalence of sleep disorders among neighborhood residents? That might be worth investigating. Maybe it would tickle Nirdosh's research interest as well. After all, apart from the obvious species difference, the sleep habits of some of her patients were almost as unusual as those of Nirdosh's mice. Nirdosh himself was a prime example. Of course, it was unlikely that a single genetic defect could provide a unifying explanation, as was the case with the mice. There were too many different kinds of sleep disorders around here to implicate a single cause. Then again . . . Was it anxiety? There was definitely a lot of that—something beyond the standard immigrant neuroses over visas and money. Everyone seemed positioned on a number line that began here and ended in India. People were constantly adjusting their position on that line, never comfortable in their current spot. Go forward? Or backward? Maybe this was what caused Nirdosh to stay awake night after night and Tiger to scream in his sleep—not to mention her patients who sleepwalked or suffered from other parasomnias. And yet it seemed too metaphysical an anxiety to affect people *so* drastically. Could that be why it manifested itself only in sleep?

One way or another, they were all sleepwalkers.

28

Missing Goddess

UNDER A BRIGHT LAMP IN A ROOM THAT SMELLED OF RUBBING ALCOHOL, Sonny removed the last of fourteen stitches from Dr. Ranjan's tongue. "All done!"

Dr. Ranjan closed and opened his mouth a few times, then massaged his jaw. "Thank you," he said in a woeful voice.

"I thought you'd be happier. Having all those stitches in your tongue must have been awful."

"*Everything* is awful these days."

Sonny pulled off his rubber gloves, tossed them in the garbage, and sat down. "Do you want to talk about it?"

"Since you first placed these stitches in my mouth," said Dr. Ranjan, "I've scarcely spoken two dozen words. A convenient excuse. I didn't want to talk. Yet my head has been throbbing with words. If you don't mind, I must release a little tension. Confidentially, you understand."

"Sure, go ahead."

Dr. Ranjan had gotten used to communicating with his hands during the past week and a half, so now they moved rapidly as words began to pour out of his mouth. "I've spent my whole life in the pursuit of truth—significant truth. Trying to strip away the infinite veils of Maya, you might say—that's what science is all about. To remove just one veil amounts to a highly successful career, though maybe a truly great scientist is able to tease away three or four. I have always believed this to be the noblest pursuit in life. I am not sure anymore. There are trillions and trillions of truths. Is it so important to know them all?"

The pain in Dr. Ranjan's voice touched Sonny. "If it gives your life purpose," he replied, "that's important."

"What if that purpose is misguided? What if it's nothing more than a delusion? If something I loved so dearly—science—something I gave myself to so honestly, so passionately, so completely, something that seemed so noble, leads to this, then what?"

Sonny leaned back in his chair and folded his arms. He had heard about the insomnin fiasco. Was Dr. Ranjan referring to this? Or could it be something to do with . . . ?

"I'm paralyzed!" cried Dr. Ranjan, sinking into his chair, shoulders slumped, his face anguished.

"I don't quite understand," said Sonny. "But maybe I understand enough. All I can say is that being paralyzed by no purpose is far worse than stopping every now and then to ask yourself a tough question. I can only imagine—"

"You can't! I've lost her! My goddess doesn't exist anymore!"

Sonny smiled sympathetically. "If your goddess existed once, why shouldn't she exist now? Aren't goddesses immortal? You just can't see her because the fools who run the world are hounding you."

"I hope that is true. During these past days of silence, I've been forced to question a number of premises underlying my life. There turns out to be little rational basis for many of them; one could argue either way. It's as if the directions on my compass are arbitrary. Or just plain wrong."

"Believe me," said Sonny. "I *know* that feeling. For most of my life, I've been using the same brand of compass."

"For *most* of your life? Does that mean you've finally found true North?"

"Hardly. Though, perhaps, after waiting all these years, I've gotten a glimpse of something. The glimpse was so brief I sometimes wonder if I saw anything at all. It's like when you look up at the night sky and you spot a quick flash—a shooting star? a UFO?—but then it's gone, and soon you're doubting yourself, and it all becomes very slippery in your mind, a *feeling* rather than a certainty."

"You're right: It *is* slippery. So how does one know?"

"I guess that's what goddesses are for."

"Precisely! And mine is gone!"

Sonny placed his hand on Dr. Ranjan's shoulder. "I have a feeling that, on a better day, you'll get another peek at your goddess. For the time being, be thankful she exists—even if she takes long vacations."

• •

"MAKE MORE!" PAUDHA HAD COMMANDED, as if Dr. Ranjan was in the doughnut business.

Dr. Ranjan had no choice. Which meant Alvin didn't, either. During the days that followed, the scientist and his assistant were fully absorbed in their tedious, uncertain mission. The various steps in the purification of insomnin had already been worked out—centrifugation, extractions, precipitations, chromatographic separations, not to mention testing the effect of each partially purified fraction on normal mice. But it all seemed more grueling than before, in part because both Dr. Ranjan and Alvin knew that they'd been extremely lucky the first time around.

One night Alvin stood in the laboratory's cold room performing an intermediate step in the purification of a new batch. It was well past 3:00 A.M. The temperature inside the cold room was only a few degrees above freezing. Alvin's concentration was so intense that he hadn't stepped into the warmth of the corridor in over two hours. When he rubbed his nose, he barely felt it. His thinking had slowed down, almost come to a stop. He knew he had to get out, but the cold, the numbness, his frozen mind, all began to feel pleasurable. He could hear his heart beating slowly: *lub-dub, lub-dub, lub-dub* . . .

Alvin had a vision.

He found himself in an extremely cold cave. Across a huge gorge was a perfect view of the summit of Everest. But that was where everyone else went. Even now he could see a group of bundled climbers struggling to get to the top of the world. Yet no one had climbed this mountain or set foot in this cave. As far as he could tell, there was no way to get in—no way out. How had he gotten here? Even great sages didn't know about this place, or had long ago stopped believing in it. He was the only one who refused to stop believing. He'd spent his whole life trying, and now, old and arthritic, he was finally here. Naked, he sat cross-legged at the edge of a gorge miles deep, gazing at the virgin sky blanketing the planet, listening to the serene music of freezing winds.

At last Alvin stepped out of the cold room, his fingers on the verge of frostbite. His mind took a long time to thaw. He was filled with a sense that he had experienced something truly wondrous—a high surpassing that induced by any of the drugs he'd done—and a deep hunger for another such experience.

• •

WORKING DAY AND NIGHT, Alvin and Dr. Ranjan eventually purified more insomnin. Less than one tenth of a microgram, it was the world's entire supply: worth $200 million.

If it worked.

When they injected it into a normal mouse, the mouse didn't fall asleep.

"It's even more potent than the last batch!" Alvin exclaimed one morning when Dr. Ranjan entered the lab. "Five days without sleep on a single dose—and still counting!"

Dr. Ranjan, who'd now gone fifteen days with almost no sleep, remained subdued.

Poor Ranjy must have had a harrowing experience in that parking lot, thought Alvin, for the normally garrulous scientist hadn't been saying much at all.

Even though Dr. Ranjan's tongue was still sore, a more serious wound bled on the inside. So that afternoon Dr. Ranjan went to see the only person in the neighborhood who specialized in that type of wound.

As soon as he entered Dr. Giri's office, Dr. Ranjan fell to his knees. "Guruji, I have sinned!"

"Please get off the floor."

"No, Guruji. I am not worthy enough to sit at your level."

"Nonsense," said Dr. Giri, unmistakable irritation in his voice. "I'm no more worthy than anyone else. Just a psychotherapist trying to make a living."

"It will be easier for me to explain from down here."

Dr. Giri frowned. "If you must. Now tell me, how have you sinned?"

"It is difficult to say, actually."

"You don't know?"

"Adultery," whispered Dr. Ranjan. "Actually, I have committed adultery."

"Ah."

"What should I do?"

Dr. Giri pointed to the chair facing him. "First, get off the floor and face me."

"No, I don't *deserve* to face you."

"I'd really prefer to look at your eyes rather than the bald spot on your head."

Dr. Ranjan seated himself on the chair, gradually slouching lower and lower. At last he said, "I love my wife and children so, so, *so* dearly."

"Then the solution isn't hard, is it?"

"But I had the most wonderful, most magnificent—"

"I get the picture."

"I see her almost every day. She's a colleague."

"Then the solution is harder."

"Can a man love two women?"

Dr. Giri scratched his chin. "I believe so, but one must distinguish between love and lust. Unfortunately, this is not always easy."

"I know I love my wife."

"Then?"

Dr. Ranjan took a cloth from his shirt pocket and wiped the lenses of his glasses. Finally he said, "I feel caged, Guruji."

Dr. Giri glanced out the window. "You aren't the first family man to feel that way. But most men are not, as we like to pretend, caged birds that would fly away were it not for familial responsibilities. If there is a cage, the door is partly open, and we know it. What we often do is flutter our wings a few times, only to realize too much will be lost by flying off. We value what we have but, yes, it's convenient to whine about being caged."

"I've done more than flutter my wings, Guruji."

"True, but you haven't flown. And you have no intention of leaving your wife for this woman, correct?"

"No . . . I mean, yes! But, well . . ."

"You just want both?"

"Oh, Guruji, I don't know! It all happened so fast—so unexpectedly! One thing after another after another. The storm led to a loss of power, which led to the thawing of the sleep inhibitor, which led that nasty CEO to threaten me, which led me to seek Menaka's advice . . ."

As Dr. Ranjan recounted everything, Dr. Giri imagined a mischievous butterfly quietly flapping its wings in some old woman's vegetable garden in Uruguay. And that made him think of the man who'd bitten his wife's buttock. A single flap, and that man's whole world had turned upside down, too.

"Guruji, should I tell my wife?"

Dr. Giri held up both hands. "First, answer some questions. Was this the only instance?"

"Yes."

"Was it a moment of weakness rather than an indulgence?"

"Actually, yes."

"Are you a good man?"

"I try."

"Are you a good husband and father?"

"I am—or I think I am—a good father. Up until now, I have been a sincere and mostly tolerable husband, although I don't know if Bhavana would say I was a *good* one. I do not help enough with the house, and I'm unnecessarily rude to her relatives."

"The average Indian husband."

"More or less. Actually, I might be infinitesimally above average—were it not for this. It really was a moment of weakness, Guruji."

"Finally—most critically—do you have the strength to stay away from this other woman's flesh, even if she offers herself to you again? Wait! Do not reply. I do not wish to bear witness to broken vows. But I will give you my opinion."

"Oh, please do!"

"If your answer is yes," said Dr. Giri, "then my answer is no. No, you need not tell your wife. If your answer is no—no, you cannot stay away from this woman—then you must tell your wife, and nobody can help you."

29

Ancestral Voices

WHEN SONNY GOT HOME FROM THE HOSPITAL ONE EVENING, THE ORANGE light on his answering machine was flashing. Gwen, he guessed. Ever since the Transplanted Man's recovery, their relationship had been strained. He knew it was mainly his doing—he'd been sullen, irritable—and he wanted to make amends. It was still early, a good evening to go into Manhattan. Dinner, a light movie, a stroll up the West Side. And perhaps the right moment would come—say, while waiting for a stoplight to change on Amsterdam and Eighty-second—and he'd kiss her hard, and maybe it would release tension in a way that sex never could.

Then again, maybe not. There were reasons why their relationship had become strained, and those reasons hadn't vanished.

He pressed the Play button on the answering machine.

"I'm in town," said the voice. "Call me at my hotel. The number is . . ."

He hadn't expected to hear *that* voice for another month. He detected a trace of urgency. His hand reached for the phone. He knew he wouldn't dial if he thought too much.

Before he uttered a word, she said, "Hi, Sonny."

He struggled against an impulse to hang up. "How come you were so sure it'd be me?"

"Nobody else knows I'm at this number."

"Oh."

"How are you, Sonny?"

"Fine."

A silence, drawn out and uneasy, though no less so than a thousand other uneasy silences that had transpired between them and, in fact, become their real mode of communication.

"Don't you want to know how I am?"

"Sure," he said in a flat voice.

"And why I'm here?"

"Uh-huh."

"It's not the kind of thing to discuss over the phone. Let's meet. Tonight— at the restaurant of my hotel. The Carrigan. It's on Fifty—"

"I know where it is."

• •

THE SUBWAY TRAIN may have been moving forward, but he felt as if he was going backward, dragged by pieces of the past. He remembered all the screaming at home—so much broken glassware that, in the end, only plastic dishes remained. He remembered the men she had been involved with: men he hated, who eventually came to hate him. He remembered how he used to lie between markers at the local graveyard, smoking joint after joint while watching stars wander across the night sky. Most of all, he remembered his dream of tracking down his father—somehow, somewhere. By the time the train slowed at the subway station, an armor forged over decades had turned into tissue paper. A short ride, and all the pain was back.

The hotel's restaurant, a large room with forty or fifty tables, was filled with suited conventioneers. He was relieved when he couldn't find her. It had to be hard for her, too, he thought. There would probably be another message on his answering machine when he got home, an apology or excuse. Then he spotted her. She was sitting at a table in the far corner. He approached slowly, each step kindling a different ache. She saw him, rose, and gave him a brief hug. He smelled the lavender fragrance she'd worn for as long as he could remember.

She was dressed in dark blue and wore a thin gold necklace. She looked stunning for a woman her age—still trim, with a stylish elegance that came naturally to her. He recalled how, even during her long bouts of depression, she had somehow managed to look good. He'd always held that against her. She had no right to look so good when everything had been so bad.

They sat down.

She tapped her index finger against her glass of red wine. "You look tired. Are you getting enough sleep on your nights off?"

"More or less."

"Less, I expect."

He shrugged.

"You get that from your father's side."

The room seemed to shrink. "My . . . ?"

She swirled her wine. "Your father was a strange sleeper, too. We had more fights over how difficult it was to lie in the same bed than anything else. He was always getting up, lying back down, tossing about. Sometimes we'd awaken with our feet in each other's faces!"

He sat erect—silent, waiting, scarcely breathing. His throat felt cottony. He stared at the design on the beige tablecloth, his eyes following a sinuous black line that became lost in an arabesque.

"His family was full of oddball sleepers," she went on. "Did you know I lived with them for the first six months after we were married? I was never cut out for a joint family. On the other hand, thirty years gives you a little perspective. I suppose it wasn't as bad as I thought at the time. But the nights were insane! People screaming in their sleep, banging their heads in their sleep, walking in their sleep. Every one of them grinding their teeth all night. Since three generations lived together, they managed to convince each other they were all quite normal. The doctors were the wackiest. That amounted to half of them: It was *the* family trade. I always found it remarkable how, despite everything, you gravitated to medicine. Your father is a doctor, too, you know. That's how we ended up in such an out-of-the-way place: Practicing where there was a shortage of doctors was the only way to get a green card quickly. I never wanted to move there, though. As things turned out, he left, you left, and I stayed."

Sonny tried to take it all in. One word, above all, stuck in his mind: *is.*

Is.

Had he heard correctly? Did she say: "Your father *is* a doctor, too"?

She was scrutinizing his face.

"You haven't spoken that many words about my father all my life! Whenever I asked you about him, you wouldn't tell me a thing: It never even occurred to me that he might be a doctor."

"A damn good one, too."

"What's this *really* about?"

"Sonny . . ."

"What!"

"He's dying. Lung cancer. We used to fight about that, too—smoking."

Sonny said nothing.

"We've had a little correspondence these past few years—just a couple of letters back and forth. He never married again. If you ask me, he wasn't meant for it. He was even more restless awake than asleep. He resented being trapped in a small Arizona town just to get a visa; he was always talking about one day traveling here or there. In the end, that's what he did. After we divorced he joined the World Health Organization. He spent a lot of time in Central Africa, and later the Caribbean. He only returned to the States two months ago."

"Why didn't you ever—?"

"He wanted to see you. But when I told him how hard a time you had growing up, I think he agreed it wasn't a good idea. And things were always so tense between you and me. Besides, I felt he hadn't earned the right."

"What about *my* right to see him?"

She looked away. "Sonny, there are many things I wish I'd done differently."

He kept silent.

"And you seem to have survived all right."

"Seem."

"That's all I can say, Sonny—all I know. I've had such brief glimpses into your life since you left home."

"Brief glimpses were all you wanted."

"Do you think that's fair?"

"Yes."

She took a sip of her wine. "I understand why you might feel that way. But *I* have tried to keep contact. Even now I call every other month."

"You make it sound like a prescription for a bitter pill!"

"Not bitter, Sonny. Just difficult to swallow. You never talk."

"There's nothing to say."

Her face suddenly looked older. "Why?"

He heard the pain in her voice. He no longer knew *why.* He could list a hundred reasons, though none was sufficient to explain why. He could see how one thing was linked to another—how it might, all together, explain why: An insecure single woman burdened by a baby. A woman who thought she had to hide her differences in order to survive in a small town. A woman who never quite managed to keep her impractical little businesses afloat. A child, stubborn and moody, like his mother. A boy exquisitely conscious of all those differences his mother was so determined to hide. An impulsive woman with poor judgment in men. A boy who sabotaged whatever was between his mother and those lovers and husbands. A boy who longed for another life, who invented alternate lives in his head—and sometimes confused them for the real thing. An adolescent who ran away three times before finally escaping for good . . .

Sitting here so many years later, the story didn't seem that different from countless other screwed-up lives incrementally damaged until beyond repair. It was more than enough to *explain* why. But it wasn't *why*.

She seemed to be trying to fathom his thoughts. At last she said, "I promised myself I wouldn't allow our conversation to go in this direction."

"Some patterns can never be broken, I guess."

She blinked a few times. "I hope that isn't so."

He kept quiet.

"Tonight is about something else," she said. "When your father phoned yesterday, I caught the first available flight. He didn't say he was in bad shape; he didn't need to. I'll be seeing him tonight. But he really called because he wants to see you, Sonny."

He bit his lower lip. He heard every voice in the restaurant, every waiter's footsteps, every clanking fork and knife.

She leaned forward and said, "I know this isn't easy for you. Meeting your father will not fix what went wrong in our lives. But maybe it will help—a little."

"Maybe it won't."

She sighed. "You'll go, Sonny, won't you?"

He stared at the ice cubes glistening in his glass of water. "I don't know him. And he doesn't know me."

"Oh, you'll know each other, all right. Your resemblance to him is—"

"*Please*, Mom."

He closed his eyes for a moment.

"Are you okay, Sonny?"

"Just fine."

She stared at him for a long time. "You need to know one thing. I never explained what happened between your father and me—why I've refused to talk about it all these years. It's not the kind of thing you want to tell your son." She glanced down at the tablecloth. "Okay, here it goes. Yes, it was he who left, but *I* was the unfaithful one. He was just unable to forgive me."

He stared at her half-empty glass of wine. His brain was burning up.

"For weeks, I pleaded and cried. Every single night! Then, after all that, when he still left, I became resentful. And scared. Think of it! There I was with a one-year-old—no way to earn a living. Your father left us what little there was, but, godammit, it was *so* hard."

The red wine in her glass seemed to congeal before his eyes.

"Sonny, I loved your father. Why did he have to leave me over a few minutes of stupidity? A mistake that I've regretted every day for almost twenty-nine years. But he couldn't forgive me. Wouldn't. He froze up completely. He had always been a rigid man. Maybe that's why I . . . Oh, I don't know! You understand, don't you?"

His jaw tightened. He looked away.

"You just won't give me a break. You *can't*. One day I hope you'll put it in perspective. At the time, I was barely twenty-three—six years younger than you are now. Think about that."

He couldn't think at all.

Not another word was spoken for two minutes. She finished her wine. When the waiter came by, she ordered another glass.

Again, silence—extended, chilly, painful.

"Don't look like that, Sonny."

He wanted to leave.

"You'll be finishing your residency soon. What next?"

"Haven't decided."

More silence.

"Sonny, is there . . . anyone?"

Her face had softened. Her eyes were clearer, deeper. In them was a tenderness he hadn't seen since . . .

"There is," he said, in a tone meant to indicate it needn't concern her.

"But it's not love?"

"Mom!"

"I'm just curious about my son, nothing more."

"Nothing more has always been the problem."

"Do you love her?"

"It's complicated."

She smiled in a motherly way. "Always is."

"You would know."

"Is there a specific issue?"

"I need to go away somewhere—be alone."

"You've always wanted to be alone."

"Not want: *Need.*"

"Your father was that way, too. He could get so alone he made *me* feel lonely. If you love her, Sonny, simplify."

"I don't know how."

"Like your mother."

"I hope not."

Her face briefly lost composure.

"I hope not, too," she said at last. She began to fiddle with the strap of her purse. "It's time for me to go. I told your father I'd be there by nine. Please go see him, Sonny."

She tore out a page from her address book and scribbled the hospital's name and a room number on it.

He stood up before she did. She kissed him on the forehead—so tentatively it hurt. She started to walk away, then turned around. She took several slow steps toward him. Now she kissed him hard on the cheek, ran her hand through his hair. He felt ready to cry. Was it all so fragile? Was he who he was because of her brief lapse more than a quarter century ago?

She was still stroking his hair. "It's been so long, Sunit."

He took a step back.

"I'll go now," she said, and walked away.

• •

THE NEXT MORNING SONNY phoned Gwen to tell her that he could be reached only on his pager, but he preferred not to be reached at all.

"What is it?"

He wouldn't answer.

"Sonny?"

"*Please,* Gwen."

He heard the anger in her silence, but she didn't push him.

After hanging up he disconnected the phone.

He rushed through his hospital duties that day. Fortunately, his patients were doing well. For once, even the Transplanted Man seemed like a routine case.

At home he drank, thought, drank more, thought more. Did his father have to leave his wife and baby over what his mother admitted were "a few minutes of stupidity"? After all, his mother had been young, and if the rest of her life was any indication, probably depressed, too. Even now he suspected that she was depressed, though as always she did a good job hiding it—just as she'd hidden a life of failures, lies. For perhaps the first time, he truly pitied her. Only he knew the depth of her self-deception. That was why their relationship could never be anything other than what it was. Had his father seen through her, too? Maybe that was the *real* reason he left. Or were matters as straightforward as his mother had painted them—that he couldn't accept her careless infidelity? Only his father could answer those questions. And now, on his deathbed, maybe he would. But then another thought crossed Sonny's mind. His mother had always had terrible taste in men. Maybe his father fell into that category, too. What kind of man would let half a lifetime pass before insisting on seeing his own son? Even if his mother had been against it, couldn't his father have still found a way? After all these years of waiting—longing—Sonny wasn't sure he wanted to meet this man.

• •

SITTING ALONE IN TIGER's restaurant, Gwen didn't know what to make of Sonny's announcement, out of the blue, that he was available only by pager. Was there someone else? But it made no sense to make such a fuss if he wanted to hide something like that. As she stared out the window at the hypokinetic man, she tried to imagine how she looked while meditating. The hypokinetic man seemed pure, elemental, anchored. Yes, she could finally see what all the hullabaloo was about—how he drew people to him, dissolved their shells, even transformed them. Did his tranquil expression reflect anything deeper? She wondered what led him to choose this particular street corner out of thousands in the city. How long would he stay? After all, for a guy like that, there must be only way stations.

For everyone?

The hypokinetic man dissolved into the darkness. For a moment, he seemed like an apparition. Then he was gone.

Three minutes later Tiger turned on a floodlight to illuminate his star attraction for the dinner crowd. Soon the restaurant had filled.

"Mind if I join you?"

Startled from her ruminations, Gwen turned away from the window. "Not at all."

Alvin sat down. "How are things?"

"Okay, I guess."

"I haven't seen much of Sonny lately. What's he up to these days?"

Gwen tapped her fingers on the table. "Who cares?"

"Oh?"

They were silent until Tiger arrived with Gwen's vegetable biryani. He greeted Alvin with a toothy grin. "I didn't even see you come in. Let me get you a menu."

"Not necessary. I'll have the vegetable biryani, too."

"Would you like an extra plate?" asked Tiger. "That way you can share until the other order arrives."

"Sure," said Gwen, even though she was famished.

Tiger left to get another plate. When he returned Gwen dished from her plate onto Alvin's. He got four spoonfuls.

"I really miss the old menu," said Alvin. "Frankly, I'm amazed at how shamelessly Tiger is pandering to the tastes of non-Indians."

"That's us."

"Sometimes I forget."

"It's a disease, and we're stricken."

Furrows snaked across Alvin's forehead. "What disease?"

"Indophilia. Like a chronic parasitic infestation, it keeps eating away at you but never kills."

Perhaps it *could* kill, thought Alvin, recalling how he'd almost died of cholera in a small district hospital thirty years ago in rural Bengal. But he objected to being lumped together with everyone else. "Neither you nor I are standard Indophiles."

"What are we, then?"

"Immigrants to Little India."

"Well, I'm thinking of applying for an exit visa," said Gwen. "Perhaps it's time to return to London."

"What's really the matter?"

"Surely you've guessed that things are tense between Sonny and me, and that's part of it. But maybe I've also seen the light. What's wrong with people like you and me?"

"There's a lot wrong with me."

Gwen looked straight into Alvin's eyes. "I don't think so."

Alvin had always been attracted to Gwen and wasn't sure how to react. Should he touch her hand? . . .

Just then a waiter showed up with his vegetable biryani.

"Half is yours," said Alvin.

Gwen took two-thirds.

Both ate quietly, reflecting on a moment when barriers had dissolved and lives might have changed—had the waiter not interrupted. Gwen stared out the window at the hypokinetic man, glowing under 200 watts.

Alvin broke the silence. "I know people around here think I'm missing a screw. Everyone views me as an anachronism: a relic of the sixties, a cliché. And in India, I'm this white guy people want to impress with their English and sell things to, but they also think I'm a nut searching for wisdom in filthy gutters. Another cliché. I'd always thought I was an original, but as I grow older, I fear that the cliché is fitting more snugly. I'm starting to think I ought do something radical before the clothes get too comfortable."

Tiger appeared with a pitcher and filled their glasses with water. "Anything else?"

"A plate of saag paneer, an order of onion khulchas, and some more mango lassi," said Gwen. She turned to Alvin. "What about you?"

"I'm full."

Now Gwen understood what was happening to her. She tried to think clearly. It was best to leave right away, buy three pounds of chocolate at the corner market, then go home to ride it out. If only Sonny wasn't acting like . . . Where was he, anyway?

Alvin was looking at her, smiling. There was clarity in his dark eyes, a refreshing candor uncommon in men his age. How old was he? Approaching fifty, probably. Sometimes he looked it, but not right now. He could almost be considered handsome. A mature man, like Santino. As a matter of fact, when the light hit Alvin's face a certain way . . .

Her food arrived. Gwen ate quickly.

She drained her glass of the last drops of mango lassi and licked her lips clean of the yellow-orange liquid. "Well, then . . ."

"I guess I'd better get going," said Alvin.

"Where to?"

Alvin thought for a moment. With Manny working tonight, he'd miss the late showing of *Sholay* at Golden Jubilee Cinema; he didn't feel like seeing the film alone. He thought of asking Gwen, then remembered how she'd complained when they saw it the first time with Manny and Sonny.

"I guess I'm going nowhere special," he finally said.

Gwen glanced down at her clean plate. "Same for me."

"You wouldn't want to come over for a drink, would you?"

Gwen stared at him for a few seconds, then said, "Do you read much?"

• •

ON THE WAY OVER Gwen had waged a fierce battle against her instincts. And lost. Now she stood in Alvin's studio apartment, confused and frustrated. All that meditation for nothing!

On the wall was a framed photograph of Alvin with Allen Ginsberg. The apartment was filled with books—crammed on shelves, piled on the floor, stacked next to the kitchen sink. Gwen felt the sadness of all those books, their pages turned again and again in this lonely room in a desperate search for a few phrases that might justify a whole life.

"What can I get you?" asked Alvin.

"Nothing."

He turned on the stereo, a John Lennon album. She sat down in the far corner of the sofa, crossed her legs, and listened to the music.

After a while Alvin sat beside her. She closed her eyes, began to breathe deeply.

Alvin took her hand in his. She felt its roughness, the result of years of laboratory work. He gently kissed her neck. She concentrated on her breathing.

Soon he was nibbling on her right earlobe. She barely felt it. She was somewhere else, standing on a pebbly shore, listening to the gentle music of waves, peering into "a mirror that no stone can crack, whose quicksilver will never wear off . . . a mirror in which all impurity presented to it sinks."

Alvin's hand slipped into her blouse.

She snapped out of her trance, opened her eyes. It took a moment to recover from her initial daze. Then she firmly pulled out his hand from her blouse, ashamed it had gone so far. And yet her guilt was tempered by a flicker of hope. The meditation—or something she was doing—had worked. Was the pathological circuitry of her brain finally getting rewired? Whatever it was, for once she had risen above the dictates of instinct just when her disease had flared up. Could she finally tame the beast, train it?

"I'd better go now," she said, getting up.

Alvin admired her silhouette in the dim light. He understood her silence. It would never happen again, and they would never speak of it.

• •

WHILE GWEN WAS WALKING HOME, Sonny was riding the subway uptown. By the time he got to the hospital, it was past visiting hours. As he took the elevator up, he debated how to address his father. Dr. Seth seemed too formal. Dad was impossible. At last he decided on "I'm Sonny." Even though that didn't sound quite right, it was a neutral enough start, and maybe the words would get warmer and still remain honest. That was the best he could hope for—honesty, a little warmth, and maybe a few answers. Perhaps that was all his father, in the final days of his life, wanted as well.

When Sonny stepped out of the elevator, the essential features common to all hospitals began to settle his mind. Both visitor and doctor, he walked slowly down the corridor, his eyes focused on the off-white tiles reflecting the ceiling lights. Soon he was standing before 912, the room number his mother had written down. All his life he had been trying to imagine his father, and ever since his mother mentioned that he resembled the man, his mental picture of his father had become less fuzzy. Now, as he prepared to knock on the door, he redrew that picture again, adding details to accommodate age and the toll of disease. He imagined a man once close to his own size, though now shrunken—a man with dry dark skin and thin gray hair, a long sharp nose like his own, the same wide eyes, but even more deeply set after many months of suffering. Perhaps his father's eyes were glazed with resignation. Or would they be full of quiet rage? That was what Sonny wanted to see: two sparks flashing from sunken sockets, even as the rest of his father's cancer-ridden body was dissolving away.

He knocked.

"Yes?"

Sonny pushed open the door. The man in the bed was white.

"Sorry," said Sonny.

He stepped back into the corridor and headed for the nurses' station.

"I'm looking for a patient named Seth," he told the nurse on duty. She was in her late forties—short, matronly, with a pleasant face.

"Naval Seth?"

"Yes."

"Are you a friend?"

"A relative."

"Oh . . . Uh . . ."

"What?"

"He passed away this morning. Such a nice man. I'm sorry . . ."

The nurse was looking him squarely in the face. Her lips continued to move, but Sonny didn't hear a word. A hundred questions and their echoes flitted through his mind. Was his father alone at the time? Did he die quickly? How great was his pain? Was there a glimmer of fire in his eyes despite all that suffering? At the very end, did he look like me? . . . *Did he mention my name?*

The nurse kept talking.

When she finished, Sonny walked toward the elevator.

RESOLUTIONS

30

Pricks of Conscience

As his "subtle mix of spices" became subtler, Tiger's business continued to boom. Food editors of the city's newspapers were raving about his new Indo-American culinary style. But Tiger felt uneasy and in time became almost as depressed as when his restaurant had been quarantined. That only exacerbated his nightmares about Ronny Chanchal, and he kept waking up in the middle of the night sweating, gasping for air. He went back to Dr. Bhushan, but she just repeated her advice to reduce stress, lose weight, and stop drinking coffee.

Tiger knew the real problem was something else. So he went to see the man with a reputation for understanding "something else."

"Guruji?"

"Yes, my child."

"I'm very unhappy. My restaurant is thriving, but I've lost my old customers."

"Have you any idea why?"

"It's the food. My food is bad!"

"Didn't you say your business is thriving?"

"From tourists, Guruji. But these people don't know curry from salsa. They like my new menu because it has so few spices, and everything isn't mixed together."

Dr. Giri leaned back in his ergonomic recliner. "I would have thought they'd want something genuine."

"Oh, they *think* it's genuine. They even think it's spicy. After eating, they often tell me how 'exotic' the food is, believing it to be praise. Exotic my foot! Of course, I can't fool the Indians."

"You want to fool Indians?"

"I want them to eat my food."

"I have been to your place several times—though not in recent months."

Tiger fingered his mustache. "Tell me, when you ate there did you order the spicy-spicy dishes?"

"Always."

"And how was the food?"

"The best I've ever had. Each dish was a work of art."

Tiger gazed down at the floor. "Now it's just junk. . . . Junk! Junk! Junk!"

Silence followed. Dr. Giri's allergies had been acting up, and he rubbed his nose to appease an itch. Finally he said, "Maybe you should cook like you used to."

"Then my profits will drop, and I've just bought a car, and my wife wants to move to a bigger place, and—"

"Now I understand the problem."

"What?"

Dr. Giri remained quiet for a long time, the way psychoanalysts do for several dollars a minute. On occasion the technique worked.

Suddenly Tiger blurted, "You are right! I *am* an artist! I have strayed, Guruji—compromised my art. I have prostituted myself for money—sold my soul!"

"That may be extreme."

"It's the truth!"

"Perhaps there is a way to make Indian food taste good without hot spices."

"Impossible! With all due respect, Guruji, you have no idea what you're talking about. Nothing can substitute for hot spices. For any spice! A great chef knows instinctively how to balance ingredients. Everything is linked. Change one ingredient, and the entire creation becomes different. The palate is *very* sensitive. That's why it has taken so many weeks to develop my Indo-American style. Every time I take away one spice, I'm forced to withdraw another. Now almost nothing is left!"

"But you've created something new, correct?"

"You wouldn't call these dishes *creations* if you'd tried them, Guruji. For Western taste buds, I've muted the emotions of my food; for Western eyes, I've separated what God knows can only be mixed."

"I see what you mean, but—"

"A great artist who can no longer practice his art might go crazy and cut off an ear! I *must* make amends. My food must once again be the finest in the city. In the land! No—*the world!*"

Tiger stood up. The wild look in his eyes made Dr. Giri uneasy.

"You shouldn't get so worked up," said Dr. Giri. "Don't do anything rash."
"Hah!"

• •

TIGER HUFFED ALL THE WAY back to his restaurant, determined to burn every last throat. When he stormed in and saw that not one of those throats was Indian, he became filled with the fury of his putative warrior ancestors and decided to free his menu from the clutches of neoimperialists.

"Out!"

A sudden silence fell. Everyone stared.

Tiger's eyes bulged. "What are you people staring at? You're not going to make an Uncle Tom of me! Do you hear? My name is Tiger. Tiger! Hear me roar!"

To everyone's amazement, Tiger roared. More amazingly, he sounded like a real tiger.

After two more roars Tiger announced, "From now on, *every* dish in my restaurant will be spicy-spicy. *No exceptions.* Now go! Dozens of restaurants will cook your kind of food. Go, go, go! The families of chefs down the street have been starving ever since you started coming here. They'll kiss your feet. Because of their like, you ruled India for two centuries. Tell them Tiger has found his stripes! Tell the world that Tiger feeds only those with courageous stomachs. If you ever come back, plan to leave with blistering bowels. Man must suffer to appreciate beauty!"

• •

WITH THE FOOD SPICY-SPICY again, the locals gradually returned to Tiger's restaurant. They left crying. Tiger had decided that a true experience of his cuisine required feeling as well as tasting the food. At first he refused to lay silverware, insisting that his customers eat only with their hands. However, when someone called him a fanatic, he allowed forks and knives to be laid out again, agreeing that it was enough that his food was, once more, the very best Indian fare in town.

The tourist crowd found the food too fiery to eat. Even so, they kept coming to view the hypokinetic man, usually just ordering coffee or tea. But when Tiger established a five-dollar-per-person minimum, the tourists started to go elsewhere.

His conscience clear, Tiger's nightmares about Ronny Chanchal stopped. He abstained from coffee and stuck to a strict diet. Slowly the pounds melted.

All wasn't rosy, though. Unable to afford the monthly payments, Tiger was forced to sell his new car at a substantial loss. Still, he wore the contented smile of an authentic man. And much to the amazement of his wife, who for years had been urging him to apply for American citizenship, he filled out an N400 naturalization application. "Say what you will about this country's past," he told her, "but no government tries so hard to guarantee that a man, no matter who he is, or where he comes from, can cook as he likes."

· ·

AMONG TUESDAY AFTERNOON's LUNCH customers were Drs. Bhushan and Ranjan. Tiger kept winking at them. This was annoying Menaka. She nonetheless smiled back professionally, since Tiger had recently been a patient. Dr. Ranjan found it more irksome. He was in the middle of an important conversation, the kind men dread, particularly if the person on the other side of the spicy-spicy dishes is . . . a mistress. Even though they'd had sex only once, it was clear to both that they were seriously involved. They also realized it had begun many months before their first caress. The fact that it had remained unspoken for so long had only served to deepen their feelings for each other. And so, when they finally did touch, their emotions had surfaced with a force neither had been prepared for. Now the time had come to talk about it.

Dr. Ranjan had no experience with this type of situation. His only guides were honesty and prudence, uncomfortable bedfellows at the moment. More than once he thought of lying. Yet he cared too much for Menaka to lie. Unfortunately, she understood his dilemma. With an intense gaze that made him even more nervous, she seemed ready to spring upon every word.

"It's a difficult situation," he said.

"You said that already."

"Did I?"

He took off his glasses, massaged his temples. Then he yawned—extending it for as long as possible.

"Do you still have sex with her?"

Dr. Ranjan hoped Menaka would accept an indirect answer. "You know how it is, Menaka. The days are so full, and both of us are exhausted by the evening, and something quick is not very satisfying, especially for her, and—"

She peered straight into his eyes. "Do you have sex with your wife?"

"Once or twice a month."

Menaka frowned. Dr. Ranjan wished he hadn't been quantitative.

"Do you love her?"

He'd been most afraid of that question. Did Menaka *really* want to know? He took a gulp of water, then stared out the window, pretending to be preoccupied with the hypokinetic man. "It's amazing that fellow is still out there."

"Don't change the subject. *Do you love her?*"

"Yes."

Evidently Menaka wasn't satisfied with the brevity of his answer. "In what way?"

He hadn't thought about *how*. He just loved Bhavana—had no doubt about it. As a matter of fact, he was a bit angry with Menaka for forcing him to defend his home. But he loved Menaka, too, which was the problem. He had to explain so that she'd understand. So he spoke, entirely unprepared, trying to think before speaking, though mainly thinking after. He babbled.

Menaka's eyes hardened. "*In what way,*" she repeated, "do you love your wife?"

Her calm was frightening, her gaze unsettling. A clock ticked inside his head, every tick louder. Again he looked out the window. Then, while he was staring at the hypokinetic man, words started to flow.

"Our marriage was arranged," he said. "We didn't love each other at the time. But somehow everything changes when you live together for so long, and you raise children, build a life, protect that life for the kids and each other, even if it's as mundane as paying the mortgage and taking Archana to Bharatnatyam class. Quite mindless when you stop to think about it—boring. Sometimes I resent it all, since it takes my mind off science, keeps me away from the lab at precisely the hour I need to be there. When I'm watching Neel at a soccer game, for instance, and an exciting idea flits through my mind. Well, I need to work it out—or I'll lose it. But I can't focus on it because my son is out on the field trying to impress me with how well he can kick a soccer ball—which isn't very, since he has unfortunately inherited his father's poor coordination. I can cite countless examples and, yes, it gets frustrating. You want to withdraw sometimes—you have to!—but you can't withdraw from the kids, right? So you don't say much to your spouse, and perhaps you bicker over trivialities and are rarely intimate with one another. In the end, though, it's all for the same purpose—to preserve your family, protect your children for as long as they'll let you: from drugs, drunk drivers, bolts of lightning. It took me forever to admit it to myself, but that's the most important purpose in our lives. In *my* life. Even more than science. And though our lives are busier than La Guardia Airport the day before Thanksgiving, there are moments in between, sometimes only seconds, when Bhavana and I look at each other and know how important it all is—how crucial both of us are to it—and that we love each other without having to think about it."

He was stunned by the depth of his own feeling, the almost eloquent defense of his home. So, apparently, was Menaka. He felt sorry for her. Now she knew how difficult things were.

Or how straightforward.

Menaka still hadn't said a word. He considered telling her that he loved her, too—more than he had so far admitted, much more than she might have guessed. But just then Tiger peeked around the corner. He still had that smug grin on his face. He winked.

Dr. Ranjan shook his fist at Tiger and shouted in a cracked voice, "Yes, you spicy-spicy bastard, I'm having an affair!"

Tiger retreated.

Dr. Ranjan glanced anxiously around the restaurant. Thank God, he thought, everyone else had left.

• •

WHEN HE RETURNED to the office, Dr. Ranjan was still trying to unravel his emotions. He sat at his desk for nearly an hour, looking out the window. Around three-thirty he went to check the afternoon mail. He tossed three envelopes into the garbage pail without opening them. Of the two pieces of mail left, one had been sent by overnight express. He opened it first.

Dr. Ranjan's heart leapt. An invitation to deliver the plenary lecture at this year's meeting of the International Society of Neurophysiological and Neurochemical Research! The meeting was to be held right here in New York City. "The Organizing Committee apologizes for the short notice," read one line of the letter, "but we could not ignore the significance of your recent findings." Dr. Ranjan couldn't believe it; he reread the whole letter. It had been nine years since anyone had asked him to deliver a lecture—and now he'd been invited to give the keynote address at the premier scientific meeting in his field!

His first impulse was to call Menaka. While reaching for the phone, he thought again. The news, exciting as it was, could wait until the bitter aftertaste of their lunch conversation had passed.

Reading the letter once more, he fell into a panic. This would be the most important hour of his career: He'd better be prepared. He needed to review the latest publications in the field. Unfortunately, the hospital library was small and didn't subscribe to specialized scientific journals. The only *real* library he had access to was the massive public one on Forty-second Street. He couldn't wait till morning. He put on his overcoat and hurried to the subway station. Thirty-five minutes later he got off the train at Times Square.

By the time he arrived, the library had closed.

Pacts with Destiny

IT HAD GOTTEN OUT OF HAND. THREE OR FOUR TIMES A WEEK, MANNY and Alvin had managed to find a few hours to catch either the 6:00 or 9:00 P.M. screening of *Sholay* at Golden Jubilee Cinema. Sometimes they even sat through back-to-back shows. Meeting for the movie had become a ritual, if not an addiction, and without quite realizing it both men had become very efficient with the rest of their time. Eventually, though, audiences dwindled. One night Manny and Alvin were the only ones in the movie hall. The next night Golden Jubilee Cinema was screening the latest Ronny Chanchal film to a full house.

Suddenly both men had lots of spare time. Much of it was spent imbibing mango margaritas and munching samosas dipped in tamarind chutney at Tiger's virtually empty restaurant. Since the samosas were scorching hot again, the two friends drank even more mango margaritas. All that liquor made the vague ideas they tossed about seem substantial.

"You know what would be fun, Al?"

"What?"

"Ride across India on a motorcycle, like Veeru and Jai did in *Sholay*—you know, when they're singing '*Yeh Dosti*.'"

Alvin squinted at Manny. "That's a joke, right?"

"I don't know. Ever since the Transplanted Man got better, I've been thinking there's something special about that song—that it's more than just a fine tune. Maybe the song is telling me—*us!*—something. Whenever you watched Veeru and Jai singing '*Yeh Dosti*,' didn't you see yourself on the screen in place of Veeru?"

"It was Jai for me."

"Yeah?"

"Yeah."

"Listen, Al, there's no reason why it has to be only in our heads. Say you and I fly to India, buy a motorcycle—can't be much in dollars—then ride around, maybe hit some touristy places but also the real India, whatever it is, wherever it is. What do you think?"

Alvin just swirled his yellow drink.

"Think about it," said Manny. "What are we doing here? Wasting time, giving up. It's comfortable, sure, but it's a sellout, man—only something to do till tomorrow. One of these days, today *has* to be tomorrow. And my tomorrow is in India: Kishore Kumar or bust!"

"Tomorrow passed me by long ago."

Manny finished the last drops of his mango margarita. Two tiny ice cubes were left. He sucked both into his mouth. "How come you're so sure it's gone?"

"I'm what everybody thinks I am, an ancient hippie. My adventurous years are over—not wasted exactly, just over. Tomorrow will be like yesterday and the day before."

"Where'd your tomorrow happen, Al?"

"Hell, I don't know. Nowhere. It was supposed to happen thirty years ago in India, I guess. Of course, it never could have. I was unbelievably naïve. Call it youth. . . . The hell with tomorrows, Manny. Today may not be the only thing that matters, but here and now is all I can deal with, all I want to deal with. There's no shortcut to wisdom."

"Wisdom—wow! That burden takes a pretty strong back. No wonder you didn't get there. And I thought trying to sing in Hindi films was something big."

A bittersweet smile crept across Alvin's face. "It is, pal. I hope you make it, I really do."

"Look, you need to find out about that wisdom stuff. Otherwise you'll spend the rest of your life wondering, 'What if? What if?'"

"You're young, Manny, real young."

"For someone who has given up on wisdom, you do a helluva job talking like you're a superwise sadhu. I guess humility isn't part of it."

"Bastard."

"Aren't we all?"

"The truth."

"Al, listen. I'm just talking about having fun. You want to go meditate in an ashram after we get done? Fine, do it. Or come back here. But let's have some fun, like in the *Sholay* song. We'll race our motorcycle past trains packed with people, tear through villages, raise clouds of red dust, ride up and down hills. Imagine a monsoon drizzle kissing your face while you speed through the countryside, or camping out in forts built centuries ago. Going right, going left, or up, or down—or just stopping—whenever you want, just because *you* feel like it. You could get into that, couldn't you?"

"Yeah."

"Well?"

"There's diarrhea."

"It's different now. And we can take antibiotics ahead of time. Sonny will get us some."

An old gleam flickered in Alvin's eyes. "Are you serious about this?"

"Am I serious?"

"Yeah, that's what I asked. Are you serious?"

"Am I serious? Shit, I don't know. Suppose—"

"No supposing. *I'm asking if you're serious.*"

"I guess I am."

"You guess?"

"*I am.*"

Alvin slammed his fist on the table. "Then let's do it!"

"You're on!" shouted Manny, slamming his fist even harder. His empty glass at the edge of the table fell to the floor and shattered.

Manny held out his hand, and Alvin shook it.

While their grumpy waiter picked up the shards of glass, Manny and Alvin excitedly discussed the proposed trip, made concrete plans. Then they went over to Alvin's apartment for a final toast to the adventure. Soon they were so drunk they could barely stand. But they had already managed to sketch a basic itinerary. They would fly to Chennai, where they'd buy the motorcycle. They'd ride it to Kanya Kumari, then climb up the peninsula and go as far north as possible without risking being kidnapped by terrorists.

Alvin lit a joint, took a few puffs, and passed it to Manny. In no time the fumes of euphoria mingled with the effects of alcohol, adding new dimensions to their dreams.

• •

MANNY HAD BEEN LYING IN BED all morning in a state of pleasant exhaustion. On and off he contemplated a large color poster of Kishore Kumar on the far wall. The original photograph must have been taken when Kishore was in his early fifties. The singer's face was full of laughter; behind the thick lenses in black plastic frames were wildly sparkling eyes. There was no intimation of the deadly heart attack soon to follow.

A song, *"O Saathi Re,"* flitted through Manny's mind as he continued to stare at the poster. He listened carefully to the voice in his head. Who owned it—he or Kishore? Manny couldn't help smiling; their voices were *that* alike. For years he had refused to accept this fact, despite what people said. Flattery, he thought. Who could sing like Kishore? Nobody—or so he believed *then*. Now, having listened to countless hours of recordings, meticulously comparing his vocals with Kishore's, Manny had concluded it really was hard to tell the difference. A pleasant chill passed from the crown of his head down into his whole body as he considered the possibility that God had placed him on earth to replace Kishore.

Suddenly he frowned. Why Port of Spain? Why New York City? If God had designated him as Kishore's heir, why put him on the opposite end of the planet—oceans away from India? That thought sparked some doubts. Having, on the spur of the moment, finally committed to chasing the only dream that mattered, he feared he might not possess the strength to pursue it to the end. Sure, it was easy to sit here in his tiny studio apartment, imagining this, dreaming that. But actually doing it was a different matter. What if he didn't get his big break? Worse, what if his voice wasn't as good as Kishore's? What if he was only *almost* as good, someone with lots of talent but not truly exceptional—not one in a million? And even if he was, India was so populous that one in a million amounted to a thousand people! There had been only one Kishore, one Rafi, one Talat, one Sehgal, one Mukesh. That was only five. Maybe he shouldn't go at all. Maybe he should simply return to Port of Spain, where he'd been happy until he started believing what people said about his voice. Wasn't it better to just keep dreaming and not face your own mediocrity?

Manny's doubts fed one another all morning. Around eleven o'clock he showed up at Dr. Giri's office.

"Can you tell the future, Guruji?"

Dr. Giri's back was acting up again, and he wasn't in a good mood. He was tired of people thrusting their palms in his face, telling him their zodiac signs, and somehow expecting him to utter a phrase that would change their lives. So, at the risk of losing a patient, he replied, "If you want someone who tells the future, five blocks from here is a woman who claims to be a gypsy. She does that sort of thing."

"They say *you* know palmistry and astrology."

"*They* are wrong. I can't read palms and stars any better than your grand-mother."

"So you *can* predict the future!"

"Did I say that?" replied Dr. Giri, without disguising his irritation.

"I need to know if I'm going to make it in Hindi films as a playback singer."

Dr. Giri stared at Manny for a long time. At last he said, "Have you ever been to India?"

"No."

"It's a different world. Not at all like the films."

"It's not just films. People, too. On slow nights at the hospital, I go to the Transplanted Man's room. One way or another, we end up talking about India, and it makes me want to go all the more."

"The Transplanted Man—how is he?"

"You know him?"

"I know *of* him."

"Wait till you hear this!" said Manny. "The Transplanted Man was going down the tube—dying—really! But Sonny, this doctor friend of mine, did something—don't ask me what, even though I was right there. And believe it or not, the Transplanted Man turned the corner. The next day he pissed a tidal wave."

"Incredible!"

"My singing might have helped, too. They say music can heal, you know."

Dr. Giri was lost in thoughts about Sonny.

"Guruji?" Manny held out his open palm. "Please read it. Tell me what it says—*what it means.*"

Dr. Giri sighed. "Well, perhaps I can tell you something." He examined the terrain of Manny's palm.

"What do you think? What does my future hold?"

"Hmmm."

"Is that Hmmm-good or Hmmm-bad? . . . Wait! Before you tell me, maybe we should also check what the cards say."

"The cards are unnecessary. How badly do you want to do this?"

"There's *nothing* else."

"Why do you want to be a playback singer?"

"Because music is the language of the world. I want my voice to be heard everywhere."

"You can do that from here," replied Dr. Giri. "Though long dead, Elvis and John Lennon are still heard around the world."

"Yes, but they are not Kishore. Being so holy, perhaps you can't understand this, Guruji."

"I am not holy—just a psychotherapist. And my job does not preclude worldly pleasure." He gestured to the stereo system in the corner of the room. "Sometimes I think the songs of Rafi and Kishore from the sixties and seventies—particularly the sad songs—are the only real bits of India left in me. Listening to them is one of the great joys in my life."

"Then you understand, Guruji! You know how hearing Kishore's 'Zindagi Ka Safar' or Rafi's 'Ab Tumhare Havale'—alone in the dark, maybe while sipping a glass of wine—can make even the hardest man cry."

"Better than you can guess. But it will be very difficult, even if you *are* as good as Kishore."

"Is it possible, though?"

"If I were to tell you that the lines on your palm are against you, and so are the heavens, would you give up your plans?"

Manny bit his lip. "Is that what you see?"

"Answer my question."

Manny looked Dr. Giri in the eye. "No."

"Hmmm."

"What do you see, Guruji?"

"Success."

· ·

AFTER MANNY LEFT Dr. Giri turned off the lights in his office. He fiddled with the knobs of his recliner, adjusting its tilt to relieve the stress on his lower back. At last he felt comfortable. He reached for the remote that controlled the stereo system, pressed a series of buttons he knew by heart. Then he took a deep breath and shut his eyes. A few seconds later he heard Kishore Kumar singing *"Yeh Jeevan Hai."*

Each lyric kindled a memory from Dr. Giri's past. Soon tender recollections of his youth in Hyderabad were dancing through his head. That remembered past was different from the original—more luminous. The music had done that, and he knew it.

After the last line of the song, Dr. Giri turned off the stereo. Wiping his eyelids, he thought of Manny. Could he really be *that* good?

· ·

DR. GIRI NEVER BETRAYED confidences, even to his wife. But sometimes he released morsels of information without divulging identities, if for no other reason than to remind Urmila that people around here genuinely needed him. Tonight, while they lay in bed with the lights off, she remarked, "You had a busy day, Shaunak." By this she meant that he had seen two patients: Manny, followed by a recent widow who was thinking of returning to India for good with her two daughters.

"Any reason?" added Urmila.

"Most of my patients have variations of the same problem, the problem all of us Trishanku types have: where to locate ourselves between the poles."

"What poles?"

"Here and *there*."

"And where do these patients 'locate' themselves?"

"More there, I suspect—though that remains to be seen. Both are trying to muster courage to search for new lives in India."

"What did you tell them?"

"To go."

"I might have guessed as much!" Urmila sat up in bed and switched on the light. "Shaunak, how can your practice survive if your patients don't stay in therapy? Other psychotherapists use their power to keep patients in therapy for years, even decades. Some they see every single day!"

"You're not being fair. To psychotherapists."

"All I know is that they retire at fifty and buy beachfront homes in California. They wouldn't be able to do that if they didn't hang on to their patients. Are your patients, for some reason, healthier than theirs?"

"I doubt it."

"Then give them therapy! Why let your patients do whatever they want? How will you *ever* develop a real practice? How, Shaunak, how?"

"Whatever happens will happen."

"Don't give me your guru talk!"

He put his arm around her. "It isn't guru talk, Urmila. It's just talk."

She rolled away. "You should have told them to stay."

"It is my duty to do whatever is in their best interest."

"I wish you'd also worry about your duty to your family. If your practice doesn't grow soon, we'll have to move to a place where you can find more patients."

He got up and left the room. He was tired of this ongoing threat. The thought of moving was downright painful. He had become part of this neighborhood, mirrored it. And he dared to think that, at long last, his own reflection upon it mattered, too. He paced in the dark for a while, then paused to look out the window at the subject of the argument, this new India of asphalt, concrete, and neon. He noticed a lean man making his way down the street, his legs moving deliberately, like those of a rock climber securing a firm foothold. At first Dr. Giri thought that the hypokinetic man had finally decided to make a move. But as the figure got closer, under the illumination of the streetlight he recognized Sonny. Walking or sleepwalking? After observing for a few seconds, Dr. Giri decided Sonny was just walking: Besides, it was barely past midnight, rather early for him to sleepwalk, and he wasn't in his boxers. Come to think of it, Dr. Giri hadn't seen him sleepwalk in weeks. Had Sonny's compass finally begun to reorient itself?

Dr. Giri went back to the bedroom and lay down. "Urmila, are you still awake?"

"Yes."

He turned on the light.

Urmila shielded her eyes. "What's the matter?"

"That's just it. *Nothing* is the matter."

"What is it, then?"

"We're *never* moving."

"But, Shaunak—"

"*This* is home. *This* is where I want my children to grow up. *This* is where I want to grow old. Not Hyderabad, not Delhi, not Los Angeles, not London, not Boston. *Here.*"

"If your practice can't support us—"

"Here!" he said, raising his voice, glowering.

By nature he was a gentle man. No more than twice in fourteen years of marriage had he given her such a look. She turned away. He shut off the light and lay in bed pondering the accretion of wounds, great and small, that gnaw at a marriage.

"If I must," he finally said in the dark, "I'll get an additional job. The children are older now, and you too can work outside the house. But we're not moving."

"Why are you being so stubborn?"

"Because I am tired and not young anymore—and maybe just a little wise."

He slid over to her side of the bed. She pushed him away.

Seconds later she said, "Shaunak?"

"Yes?"

"I'm sorry."

She kissed him. Under the covers, he placed his hand on her waist and ran his fingers over a long central cesarean scar, souvenir from the last of three pregnancies. Then, beginning at the top of the scar, he kissed her all the way down.

32

Of Love and Lust

THE ELEVATOR SEEMED TO TAKE FOREVER. AT LAST THE METAL DOORS opened. Menaka Bhushan squeezed into the packed electric box, which stopped at nearly every floor on the way down. Finally the doors screeched open on the ground floor. She darted out, rushed across the lobby, and spun through the revolving doors of the main entrance.

She had gotten tied up with an ICU case, and now less than forty-five minutes remained before Dr. Ranjan's big lecture on the other side of town. Yesterday afternoon—after he had practiced before her for the eighth time in three days—he'd made her promise to sit up front so he could see her from the podium. Now, with all this traffic, she'd be lucky if she got to the convention center before the lecture began. She waved frantically at every passing cab.

A taxi dropped off someone. Menaka hurried over, but another woman beat her to it. She glanced at her wristwatch. Only thirty-six minutes before Nirdosh's lecture!

At last another taxi pulled up at the curb a few feet away. Afraid of losing this one, too, she rushed over and gripped the door handle while the man inside paid. He got out; she got in.

"The convention center. *Fast.*"

"Nothing's fast at this time of day," said the driver.

Menaka had been to the cash machine in the hospital lobby only an hour earlier. "There's a hundred-dollar tip if you get me there in fifteen minutes. I'm timing you."

"Are you serious, ma'am?"

She opened her purse and flashed some money. The driver floored the pedal. The taxi swerved right and left, ran lights, raced down side roads and alleys.

While the cab crossed the bridge into Manhattan, Menaka gazed at the gray water below and told herself to control her excitement. This was Nirdosh's big day, not hers. She was just . . . well . . . Perhaps not even that. During all the practice sessions this week, Nirdosh had behaved so collegially it was painful. She had said nothing, though.

The taxi skidded in front of the convention center. Menaka counted out five twenty-dollar bills and handed them to the driver.

"You said the *tip* would be a hundred. The fare's nineteen."

Menaka passed him another twenty.

She hurried to the main auditorium and strode down the aisle to the first row. A couple of seats were still unoccupied. She glanced around the immense hall. Across the front wall was a huge screen to project slides and a large monitor behind the podium to televise the speaker's face, magnified several hundredfold. Poor Nirdosh must be terribly nervous, she thought. She was glad they had practiced so many times. Even so, she feared he might panic onstage. It would be just like him. Had he slept well last night? That was too much to expect. She hoped he had at least managed to shut his eyes for an hour or two.

The lights began to turn on and off, signaling the start of the plenary session. The society's president walked across the stage to the podium. The auditorium fell silent. Until then Menaka had been oblivious to the background noise. Now she looked behind her. Not a single empty seat was in view.

"I'd like to bring the session to order," said the society's president. "In recent weeks there has been so much in the press about our speaker that he needs little introduction. Nevertheless, I'd be remiss if I didn't say a few words . . ."

• •

"SLEEP IS A MANY-SPLENDORED THING," began Dr. Ranjan, repeating a line he'd rehearsed all night in a deep voice—although now the words squeaked out of him. "But I will do my best not to put you to sleep."

Even though he would have preferred to hear his audience break into uncontrollable laughter, Dr. Ranjan was only mildly disappointed that his first one-liner had fallen flat. Ready to deliver the lecture of a lifetime, he could see Menaka smiling in the front row. Her approval swiftly thrust him into a new mode. All of a sudden he felt like a talk-show host doing his thousandth performance: charming but not cocky, cogent but not glib, amusing but not offensive.

"Sleep, sleep, sleep! We spend more than a third of our lives in this state, though some philosophers have argued that we sleep through our entire lives."

He heard a few snickers in the audience. His confidence soared.

"The mind unravels in our sleep, reliving our past, changing it, inventing futures we may or may not live but that remain very much part of us. Surely there are few matters of greater importance. Without sleep, we are miserable. And yet sleep is one of those areas about which we understand precious little. As scientists, we have collectively learned the secrets of so many phenomena, often in great detail. Yet, for the most part, the secrets of sleep remain secrets. I do not mean to diminish the work of others. It is amazing that they have discovered as much as they have, given the difficulty of the problem. Yes, a difficult problem, very difficult. The answers will be many, and together they will combine into an unexpectedly complex whole. Today, I will tell you the story of one such answer, a factor discovered in my laboratory with the invaluable help of my colleague, Alvin Quimby. We call this factor insomnin."

For the next forty-seven minutes Dr. Ranjan recounted the story of insomnin. He was Darwin, he was Freud, he was Einstein, he was Bose, he was Schweitzer, he was Pythagoras, he was Ramanujan. He was many people, but—thank God!—he wasn't himself.

Toward the end of his address, he waxed philosophical. "The Greeks used to believe Sleep was the brother of Death. What, then, of the person with a chronic sleep problem? Not someone who passes a difficult night every now and then. Rather, a person who spends a large portion of time trapped in that mysterious limbo between sleep and wakefulness scarcely understood by scientists and physicians. What must be the effect of inhabiting that no-man's-land night after night—over an entire lifetime!—on that person's outlook? On that person's whole life?"

Menaka signaled that his allotted time was up. Dr. Ranjan was right on schedule. He concluded as he'd begun: "Sleep is a many-splendored thing. I hope I haven't put you to sleep."

The man and his phenomenal science led the tight-sphinctered audience to smile, then laugh. And row by row former skeptics—including those who had once called him a charlatan, a mystic, and worse—rose and clapped.

• •

"You were wonderful," breathed Menaka as soon as she entered Dr. Ranjan's office an hour and a half later. "Wonderful, Nirdosh!"

He was sitting in his chair, elated, the thunderous clapping still resounding in his head.

With a different kind of elation, he watched Menaka take off her blouse, her skirt, her slip—then step forward. She stood before him, her taut waist inches from his quivering lips, her black pubic hair glistening in a slant of sunlight.

"Here I am, Nirdosh."

Dr. Ranjan watched goose bumps develop on Menaka's dark skin. He wanted to grab her and kiss her navel.

"It isn't necessary," he said in a eunuchy voice.

"I want to, Nirdosh. I want to give myself to you. *Completely.* Devour me, Nirdosh. Devour me!"

Every pore on Dr. Ranjan's skin exuded sweat. He closed his eyes. His heart raced past his brain and conspired with other organs. He squirmed in his seat. Oh, how he wanted her! His fingers gradually moved toward his belt buckle. Then they stopped.

"I can't, Menaka," he said, almost inaudibly. "I just can't."

Menaka the neurologist and Menaka the woman knew a great deal about men. Yet she was flabbergasted by Dr. Ranjan's response. Nobody had to inform her that most men who cheat on their wives ultimately return to them. But she had never expected Nirdosh to resist at that moment—and so absolutely!

Even as she hastily slipped back into her blouse and skirt, her hurt feelings melted into an emotion far from anger. She truly loved this man. She was proud of him, not nearly as much for his incredible lecture as for his self-control, his genuine goodness. Whether or not she could convince anyone else, before her stood the ideal man, perhaps the mortal son of a minor deity. And she knew from the flaring nostrils, twitching face, and trembling fingers she'd witnessed just moments ago that he wanted her as badly as she wanted him. Maybe more.

Dr. Ranjan had been facing the other way, staring out the window, sobbing quietly.

"Nirdosh?"

He didn't answer.

"Nirdosh?"

Still no answer.

She became afraid and rushed over.

His face was ashen. Blood dripped down his lips.

"Oh, my God, Nirdosh! Please don't bite your tongue! Please! Not again!"

Tears came to her eyes, and she fought off the impulse to lick the blood trickling from his lips. She understood. Last time he had bled for his wife. This time he was bleeding for her.

HERE, THERE—ELSEWHERE

33

Aftermaths

EXHAUSTED FROM FLYING HALFWAY AROUND THE WORLD, NISHAD AND Sonali, together with 351 other people, got off an Air India jumbo jet and lugged their carry-on bags down a corridor at Kennedy Airport. They turned, tramped along another corridor, then down an escalator, following the signs for IMMIGRATION AND CUSTOMS. At last they arrived in a huge room with many booths.

"Foreign nationals in the right lanes, citizens and permanent residents in the left," shouted a uniformed woman, as if addressing a group of prisoners.

The group split, most heading for the right lanes.

Nishad and Sonali went left. From sleeping in an awkward position on the plane, Nishad's back ached horribly, and tingling sensations traveled down his leg into his great toe. "It feels good to walk around," he said.

Sonali, virtually silent during their twenty hours of travel, didn't reply. On her face was a look of failure, disillusionment, damaged pride. Nishad wanted to utter something sympathetic, but he knew he had to be careful with his words. Setting foot in New York City had surely intensified Sonali's memories of the bite on her left buttock.

And the aftermath.

India hadn't gone well. At first Sonali had been so excited by the country's entrepreneurial spirit that she seemed to forget the strange circumstances that had brought them there. She couldn't get enough of the Delhi where she'd been born and raised. All over the city Marutis and other small cars filled the streets, and in every fourth or fifth car someone was gabbing on a mobile phone. Billboards advertised this or that dot com. Many South Delhi colonies had fashionable shopping centers, clinics boasting the latest ultrasound equipment, computer rooms that rented Internet access; some even had a McDonald's or a Pizza Hut. There was construction everywhere, old single-story edifices being replaced by modern multistory buildings.

But despite all the evidence of change, Sonali's enthusiasm diminished day by day. Living with her conservative family for the first time in years—in the same Green Park house where she grew up—only served to hammer in the fact that America had changed her more than she cared to admit. Her tolerance for the inconveniences of Indian life—the crowds, the power failures, the dust, the smog, the imprecision of "Indian time"—had vanished. With each passing day she spoke less about her grand plan of setting up an engineering firm.

Sonali's mood was painful enough for her, but she had a way of infecting others. Soon her whole family was on edge. Nishad wasn't happy, either. His mother-in-law found fault with everything he did, made snide comments about his family, and somehow managed always to be in the bathroom when he needed it. But because it was *her* family—and because he'd made the initial mistake of whispering a few impolitic remarks to her—Sonali refused to grant that the return to the homeland hadn't turned out as she'd hoped.

One afternoon she came back from the corner market, where she'd gotten into a heated argument with the fruit vendor over the quality of his mangoes. She was still furious. "Why is the underside of every mango bruised?" she shouted at her parents and sister, who were watching highlights of a beauty pageant on TV.

Nobody understood what Sonali was talking about.

"This new India is really no different from the old," she continued. "The milk still has water mixed in it, and the cement is still half dirt. *Nothing* has changed." Then, looking at her parents and sister, she added, "*No one* has changed."

Her parents and sister exchanged troubled glances but didn't reply. Sonali went on. Little by little her criticisms of modern India became direct attacks on her family.

Her sister couldn't take any more. "You're no longer one of us!"

"Thank God for that!" snapped Sonali.

Her parents got involved.

The altercation went on into the evening. Nishad did his best to stay out of the fray and was thereby relatively spared, though in passing his mother-in-law referred to him as a "buttock-biting maniac." From the scorching look Sonali flashed her sister, Nishad gathered that she'd told her sister, who had then betrayed the confidence to her mother. He was pleased that Sonali was angry on his account, even if he could no longer look any of her family in the eye.

In the bedroom that night Nishad wanted to console Sonali in some way. He was reluctant to open his mouth, however, since he appeared to be rising in her estimation simply by keeping quiet. Even so, while they lay in bed he couldn't help voicing his thoughts. "Do you think we ought to go back?"

At first Sonali just ground her teeth some more. Nishad feared his tenuous stature had taken yet another nosedive. He turned off the lights, resigned to a miserable future.

In the dark Sonali muttered, "I want to be on the next flight to New York."

A smile stretched across Nishad's face. "Are you sure?"

"*I said* the next flight!"

In the flattest tone he could manage, he said, "I'll go to a travel agent tomorrow morning. Of course, it will probably be a couple of weeks before we're able to obtain a reasonable fare. One-way tickets with no advanced booking cost—"

"I don't care what it costs."

The next morning Nishad paid seven thousand dollars for two tickets on that night's flight. Then he went back to Sonali's parents' house and relished ten hours of chilly silence.

And here they were, back in New York City. They didn't have jobs, didn't have a place to stay, didn't even have a bank account. It was as if they were arriving in America for the first time. Maybe, thought Nishad, that was as it should be.

"May I see your green cards, please?" said the immigration officer.

Nishad couldn't keep from grinning as he handed the two cards to the immigration officer. Then, catching Sonali's nasty look, he bit his lip and tried to appear grave. But the grin burst upon his face again, broader than before. She scowled. Nishad embraced Sonali and pressed his lips firmly against hers.

Sonali's lips had never been so unwilling.

• •

THEY TOOK A TAXI to Little India and found a cheap weekly rental with a kitchenette situated directly across from the X-rated movie theater. After settling in they walked to Tiger's restaurant. Inside, Nishad spotted Sonny sitting at a window table with Manny. Nishad didn't want Sonali to be reminded of the whole saga again, so when Tiger strode up to greet them, Nishad pointed to the opposite side of the restaurant. "Do you mind if we sit over there?"

"Anywhere you wish," said Tiger. "It's another slow night."

Nishad chose a table in the corner of the restaurant farthest from Sonali's former doctor and made her sit with her back to Sonny.

"Well, then," said Nishad.

Sonali stared indifferently at the menu.

Tiger came by and filled their glasses with water. "Ready to order?"

Nishad glanced at Sonali. She didn't look up from the menu.

"I think we need a bit longer," said Nishad.

"No hurry."

Five minutes later Sonali was still staring at the menu. So far she hadn't said a word. Nishad was worried.

"The mutton pullao here is the best I've ever had," he said cautiously.

Sonali's eyebrows angled sharply. "Don't think I haven't seen the way you've been smirking all evening! And don't think I didn't notice Dr. Seth on the other side of the room—and how you're trying to keep me from seeing him! Don't think you've gotten away with anything, Nishad! Don't think . . ."

• •

WHILE SONALI WAS DON'T-THINKING Nishad, on the opposite side of the restaurant, Manny was detailing "the plan."

"*Really?*" said Sonny. "You and Alvin are really going to ride around India on a motorcycle like those guys in *Sholay*? Really?"

"Really, really, really."

"Watch out for Gabbar Singh!"

Manny grinned. "Thakur broke his arms, and he's in jail."

Sonny shook his head. "Not a chance, my friend. Gabbars are on the loose everywhere."

Manny drank some water. "Whatever happens will happen. Maybe I've got a shot, though. Have you ever asked yourself why so many people around here keep listening to film songs from the sixties and seventies when they can listen to whatever they want? Because the new voices don't touch you in that deep way. The music still hasn't recovered from the disco era."

"That may never happen."

Manny nodded slowly. "Maybe I'll just starve and cry. But I'm going to sing until my vocal cords rip—or they hand me a recording contract. What about you, Sonny? Any answers?"

"Believe it or not, I've been thinking that *maybe* Trinidad is—or has—an answer."

"If the question is 'What island off the coast of South America sits near a latitude of ten degrees and a longitude of sixty-two degrees?' then the answer could be Trinidad."

"That's not the question."

"It's a question of place, right?"

"Not so much geographical place, if you know what I mean."

"I'd have guessed that, if you went anywhere, it'd be back to Arizona. The way you talk about the desert, the ancient ruins, the canyons—"

"That's just it. I'd probably end up hiding in a canyon. Life may be a circle, but I'm not ready to go all the way around yet."

"Why should Trinidad be on *your* circle?"

"I'm not sure it is. Arizona is on one side; I still don't know what's on the other. But Trinidad makes sense to me, at least in the abstract. It's far from all the places that exert a pull on me, and yet from what I can tell—and from what you've told me, Manny—it also contains something of all those places. The right mix, or close to it. Different but the same. So it still could be—"

"On the circle?"

"Right."

"Sounds circular."

"More than you think. It turns out that my father spent a few years in the Caribbean, though I'm not sure exactly where."

"That's not a circle, Sonny. That's a tangle."

"It's just one more reason that keeps me wondering. Even in dreams I often find myself on an island."

"Manhattan's an island."

"Yeah, but . . ."

"Sonny, a place has smells and tastes and sounds. Trinidad has lots of that—a real powerful buzz."

"That's part of the attraction. It's like you and India."

"Is it, though? I know *why* I'm going to India, what I'm going to do when I get there. Do you know why you want to go to Trinidad?"

"I can't say."

"You can't say, or you *won't* say?"

• •

When Sonny got home that evening, the dog was gone.

"Tandoori!" he kept calling out. He checked under the bed, inside the closet, in the bathtub. Then he stuck his head out the apartment door, looked up and down the hallway.

"Tan-doo-ri!"

No dog.

He noticed that the window next to the fire escape was open. So, flashlight in hand, he went outside and combed the neighborhood. Soon he was shouting, "Tandoori! Tandoori!" at every street corner. Since he had no grilled chicken in his hands, people stared at him the same way they'd stared at the hypokinetic man when he got stuck between the subway doors.

Hours passed. Sonny searched the dark streets of surrounding neighborhoods. Still no dog. At 11:00 P.M. he returned to his apartment, exhausted. He called Gwen: After three rings he remembered she was working tonight. He dialed the hospital. The operator placed him on interminable hold. He lost patience. He went to his desk and, on a sheet of notebook paper, wrote with a big black marker:

Lost Dog. Reward $100. About 2½ feet long, 1½ feet high. Red-brown fur. Brown eyes. Male. Answers to Tandoori. Call . . .

He read it over, then changed the reward to $1,000. Since he didn't own a computer and had no idea where to find a photocopy machine at this time of the night, he wrote the same words and numbers on sheet after sheet, until his right wrist felt shaky. For the next hour and a half, he posted the sheets on neighborhood walls, lampposts, telephone booths, shop windows—wherever he found space. Once he thought he saw a dog lurking in the shadows near the hypokinetic man. He raced to the corner, but Tandoori wasn't there.

Sonny knelt in front of the hypokinetic man. "Hey, buddy, seen my pal? My *other* pal."

There was no response.

"Man, I wish you could talk."

Sonny patted the hypokinetic man on the shoulder, then crossed the street and taped the last of the eighty-seven sheets to a lamppost. He tossed the nearly empty roll of tape in a trash can. For another half hour he roamed the streets, periodically shouting Tandoori's name. Eventually he gave up and trudged home.

..

Tandoori had, in actuality, been with the hypokinetic man when Sonny thought he'd spotted the dog. After Sonny left, Tandoori emerged from behind a Dumpster, licked the hypokinetic man's face a few times, then settled into his lap—which had recently been emptied of dollar bills and change by Jay and Atul.

A short while later Tandoori heard footsteps. He crept back into the shadows.

It was Atul again, but this time he'd come without Jay. Atul's expression was grave. Although he was relieved that his father had stopped pandering to the tourist crowd, the spectacle outside Tiger's restaurant had transformed a sensitive, fuzzy-faced youth into a world-weary adolescent who had experienced his first wet dream and begun to shave. He no longer believed in the pose-for-the-ism; in fact, he was amazed that he had ever been so naïve.

Tonight Atul sat down beside the hypokinetic man with the intention of setting everything straight. "I want to make sure you understand that I never liked making money off you," he said. "That was Jay's idea. Sure, I'm guilty for going along with it, but remember, I'm giving it all to UNICEF . . ."

The hypokinetic man sipped from the glass of mango lassi that Atul had brought along. The slightly bent straw made a whistling sound. Atul straightened it. Unobstructed flow—six ounces an hour—was restored.

"Call me foolish," Atul went on. "But for a while I really thought we— *you*—were onto something."

A blast of air, brief but cool, blew down the street. Atul noticed that the top button of the hypokinetic man's jacket had come undone. He refastened it.

"It has been an unusually warm month," said Atul. "But it's starting to turn cold. And I might have a girlfriend soon—could be Madhvi Giri, Guruji's daughter. I've caught her looking at me in class. Of course, with her dad being so saintly and all, her parents might not let her hang out with guys. But who knows? If I don't start working on it myself, before you know it my mom will fix me up with some Indian girl from Kansas or Kanpur that she finds in the newspaper. Believe it or not, Srini's mom did that to his older brother the other day . . . Well, I guess you know what I'm trying to say."

Atul put his arm over the hypokinetic man's slender shoulders. "You're making this awful hard for me," he said in a choked voice. "I've got to say it, though. I think it's time for you to make a move."

The hypokinetic man stopped sipping the mango lassi.

"Don't look like that! I didn't say you have to move *right this minute*. We've just got to be realistic. I *know* you understand. I can tell from your face that you're getting better. Maybe if you just *try* to get up?"

The hypokinetic man stared blankly into the night.

"At least start thinking about it. Okay?"

• •

SONNY WAS OFF the next day, a Sunday so bright it was depressing. All morning he sat by the phone waiting for someone to call about Tandoori. After lunch he wandered through the streets. By then he was certain Tandoori would never come back. Eventually he found his way over to Gwen's. She'd been sleeping off a busy night shift and answered the door in her robe. "What is it?" she asked, rubbing her eyes.

He explained.

"Let's go look for him, Sonny. He must be somewhere nearby. Tandoori is as street-smart a dog as they come. Don't worry."

"I'm not worried anymore. Just sad. You're right. He *is* a street dog. He had to get back on the street. When I think about it, I'm surprised he stayed so long."

"It'll be light outside for a few more hours. Between the two of us, I'm sure we'll find him."

"And if we do? I'm not going to drag him back."

"He's a dog, Sonny, not a person! I can't believe he'd think that way!"

"What way?"

"The way you think."

A long silence passed. Eventually she said, "Maybe Manny or Alvin has seen him."

"I've already called them. They're busy making plans."

"For what?"

Sonny told her.

"You mean they're going to ride across India aping those two buffoons in *Sholay*?"

"That's one way of putting it."

"How utterly ridiculous!"

"It requires guts."

"Guts? It sounds adolescent—puerile!"

Sonny kept quiet.

"Would *you* do it?"

He didn't answer.

"It's exactly the kind of thing you *would* do, isn't it—ride a motorcycle across India?"

"Or somewhere."

She folded her arms and stared at him. "Really?"

She was getting at something—demanding an answer. He felt he had to make his point. At last he mumbled, "I'd ride solo."

• •

THAT NIGHT SONNY SLIPPED OUT of Gwen's apartment and went for a sleep-walk, his first since the Transplanted Man's recovery. He passed the Dumpster next to Tiger's restaurant, where Tandoori was simultaneously copulating and munching on a leftover spicy-spicy kebab.

Tandoori took care of the business at hand and caught up with his ex-roommate. The dog followed Sonny as he zigzagged through the neighbor-hood for twenty-five minutes before heading back to Gwen's place. At the entrance to the apartment building, Tandoori turned away.

Gwen hadn't been aware of Sonny's absence. When he knocked over the coat stand, she woke up screaming. She hurled three volumes of Proust from her bedside bookshelf into the dark. The last barely missed Sonny's head.

Sonny remained asleep through it all, but the racket woke other tenants. One phoned the police.

With uncharacteristic promptness two officers from the local precinct thumped on Gwen's door. The noise awakened Sonny. The policemen asked questions, which Gwen, wrapped in her robe, answered. The policemen saved the most obvious question for last: "Why is the gentleman in only his boxers and jogging shoes?"

Sonny was still too dazed to explain, but Gwen hinted that it had something to do with kinky sex. The officers evidently identified. They winked and left.

After a long silence, Sonny asked, "Did I sleepwalk again?"

"Yes!"

"That's *so* weird."

"If it were only *that*." She sounded tired, sad. "Sonny, I'm not really talking about the sleepwalking. I don't think you can help that. All of us carry bag-gage, and you unload yours in the middle of the night. What I'm talking about is *us*. I've been wondering, thinking, and now I want to know what you think. *Frankly*. Does this make sense, you and me?"

As far as Sonny was concerned, now wasn't a good time to delve into this. So he tried to formulate a vague yet cautiously optimistic answer. Even that was hard for him right now—since he was groggy still, his thoughts scattered. All he could say was "I don't know."

That answer was too frank.

"Why do you always not know, Sonny? In the ER and ICU, I've never seen anyone as skilled, as smart, as decisive. When a difficult situation arises that no one else can handle, somehow you improvise a solution that pulls the patient through. If I became gravely ill, you're the doc I'd pick. Why can't you translate that into the rest of your life? Why? Why am I in love with a shilly-shallying, namby-pamby, fence-straddling, wishy-washy, vacillating, immature . . . ?"

He might have tried to defend himself had she not said *love*. It was the first time either had used the word outside of sex.

Love. At first the word floated through the air. In the ponderous silence that followed, it became weightier. Sonny and Gwen braced for its crash on the floor of her apartment.

Gwen fell into a fit of blinking. She thought that maybe she ought to add a few more epithets in order to diminish the impact of the *love* part. To hell with it: She'd said it—meant it. Maybe it wasn't the best time, but she was awfully curious about Sonny's reaction. She scrutinized his face.

At last he said, "Immature?"

"God damn you!"

During the next few seconds she was, oddly enough, relieved that Sonny had sidestepped the issue. Her better sense told her to use the moment to cool down. But the box had been opened: Everything had to come out.

"Where are *we* going?" she asked. "Sometimes I feel like a player in a game of psychobilliards. But who am I playing with? Against? Sonny, there's a barrier around you that I can't get through. Obviously a lot is going on behind it. Every day I'm with you—every night!—I see another sign. Like the sleep-walking. I can't help but wonder what it *means*. After all, it's not just sleepwalk-ing, it's *strange* sleepwalking! And then there's the pot. . . . And what *did* you do to the Transplanted Man? It's as if you went into an altered state and now have amnesia. I know you think the sleepwalking is part of it. Part of what, though? Have you any idea how much all this upsets me?"

He said nothing.

"Sonny!"

"There are some things . . ."

"*Some things?* What does that mean? And don't give me that trite bit about 'riding solo.'"

It *was* about that, he thought—but not only that. It also had to do with what he now knew about his parents. And what he didn't know—what he could never know. He realized that, with his father's death, he had lost much more than the chance finally to connect the triangle between himself and his parents. Maybe he'd also lost the chance to extend new lines.

"What do you mean by *some things?*" insisted Gwen.

She had turned on her "professor of literature" voice. He knew it was best to back off, but he couldn't.

"Some things you've got to keep to yourself, some things that can't be translated, some things you can't share."

A tightness came over her face. "Amazing! From where do you get these profound ideas? Conrad? Heidegger? Dostoyevsky? Or does a chunk of rose quartz sitting in your apartment transmit the wisdom of time to you?"

"Lay off, Gwen! I'm not ready—" He stopped short.

"Go on. Ready for what?"

"The rest of this conversation."

"What makes you so sure there is a 'rest'?"

3 4

The Great Mouse Robbery

EVER SINCE THE INSOMNIN DEAL, UNIVELTA BIOPHARM SHARES HAD skyrocketed. The stock had already split; a second split was long overdue. Meanwhile, in a fickle market, the shares of other pharmaceutical companies that were overinvested in less promising approaches to sleep problems continued to tumble. Many billions in value had evaporated. Executive salaries had been slashed drastically; layoffs were about to go into effect. Was insomnin *the* major factor regulating sleep? Market analysts began to speak of the sleep market as a zero-sum game—which Univelta had won.

So seasoned observers of corporate America were not surprised when it was reported that someone had broken into the hospital's research wing and stolen Dr. Ranjan's sleepless mice. Of course, no company could use the mice without implicating themselves. But it didn't go unnoticed in business circles that, since the authenticity of Dr. Ranjan's data could now be challenged, others could produce insomnin using a different approach and claim they had "discovered" it independently. In the eyes of investors, the shares of other pharmaceutical companies with sleep remedies in the pipeline were suddenly valuable once more—at least until insomnin was available again, a prospect that, without the mice, seemed remote. The news had a predictable effect on Wall Street. Within days stock prices of major pharmaceutical companies, save one, had rebounded. Univelta, at its lowest price in over a decade, was still falling.

Although the efficiency of the burglary suggested a highly organized operation, rival pharmaceutical companies weren't the only potential culprits in what the tabloids dubbed the "Great Mouse Robbery." Publicity surrounding Dr. Ranjan's discovery had been so great that the police were entertaining a broad range of suspects, even bioterrorists.

And then there was Dr. Ranjan himself.

One of Dr. Ranjan's scientific competitors suggested to the press that the whole insomnin story had been cooked up, a figment of his renowned imagination. With so much at stake Dr. Ranjan had to show something or get rid of the mice. Since there was nothing to show, he'd chosen the latter course. Wasn't this the same "scientist" who, a few years ago, claimed he'd figured out the biochemical basis of love? In which scientific journal had the data been published?

Many leads were followed, but the half dozen detectives on the case came up with nothing.

• •

DR. RANJAN LOOKED LIKE a walking corpse. He didn't say much to anyone except the detectives; even with them he mostly nodded or shook his head, depending on Alvin to fill in details. He had tried four times to make an appointment with Paudha, but the CEO refused to see him. Dr. Ranjan feared his job was in jeopardy—the ignominious end of his checkered scientific career. Day and night he swam in an ocean of anxiety, wave upon wave surging over him. His jaws ached from incessant clenching, deepening the cracks already present in his molars. His eczema had been acting up, and once he started scratching, there was no end to it. He even developed pains in his chest. Once, they were so bad he feared he was having a heart attack, but the pain subsided just as he began to dial 911. Everywhere he saw impending doom. He was certain Univelta Biopharm would sue the hospital. The hospital would blame him. He would be arrested and, after a very public trial, convicted. He'd spend the next twenty years of his life in a prison with murderers, robbers, rapists, investment bankers!

Bhavana was understanding. But she was also openly worried about the practical issue of how the family would manage if he lost his job. That didn't help.

He yearned for Menaka to gently stroke away his misery. His longing only became greater when she sent him a note, seemingly collegial.

> *Dear Nirdosh,*
> *I'm so sorry about the mice. Let me know if I can be of any help.*
>
> *M*

He knew exactly how she could help. In the moments of weakness that accompanied his despair, pinpricks of lust tickled his anxieties: He couldn't get his mind off Menaka's warm flesh. With every heroic molecule in his body, Dr. Ranjan resisted the impulse to call her. But that left no heroic molecules to face the difficulties at hand.

• •

ALVIN WAS ABOUT TO BACK OUT. In part it was because he was feeling guilty about leaving Ranjy at so difficult a time. But there were other reasons, too. While he liked the idea of riding around India on a motorcycle, in the back of his mind was the thought that Jai had died at the end of *Sholay:* It forced him to admit that he'd arrived at a point in life when mortality lurked a few bends down the road. It also reminded him of how he once lay in a bed with his buttocks over a seven-inch-wide hole through which his watery stool poured into a bucket. He had been sure, back then, that the cholera would kill him, just as it had taken the lives of three others in the ward. Thirty years had, fortunately, added perspective. Even as he thought about those terrible weeks shitting his guts out in a small government hospital eighty miles from Calcutta, Alvin realized a fragment of him could never have ended up in that bucket of watery stool, a fragment that still yearned now as then. That was why he'd enlisted in Manny's half-crazy proposal. And yet the mouse robbery had reminded him of life's perverse vicissitudes, rekindling old doubts. Was there anything for him in India? Had there ever been? For three decades he had felt the country's pull, but he still couldn't explain exactly why. Had he simplemindedly accepted myths perpetrated by countless Occidental romancers of the East—and exploited by Eastern charlatans? He needed to talk to someone who truly understood what mattered, what didn't. And who better than the Transplanted Man, someone who'd crawled through the pit of despair so many times?

Late Thursday evening Alvin knocked on the Transplanted Man's half-open door.

"Yes?"

Alvin stepped inside. "We've never actually met. I'm a close friend of Manny's. Also Sonny and Gwen's."

"You have good taste in friends," said the Transplanted Man, putting aside *Mansfield Park.* "What can I do for you?"

Alvin wasn't sure where to begin. "I'm getting older."

"I sympathize."

"It's more than that. It's time for me to attempt, one last time, to find out what it's all about."

"*All* is a lot."

"Meaning with a capital *M*. Truth with a capital *T*."

"Do you have something against lowercase letters?"

"You know what I'm talking about. I need to decide what to do with my life."

"One must decide that every day."

Alvin's brow wrinkled. "Nobody decides every day, and few think about it as often as once a month. You'd drive yourself nuts if you kept asking, Is my life worthwhile? But there are times when you *must* ask. From my boss, Ranjy—uh . . . Dr. Ranjan, the scientist here who's been in the news—I've learned that you've got to try any way you can. Science is powerful for answering small and medium-size questions—and in that category I put relativity, evolution, and the existence of life elsewhere in the universe—though it takes you only so far toward the Big Questions, the only ones that ever mattered to me. But you can't just quit asking because science can go no farther, right? You've got to keep trying—whatever gets you a tiny bit closer. Don't you think about the Big Questions?"

A wistful look came over the Transplanted Man's face. "I only began thinking about them in a serious way when I was older than you. Until then, I assumed my life was worthwhile. But life has a way of testing your assumptions. For me, it happened when my wife and son died within a year of each other. She of cancer, he in a motorcycle accident." The Transplanted Man slowly shook his head from side to side. "You know, I still keep Arvind's cracked helmet by my bed back home. That was a very hard time for me— perhaps even harder than what I've just gone through—and I couldn't stop thinking about those Big Questions. I am no philosopher or mystic. I am just an ordinary man who has lived an unusual life owing to an unusual disease and considerable luck in politics—although lately that luck has changed. You may have heard that I'm no longer a minister."

"I didn't know."

"Perhaps it isn't an altogether bad thing, considering the tenuous state of the current coalition. But back to your question. I have opinions—rather strong ones. You see, I was once involved in trying to determine what a life is worth."

"You sound like you're talking about dollars and cents!"

The Transplanted Man drank from the glass of water on his bedside table. "Much is lost in the exchange rate."

"I don't get it."

"I tried to unsettle the Bhopal settlement," said the Transplanted Man. "Or did what I could. But I didn't have the same kind of clout then. Indians sold themselves for less than three thousand dollars each. I couldn't believe it! Blindness was valued at roughly the cost of a weekend stay at a hotel in Manhattan! An Indian life was judged to be virtually worthless! On the other hand, here in the United States if a man dies in a car accident due to a defect in the car, his survivors are paid thirty million dollars. Here, life has almost infinite value. Yet I, an Indian, am worth one ten thousandth of an American. Or perhaps my value increases now that I am lying in a hospital bed here?"

"I don't see what this has to do with—"

"In my own case, it gets even more complicated. On the black market, tycoons who need transplants will pay $100,000 dollars for a kidney, $250,000 for a heart, almost as much for a liver, $20,000 for a cornea, $80,000 for a pair of lungs, $500 for a pint of blood, $40,000 for a quart of bone marrow. Looking at it this way, I have, by virtue of my multiply transplanted body, an accumulated value approaching one million dollars. Pretty good for an Indian, eh? Of course, that is still only one-thirtieth as much as an American is worth."

"You're mocking me," said Alvin.

"I'm mocking myself," replied the Transplanted Man. "As far as I'm concerned, there is only one Big Question. Without dollars or rupees, stripped of all masks and postures—with no labels at all—what's left? If the answer is nothing, then life isn't much more than a lit beedi slowly turning into smoke. But what if, stripped clear, that elemental self is warm with passion and yearns for something that is—for lack of a better word divine? Then there is a *chance* of meaning. And if that chance is wasted, as far as I'm concerned, no life is emptier."

• •

WHEN ALVIN FIRST ANNOUNCED that he was leaving, Dr. Ranjan had been saddened, though he understood Alvin's reasons. That was ten days ago: before the mouse robbery. Then, Dr. Ranjan had thought he could bear the loss. But this afternoon—as he paced back and forth between the fume hood and the incubators, his heels clopping on the lab's old linoleum floor—he felt utterly helpless. How had everything gone so wrong? Any day now he expected to receive a phone call from Paudha ordering him to pack up his office and lab. Then what? At his age, with his sullied reputation, no one else would hire him. Bhavana's salary wasn't enough to take care of the mortgage;

they'd be forced to move to a more affordable neighborhood, place the kids in a new school. Would they even be able to send Archana and Neel to decent colleges?

The mix of sulfurous and phenolic odors wafting through the lab started to bother Dr. Ranjan. He went down to the cafeteria for a cup of coffee. While sipping the hot liquid at a corner table, he stared at the plain gray tabletop. There was something soothing about that particular shade of gray, something that perfectly matched his mood.

"May I join you?"

Startled, Dr. Ranjan looked up and flashed a faint, almost sickly smile at Sonny.

Sonny set his cup down on the table. "Sorry to hear about your mice."

Dr. Ranjan was silent. Sonny tore open a packet of sugar, poured it into his coffee, and stirred. Both men quietly sipped.

After a while Sonny said, "You've got a family, right?"

"Funny you should mention it. I've been thinking a great deal about them all day."

"Listen, I don't mean to pry," said Sonny. "But I don't know too many family men and, well, I've got a few questions."

A slight grin appeared on Dr. Ranjan's face. "You're thinking of marriage?"

Sonny took another sip of coffee. "At some point in a relationship, you have to go in either one direction or exactly the opposite. You know what I mean?"

Dr. Ranjan's grin abruptly vanished. "All too well."

"So?"

"A complicated business: marriage, families, fatherhood. I'd have thought that if any man was ideally suited, I was that man. I'm no longer so sure."

"It ties a man up?"

"It does—although not the way you think. Well, that way, too. More significant is how it changes your attitudes. You find yourself compromising in ways you never imagined."

"Doesn't sound very appealing."

"Sometimes it's the most wonderful thing in the world. Only when I look at my children—on that rare day I'm not preoccupied with experiments—do I understand how distorted a person's thinking can get, how puny these other things we pursue in life are. It's impossible for anyone else to comprehend how much you love your kids. What's more, even if its purity gets stained with the resentment that is intrinsic to family life, the love somehow repurifies itself in time. At least on the parent's side. With your spouse, on the other hand, it's often a more difficult matter. But you know, on late summer nights Bhavana and I sometimes sit quietly in the backyard, listening to the buzz of winged insects. At those times I feel overwhelmed with the satisfaction of building something only *we* could have built—together. That's genuine happiness, almost bliss. Of course, it only lasts a moment or two. Then Bhavana has to make the kids' lunches for summer camp the next day, and there are bills to pay—the electricity, the orthodontist, half a dozen kinds of insurance. It all serves to remind you how fragile everything is. A calamity, a mistake, a spell of bad luck, and it can all fall apart, throw you into the most profound despair that exists—much worse than what happened to me over insomnia. Unfortunately, no one really prepares you to be a husband and father. That, I think, is why it feels like a series of jolts."

"Harsh ones, it seems."

Dr. Ranjan nodded solemnly. "*Who* you are clashes with *what* you are: husband, father, breadwinner, role model, whatever other labels weigh you down on any given day. Should you try, for instance, to teach your son to dribble a basketball—it's just a recent example that comes to mind—or should you instill in him a sense of what's important, what counts and what doesn't? Believe me, that's a lot more difficult than a clumsy father learning how to bounce a basketball so he can teach his son. It all takes time. And it's hard. There aren't many who manage to be good family men while fully pursuing what mattered most to them before they had families. But I'm beginning to think it doesn't have to be that way. After all, how did Bach father twenty kids *and* create hundreds of magnificent compositions? Maybe the trade-offs and compromises are largely artificial."

"Artificial? How?"

"Can you teach your son what counts in life without doing it yourself?"

"But to your son, what counts is learning how to dribble that basketball. Will he let you teach him about life if you can't teach him how to dribble?"

"I worry about that, too."

"What if you're wrong?"

"Then it's a tense state of affairs. Lots of minor skirmishes, threats of major battles. Since the strife is with those you love, you'll always lose, no matter what. And if you're not careful, you'll lose ninety percent of your ambitions along the way. Your muscles soften, your edges dull. You won't even realize it—until something happens. And I'm not talking about the mouse robbery."

"Are you talking about something that makes you shred your tongue with your teeth?"

Dr. Ranjan stared at Sonny for a long moment. "Maybe you didn't know *this*," he said. Then he stuck out his tongue, displaying twelve stitches across the middle—in almost exactly the same place as before.

"Again!"

Dr. Ranjan nodded.

"Those stitches look like they're ready to come out."

"They were supposed to be taken out yesterday. I didn't feel up to it."

Neither spoke for a while.

"Do you think you can stay away from her?"

Dr. Ranjan's eyes widened. "How do you know?"

"Don't worry. After I stitched you up the first time, one of the ER nurses mentioned that Dr. Bhushan had called three times to find out how you were doing."

"Oh."

"So can you stay away?"

"It's a decision."

35

The Rebirth of Venus

RONNY CHANCHAL SAT ON A SOFA IN HIS NEW DELHI RESIDENCE, star-ing at glistening ice cubes in his glass of whiskey. It was one of those increas-ingly frequent moments when he wished he hadn't forgone marriage and children. Over the past week he had mentally made the decision to retire from the screen, having at last reconciled himself to the fact that he'd never create a great work of art. Though not generally prone to self-examination, he finally saw his desire to make a monumental East-West film as the desperate hope of an aging actor. Peering inside his artistic self had also confirmed how little there actually was. He thought back to the beginning of his acting career, when he was one of thousands of would-be heroes on the streets of Mumbai, waiting for a break. What had distinguished him from the throng? He wanted to believe that there had once been a kernel of talent and that someone had seen it: the actor he might have been. He wanted to believe that he could have become that actor if he hadn't embraced Bollywood's commercialism with his whole soul. Was there any truth in that? It was nice to think so. Of course, all was moot now, his decision final. From here on his energy would be focused on politics. Politics and nothing else.

He had nothing else.

As he sipped his whiskey he wondered how the Transplanted Man was far-ing on the other side of the world. Only a few weeks ago he had spied him sit-ting up in his hospital bed, although so far no news report had confirmed his recovery. But even if the Transplanted Man survived and reentered the fray, Ronny Chanchal believed he no longer posed a serious threat. After going through so much, the Transplanted Man was probably too frail to mount a forceful campaign. Even his opposition could be only the kind of feeble coun-termove that would prove to everyone that he, Ronny Chanchal, was the most realistic hope for a country fed up with confused coalitions and impotent leaders. In certain respects it would be best if the Transplanted Man shuffled on for a while. Ronny Chanchal could then publicly mourn the Transplanted Man's plight while clearly positioning himself as heir to the dying leader—and so much more competent by comparison.

As he poured more Red Label into his glass, Ronny Chanchal felt his conscience, slight as it was, begin to prick him. A man who fakes heroism for living is an excellent judge of true heroism. For over a decade he had watched the Transplanted Man's ordeal, his struggle against the repeated thrusts of death. It was as if the gods couldn't decide whether he was mortal or immortal, so they kept trying to kill him to see if he'd survive. Ronny Chanchal was also convinced that the Transplanted Man knew India like no other politician, that he was the last of the great ones. If Ronny Chanchal had cared even one-tenth as much for the country's future as he did for his own, he would have been the Transplanted Man's most genuine ally, the guardian of his legacy.

This was not the case. He lifted his glass and swirled the golden liquid, thinking that the time had come to topple the government once and for all. There was virtually no chance it would survive another no-confidence vote. As far as he was concerned, all that stood between him and the prime ministership was one man.

• •

ALL THINGS CONSIDERED, Sonali was glad to be back. Although neither she nor Nishad had been able to find jobs in the New York area, one of Nishad's ex-IIT batchmates had recently offered both of them positions at a start-up company outside San Jose. The salaries were low, and in these uncertain times the whole enterprise could fail, but there were no other immediate options. Sonali was looking forward to moving out of their dilapidated weekly rental across the street from the X-rated movie house. Also, moving west. New York City contained too much of the past; the Bay Area promised a new future—professionally as well as personally.

She was pleased that Nishad was no longer critical of her figure. As a matter of fact, now he claimed to prefer it that way. And that wasn't the only change in him. This new Nishad was understanding, tender. He cooked dinner three times a week, did all the dishes, even scrubbed the bathroom tiles.

Of course, Sonali would never concede her satisfaction. She had become a proud woman; in the face of the defeat in India, a new defiance had grown within her. And deep down she remained suspicious of her transformed husband. The more she thought about it, the more intense became her skepticism.

After all, wasn't this the man who had *pretended* to suffer a temporary memory loss when he was really doing who knew what while she slept? What kind of man would come up with an excuse so absurd it was almost believable? Even now she didn't know exactly what he'd been up to the night he bit her buttock. Was this "reformed" Nishad, in reality, the same old fiend up to some new deviousness?

Sonali wanted to test the sneaky bastard. So she began to eat. Cashews, potato chips, ice cream, avocados, olives, chocolate bars, pepperoni pizza with extra cheese—and lots of deep-fried Indian food. It helped that Tiger's restaurant was only three blocks away. She ate plate after plate of his spicy-spicy samosas and quenched her thirst with thick mango milk shakes.

Remarkably, Nishad said nothing about the additional pounds. Just to make sure the message wasn't missed, she began to traipse around the house in skimpy underwear. Often, nothing at all. Alone, she sometimes stood before the mirror naked. She liked the look of her new body, which bore a resemblance to a Paleolithic Venus figurine.

Could she rise to the part?

One evening Nishad returned with a bag of groceries. He put the perishables in the fridge, then donned an apron. "What are you in the mood for, Sonali? I was thinking of cooking aloo-matar and rice."

The only dish on Sonali's mind was Nishad.

While he peeled a potato, she slipped out of her panties. She wiggled her body alluringly before him.

Nishad set the potato aside. "Who do you think you are?" he said, grinning. "A fertility goddess?"

"Possibly," she replied in a husky voice. "Come, Nishad, let's find out."

She went over to the sofa and parted her thighs.

As he stared at the curvaceous woman on the sofa, he recalled the overwhelming passion he'd felt the night he bit her. He started to unbutton his shirt.

"Hurry!"

Suddenly he became uneasy. There was an intimidating note in her voice. And the way she lay there—with that voracious look in her dark, shiny eyes—did nothing to allay his uneasiness.

"Undress, Nishad. Now!" Her voice was military. He obeyed.

For a while his small, bony body swam upon her ample flesh. Then he shut his eyes and dove. His body was swallowed by Sonali's. It felt wonderful. What the hell, he thought, let her do with him what she wished.

She did.

Eight and a half minutes later, smiles of immense satisfaction on their faces gave way to a deeper tranquillity as they lay on the sofa, unaware that Sonali's ovary had, improbably, launched not one but three eggs this month. Flickering like stars, the eggs drifted, each waiting for a single sperm to penetrate its tough shield. Normally, all of Nishad's sperm would have died en route; the unfertilized eggs would have been swept away. But this evening three wily sperm with wildly tacking tails persisted—each carrying the gene pool of a strange, shy man who had bitten his wife's buttock and almost gotten away with it.

All three of Sonali's eggs were fertilized.

While Sonali and Nishad lay snoring in each other's arms, three shiny zygotes—eight and a half months later to emerge as triplet girls who would alter every dimension of Nishad's life—floated toward the hospitable lining of Sonali's womb.

36

Dosti

THE TAXI HAD GOTTEN STUCK IN TRAFFIC ON THE WAY TO THE AIRPORT; Manny and Alvin arrived at the gate just in time for the final boarding call. Now the two friends stood at the end of a rapidly shrinking line, only several feet from the Air India ground personnel who were examining boarding passes held out by the passengers in front.

"I've been meaning to ask you something," said Manny. "Have you ever ridden a motorcycle?"

"I haven't even ridden a bicycle."

"Shouldn't be that hard, right?"

"Shouldn't be," replied Alvin in a flat voice.

Both became absorbed in their own thoughts. Alvin grimly peered through the huge window at blinking red lights of planes taxiing along the runway.

"Boarding pass?" said the Air India staff person to the passenger just ahead of Manny.

Alvin suddenly felt cramps in his belly, which proceeded to broadcast loud, gurgling noises.

"Did that come from you, Al?"

"Only nerves, I think. No big deal."

But just as Alvin finished saying this, he experienced more severe cramps, followed by a fluttering feeling lower down. Memories of cholera assaulted him in full force. He pointed at the men's room less than fifty feet away. "I have to go. *Badly.* Here, take my backpack. I'll see you in a minute."

"Hurry, okay?"

• •

EVEN THOUGH MANNY's boarding pass read 37C, an aisle seat, he chose the middle one, 37B, since Alvin was half a foot taller and needed more leg room. Besides, if it turned out Alvin was sick, he'd be getting up a lot to go off to the lavatory. Who'd have expected something to start even before they boarded the plane? Since the overhead storage bins were full, Manny squeezed Alvin's backpack under the aisle seat, then stored his own. He fastened his seat belt and smiled at the man next to him in the window seat.

It was stuffy. Manny adjusted the air nozzle so that a stream of air hit his face. Then he pulled the airline magazine out of the seat pocket before him. While he flipped through the pages, his elbow began to joust with the elbow of the man in the window seat, who seemed determined to occupy the whole armrest. After a while they achieved a truce. Manny glanced at the digital display of his wristwatch, then at Alvin's backpack lying on the floor in front of the empty aisle seat. What was taking him so long?

"Prepare for departure," announced the captain over the intercom.

Flight attendants strode up and down the aisles, their eyes scanning each row for unbuckled seat belts, loose luggage, reclining seatbacks.

Manny stopped a flight attendant.

"You *can't* take off yet! My friend—the guy who's supposed to sit right here—is outside waiting to board. He had to run to the bathroom. He must be—"

Just then Manny spotted Alvin rushing down the aisle. He plopped in the empty aisle seat. He was breathing hard.

"You okay?" asked Manny.

Alvin nodded, barely.

The jet began to slowly back out from the gate.

"Please turn your attention to the safety demonstration at the front of the cabin . . ."

Manny and Alvin watched the flight attendant as she demonstrated how to slip on the life vest and breathe through the emergency oxygen mask. Even after the demonstration was over, Alvin kept staring straight ahead.

"Flight attendants, please seat yourselves for takeoff."

A sudden lightness. Almost simultaneously, Manny and Alvin sighed.

Soon the flight attendants were moving about the cabin again. In the row ahead a woman was laughing. Somewhere in the back a child complained that her ears hurt.

"You know, Al, for a moment, I thought you ditched me."

"For a moment," replied Alvin, his eyes still directed straight ahead, "I did."

• •

DR. RANJAN SAT in his office all day, trying to avoid sinking deeper into depression. He kept sinking. He needed someone to show him how to control the fires raging within and without, someone to apply a salve to his burns. On Friday morning he arrived at Dr. Giri's office with three days of stubble and dark semicircles under his eyes.

"Guruji, I'm anxious all the time."

As usual Dr. Giri struggled with the question of whether to play the guru or the therapist. The guru would have said something wise or comforting; the therapist ought to keep it entirely open-ended. He really wanted to handle this case as straight psychotherapy. After all, Dr. Ranjan was a man of science, a fellow Ph.D. So all Dr. Giri said was "Hmmm."

Dr. Ranjan appeared puzzled. "I feel lonely."

Dr. Giri folded his hands but said nothing.

Dr. Ranjan looked as if he was going to get up and leave.

"It must be difficult," Dr. Giri added hastily.

Dr. Ranjan pulled a lens cloth out of his shirt pocket, then wiped his eyeglasses. "I have always tried to be an optimist, Guruji. Whenever things were going badly, I would tell myself that, on just the right day—maybe with enough cloud cover, or on the coldest morning of winter—Icarus could have flown much higher. And for believing this, I have been singled out for pain and humiliation. It's so unjust!"

"Ah."

"Now I need Menaka more than ever, even though I've vowed never to become involved with her again."

"Huh."

"She understands certain things about me that Bhavana doesn't. *Important* things. It was no casual affair. Menaka was my support, and now . . ."

"Hmmm."

Dr. Ranjan sighed loudly. "There must be some sense to all this, Guruji."

Dr. Giri became reflective. An old Rafi song from *Waqt* could be heard from the beauty salon next door. As Dr. Giri listened he wondered what it took to be a genuine guru. What was required to qualify? Did he have to meditate in an ashram in the shadow of a great mountain until he experienced a mystical vision? Stand on one foot for days until the pain grew so great he no longer felt it? Study ancient scriptures until he knew them by heart? And suppose he embarked on the journey to guruhood, how would he know when he'd arrived? As best he could tell, there were no objective criteria. Would he just know?

The Rafi song finished.

"I need courage, Guruji. Courage to never be false to my wife again, courage to outlast everyone who is after me—courage to prove my claims true."

Dr. Giri fought off an impulse. At last he said, "Uh-huh."

"Can you help me find that courage?" asked Dr. Ranjan, his voice impatient.

Again the impulse assaulted Dr. Giri. It had gained in strength now, become a conviction threatening his balance. What was courage, anyway? Before him was a man of integrity whose whole world was falling apart, a man who, despite his misfortunes, still refused the tepid drink that satisfied most mortals. This man was going to tempt fate again. He wouldn't run away, wouldn't shirk responsibilities. And he wouldn't give up. Beginning right now, he would try to rebuild. Day after day, year after year, he would keep trying. Was this man any less courageous than a gladiator?

While Dr. Giri was lost in his ruminations, Dr. Ranjan began to fidget. Once more he looked as if he was about to get up and leave. "*I said*, Guruji, can you help me find that courage?"

The struggle within Dr. Giri was over. He took Dr. Ranjan's hand, looked into his eyes, and smiled warmly. "Yes, my child."

• •

BEFORE LEAVING DR. GIRI's office, Dr. Ranjan made another appointment. But the immediate problem that had brought him to Dr. Giri was solved by aid of an altogether different nature.

In the far corner of the animal room—in the very last cage—was a mouse with red eyes and green ears, a mouse that wouldn't sleep. A couple of weeks ago, during routine cage cleaning, Alvin had mistakenly placed the animal in a cage full of normal mice: a cage left untouched by the mouse robbers. And late that Friday night—after most singles' bars had closed and more people were making love than any other time of the week—Johny Walker's great-granddaughter found a mate.

Skipped Beats

WHILE WALKING HOME FROM THE HOSPITAL AT NIGHT, SONNY WENT BY the X-rated movie house. Showing was *Bertha Does Silicon Valley*, a controversial film in which several Indian American actors and actresses were making their porn debuts in supporting roles. Outside the theater Sonny watched two teenage boys being handcuffed by a pair of provocatively dressed women—apparently undercover cops posing as prostitutes. One of the boys was Tiger's son.

"It's all a big mistake, Officer," said Jay, who wore a sports jacket and shiny shoes with two-and-a-half-inch heels. "We were just being friendly, that's all. Being friendly isn't a crime, is it?"

"Shut up, kid!"

Atul—who ten minutes earlier had warned Jay to stay away from the women—hung his head in shame.

"Now I get it," said Jay. "You thought I said *coke*, as in *cocaine*. No, Officer, I said *smoke*. Didn't I, Atul? Smoke! S-M-O-K-E. Of course, I know it's not good for you, with lung cancer and all—the surgeon general is definitely right about that—and technically I'm a minor, but don't you think handcuffs is overdoing it?"

"Quit bullshitting me, kid!"

"No, really! All I wanted was a cigarette! Isn't that true, Atul?"

Atul didn't look up.

"This is serious business," said the policewoman.

"I know, I know," replied Jay. "Are the handcuffs necessary?"

"Standard procedure, kid."

"Atul, why don't you tell the officer we're okay? Go on, Atul, she'll believe *you*."

Atul broke out in tears. "What about *him*, Jay? Who's going to take care of *him*?"

"Oh no! I forgot about him!"

"He'll wither away!"

"Officer," said Jay. "I have to explain an extenuating circumstance. See how my buddy is crying? It's not for himself but for a friend of ours. This man really *needs* us. A sad story, Officer. A typical example of what can happen to good people in this city. We're the only ones who've taken the trouble to care for this unfortunate gentleman. Social service, you might say . . ."

· ·

AT THE LOCAL POLICE STATION Jay and Atul were fingerprinted, photographed, and booked for soliciting drugs and sex. Their horrified mothers refused to pay the nominal bail.

Atul's mother blamed Jay for her son's moral plunge. "Atul was such a sweet boy before he met Jay," she told Jay's mother. "I'm sure it was all Jay's doing."

"Jay may have a naughty streak," retorted Jay's mother, "but my son isn't stupid. His teachers used to say he was a genius! Only by being with a fool like Atul could he have gotten into all this trouble."

Eventually the two women stopped communicating altogether.

At home Tiger told his wife she was overreacting. "Let's just pay Atul's bail and forget it, Sushma. Boys sometimes do silly little things."

"Drugs and prostitution are not 'silly little things'!" she replied. "You just want all this to die down quickly because it might hurt business. If you hadn't been so caught up with making money instead of being a father, Atul would have never gone astray in the first place. Or is it the old royal thing? Ah, that's it! How can the crown prince be in jail? I'm sick of your imaginary kingdom. Sick, sick, sick! It doesn't exist. Hear me? It *never* existed!"

Tiger lost his temper. Grandly. Soon he wasn't speaking to his wife.

The general lack of communication didn't help the prospects of the two delinquents.

Meanwhile the hypokinetic man hadn't seen his youthful benefactors all weekend. He missed them, especially Atul. Now that Sonny knew the boys had been caring for the hypokinetic man, he tried to nourish him with protein-rich liquid supplements. But Sonny was on call that weekend, and at his harried best he was no substitute for Atul. Every night the hypokinetic man's lap was emptied by bandits, who neglected, however, to take care of his basic hygiene.

Time to get up—to move on. So the hypokinetic man did just that, inching in the direction of the Esmoor Street subway station.

· ·

WORD HAD FINALLY GOTTEN out that the Transplanted Man had escaped death yet again, lubricating the myth of his invincibility. In recent weeks major faults had ruptured in the Indian political landscape. With the prime minister facing a no-confidence vote that was a foregone conclusion, on the minds of many was this question: Did the Transplanted Man possess the strength to lead?

The Transplanted Man thought so—knew so. He didn't need to hear the results of his latest blood tests to realize he was enjoying his best health in years. Of course, his heart, always a problem, sometimes beat erratically. And his vision remained dim. So many drops of steroid solution had been placed in his eyes that he was developing dense cataracts. Normally the decrement in his vision wouldn't have bothered him much. Right now, though, he wanted to see the world in all its brightness and color. The dark haze seemed like a warning to proceed carefully, and he was in no mood to heed it. The current political situation demanded boldness.

After Sonny finished examining him one morning, the Transplanted Man announced, "I'm leaving—tomorrow."

"Tomorrow?" gasped Sonny.

"Elections. The prime minister just lost a no-confidence vote. See?" The Transplanted Man reached over to his bedside table and handed Sonny a fax that had arrived only an hour before from his party's headquarters.

Sonny felt a sudden ache. "You can't go just like that!"

"It's not 'just like that.' I've been here for months! A few weeks ago the world had given me up for dead. Now I'm the center of attention again. My advisers tell me I can lead the country for the asking. But first the people need to see me in flesh and blood. And I need to see them. *India.*"

"Yes, but . . ." Sonny did his best to summon some clinical authority. "Your heart isn't . . . I don't think you're strong enough."

The Transplanted Man smiled. "In the past day my strength has doubled. It will double again in another day."

"You need rest," said Sonny, doctorly firmness back in his voice.

The Transplanted Man shook his head from side to side. "An election is what I need. Approaching the campaign, I feel like . . . a divine emissary. Soon I'll be fully recovered. We will win big this time. And then I will do *big* things, unselfish things. It's time to turn the country around."

"Is this it?" said Sonny, almost in a whisper.

"I hope not. I've been thinking about you, Sonny. In another seven months your training will be complete. Why don't you come to India when it's over?

You could be my personal physician. God knows, I need one! That would engender a lot of publicity for you. You would be known as the doctor who cured the incurable."

"You cured yourself."

"Not this time. *You* saved me. You know it. *I* know it."

Sonny said nothing.

"If you come to India," continued the Transplanted Man, "I will find just the right shantytown in Delhi where you can use your gifts. Unless, of course, you prefer a lucrative practice of politicians, crorepati industrialists, and underworld bosses? . . . No? I didn't think so. . . . Please seriously consider my proposal, Sonny. I, for one, would be most grateful. And it might be a very good thing for you, too. India can't come to you, but you can go to it. You must face the reality of India, its passion and pain. Here, there is too much numbness, a whole culture under anesthesia."

"If you ask me, India could use some injections of anesthetic. People kill each other over things that happened hundreds of years ago; they die of scourges conquered almost everywhere else. Is that the kind of passion and pain you're talking about?"

"Mostly, it isn't. The pull of one's homeland—there is nothing like it. Sonny, I wish you really knew how India feels, day after day, year after year. It would mean a great deal to you. Its *thickness.*"

"I've seen a lot of what you call thickness right here in this hospital over the past two and a half years. And besides, India is too Indian for me."

"What are you if not Indian?"

"Who knows? Every month, I have a different theory."

"It sounds complicated."

"It is."

"And what about Gwen?"

"That's also complicated."

The Transplanted Man stroked his chin. "So then, this really is it. I understand something of what has happened to you during these past months, and I'm sure you won't stay put for long. Of course, all our adventures are, in the end, impossible. Even what we call success is mostly failure."

"Then why try?"

"Because there is, all told, no choice. So what if we run around in circles? The thing that matters most is the experience and the memories it leaves, which get polished a little more with each passing year. Sometimes they take decades to develop a subtle glow."

"That's a lot to go through for a little glow."

"Subtle—not little. And there is more. How does one speak of it? It is different for everybody, moving and deep, whatever name it goes by. That is why I listen—and why you must, too. Not listening is like taking two pills of poison three times a day. So now, both of us will listen to ourselves, eh? But you will hear about me in the news. How will I know what becomes of your adventure? After my own, I can't think of any I care about as much."

"I'll stay in touch."

"So you say now. Come here. Sit beside me."

The Transplanted Man shifted in his bed to make room.

"I would like to say many things to you, Sonny—tell you where I've been, where I'm going, and so much more. But suddenly there is no time. So I can only let you know that I wish to say all this. It is what a father wants to tell his son but never gets around to it, what a grandfather wants to tell his grandson but the boy is too young. Do you understand?"

Sonny nodded. "We'll meet again."

The Transplanted Man took Sonny's hand and clasped it between his own. "If we meet again, Sonny, the circumstances will be different. There is a reason why a father never gets around to telling his son."

• •

DUSK APPROACHED. The Transplanted Man went over to his ninth-floor window and gazed down at Little India. Even after all he had gone through, he would miss this place. As he absorbed the local landscape, he was struck by a change. The hypokinetic man was no longer at the corner of Esmoor and Forty-third. Instead, he was walking—so to speak—down the street. With great interest, he observed the hypokinetic man's movements. He timed a single step with his wristwatch. Twelve minutes, forty-seven seconds. Another: eleven minutes, four seconds. Then another. The hypokinetic man was, indeed, moving faster—nine minutes flat on the fourth step. Where was he going?

Eventually the hypokinetic man faded into the evening, and Manhattan began to glow in the distance. The sight propelled the Transplanted Man's thoughts to the other side of the world. Suddenly he couldn't wait to see the cities back home: Mumbai, Kolkata, Delhi, Chennai—they were all so big now! It used to be said that the real India was its half million villages. Did that still hold true? Not for long, it seemed. It was hard to believe that he'd soon be speaking to thousands upon thousands in those cities and villages: arguing for stronger child labor laws in Kanpur, ranting against rising edible oil prices in Ramgarh, championing farmers' rights in Sandhela, urging the building of more power plants in Haryana, dedicating a new medical college in Orissa, promising extra irrigation water in Kurwar, supporting low-interest loans for high-tech companies in Hyderabad . . . In no time lines from a hundred different speeches became jumbled in his head. Yet he knew that, when the moment came, the words would flow effortlessly. Already he could hear the crowds cheering him on.

He smiled. He hadn't expected to see India again, so sure had he been of death this time. How many more lives did he have? He'd squandered so many—just as the country had. Thirty years ago he hadn't appreciated the tremendous burden that rested upon his generation of leaders. Twenty, ten, even five years ago he hadn't fully understood that responsibility. If he and others had risen to the task—if the real problems had been faced with honesty and fortitude—what might India have been? *Could it still be?* Yes, he believed it could. But the task required vision. He knew that some deemed his particular vision reactionary, a Gandhian regression. They misunderstood: He had nothing against computers and missiles. But hype about cyberspace and outer space had diverted attention from the other India, the very marrow of the country—the India he hailed from and, for an unforgivably long time, had nearly forgotten. As far as he was concerned, that billion-headed behemoth, with its 2 billion feet stumbling every which way, was the future—always had been. Even if the wagers on high tech paid off for the smaller, wealthier India, what guarantee was there that the India of villages and slums would reap real benefits?

His mission was to make sure that happened. Many could pretend to lead, but no one had yet demonstrated the genius to make the behemoth march. And now, during his very last life, he would attempt exactly that. For he understood the strength beneath the behemoth's recalcitrance, the nobility of its suffering, its aspirations to greatness. Call him a self-deluded fool, but if anyone was up to the superhuman task of guiding it into the future, he was the one, and now was his time. Based on the past few months, he couldn't tell whether Fate currently favored him or was opposed. He had almost died a month ago, yet he'd never felt more alive than at this moment. But if Fate was against him, he was ready to challenge it—and the cynicism of three post-Independence generations—from the second he set foot in India. To walk barefoot on the warm earth of the Indian plains, heir to thousands of years of continuous civilization! And he could be its next leader!—the descendant of

Maharana Pratap and Tipu Sultan, of Chandragupta and Ashoka, of Gandhi and Nehru. He would prove himself worthy of such an ancestry. He would . . .

His heart skipped a beat.

Then another.

And then it began to race—faster, faster.

His hands trembled. Beads of sweat trickled down his forehead. He leaned against the wall—light-headed, nauseated, breathing rapidly.

The palpitations continued.

They will go away, he told himself. They *always* go away.

They didn't.

A heaviness entered his chest and quickly invaded his shoulder, his upper arm. His throat felt tight. Gasping, he staggered across the room. By the time he reached the bed, his shirt was drenched with sweat. As he lay down, he clutched the left side of his chest. He began to whisper a prayer he remembered from long ago.

He didn't finish.

38

Unstuck

THE PATIENT WAS THOUGHT TO HAVE GONE TO SLEEP EARLY, AND MANY hours passed before he was found dead in his bed. It quickly turned into a matter for diplomats, not doctors. It was only when the resident on call phoned in the morning—while Sonny and Gwen were watching the weather forecast on TV—that they learned of the death.

Sonny pressed the remote to turn off the TV. He was breathing fast. One by one, then simultaneously, tiny holes of extreme hypersensitivity formed inside him. Soon he was full of holes. He felt weightless, as if one more hole might permanently disembody him. He stared at Gwen. She was looking at him, too, her face expressionless. She seemed far away. In her eyes, also, he saw that distance. It had grown in recent weeks, but now the distance seemed greater, increasing by the second. Unbridgeable?

"I'm going," she whispered.

"I know."

Silence.

She stared at the floor, he at the wall. After a while he went over to the window. A few raindrops were clinging to the windowpane. Low, gray clouds stretched across the sky. He felt on the verge of tipping over.

"Sonny—"

"Don't explain."

She picked up her clothes from the sofa. Within minutes she had dressed. She walked over to the door, opened it slightly. She stood at the threshold, her hand on the doorknob. She remained like that for a long time. He heard her soft sobs, but he couldn't look at her. The walls of the room seemed to draw toward him—until he'd become enclosed and Gwen was on the other side.

The door shut.

He closed his eyes. Why had it become so quiet? At this time of day, rush-hour noise usually filled the apartment, yet now he seemed encased in the deepest silence he had ever known.

He tried to speak to it. Might it speak back?

It couldn't.

Not here. Not now.

Suddenly he heard everything: angry horns in the street, dogs barking in the hallway after returning from their morning walks, doors banging shut as tenants left for work, the man next door complaining about the elevators. All the noise was painful.

He fell back on the bed, dazed. A massive emptiness yawned before him, a great hole covered with groundless assumptions that people cry and kill for. All appeared as grand deceits invented to protect human eyes from searing visions of that hole.

Tears.

For what—for whom? His mind became a rushing collage of images that refused to settle.

The sound of a police siren brought him back to the present. He glanced at the wall clock.

Two and a half hours late for work.

· ·

WHILE SONNY WAS MAKING his way to the subway station, the drizzle turned into full-fledged rain. He hailed a cab. As the taxi sped down the street, his eyes focused on the intermingling streams of rainwater coursing over the windshield: the changing patterns.

Three minutes later the cab stopped in front of the hospital. It was really pouring now. Sonny paid the driver, then stepped right into a deep puddle. He stood in the downpour, unable to move, water from the puddle seeping into his sneakers. In a short time the rest of him was soaked as well. He watched the revolving doors at the hospital's entrance: people going in, going out. Last night the Transplanted Man had died, front-page news on the other side of the world, but this morning everything looked the same. The Transplanted Man had become just another inactivated number in the hospital's computer system. Already his thirty-two-volume medical record was probably stacked on a shelf for the dead, his corpse zippered in a vinyl bag—awaiting an autopsy that would reveal that the Transplanted Man was, in fact, not so different from anyone else.

Sonny took several steps toward the revolving doors. Then he stopped. He couldn't go in. He turned around and crossed the street, taking shelter under the canopy of New Dariba Jewelers. He stared at the dark brick walls of the hospital. Two and a half years there: an eternity and a moment. Because he had passed multiple-choice tests, he'd been allowed to witness the fronts and backs of people's lives, the shadows cast. What experience was like it, except war? But this war would never end. Screams would keep echoing through the hospital's corridors, and blood would keep splashing on the tiles. Day after day he'd been trapped in this weird war that lacked an enemy. Not long ago he had found it hard to imagine an existence without the crossfire. But now, the veteran of countless battles, he couldn't wait to be relieved of duty.

Less than seven months to go. Then what?

The rain had nearly stopped, and Sonny began to walk down the street. The air smelled different today. Garbage, automobile exhaust, lunch buffets in preparation, a dozen other odors, acrid and sweet. The moisture had diminished each odor's separate intensity, and their combined effect didn't saturate the senses as usual. The whole smell was almost comprehensible.

Almost.

He stopped, closed his eyes, inhaled deeply. A place, *his place,* had to smell just right, and he wanted to remember this smell, always.

Did Trinidad smell like this? It seemed terribly important to know. It was not here, there, or where he'd come from. Not New York, not India, not Arizona. Trinidad was elsewhere, though with the attraction of those other places. Was it free from what drove him away? Did this Afro-Asiatic Caribbean island off the coast of South America represent a solution? Probably not. A temporary destination? Perhaps. For him, there could be only temporary destinations. He wished Manny were still here so he could ask him how the streets of Port of Spain smelled. But by now Manny and Alvin were probably riding their motorcycle down a dirt road somewhere near the southern tip of India.

Had he decided? Yes.

But now?

Now!

Did he really need to complete his residency? He already had his medical license. If he wanted to be certified as a specialist, those extra months mattered. But he didn't *need* them. All his primary care months, the work he found most satisfying, were over. Only subspecialty electives were left, during which he'd follow around senior physicians, listening to their long, esoteric discussions. That wasn't his style.

When he got home he would call the hospital to resign. Brief, pleasant, without explanation. His residency had been a way station on the road to somewhere; resigning would make his commitment to that road irreversible. And then he'd go. Tonight, if possible.

He turned in the direction of his bank, intending to withdraw all his savings. Again the rain pelted down, much harder now. No vacant taxi in sight. The bank was only two subway stops away, so he headed for the station. As he approached he saw a dozen people rush into its depths. He'd probably miss this train, but what the hell, it was worth trying. He darted across the street, dodging a furniture truck.

He raced down the steps. Why hadn't the train left yet? Pulling a token out of his pocket, he charged through the turnstile. The train was still there, its doors open.

As soon as Sonny stepped inside, the conductor shouted over the intercom, "It's you again!"

At the other end of the car, trapped between the closing doors, was the hypokinetic man. He looked like he had just boarded, and yet he seemed to be stepping backward—as if he'd changed his mind and was now trying to get off.

"Move!" yelled the conductor.

Sonny flipped his middle finger at the intercom, then ran over to the hypokinetic man and carefully eased him back onto the platform. The doors closed, and the train started to move.

Now Sonny stood alone with the hypokinetic man. Echoes of the departed train reverberated through the station. Soon the echoes were gone. It was oddly peaceful. Sonny stared at the hypokinetic man for a long time, struck by the fact that his face was no longer stony. Even his eyes seemed clearer.

After a while Sonny heard the approaching rumble of the next train. Seconds later its headlights were visible. The train came to a halt, and people rushed out.

Sonny rested his hand on the hypokinetic man's shoulder, only to feel the taut muscles gradually twist away from the train. The hypokinetic man took a step toward the station's exit. Then another.

From inside the car the conductor's voice bellowed over the loudspeaker: "Please stand clear of the closing doors."

Sonny squeezed between the doors just before they shut. The train gathered speed.

So did the hypokinetic man.

ACKNOWLEDGMENTS

Above all, I must thank Julia Serebrinsky for believing a novel existed in the more than six hundred pages (small type, narrow margins) that one day landed on her desk and for guiding me through many revisions with wisdom and warmth; and Neeti Madan for faith, patience, enthusiasm, and a fine critical eye. I also wish to express my deepest gratitude to Doris Cooper, David Davidar, Marina Budhos, Amy Johnson, Diya Kar Hazra, Marc Aronson, L.H., and Stan Mendoza for their support and/or valuable critiques. Parts of this book were written during residencies at the Corporation of Yaddo and the MacDowell Colony, which are gratefully acknowledged. Finally, and perhaps needlessly, a note to dear ones, colleagues, and others: The characters in this novel speak and act for themselves, not the author.

The portion quoted of *Gitanjali* by Rabindranath Tagore, originally published by Macmillan in 1913, is from the Dover Thrift Edition (Mineola, N.Y., 2000). The portions quoted of *Walden* by Henry David Thoreau are from the Barnes & Noble Books edition (New York, 1993).